STRANGERS AND

Book Seven

MILLENNIAL KINGDOM

THE FINAL CHAPTER

By John and Patty Probst

Strategic Book Publishing and Rights Co.

Strategic Book Publishing and Rights Co., LLC
USA | Singapore

For information about special discounts for bulk purchases, please
contact Strategic Book Publishing and Rights Co. Special Sales, at
bookorder@sbpra.net.

ISBN: 978-1-946540-87-4

Book Design: Suzanne Kelly

DEDICATION

Three people took special roles in the completion of this book. It is on our hearts to mention each one with tender love.

We first met Dr. Ruth Wilkins in the early 80's when she assisted us with Mission work in Arizona and California. She has been a dear and faithful friend ever since then and an avid reader of our books. When she learned we were seeking someone to transcribe our hand written manuscript, she messaged and asked us to consider her. We agreed and Millennial Kingdom became a labor of love as she took our pencil scribbles with mark-outs, inserts, misspelled words, and converted our manuscript into something readable.

When we needed an editor for three of our books we sought the Lord to lead us to His choice. In our research one name stood out, Kathleen Marusak. She was shown to be very professional, being listed in a major writers' publication. We found not only an excellent editor but also a sister in the Lord who became a unique and special friend. She edited three of our previous books and 'Kat' truly sacrificed to do Millennial Kingdom. This was her concluding comment following completion of an incredible job of cleaning up and sweetening our work, "I don't think I have ever worked on a book that took me on such a stupendous journey! King Jesus was there every minute, and He made every word shine! What a powerful work this is. I know He will use it to His Glory!"

Years ago while we were pastoring Skyway Church in Glendale, Arizona, our youth pastor showed up at our trailer house one night around midnight with a young man who was half drunk. He wanted to argue religion. We sat outside and discussed life, religion, Christ, church, heaven and hell until four in the morning. The next day he came to the church office and after an hour of battle and struggle with God, Mike Ritchie accepted Jesus Christ as his Savior and was powerfully and gloriously born again. His whole future transformed. He cleaned up his life, was a faithful church member, good leader and took a job with a company he still works for today. When I contacted Mike to ask if he would be interested in helping complete this project since he is a faithful friend and reader of all our books, he agreed. Mike Ritchie covered the publication expenses of Millennial Kingdom.

To these three we gratefully dedicate this book.

—John and Patty Probst

STRANGERS AND PILGRIMS SERIES

FOREWORD

We began writing *Millennial Kingdom* in August of 2010 and a book that should have been completed in a year or two has taken six. The story of the writing of this book has become a story within a story and deserves to be told, because it is so intertwined and cannot be left apart.

In 2010 I made several feeble attempts to begin this story; however words would not come. I immediately faced a gigantic writer's wall that seemed impossible to surmount. A problem that defied my comprehension blocked my path forward. I wrestled with the question of how one thousand years could be condensed into one book. Patty and I both staggered with the enormous expanse of the work and thus writing stood still.

Then in 2011 an idea came to me and I rushed into writing. Sadly, after forty-eight pages the story bogged down and eventually went into a wastebasket. Alas, back to square one.

Patty and I took to prayer since the previous six books were all given and inspired by the Lord, and unless He gave us this one there would be no book 7. Months of silence passed.

But because He is faithful to complete the work He called us to, suddenly God gave the opening. It was genius and one we would never have thought of. PTL! The words flowed, yet only for five chapters. Where to go from there with the story? He was silent. We waited.

Then in the darkest part of a night, the Lord woke me and blocked out seven incredible segments spanning the entire thousand years. At the same time He filled my mind with the first Segment.

By now we were in early 2012, I feverously wrote and Patty was first reader and such a vital part with comments and doing initial editing.

Suddenly, to our dismay the Lord stopped us on the next to the last chapter of Segment One. I knew what that last chapter would contain, yet was not allowed to write it. Beyond that, the rest of the chapters in all remaining Segments of the book carried only sketchy thoughts. A dream revealed one scene, a few unattached images for others, Scripture from Revelation concerning the end, still no flow of plot, dialogue, nothing.

Then life happened. Patty started a home-based business upon retirement from her job. With that, an active ministry in Media Focus, travel, and conventions, each took their part in placing Millennial Kingdom on a shelf. This delay troubled and perplexed us both because we sensed a need to finish this book, all the while seeing days and months slip away.

That closed door opened in August 2016, six years from the date we first started Millennial Kingdom. The Lord spoke clearly, "It is time to finish!" I felt strongly He wanted us to complete writing by December 18, 2016. Impossible! Could it be done? Write the bulk of the book in less than four months? That would truly require a miracle!

A miracle it was! Patty and I both immersed ourselves into the writing. The Holy Spirit was all over it and poured the story into us with such force and direction until I felt I simply just held the pencil.

Chapter upon chapter filled my mind coming from places I never knew existed. Plot, action, dialogue, and characters emerged from somewhere far beyond my knowledge and ability. Patty was astounded and we both were overwhelmed by the Lord's anointing on this story.

Now the spiritual warfare became the most intense we have ever encountered. It was obvious the enemy hated this book and especially the final chapters. One night the battle escalated in the room where I wrote to a frightening level. It was demons against angels and at one point so fierce my hand, fingers, and arm locked up and they could not move. That attack to block the writing took place at the very point in the book which I believe satan hates the most. The reader can guess which passage it was.

To conclude, Patty and I give God the Glory! It is His story. On December 16, 2016 I wrote the final two words, The End.

CONTENTS

THE OPENING

CHAPTER 1

HIDDEN MONTHS

"Mommy, you promised to tell me of my hidden months," Johanna Hillag pleaded.

"I promised to tell you when you were old enough."

"I'm ten and that's certainly old enough!"

"I'm not sure you would understand . . . yet." Her mother seemed to waiver.

"Oh Mommy, my mind is expanding faster than I can learn. I want to know everything! Why won't you tell me? It's about me. I never hear you and Daddy talk of 'before'! Why?"

"Those times were dark and evil, and seldom spoken of by those who –."

"Night is dark, but I don't understand what evil is." Johanna followed her mother over to the kitchen sink.

"And well you shouldn't." Her mother stopped what she was doing to look deep into Johanna's persistent eyes.

"Please," she asked again. "I'm ready to listen. I want to know about my hidden months. I'm old enough. Please, Mommy." Johanna tugged at her mother's sleeve.

"Best we wait for your father to return with your brothers."

"John isn't interested. Besides, just because we're twins doesn't mean we have to do everything together!" Johanna stomped her foot. She was tired of waiting. "John can ask for himself – when he's eighteen!"

"Johanna Hillag!" Her mother was taken aback. "Are you angry now?"

"No! Yes! I'm ready to hear, learn, to know about – 'before' – and my hidden months. John is not, and Adam is – different – and doesn't need to know. You said so yourself."

"Adam is six, and yes, he is different. A millennial child."

"Mommy, you keep saying that, but you won't tell me how I am different," she cried as a tear ran down her cheek. "John and Adam have their time with Daddy. Can't this be just our time now?"

Her mother wiped Johanna's cheek, her brown eyes softening. "OK," she spoke gently. "Come." She led Johanna into the bedroom. "Sit," she said as she pointed to the bed. Johanna complied, watching her mother enter a closet. She emerged a few moments later with a locked metal box and placed it beside Johanna. Johanna gave her mother a questioning look.

"I keep the lock on this chain around my neck to remind me that the contents of this box are close to my heart. No one has seen this besides your father and myself. I will show it to you now and tell of your hidden months."

CHAPTER 2

THE BOX

Johanna eagerly peered into the box. The first thing to catch her eye was a small Bible. She glanced at her mother, who nodded for her to pick it up.

"Careful, the pages are brittle."

Johanna gently opened the Bible. She read on the presentation page: 'To Nikki. Love, Mom and Dad.'

"Grandma and Grandpa Savage gave me that Bible when I was about your age. It was in my purse the – the – night, or it would have been – burned up like your father's. I wish we had it still. It was your Papa Hillag's."

"Your Bible is strange, so old and worn. What's this?" Johanna reached into the box to pull out a tiny collar.

"That belonged to our little dog, Chesterfield. He didn't survive," Nikki said, sadly.

"These look like ancient SATs." Johanna held up two phones.

"They are, but they're not that old. Faithful SATs your father and I got in Atlanta."

"You were in Atlanta? Wow! When?"

"For a while. These SATs worked until right after you were born. Now, let me tell you about – ."

"Was this ring one Daddy gave you?" Johanna laughed. "It looks like he made it."

"He did." Nikki turned her head away. "He slipped it on my finger the day we were married in the Colorado woods . . . it was all we had," she murmured, lost in her memories.

"Oh, Mommy, I'm so sorry. I didn't mean to be disrespectful and make fun." The child put her arms around her mother and held her tight.

"I know you didn't. Those were horrible, desperate times. Here, let me tell about – ."

"Wait! I want to know everything. Pictures? Pictures we can download from the SATs or memory bars?"

"Everything was lost as we ran for our lives time and again. Lost, but for the memories that the Lord has graciously allowed me to keep. Perhaps I can paint mental pictures for you."

"Wonderful! What's this?"

"A walkie-talkie. It was given to me by Cheyann Armstrong. She owned the General Store in Douglas Landing. We used these to talk to each other."

"Why didn't you call on your SATs?"

"Too dangerous! Combats monitored calls."

"Who are Combats?"

"They were the military forces of the antichrist."

"Oh. Is your friend here now?"

"No, she was killed in a combat raid."

"I don't understand, Mommy."

"I know. You have never seen death, but I have . . . many times. What's left in the box?"

"This cracked cup."

"Silly, silly old cup." Nikki laughed, taking it from Johanna, touching it tenderly. "This opens a whole new set of memories for me," she began. "This is one of the cups from Atlanta Rona used to serve your father coffee."

"Rona?"

"Yes, our fourth generation Gamma robot."

"You mean like Chloe?"

"Chloe is newer and does things Rona couldn't; but let me tell you, Chloe can never be Rona. Rona had – personality." Nikki grew quiet. "She fought combats off while we escaped."

"Did she die?"

"You could say that." Nikki seemed to snap back from her thoughts. "Anyway, this cup reminded me of your father. I took

6

it to the Lake House and later packed it in the air van. 'Course that was before your father knew I was madly in love with him."

"Oh, Mommy, you have never told me how you met. Was this all in the 'before'?"

"Yes, but after the Rapture. I read about that to you in your Bible."

"Yes."

"When the Rapture happened, I was with my family, vacationing in Mexico. In the night, my mommy and daddy vanished. I was fifteen and so frightened, I panicked. I locked myself in my room and wouldn't come out. I was too sick to eat. That's when your father rescued me. I think it was love at first sight, at least, for me."

Johanna rolled over on the bed, propping her chin up in her hands. "How romantic." She sighed.

"Not so," Nikki corrected. "We were two kids, orphaned, and scared crazy. Your father's mommy, daddy and sister vanished, too. Can you imagine if five years from now we all disappeared and left you alone?"

"What did you do?" Johanna hung on her mother's every word.

"Ran for our lives. Your father was determined to survive."

"Did you?"

"Of course, but many of our friends and team members didn't." Nikki grew silent again.

"When did Daddy fall in love with you?"

Nikki laughed and wiped her eyes. "I used to tease him that it wasn't until I was the only one left and we were alone in the deep forest."

"Was it then?"

"I don't know, Johanna. He says he loved me from the time we met. He just wouldn't admit it; and he certainly didn't show it. I can tell you this much, child, Daddy has loved me as much as any man can love a woman. He would have given his life for me."

In that moment, Johanna saw something in her mother's eyes she had never seen before.

"He was my protector. With God's help us, we survived."

"Mommy," Johanna whispered. "Where are all your friends who got – killed?"

"I'm not sure, Sweetheart. We have not seen them, but I think they are with the Father, as it says in scripture: 'Those martyred in the Tribulation are before the Throne of God day and night. He wipes away their tears.' Perhaps we must wait until the end of this age for that reunion."

Johanna thought for a moment before forming her next question. "Were you and Daddy the only ones who survived the 'before'?"

Nikki smiled and hugged her daughter. "You and your brother did, too, and Chloe."

"Aw, Chloe's a robot. I mean people."

"Two others that we know of." Nikki grew serious.

"Steven in Colorado. How terrible of me; I can't remember his last name. Waaleen told me he was alive," Nikki smiled at her guardian angel positioned nearby. "And, old Shag is somewhere."

"I want to hear his story." Johanna hesitated, then added, "Should he ever come here."

"He may never speak of it . . ." Nikki's voice trailed off. "Some memories are better left behind, along with the past . . ." Then, she brightened up. "I see you have emptied the box. Are you ready to hear of your birth and the hidden months?"

Johanna took a deep breath before she responded. "Mommy, you are right. There is so much I don't understand. I'm just a little girl and my head hurts from all you have told me. But something in my heart yearns to know, to search for all that I must hear. I want so much to understand. I – I think I'm ready, Mommy. Please tell me everything!"

CHAPTER 3

TWIN BIRTHS

"It was July in the year two-thousand thirty-two," her mother began.

Johanna's eyes grew big. "How can that be? This is only the year ten," she exclaimed.

"True. It is year ten of the thousand-year reign of our Lord Christ. In 'before' time it was two-thousand and thirty-two years after the Lord's first coming."

"When He died on the cross and was resurrected?"

"Yes. Anyway, that July God poured out His wrath upon the earth with fierce heat. The sun was scorching. People all over the world were dying and cursing God. Power outages darkened the nations as air conditioners struggled to pull temperatures down. Plants and vegetation burned up; many of the beautiful trees and bushes in our forest died. To stay cool, your daddy and I and little Chesterfield sat in Cold Creek under shady spots and poured water over each other; that is, until the water got so hot we had to get out."

"Cold Creek was hot?" Johanna gasped in disbelief.

"It was like a sauna, and I thought for sure I was going to die. Your daddy took us to a cave he had discovered, but the heat and air inside was suffocating. Toward the end of July, when we were certain it was the end for us, the weather suddenly changed to freezing cold – in July, Johanna. We all got sick with colds and fever and that's when our little dog Chesterfield passed . . ." Nikki's voice broke.

"Aw," Johanna grew sad. "I wish . . ."

"I know, dear. Me, too! July 30th, we were trying to stay well and warm in our old log house – ."

"This one?"

"No. Anyway, I went into labor. I was scared out of my wits and trying to be brave. I can't even imagine what your father was feeling. There were no hospitals; at least, none we could get to."

"What's a hospital?"

"It was a building full of rooms with beds for sick people went. Doctors and nurses there treated them and gave medicine so they could get well."

Johanna sat up in the middle of the bed, her attention on her mother. "What was it like to get sick?"

"When sin came into the world, disease and sickness came with it. Your throat might hurt or your nose run or feel stuffy. You could have fever, coughs, and your body would ache. I used to get terrible headaches."

"My head hurts sometimes," Johanna commented.

Her mother laughed and playfully ran her fingers through Johanna's hair. "That's because you strain your brain, girl, not because you're sick. There is no disease or sickness any more . . . not since Jesus came. Anyway, a hospital was where doctors could assist women giving birth and provide medical care."

"Why didn't you go to one?"

"Your daddy and I were believers in the true Christ and considered fugitive Non Coms. To be discovered or captured meant taking the mark of the Antichrist Justus Christos or immediate and certain death by – beheading!"

Johanna drew back in horror. "That is awful! Lord Jesus would have none of – ."

"He hadn't returned yet, dear, and the world was dominated by an evil monster, Christos," her mother's voice ended with a hiss. Johanna saw anger in her mother's face, unusual and unbecoming; then, quickly her expression transformed to one of love. She touched Johanna's face gently.

"Your father was as scared as me. He had to be doctor plus carry responsibility for my life and yours on his shoulders. John cried in such a tiny frail voice when he was born, and your daddy was so excited he shouted, 'He is a miracle and a gift from God. We must name him John!' Then, to our total surprise, you arrived. We never imagined there were two gifts from God; so we named you, Johanna. Born July 30, 2032, you stole our hearts."

CHAPTER 4

DIFFERENCES

"You see, Joanna, there are fourteen months added to your age. Those are the months from your birth until the return of our Lord Jesus that we left hidden until you were old enough to understand. We just counted your birth from year one of the Millennium," her mother explained.

"Is that what makes John and I different from Adam?"

"When you were born, yes, you are both Tribulation children, and Adam is a Millennial. From this moment on, my precious daughter . . ." her mother paused to look deep into Johanna's heart and soul with kind eyes. "From this moment on, you will remember you were born during the worst time in the history of mankind. And you are not ten, but actually eleven, going on twelve. In a few months, you will have your twelfth birthday."

Johanna sat motionless, stunned, staring at her mother and trying to assimilate what she had just been told. She began to giggle.

"What?" her mother frowned.

"Wait until I call John, 'Little Brother'; I'm fourteen months older now." Johanna laughed.

"Silly girl! John was born a few minutes before you and will always be your older brother. But have your fun with him, and your daddy and I will explain his hidden months. We'd better go to the kitchen." Johanna's mother started to get off the bed, but Johanna grabbed her hand and pulled her back.

"No! Wait! I want to hear more, Mommy. Please!"

"About what?" her mother looked surprised at Johanna's persistent interest.

"I know I am different than Grandma and Grandpa Savage, Papa and Mema Hillag, and my other relatives, but you have never told me why. They can do so many wondrous things that we can't. We have to travel in cars and transports, but they just, go! Poof! I still remember trying to walk through a door like Grand Papa Farmer does, and I nearly broke my nose."

"True, so true," her mother said as she laughed. "They are wondrous, indeed. You see, child, they lived during the Age of Grace – the Church Age. When our Lord Jesus Christ came for the Church, they were all given glorified, resurrected bodies, flesh and bone, perfect in every way; spiritual bodies, able to move in space, and yes, go through doors and walls, just like Jesus when He rose and appeared to His disciples. They never grow old, get tired, feel hunger or pain."

"But Grand Mema Emile will lie down and rest with me, and all of them eat with us, Mommy."

"Yes, but not because they must. We are different, Johanna, because our bodies are flesh and blood. Put your head against my chest. Hear my heart beating?"

"Yes."

"Yours is, too, and we get hungry, tired, need to breathe air, and can burn our finger on a hot pan. They are Resurrected Saints; we are Tribulation Saints, and Adam –."

"I know, a spoiled Millennial child with no angel."

"Stop that!" Her mother swatted at her playfully. "There is no need for Guardian Angels during the Millennium. Lord Christ guards them."

"Then, why do I have Ofinian, and Lonsu is always with John? Couldn't they be of better use with the Choir Angels, or as Messengers or Gathering Angels, instead of following us around with nothing else to do?"

"I was assigned to be with you at the moment of your conception, never to leave for all of eternity," Ofinian answered Johanna's question. "My duty did not change with the coming of the Master, O little one."

"What an incredibly, fascinating age we live in, Johanna." Her mother squeezed her hand. "Such an interesting, indescribable mix of creatures all living together; a perfect existence in unblemished harmony; well, at least for now."

"Think of the differences we each possess, Johanna. Angels like your Ofinian, my Waaleen, your daddy's Detrius, John's Lonsu –!"

"And Great Auntie Janee's Miglia. I really like her angel," Johanna gushed.

"Angels, Resurrected Saints, us, and children born in the Millennium. A lion plays with a lamb instead of eating it. What miracles," her mother murmured.

CHAPTER 5

THE RETURN OF CHRIST

Johanna marveled at the world she lived in. She was lost in thought until her mother once again started to get up. Johanna lunged for her hand, to hold her back.

"No! Not yet, Mommy! Tell me what happened next."

"Next?"

"After I was born."

"Let's save that for another time. We need to start dinner before your daddy and brothers return."

"I won't eat!"

"Johanna!"

"Please, Mommy, tell me the rest. What was the last fourteen months like, and I want to hear about when King Jesus came with His angels, and army, Papa, Mema, and all the rest. Please finish, Mommy," Johanna pleaded. "Don't make me wait any longer. Please!"

"You think you are ready to hear about the last of the 'before' time?"

"Yes, oh yes!" Johanna bounced on the bed and sat up straight.

"All right, but we must hurry." Her mother fluffed a pillow to prop herself up on and settled in. Johanna gave her full wide-eyed attention.

"A darkness fell upon the face of the earth," Nikki began. "A darkness so hideous and sinister words fail to describe it. It wasn't a dark like the nighttime after the sun goes down, but a heavy dense spiritual darkness. A black full of godlessness so painful, men and women cried out curses to a God they didn't believe in. They gnawed their tongues until they choked on their own blood."

Johanna shivered. A chill ran up her spine. "Did – did you and daddy do that?"

"No, we were believers and the Holy Spirit was beside us; but let me tell you, my child, we felt its terrifying effects.

"By then, most of the earth's water was polluted. Oceans and lakes were dead and stagnant. Nothing could live in them, and there was a severe shortage of drinkable water. Even Cold Creek was polluted. We had to boil the water an hour before it was safe!"

"Oh, no!" Johanna gasped. She had no idea what polluted meant, only that it sounded ugly.

"Many of the world's rivers dried up. Our Mississippi River was merely a stream in a dry, caked riverbed. The Great Euphrates River completely gone. The evil Antichrist, Christos, who made the world believe the real Christ was an alien who abducted men, women and children in the Rapture, now told everyone that the alien Christ was coming back to destroy the earth. He urged all nations to amass their armies to a place called Armageddon, to fight and defeat this alien Christ."

"But He wasn't really an alien, was He, Mommy? "

"Not on our life, Johanna, nor did they defeat Him. But before that battle was fought, terrible things took place. I shudder to think what might have happened to all of us, if we would have been in the old log house."

"Our house, Mommy?"

"Not this one, dear. The old log house had stood solid and firm for over one hundred years. It was dilapidated when we moved in. All the windows were broken out, and the doors missing. We had two poles in the main room propping up a sagging roof."

"But our house is so beautiful and strong!"

"I'm getting to that, dear. It was mid-afternoon on that day. Our SATs no longer worked, so we were isolated from world news. What we didn't know was that the earth shook violently, like it was attempting to cast off a cloak concealing all the evil underneath. Unbeknown to us, a great and powerful earthquake was racing across the face of the planet. Cities were leveled, mountains crumbled, islands disappeared into the ocean's waters and Christo's temple collapsed as Jerusalem broke into three parts.

"I was in the log house with you and John when suddenly I felt an uneasiness and urging I didn't fully understand."

"It was Waaleen trying to guard you, wasn't it, Mommy?"

"I think it was all three angels," her mother reflected, 'but mostly the Holy Spirit. Just then your father ran in from outside, yelling for us to get out. We barely had time to run down by Cold Creek, when the quake hit. The earth shook with such force and vengeance, we were thrown flat to the ground. Trees toppled, the earth cracked with a loud bang, rocks and branches literally flew through the air. Your father tried to cover us with his body, but we were tossed about like bugs. I managed to look up to see the roof of our house cave in, then the logs seemed to explode into a heap. One log almost rolled over us!"

"I don't understand what it means to be scared or afraid, Mommy, but I must have been."

"You and your brother were just babies, but yes, you cried, no, you screamed; it took us a long time to quiet you both. I'm sure you sensed our fear."

"If our house was ruined, where did we stay? How did we get this one?"

"We rebuilt the log house after King Jesus returned." Her mother swept her arm around the room. "Bigger, and beautiful; a truly amazing home in the image and spirit of the old one. But back then, in the 'before' time, we retreated to the cave your daddy had discovered."

"Was that the end of God's anger?" Johanna asked.

"No, it wasn't, child. The sky grew dark with hideous, foul storm clouds. They neither moved, nor produced rain. Day by day they became more and more ominous. There was no wind, only a death-knell of silence."

Johanna drew in a long breath, aware of her heart beating faster. She dreaded hearing what happened next, but was almost

17

compelled for her mother to continue the story. Her eyes and expression must have conveyed her eagerness.

"Then it started! The sky split apart with blinding flashes of lightning, one after another after another, on and on with no letup. The thunderclaps made our ears pop until we thought we would go mad.

"We huddled in the cave, plugging our ears, trying to keep you children covered and quiet, fearful we could be buried at any moment. Then it happened! A Bang! A crash! Shaking! I couldn't imagine what it was – until – there in a blinding flash! A chunk of ice the size of a boulder hit!"

Johanna drew back with a scowl. "What was it, Mommy?"

"Hundred-pound hailstones!"

"I've seen hail, but they are always tiny."

"As they should be, but these were huge, knocking down trees. One smashed into the basement of what was left of the Parrigan house. Your father and I and little Chesterfield hid from Combats several times in that . . . secret basement . . . ," her mother murmured. "Humm, anyway, the hundred-pound hailstones were foretold in the Book of Revelation, and they proved smashing."

"Mother! They weren't funny!"

"Indeed not! After that the sky remained a dismal gloomy black. We never saw the sun, only grey in the daytime; starless skies at night with only a hint of a glow for the moon, when it was out."

"That sounds awful."

"It was. So many people were dead; cities demolished, the earth completely ruined; yet Christos was still demanding the worship of every person, and the taking of his mark. The whole world was thrown into utter chaos and the antichrist began feverishly gathering a massive army to battle the One he referred to as the alien Christ."

"Was that when Lord Jesus returned?"

"Yes. We had no outside news because our SATs no longer picked up any signal, but we knew when it happened."

"How, Mommy?"

"It grew light when it was night. The clouds rolled away, Praise the Lord." Her mother began to weep, but kept talking through her tears. "Light shined in a clear blue sky – oh, it was glorious! A miracle, grass and trees grew green before our eyes. Oh, child, we heard birds sing, for the first time in months and months. We walked to the creek in the warmth of the light and there, we didn't have to be told, but we tasted it. The water ran cold and pure! Jesus Christ had returned! We sensed His Presence all around us and heard His loving and gentle voice in our hearts and minds . . . calling us. Oh, Johanna, I can't describe the healing your daddy and I saw in the world around us and in each other's faces. You children glowed in the brilliance, and we were filled with such joy!

"Later, we found out when everyone was gathered for the Judgment of the Nations, that the armies of the antichrist were consumed instantly by the glory of the Lord's countenance. The end of the antichrist, Justus Emmanuel Christos and the false prophet, Elias Noostradam, came swiftly. Both were judged eternally damned and cast into the Lake of Fire."

"Wow!" Johanna gave an excited whistle. "And Lord Jesus took His rightful place as King, huh? What did He do next?"

"Your daddy and I were each holding one of you. Everyone had traveled to Jerusalem to gather before the Son of God, Jesus Christ. It was awesome to see Him. We, along with others who had believed on the true Christ, were sent to His right. Those who also had not taken the mark, but didn't believe, were ordered to His left. They began to scream and plead with the Lord, but He told them that He never knew them, and they were banished to the place of torment to await final judgment."

"That scares me, I think," Johanna said dropping her eyes. "Did you know any of them?"

"Seems there were a few from Douglas Landing and Applegate that we knew by name only. The great news is that we met other believers from our area, who also survived the Tribulation and are our neighbors now."

"After that you came home?" Johanna snuggled next to her mom.

"There was the Judgment of the Nations. The ones who mistreated Israel no longer exist. The United States was restored to the greatness we once had."

"We're home!" Johanna heard her daddy call from the other end of the house. "Where is everybody?"

"That's the story of the end of the Tribulation and the Glorious Return of Christ." Her mother smiled as she helped Johanna hop off the bed.

SEGMENT ONE

FARMER & EMILE'S REIGN

CHAPTER 6

DAWN OF A SPECIAL DAY

Farmer walked the banks of Cold Creek slowly, lost in thought. The newly risen sun made its warmth felt, its light breaking through the trees. He paused at a spot where the bank overhung a sharp bend in the creek. Little eddies swirled in vanishing circles, as the water swiftly disappeared from Farmer's view into a deep pool beneath the outcrop where he stood, only to reappear seconds later on the other side.

"Hum." Farmer rubbed his chin. He tried to form mental images of an event that took place at this location some years before.

"Ya can't see it atall can ya, Adreen?" Farmer asked his Guardian Angel who stood nearby in the trees.

"I cannot. What took place in those years was shut out of Paradise."

"I reckon it ta be best we didn't know then, but it sure be painful ta learn of it now . . ." Farmer spoke in a low voice. He gazed on the tumbling motion of the water over rocks as his eyes followed the creek downstream in its endless journey to flow into the Shanko River. How many times he had walked these banks.

"Course, thet be over a hundred years ago." He smiled at the thought, then grew solemn. "Thet was 'before' . . ."

"Here you are, Farmer," Emile appeared beside him. "Froton told me you were walking Cold Creek."

Emile studied Farmer's face a moment. She, too, grew serious.

"What are you thinking, Farmer? I sense sadness."

"See right there where the water goes outa sight?" Farmer pointed.

"Yes."

"Mark tol' me best he could recollect, thet be the spot he and Nikki hid in thet pool under this bank while the enemy soldiers of the antichrist walked by; here where we stand, Emile. It was dead of winter with snow an' Nikki pregnant with the twins, in ice-cold water, they was scared, running fer their lives! Just a wanten to live!" Farmer shook his head. "I can't even picture in my mind the horrible – !"

Tears filled both their eyes as Emile gently put her fingers on Farmer's lips.

"But they did live, Farmer, and John and Johanna were born. What a blessing during such a terrible time."

"Aye, what excitement – an' relief when we all returned ta earth ta find out Mark hed believed in the Lord and not be lost," Farmer declared, remembering.

"And we met Nikki for the first time, to learn they believed in Jesus together," Emile reflected.

"Reckon she be the perfect mate fer Mark, fer them both ta go through the Tribulation."

"And the first time I held the twins they kissed me! I felt like a grandmother all over again!"

"Thet ya air, many times over, Emile." Farmer laughed.

"Oh, Farmer! This is their special day and we ought to have only happy thoughts and memories."

"Reckon so, Emile." Farmer grew pensive again, throwing a quick glance at the pool beneath the creek bank. "But still we be rememberen', bad memories mixed with the good. Ya think thet will ever change?"

"Perhaps in the New Heaven and Earth," Emile reflected. "God will wipe away all the bad times – along with our tears . . . for eternity."

"He will hev ta do it, 'cause right now I can't forget what we've been told; the awful unthinkable events an' conditions of the Tribulation years an' the dark times when John and Johanna were born."

"Shh," Emile soothed as she patted Farmer's face lovingly. "Remember, this is their special day and no dark memories are allowed to cloud it. We live in a perfect world filled with light and joy. Every day is precious, Farmer."

Farmer smiled at the sight of Emile's shining face; then held her tight. "I love this place and I love you," he murmured.

"I love you, too, forever and always." She kissed him as she stepped back. "I have coffee going at the house. Want some?"

Farmer nodded. "Walk or fly?"

"Let's walk and savor each moment."

CHAPTER 7

BACK HOME

Farmer took Emile's hand as they walked beside the creek towards home. Farmer grew quiet and was soon lost in thought. He remembered when they first returned to Douglas Landing, how thrilled they were to learn of Mark and Nikki taking up residence in the old log house that had stood strong and silent for a century. Instead of their moving somewhere else or into Douglas Landing, they insisted the young couple remain at the original homestead site and rebuild the log house, bigger and better than it had ever been. Of course, Mark and Nikki were eager to comply, since their married life began in that house with good times spent there despite the horrific conditions of the world around them.

Returning Resurrected Saints pitched in to help Tribulation Saints with a glorious house rising. Clarence Judd supervised the replacing of stones in the fireplace. Memories flooded Farmer's mind as he pictured it happening again. 'Reckon we did this once before, Clarence,' Farmer remembered teasing his former neighbor.

'Yep, but I like it better this time,' he had replied.

'How so?' Farmer asked.

'No backache.' The corners of Judd's mouth had curved up slightly.

'Quit the jawen' and get to worken.' Joe Baltman walked up and smacked Farmer's shoulder. 'We got walls to put up and a roof to raise so's we can get these youngens settled in!'

Useable logs from the old house were set in place with the help of an old log loader Donald Parrigan found in one of the lumber mills sheds. New logs were cut to expand the original two-bedroom home into a four-bedroom, complete with a large family den. However, at Mark's insistence the loft was retained.

The saints worked long hours from dawn till dark, bringing Mark to the point of exhaustion.

'Don't you dudes ever get tired?' he cried out the fifth day while slinging a hammer across the newly laid floor.

'No!' the rest responded in unison.

Meanwhile Emile, Sally Baltman, Beth Parrigan and Ella May Brooks set about helping Nikki put the final touches on the interior of the house.

And, what a sight it was to see when finished! Farmer reflected.

'O, dear God! It's a mansion!' Nikki burst out, clapping her hands, then covering her mouth as tears welled up. Mark took her in his arms, as seven years of pent-up tribulation horror were washed away.

'Probably they was a thinken o' the hard times they hed come through!' Farmer thought. 'Fearen' every moment in the old log house thet the enemy might break in on them. Hiden' other times in the neighbor's secret basement – like rats ,as Mark tol' it – and finally holed up in a cave. Then ta have a mansion of ther own!' "Umm, Umm," Farmer mumbled.

'Nikki and I can never express our thanks,' Mark spoke through tears. 'In our most elaborate dreams we could never have imagined this!'

'Thank you all so much, we love you more than words can express!' Nikki added, reaching down to pick up Johanna, who had just toddled up to wrap her little arms around her mother's leg.

'Reckon the joy we all see in yer faces is plenty of thanks fer – !'

"Farmer, I declare!" Emily broke into his thoughts. "You have been off again in another world this morning. Here is your coffee, my dear."

Farmer took his cup from Emily and they both went outside to sit on the porch.

"Were you still thinking about what Mark, Nikki and the twins endured during the Tribulation?" Emile looked deep into his eyes, in an attempt to understand what had preoccupied him so completely during their walk to the house.

He snapped back to the present, shook his head, rubbing his hand through his hair, and chuckled.

CHAPTER 8

COFFEE TALK

"Actually," Farmer smiled, taking a sip of coffee. "I was thinken how coffee was one o' the things I surly did miss in Paradise." He turned his head to gaze at Cold Creek. There, the morning sun glistened on the water.

"What?" Emily blurted out. "But Farmer, we had such wondrous, exotic, exquisite things to drink, and certainly not of this world."

"Weren't coffee," Farmer declared, then burst out laughing.

Emile stared at him, then playfully poked him. "Silly, you weren't thinking that at all!"

Farmer wiped his face and took Emile's hand "I was actually remembering when we rebuilt the old log house."

"Oh, yes!" Emily brightened. "What a glorious start to the Millennium. It was our very first project."

"Emile, I knew how much thet place meant to you. Air ya sorry we didn't fix it fer ourselves?"

"Absolutely not! Besides, I spent more of my life in our home on Breach Street."

"Do ya regret not fixen our place there? We hed lots o' memories in thet little house."

"The only memory I have there is of an empty house and lonely life with you gone." A tear trickled down Emile's cheek. She squeezed his hand and dropped her eyes. When she looked back up, she smiled. "I love our home. You chose the perfect location on Cold Creek. Our house is magnificent, tucked away in a beautiful setting, and we are still here on our homestead. You made sure we had a porch just like before, but most of all, Farmer, I love our home because you are in it."

Farmer took a deep breath, deeply touched by Emile's words. He remained silent for some time. He withdrew his hand and drank more coffee.

"Farmer, do you ever miss the home that the Lord prepared for us in Paradise?" Emile asked, reaching up to touch his face.

"Thet fer sure is a place beyond compare, and I admit, I do long fer it at times. But then I think, we be here a thousand years. I reckon the Lord Jesus done made it strong enough ta last thet long!"

Emile laughed.

"But Emile, what a home this be for us."

"I know, I know, lots of room, and even electricity," Emile laughed. "Not that we have to cook unless we wish to for those who came out of the Great Tribulation – ."

"Or were born in the Millennium," Farmer added. "Which reminds me, I did miss eating meat, and chicken, even fish while we were in Paradise."

"Oh, phooey; and you wouldn't have those now if it wasn't for the flesh-and-blood people needing to eat meat, mister Farmer. Those like Mark and Nikki, the twins and Adam – and a growing number of others. Anyway, I do miss the fabulous delicacies we enjoyed in Paradise that aren't here, let me remind you." Emile's eyes sparkled.

Farmer grinned. He finished his coffee.

Emile grew solemn. "I truly hope the children are pleased with the gift we are giving them," she said, quietly.

Farmer got up and took their empty cups. "They gonna be most excited," he exclaimed.

"Well, I know two things you didn't lose in the resurrection," she called after him as he ambled towards the door.

"What thet be, Emile?" He turned to look at her, curious.

"Your love of coffee and that sweet Texas drawl."

CHAPTER 9

FIRST CELEBRATION ARRIVALS

"Reckon we just go on in?" Farmer inquired of Emile as they arrived outside Mark and Nikki's house.

"Farmer, you know it frightens the twins and Adam when we just appear inside." The couple walked to the door, which was wide open and inviting. Farmer raised his hand to knock, then held back.

"Do there be any birthday children hereabouts?" Farmer hollered his greeting instead.

"There be," came an excited response and the scramble of running feet sounded. The twins appeared first, tearing across the large open space of the living room, dodging furniture pieces, followed closely by Adam.

"Grandpapa Farmer! Grandmamma Emile!" John and Johanna screamed, flying into waiting arms. They were held lovingly and tenderly for some time as the children spoke all at once, telling of their plans for the day.

"The house is decorated and so pretty," Johanna exclaimed.

"Papa and Nana Hillag are coming." John was excited and couldn't wait to tell the news. "All the way from Lugar de Paraiso – wherever that is, and it has been so long since – well, I have trouble remembering what they look like." Both children laughed.

"And your Grandma and Grandpa Savage? Will they be here?" Emile inquired.

John and Johanna dropped their eyes and sadness clouded their faces. "We haven't heard anything," they said in unison; then Johanna brightened. "I asked King Jesus if He would remind them," she declared with determination.

"An' I reckon He answered?" Farmer asked.

"He always answers." Johanna smiled. "He said that our birthdays and those who would celebrate them is all planned out."

"Which doesn't tell us a thing," John mumbled.

Farmer and Emile laughed out loud and squeezed the twins in a hug.

"You bring them a gift?" Adam broke into the conversation. "Ain't my birthday and I ain't getting any gifts so I don't really care who shows up," he remarked, with a sullen smirk.

"Oh Adam, you don't really think that," Emile responded with concern. She reached out to hold Adam but he drew back.

"I do! And don't touch me. I don't want you here or anyone else!" With those cutting words Adam spun around and ran down a hallway.

"Well, do tell." Farmer scratched his head. He was perplexed by the actions of this grandchild.

"Adam has acted selfishly all morning. I told Mother he is such a spoiled Millennium brat," Johanna explained.

"Child, don't be harsh and unkind with yer words. Adam be yer brother," Farmer chided.

"He is different, Papa Farmer, and often mean. The rattlesnakes show more compassion than he does."

"He was cross and argued with Daddy while we were gathering party things in Douglas Landing," John added.

"Well, we shall not let Adam's words or actions spoil your birthdays. He will be better, you'll see," Emile said, her words meant to defuse tension.

"Welcome," Mark and Nikki greeted them. "What a glorious day, and we have such a celebration planned."

"We left the front door open so you wouldn't have to come through it," Mark said as he grinned.

"And scare the children," Emile added. "Nikki, what a beautiful dress. You are gorgeous; let me see your earrings, and your hair. Oh, my!"

"Mother, Adam was mean and shouted hurtful words," Johanna blurted out.

"We know, Johanna." Nikki pulled her daughter to her. "Your father has dealt with that and sent him to his room. And don't you tattle."

"Come back to the kitchen with us. We are so pleased you are here. It is especially important to the twins today." Mark motioned them to follow.

"Ya reckon us ta be equally excited and anxious when they reach their 730th birthday?" Farmer laughed.

"Oh Farmer, the resurrection has certainly not hampered your silliness. Why 730?" Emile swatted his arm.

"Good spiritual number, as I see it."

"Even though we are close enough to walk to your house," Mark continued, "the children, Nikki and I never tire of seeing the two of you. I love our coffee times on your porch." Mark led them into the kitchen and over to a table filled with delicious-looking, quartered sandwiches, a variety of chips, and trays filled with veggies and fruits. On a smaller table sat a beautiful birthday cake decorated with frosted flowers, the edible glitter sparkling in the morning sun streaming through the window. Twenty-four candles circled the top layer.

"Oh my, children, you are expecting a houseful!" Emile gasped. "Look at the size of that cake."

"Indeed!" Nikki laughed. "And you are the first arrivals."

CHAPTER 10

THE HILLAGS

Deafening shrieks from the Hillag twins suddenly filled the house. Everyone froze.

"The children!" Nikki shouted.

Farmer and Emily were instantly in Johanna's bedroom. Mark and Nikki were right behind, busting through the door. Nothing of the twins was visible except thin arms wrapped around the necks of a striking figure of a man and a radiant woman. Tanned legs clung to waists of the adults, while small feet kicked in time to their excited laughs, giggles, teases, hugs and kisses.

"I declare," Farmer exclaimed, taking in the sight. "Reckon it be a handful o' moons since I see youngens this stirred up ta see their Grandma and Grandpa."

"It's Papa Caleb!" John proclaimed as he slid down to the floor.

"And Nana Sarah!" Johanna bubbled, holding tight to her grandmother.

"Dad, you scared the life out of all of us," Mark declared.

Caleb turned to Mark. His keen eyes were penetrating, taking in every feature of his son's face, peering into his mind and heart, his very soul. No words were spoken, but Caleb's facial expression changed from a strange sadness to one pleased with what he beheld. His eyes welled up to overflowing and tears tracked down his cheeks. He pulled Mark to him in a heartfelt hug, meant to convey the joy he felt.

"Son, in our 'before' life, I was always only 'Pops.' I can't tell you how special it is to hear you call me 'Dad'; and, even though we have seen you numerous times since Christ's return, – your – I – my heart –." Caleb choked up and couldn't go on.

34

Mark laughed; then grew serious when he saw Caleb's distress.

Everyone stood in silence. The twins looked bewildered, trying to understand what was happening.

"What is it, Nana?" Johanna whispered to Sarah, who responded with a soft, "Shhh."

Caleb turned his eyes towards Sarah with a slight nod that carried a meaning so rich and vast it slipped by Mark, Nikki and the twins unnoticed. However, Farmer and Emile caught it and understood full well the memories and emotions carried in Caleb's glance and tip of his head.

The four of them were keenly aware of the sights, sounds and glory they experienced in Paradise. Joyful memories of being gathered to the river to greet family and friends who had passed from death to a newness of life, into a marvelous place prepared for God's children. What incredible and blessed reunions filled Paradise! The relief they felt to discover a loved one had believed on Christ, became born again and was now in Paradise, assured them there would never be another separation.

But Farmer, Emile, Caleb and Sarah also painfully remembered loved ones they longed to see and worried that they might not ever know in the new kingdom. Hoping against hope each time they gathered at the river, it would be those they thought about; yet, sadly, they never arrived. Then, one day they would learn those loved ones had died, and were not to be found in Paradise. Such grief and deep sorrow ravaged the saints facing the stark truth of their loved one now lost forever. Never a glad reunion, left only to see them one final time at the Last Judgment and listen to their pronouncement of doom: 'Your name is not written in the Book of Life. Be cast into utter darkness and fire for eternity!'

Farmer and Emile remembered that Caleb and Sarah faced that unthinkable possibility their entire time in Paradise, never knowing for sure; clinging to hope that Mark would accept Christ. No doubt the Savages had held to that same hope for their daughter, Nikki. How easy it would have been for two teenagers, orphaned by the Rapture, in fear for their very lives, to embrace the dark side and follow the antichrist; or, be destroyed by evil forces before they had an opportunity to believe.

"You didn't follow darkness, but sought the Light, which is Jesus Christ," Caleb declared with almost a shout that startled everyone. "How excited and elated Sarah and I were to discover both you children not only were saved but survived the Tribulation and the forces of the antichrist," Caleb continued, as he drew his family into his arms.

"Oh Caleb, why do you have such a capacity to bring us all to tears, then make us laugh? But you shouldn't discuss such matters in front of the children," Sarah chided.

"It's OK," Johanna piped up. "Momma told me about the 'before' years."

"She did?" Caleb kissed her forehead. "We must discuss that, and you will tell me all about it."

"What have you been doing?" Esther walked into the bedroom. "I've been ringing the doorbell until I gave up and came on in."

"Auntie Esther is here!" Both twins leaped into Esther's arms, nearly toppling her.

CHAPTER 11

A HERO

The initial excitement of the children over having their Papa Caleb, Nana Sarah and Auntie Esther began to fade by mid-morning. The sun was warm and inviting, calling John and Johanna outside to play. Adam joined them, hardly acknowledging the adults on his way through the family room.

The house was brightly decorated for the twins' birthday party, and the food was prepared, so little remained to do except await the arriving family and guests. Who would come to the celebration was, however, uncertain. In the Millennium, one did not send out cards with a personal invitation and request for an RSVP. It was the guardian angels that spread the word, and Caleb's angel, Herculon, responded immediately, "They will be here."

Clifton and Rachel's angels sent word days later that they wished to attend, but had some uncertainty over a project Lord Jesus had them supervising. It must be completed first. The silence from the rest of the family and friends, was their way of saying, 'We will surprise you when we appear in your house!' Or, there would be a knock on the front door, if the guests would happen to be Tribulation Saints or Millennials. This uncertainty didn't foster disappointment or even discouragement, but rather generated a sense of mounting excitement. Who would be next?

The women busied themselves in the kitchen and dining area, while Farmer and Mark, coffee cups in hand, along with Caleb holding his juice drink, made their way into the office den. An unplanned reaction among the three men began touching their emotions.

Caleb studied shelves lining one wall of the room, mostly bare except for a handful of worn and pitiful books. Caleb would never be critical of a single page, for he knew each copy carried precious meanings of indescribable sacrifice and worth. He spoke with reverence befitting the moment.

"Son, I perceive you built this room in faith of what will be; not what is now."

Mark followed his father's gaze to the sparse copies of books to understand the meaning of Caleb's insightful comment.

"Yes, Dad. Too many great works were destroyed in the Tribulation, yet I do have faith that, as our Lord Jesus Christ brings restoration, these shelves will be filled with the best, the purest writings, and all will be historically accurate; books that have value and worth; that build up and not tear down; stories that reflect Light, not darkness – truth, not lies. God's Word, the Holy Bible, will take its rightful place of honor over and above every book." Mark smiled as he offered his conclusion. "And, we have a thousand years to read them all as well as forever to explore the unfathomable depths of God's Word."

"I reckon what ya just spoke deserves an Amen," Farmer replied in reflection.

The three men took seats in cushy recliners that seemed perfect for this den. No word was uttered as they sipped coffee. Caleb finished his drink, quietly taking in the magnitude of the moment. Their minds recounted in thoughts and images what had already transpired in only ten years of the Millennium. They could not even imagine their lives forged over a thousand years, when the earth would be repopulated and rebuilt into a perfect world ruled by Christ, the Prince of Peace, The King of kings; a world void of sin and evil – yet, would it come? From the first day of the Millennium, that Glorious day when Christ took His rightful place in the Temple and all people as one worshipped Him, a foreboding realization sprouted up like a tiny weed.

As days passed and time progressed, it seemed that the creative force of God, which controls mankind and all of nature, was sent back to the Garden of Eden. To restore the earth as it was originally intended, a world that sin could not invade again. Yet, would that truly be?

From that very first day of the Millennium, an unsettling dread wrestled its way into the thoughts and minds of the Resurrected Saints and some of the Tribulation Saints. That fear sought a dark, hidden secret place in shadowy recesses, waiting to manifest its unsettling lies in its unholy quest to dampen Christ's priceless gifts of Joy and Peace. But what was to come could not be denied, for the Scriptures were quite clear and descriptive concerning events at the Millennium's end. That sickening reality exposed itself in flashes of images forcing the three men to mentally acknowledge the evidence that a horrific final battle would come as surely as each second marched slowly but steadfastly towards that day.

Smiles vanished and a strange sadness clouded the men's expressions. Farmer sensed what they saw and felt; his own thoughts were kin to theirs.

"Best we not speak o' wicked doings to come fer they can never be a part o' the world we live in now," Farmer said.

Caleb shuddered and nodded his head, pushing the foreboding predictions back to their hiding places. His gaze focused on Farmer and his demeanor brightened.

"When I first met you in Paradise, Farmer, I was awestruck. I had heard stories about you from Grandfather Clifton, so the day I stepped foot on the porch of the old log ranch house, it felt like your presence was still there. You became my hero."

"Reckon me ta be a sorry example of a hero, Caleb, compared ta all ya did in life; or Mark, fighting ta live in the Tribulation. I fer sure never earned no hero medals. Was only a simple man with a dream, which I took a chance on – followed only ta lose it all. Emile was the hero fer goin' on alone. Yer Grandpa was a hero who fought in a terrible war and forged a life in the virgin territory o' Alaska. Janee was most a hero fer overcoming her own demons and making her last days on earth count fer the Lord!"

Caleb's eyes brimmed with tears, which he quickly brushed away. Mark buried his face in his hands, then looked up when Farmer continued.

"Only two heroes in this room, as I see it." Farmer leaned forward in his chair, directing his attention towards Caleb. "Caleb and yer helpmate Sarah – ya pulled up stakes and left yer home and all ya knew, ta be missionaries in a most beautiful place; but full o' closed-minded and cold-hearted people. Ya faced Satan's emissary in spiritual battle an' had victory."

"An ya, Mark, robbed o' youth but still young, ya became a leader o' men an' women an' faced death more'n any man should hav' ta. Ya braved forces o' evil ta take yer stand, determined ta survive, an' all the while pertectin' yer wife an' babies. I could never o' done all that! The only thing I ever did thet would give even a speck o' notion ta greatness were ta hav a family thet fer a century built a most profound an' impacting legacy. Ya air my heroes – all o' ya!"

With that, the old patriarch rose from his chair and bowed in humble respect to his great and great-great grandsons. They both jumped to their feet and stood by Farmer's side. He drew them both to his chest, holding them tight. Then, he kissed their foreheads with a light touch of his lips as though passing on a blessing – first to Caleb, then to Mark. How he had longed for this moment all those years in Paradise; family he had never met, and only heard about, until the Raptured Saints arrived and he looked upon Caleb, Sarah and Esther for the very first time. Then, the fleeting remembrance of the seven years of worry and agony that Mark might align with the Enlightened One and give his allegiance to the antichrist flashed past him. Now Farmer held them both in his arms. He wished that this moment filled with such rich emotions could go on forever . . . 'I reckon thet ta be why eternity be endless,' Farmer thought. 'All the stories and talk 'bout moments like this an' so many baring witness from life ta recollect an' cherish; then just ta be thankful fer all the Lord's blessings. I truly be most grateful ta Ya, Father God! A thousand years won't be near 'nuff time.'

CHAPTER 12

AN INVITATION

Conversation in the den took on a more contemporary flavor. It was Caleb who changed the subject.

"What work does the Lord Jesus have you overseeing Farmer?" he asked.

"I be supervisin' mill work o' Pacific Timberline," he replied with a broad grin. "With all the rebuilden' a goin' on, demand fer lumber has leaped far beyond what we can cut. I reckon us ta hev work a goin' fer the whole thousand years."

"Then it will all burn up at the end," Mark joked, then grew instantly somber, realizing the severity yet necessity that the old ways would face destruction to allow the arrival of a new heaven and earth. His mind staggered trying to conceive of it.

"Who's your companion Resurrected Saints?" Caleb asked, not commenting on Mark's ill-conceived remark.

"There be quite a number in Applegate," Farmer answered. "Ones I be closest ta be here in Douglas Landing. Donald an' Beth Parrigan be in charge o' the cutting o' the timber. Joe an' Sally Baltman be watchen' over the horses, cattle an' t'other animals. Clarence Judd, he checks out all construction here a bouts." Farmer hesitated, dropped his head and remarked sadly, "Locust Tree Judd, Clarence's missus is not here . . ." his voice trailed off.

"Reckon it be best not to speak o' those who never knew Christ, fer there be far too many who once were dear an' precious friends, who not be with us now or ever."

"Gordon and Ella Mae Brooks air like – well, kinda' like the Mayor o' Douglas Landing, an' you could call Ella Mae the Principal o' the school." Mark broke into the conversation. "Our

41

children attend there and Donald and Beth Parrigan's daughter in life, Beverly Ann, trains the teachers at the school."

"Beverly's son an' daughter-in-law in life, Donald, Jr. an' Macy, regulate all hunting an' fishing thet go on in this area by Tribulation Saints an' Millennials," Farmer added.

"There are two lumber mills, so who supervises the second?" Caleb asked.

"Cascade? Tis a Resurrected Saint by name o' Alex Holder. I never knew him in life but found out later he lived in Applegate, was saved in a church there and attended most ever' service. He faithfully drove out ever' night ta work night shift. When the market for lumber caved in and Cascade was forced to shut their night work down, Ol' Man Weilheim kept him on ta clean up an' watch the mill nights. He suffered a deadly heart attack an' mill hands found him next morning. Now he runs the place. Ain't thet just like the Lord?" Farmer remarked with a bit of Texas drawl and humor.

The three men sat in quiet contemplation for a few minutes before Caleb turned his attention to his son, Mark. His eyes narrowed.

"Son, are you working in one of the lumber mills?"

"No, Father, why?"

"Won't you, Nikki and your children come to Lugar de Paraiso? " Caleb's eyes danced with excitement over the possibility. "We have so few to work," Caleb's speech was rapid as he made his appeal. "The restoration of a fitting resort town is slow. We have to wait on Tribulation Saints to have children, and those Millennials have to grow up and have children. Master Jesus has sent families and singles to shore up our workforce." Caleb shook his head. "Not enough – not enough! The Resurrected Saints saved in the Global Missions Church are there with us, but – ."

Mark looked away. He knew without being told drunken Tasada was not numbered in the Global Missions group.

"I don't know, Dad. I just finished assembly of a Transporter in Applegate, and I've been assigned to build a second station in Springdale to accommodate the growth in that city."

"Please, Son, I am pleading with you to bring your family and come help us. Think of it as an extended vacation. Your mother and I so long to have you all there with us." Tears filled Caleb's eyes. "We missed too much of your life, and had none with precious Nikki and the grandchildren. Please, Mark, come stay a hundred years."

All three men burst into laughter!

"Dad, you know I can't accept your invitation without the Lord Jesus' permission," Mark said as he wiped his eyes.

"Then let's ask Him." Caleb hugged his son in agreement.

"I reckon ya best let Nikki in on this here invitation," Farmer quipped, "afor' doen thet asken!"

CHAPTER 13

FAMILY NEWS

"Your great-grandparents, Clifton and Rachel have just arrived," Mark's angel Detrius joyfully announced. "Grandmother Morgan is with them, also."

The three men hurried to the living room where the rest of the families were gathering. Loving, joyful hugs passed among the members and everyone was speaking at once in loud excitement. Clifton and Rachel were radiant; their resurrected bodies giving off a glow which indicated the happiness they felt. The clothes they wore held a regal appearance to indicate the importance of the occasion. Both of these patriarchs bowed slightly to Farmer when he entered the room; then the couple squatted to hold John and Johanna a minute before speaking.

"Oh children, you have grown so!" Rachel exclaimed.

"Old enough to know all about our 'before' years," John declared proudly.

"Momma told me everything, even before John." Johanna grinned.

"And Papa, Nana and Auntie Esther are already here all the way from Lugar de Paraiso," John pointed out.

"So we see," Clifton laughed, "and we hail from Alaska," he continued, winking at his 'before' life dad, Farmer.

"Wow!" Johanna whistled. "Is Alaska far away? If Mamma and Daddy drove us in our air car, how long would it take?"

"With so many roads still in disrepair, well over a week," Great-grandmother Morgan injected into the conversation. "That is why Transporters are being erected to make travel so much quicker. Great-grandfather Joseph and your Great-great Uncle Walter are supervising the building of one right now in

Fairbanks and therefore could not come today. They both miss you and wish you a most wonderful and fun-filled birthday." Morgan hugged and kissed both twins.

"If God and Jesus are so powerful, why don't they just say the word, and 'poof,' all the transporters would be built and operational and the roads fixed?" Adam, who had been standing to one side, questioned.

All the family turned their attention to him. Mark started towards his son, but Caleb grabbed his arm and with a slight 'no' and shake of his head, then whispered, "You were once like that, Mark, remember?"

"Why not?" Adam demanded.

"Oh, child," Rachel addressed Adam's question. "God doesn't do what man can rebuild."

"That is just super!" Adam retorted. "God sits back and watches over all of you boss us around, and we Millennials do the work. Hardly fair!"

"Why are you so angry, Adam? We love you!" Morgan reached out to him.

"No! No, you don't," the boy objected loudly. "Not my birthday. No presents for me. If not for my dumb brother and sister, you wouldn't even be here."

Emile moved towards Adam to hold him. He drew back while his face grew crimson.

"Don't touch me!" he hissed. "You are no better than the rest of them. You live a mile down Cold Creek. You never come to see me, but here you are for – for – them. You don't love me because I'm – different!"

"Adam, you know that isn't true." Emile was cut deeply in her spirit.

"That is quite enough, young man," Nikki shouted. "Back to your room. We are going to have a talk."

Adam fled to his bedroom with Nikki right behind. Mark glanced at Caleb and Sarah with a pained expression of concern over Adam's attitude before following Nikki to deal with Adam.

Caleb pondered a disturbing thought as he heard Adam's bedroom door slam shut and the muffled voices of an argument

45

evolving. 'How is it possible for this kind of action and words to happen in a perfect world?' he wondered. He voiced his unsettling question to Farmer, who was standing nearby.

"Ever'one born from the fall o' the first humans, has been infected with a sin nature, and I reckon thet sin nature keeps comen' along, even in a perfect age. So ever' person born must accept Christ jus' as it was fer you an' me, Caleb, an be borned again. Iffen thet weren't true, why else will so many turn from the Lord Jesus, with Him bein' here in our very midst, and follow Satan in a last-ditch rebellion?"

"Aye, Farmer, I see a turning from Christ in Adam and leaning towards darkness and impending doom. There is so much of Mark in him."

"An' what turned Mark?" Farmer asked.

"The Rapture scared the hell out of him," Caleb mused.

"Then I reckon a most frightenin' scare may be needed fer Adam," Farmer concluded.

The family went on with their visiting and the conversation once again picked up an air of joy and excitement.

Morgan came to Caleb and Sarah. "Caleb, your father is so sorry he is not here. He misses you both deeply and truly wanted to see the twins and Adam. But, he is heading a very critical reconstruction in Alaska and in the final stages of a new Transporter station. Lord Jesus wanted him to finish. He will have time with all of you soon. Jesus promised."

"Uncle David, Aunt Cynthia and your cousin Mary should be here in two more hours," Morgan continued. "Your mother, Hannah, and your family are coming, aren't they?" she asked of Sarah.

"I think so," Sarah murmured. "I'm not sure about my real dad. His angel told him about our party, and my step-dad . . . isn't –."

"Yes dear, we know." Morgan squeezed Sarah's hand.

"Grand Nana." Johanna tugged on Morgan's sleeve.

Morgan gazed into the golden face of her Great-grandchild, Tribulation-born, Johanna Hillag. Her eyes were filled with wonder and a strange exuberance to learn and know everything. She seemed most serious.

"Yes, child." Morgan took Johanna in her arms.

"Have you heard if your cousin Janee is coming to my birthday party?" she asked wistfully.

"Yes, she should be here this afternoon, and I think her mamma and daddy, Leah and Harold, are coming with her."

"Perfect!" Johanna drew away, satisfied with the answer. "There are some kids coming from Douglas Landing and a bunch more from Applegate to my – I mean, our party. They have all seen the children's programs that Janee is producing in Hollywood. They idolize her as a celebrity, and I think they are more interested in her than the party with John and me." Johanna shrugged. "They will ask her for a story." An impish grin curled the corners of her mouth. "Perhaps she will tell a scary tale of the 'before' years –."

"Oh Mom!" Sarah cried out as her mother, Hannah, appeared in the room. Some party members jumped with a start at the announcement of this new, sudden arrival. Sarah leaped into her mother's waiting arms.

"It has been so long!" Sarah sobbed. "I have missed you so."

"Much too long, Sarah." Hannah held her for a long time. No word was spoken, just two Resurrected Saints caught up in the moment of a glad reunion. Suddenly Sarah pulled away, taking in the room with one full sweep of her eyes.

"Where are Penny and Toe Jam? Are they with you?"

"They could not make it, but Lord Jesus will send them to see all of you later. In His time."

"I hesitate to share this with you, because it's such a special occasion today," Sarah announced as she dropped her eyes.

"Tell me." Hannah was instantly intent.

"Coming back to earth, and now seeing you, brings back fearful memories."

"There is no fear now, my dear."

"I know, I know." Sarah averted her eyes. "But I do remember the fear and trouble Stoner brought on us. He wanted to destroy Caleb and me, and violate our children. He attempted to draw Mark in to worship Satan and tracked him down during the Tribulation to kill him because he refused."

47

"Yes, I heard," Hannah whispered.

"Stoner might have succeeded in taking Mark's life, and killing him and Nikki before the babies were born."

"But he didn't succeed, Sarah."

"Only by the Grace of God, and Shag's taking him out . . ." Sarah brushed away tears.

"Sarah, there is no place for fear now. Stoner can never hurt you again."

"I know, Mom, I know; but why do I dread facing Stoner at the White Throne Judgment? I guess I just needed to tell someone – you!"

"I'm so glad you did. Now, you must put this from your mind." Hannah held her again.

Just then Mark and Nikki walked into the living room followed by a downcast Adam. His face was splotched and his eyes bloodshot from crying. He wiped his nose with one hand.

"Adam has something to say to everyone," Mark said. "Adam?"

"I'm sorry for what I said." Adam was nervous and embarrassed; however, he held strong eye contact with each family member as he spoke. "I asked Jesus to forgive me. I get angry at things and say hurtful words. I don't want to be that way, or feel ugly emotions and, and, have hateful feelings, but I don't know how to stop. Please forgive me; I am so sorry! Please forgive me and love me, too." At that Adam dropped his head in shame.

The family gathered around the humbled boy and loved on him with hugs, tender words of acceptance and compassion, giving him much-needed affirmation. He bawled and clung to John and Johanna when they expressed in simple childlike words their love as his brother and sister, and their need for him. The last of it broke Adam's heart.

Soon the children were off to another part of the house laughing, playing loudly, having fun, the incident already forgotten.

"Where's Esther?" Nikki questioned, looking around.

"She is walking along Cold Creek," Nikki's angel Waaleen spoke softly. "She may be troubled or sad."

"Lead me to her, Waaleen," Nikki asked, as she left out the front door and headed down to the creek.

CHAPTER 14

ESTHER AND NIKKI

Nikki made her way carefully along the creek bank, peering intently into the surrounding forest of trees and brush. She stopped.

"Esther?" Nikki called out. No answer.

"Esther!" she called out again. "Where are you?"

There was a slight rustle of breeze in the cedars. The distinctive odor captured Nikki's attention for an instant; however, she quickly dismissed it. Where was Esther, and why did she leave the party to come out here alone?

"Oh Waaleen, where is Esther?" Nikki climbed over a fallen log.

"She is a quarter mile ahead of you." Nikki's angel pointed downstream. "She is sitting on a rock at the edge of the water."

Nikki plowed through thick patches of brush and open areas of pine trees, her shoes crunching the needle-covered ground.

Thick undergrowth forced a slower stride, as the path hugged the water's edge. Rounding a bend in the stream's flow, Nikki caught sight of Esther standing in a small open meadow. Nikki was struck by the strange grandeur of the scene before her. Esther was resplendent, her body shining with a dazzling bluish hue. Her angel stood directly behind, wings partially unfurled, providing a canopy covering. Nikki instinctively sensed something was amiss. She rushed to reach her sister-in-law.

"Esther, are you – OK?" Nikki tried to catch her breath.

Esther gazed a long time across the tiny meadow and into the trees.

"It is so beautiful and peaceful here. I watched a herd of deer pass along by those flowers over there." Esther nodded in that direction. "A cougar was with them. How different – from 'before' . . ." Esther's voice trailed off.

"You are not yourself! What is it?" Nikki pressed.

Esther glanced at Nikki, before turning her gaze back to the meadow. A deep sadness filled her eyes. "You needn't have come, dear Nikki. This is a special day for you; your twins' birthdays. You should be with them."

Nikki laughed. "Everything's patched up and they are playing with their friends from Douglas Landing. Believe me, I would just be a boring, 'in-the-way' mom."

Esther reached out and took Nikki's hand. Esther's face scrunched up and her lip quivered.

"Oh, no, Esther," Nikki cried. "Tell me, please, what has made you sad?"

Esther held her gaze. Nikki wanted more than anything to look into the depths of her soul. She had no clue what was troubling her sister-in-law. Her face glowed, but mingled in her features was a disturbing sign Nikki had never seen before. Oddly, it seemed out of place.

"I was sitting on that large rock, thinking," Esther spoke low. "Will you stay and listen awhile?"

Nikki nodded and the two women slid down the bank and hopped a small space of water onto the rock. Esther sat with knees under her chin, while Nikki kicked her shoes off and sled her feet into the water. No word was spoken. Nikki loved the feel of a warm July sun tempered by an occasional hint of breeze in her long black hair. There was no song of meadowlarks or hacking cry of the blue jays, only the ambling of Cold Creek over rocks. Suddenly Nikki was aware of Esther watching her closely. She turned to catch Esther staring intently.

"What?" Nikki laughed, embarrassed.

"I often wondered what kind of woman would snag my brother," Esther attempted a smile, but that strange sadness would not be denied. "I would try to picture what she would look like; how she would act. The ones he hung out with at Lugar de Paraiso were spoiled tourist tramps and not good enough for him. Mom, Dad and I were so afraid he would leave Mexico City and go with – the – er – last one –."

"You mean Kim?" Nikki bristled.

"Yes. She took his youth and gave him nothing in return. She would have ruined his life."

"She was a bitch," Nikki snarled, wanting to change the subject. "Did you picture me?" She turned her head and kicked water with her foot.

"I did. Well, with lighter skin and hair."

"Oh please!" Nikki swatted at Esther. Both women fell silent until Esther picked up the conversation.

"Mark could never have found a more beautiful, loving wife. Thank you for never giving up on him. Watching Adam today, I saw Mark all over again, when he was eight. I know how he was when the Rapture took – us . . ."

Nikki studied Esther's face before she made an observation.

"Esther, are you sad? Is it because of Mark and Adam?"

"That is part of the reason."

"I don't understand, Esther. How can you be downhearted? This is the Millennial Kingdom, Christ's perfect world. How can you – feel things I do?"

Esther's eyes filled with a great love, her voice carried a gentle understanding of Nikki's confusion.

"I am sad because I can remember. I remember the 'before' life. I don't count memories as a curse, but a gift God gives us; and that gift will remain until the New Heaven and Earth. Being here today triggered memories, lots of them, some filled with regrets."

"Regrets? I don't understand." Nikki began to cry.

"As I watched you, Mark and your children, I realized what I . . . have missed. I was so young when Christ caught us up. I was in college and praying a handsome guy would ask me out. Oh Nikki, tell me what it was like to fall in love?"

Nikki dropped her eyes. "It was pure heaven and absolute hell. If Mark gave me the slightest notice, I was elated. I longed for his love and ached to love him. At times, when he acted sweet on this French girl, Dulco, I died, wallowing in doubt and self-pity. A hundred times I feared I had lost him, yet, inside my heart, I knew I would follow him to the ends of the earth – if he would only ask; and when he did and kissed me – and that first time we – we made . . ." Nikki reached down to scoop up water and wash her face. "That part is private," she giggled.

"I never experienced any of that but often dreamed of it; even as a little girl. I, too, was thrilled when a cute boy kidded me or wanted to carry my iPad. And a simple touch? Oh, bless my soul! A young man's hug or touch sent chills and warm sensations all over me. Then it all ended – raptured. I lost all those hopes." Esther wiped away tears; then laughed. "Yep, I still cry, too, and that stays 'till the New Heaven and Earth."

Esther grew solemn, showing keen interest. "What was it like to carry a baby and give birth? I want to know everything!"

"No, you don't, girl," Nikki flung water at her. "Parts of it I wouldn't wish on my worst enemy. Puking your guts out with morning, noon and night sickness. The weight and uncomfortable backaches and labor grew worse with each passing month. The last month, if ever I wanted to murder Mark . . . but I couldn't, you understand. He was my doctor." Nikki paused with a grin, which slowly faded.

"That was the bad part. The good part was the sense that the love you and your husband had for each other conceived a baby. Our lives evolved, and our fight to survive took on new meaning. Now we fought as one to save and protect our child. There was that moment I felt, it was like – a flutter. Then I felt more movement and as the baby grew I thought it was kicking a soccer ball around."

"You didn't know you were having twins?"

"How could we? Mark, towards the end, would lay his head on my belly and say he could hear the baby's heartbeat; it was strong, ready to face an ugly world and fight for its life. What a shock to discover twins! But then to – to hold them! I experienced something I have no words to describe. I only knew I was a mommy and would be forever. I was determined I would move heaven and earth to love and protect my John, Johanna and later, Adam."

"I will never know . . . any of that." Esther sighed. "I only imagine; but I am thrilled for you and Mark. I am very proud of both of you, and I love the children with all my heart."

Sadness appeared to once more envelop Esther. She watched the water make its way downstream and out of sight. Both women were aware of each other's nearness, but nothing was spoken. Nikki realized her descriptions could never substitute for the actual experience.

Esther glanced at Nikki before dropping her eyes. "When I was a little girl," Esther began slowly, "I saw this movie about a homely little girl. The boys freaked her out with their taunts and crude jokes. I never forgot one scene. She so desired to be asked out on a date, but was only ignored. She dreamed of going to the High School Prom, but prom night came and she sat home – alone. Tearfully, she looked in her mirror and cried, 'What's wrong with me?' Then she buried her face in her hands and wept. I cried with her in that movie because I knew down deep I wasn't pretty."

"Oh, but you are beautiful!" Nikki injected tenderly.

"Ha!" Ester laughed and wiped her eyes. "It took the resurrection to fix that."

"Not true," Nikki replied, straight-faced. "Surely, the movie had a happy ending?"

"It did, but not for me. The girl graduated High School and went to college. In one of her classes a boy took interest in her and love blossomed. The story ended with his proposal of marriage. The final scene was a beautiful wedding and her dreams coming true. As the final credits began to come up they fast-forwarded to the future: a home, kids, travel and holidays. In that moment something happened to me, Nikki. A deep hunger and longing began growing in my heart to fall in love, and to be a wife and mother. I wanted it so much I could taste it; and every time the guys passed me by for the pretty girls, I died inside. Rejection chipped pieces of my dream away day after day. I was the school nerd, the proverbial wallflower who sat on the sidelines during every dance."

"No one ever asked you to dance?"

"Well, yes, a few times, but never the boys I had crushes on. They were not attracted to me and many shunned me because I was a Christian and a Preacher's daughter."

"I understand about being a Christian. We were far from popular in those last days," Nikki murmured.

"When we moved to the resort in Mexico, my chances at romance became even more remote. There weren't many desirable boys who were local, and the tourist crowds of college kids were obnoxious. So, I decided to enroll in college. Mom and Dad thought and believed I was going for an education and to find my 'calling,' but the truth? I was husband hunting, and my desire for love was so powerful my heart ached. If a guy showed interest, I could have easily –."

"That's how I was with Mark," Nikki responded, understanding in her response. "I can not tell you what it did inside to me when he finally whispered, 'I love you!' The world in all its evil darkness became – heaven. But tell me, Ester, did you meet someone at college?"

"I did. I watched him from a distance and maybe even then I was beginning to fall for him. I had urges so strong I began losing control and my senses took over. I did silly things, stupid me, to get his attention. If I could only get a 'hello,' or a 'hi,' I was so excited I acted giddy."

"I can identify with that, but did –?"

Esther held her finger to her mouth cutting off Nikki's question. Nikki instinctively sensed a mood shift in her sister-in-law. Esther was grave and deathly serious in what she was to say next.

"What I tell you now, Nikki, must not and shall not ever be spoken of again. Do you agree?"

Nikki nodded, never breaking eye contact.

"At the height of my longing for love and passion, my evil step-brother, Stoner, came into my mind and offered to fulfill all my desires. His presence was so powerful, so overwhelming, I could feel his touch, a cold touch, yet thrilling as his hands and mouth moved . . . over my body."

"How awful!" Nikki cried aloud, reaching for Esther. "Oh, no!"

"I was scared out of my wits, but you know what frightened me the most? It aroused me and I wanted it." Esther covered her mouth and whimpered in low moans that came from somewhere deep inside.

"Oh, Esther, you didn't? What did you . . .? How . . .?"

"No, Nikki, I fought an invisible demon with every ounce of my strength and screamed to the Lord Jesus for His help and protection. The instant I called out to Master Jesus, Stoner and all his evil vanished. I wept uncontrollably for hours!"

The two women held each other for a long time. A wind blew gently in the trees, and from the meadow the soft mooing of the cattle joined the song. Other birds made up the chorus and for a moment a magical kind of music was heard bringing peace and closure to a terrible nightmarish memory.

CHAPTER 16

DESCRIBING PARADISE

Esther nodded her head in the direction of the house and held out her hand to Nikki.

"Come. Let's walk and I'll tell you. It is a place of absolute perfection." Esther smiled as she began.

"I hear there are cities and villages, with mountains and forests," Nikki gazed ahead through the trees, "and streams like Cold Creek."

"True, and what struck me most when I first saw Paradise was the brilliance and crispness of the sky and colors. The shades and hues were unlike those of earth. Grassy fields to run across and flowers to delight the senses. No weeds; no dead things; and the cities and towns? Oh my, Nikki, shining and shimmering in the light beaming from the very Throne of God. Each town was perfect in its architecture and design; each with a given function; occupied by various groups of people. Our city was named, 'Sent,' and made for those who were missionaries in life. I was there because of Mom and Dad. Oh Nikki, no place here compares, even in the Millennium. It was beyond any dream or thought. How can I describe it to you? If only I had a picture to show you . . ."

The women climbed over a log and pushed through brush, not speaking until they broke free into a clearing.

Nikki asked with reverence, "Did you see," she swallowed, "Him?"

"Father God? No, but we went before His Throne. Holy beasts surrounded the Throne of God and angelic beings of all kinds were everywhere. There was dense smoke, lightning and thunder, and I heard His voice. I fell on my face!"

"Were you scared? I mean, was His voice frightening?" Nikki asked.

"Actually, it was majestic and firm, yet it held a love and gentleness I never felt before – only in King Jesus. When I heard God's voice, I didn't understand His words, but oddly knew what He said."

"What did He say?"

"He said, 'I love you, my child!' Those words flooded my soul and spirit, and I hear them often in my mind, like He wants to be sure I know."

"I hear Him say that too, Esther, but I'm sure not so distinctly, but still, I hear Him."

"My house was truly a mansion just as Jesus promised," Esther reflected, "grander than where I stay now in Lugar de Paraiso."

Nikki brightened with excitement as she changed the direction of the conversation.

"Did you meet any Biblical celebrities?"

"Biblical celebrities?"

"You know, Peter, James, John, Jeremiah, Moses?"

"Humm," Esther broke out in a mischievous grin. "Yes, I met Caleb once."

"You did?" Nikki's eyes grew big. "Caleb, who led the children of Israel in battle to conquer the Promised Land? What was he like?"

"I met Caleb Hillag who did battle with the Enlightened One, Stoner. Caleb was a strong preacher, a battle-hardened warrior, my dad . . ."

Nikki saw the joke that in the telling lost its humor. She dropped her head and continued following Esther on an overgrown deer trail.

"We saw little of the Old Testament Saints; they were in another part of Paradise. The prophet Nahum came to our village once and told how The Lord had called him to prophesy judgment on wicked Nineveh. Phillip from the early church also came to visit for a while. He was a missionary called to Samaria, and out to the desert, then to Caesarea. "

"Wow," Nikki sighed. "That had to be totally awesome! I've never experienced any of that."

"You will some day, Nikki," Esther reassured her.

"Janee just arrived at your house." Nikki's angel interrupted.

CHAPTER 17

JANEE STEMPER

Nikki and Esther emerged into the large main room of the log home. Nikki was out of breath and completely taken back by the scene before her. Instead of the commotion of greetings and excitement she expected, the room was completely still. The hugs and hellos were over and in the center of the room surrounded by children stood Janee Stemper.

Her long golden hair flowed across her petite shoulders and down the back of a greenish-gray satin dress. Janee's resurrected body was a resplendent version of her former self. Her face and skin were white and flawless. Her beauty was captivating and not a word was spoken; not by the adults who filled sofas and lined the walls; nor the children who crowded to get near this woman still so idolized by the world.

Janee was holding John and Johanna tightly to her breast, kissing their smiling faces and speaking birthday wishes to each of them in a rich, full voice. Her words were gentle, yet bold, and all the children were awestruck.

Janee suddenly released John and Johanna, lovingly patted both their heads, kicked off her heels, and in a swift eloquent move sat down on the floor. This signaled the children to sit also. Amid the claps and laughter of the family and guests, one very young millennial child scooted in and touched Janee's hand and giggled with glee.

Janee looked intently at each child, fixing them in her mind. Everyone grew quiet again awaiting a further response. Her eyes scanned the family, spending a few seconds of eye contact with every member, ending this silent greeting with Esther and Nikki. Now with a slight twist of her head, a glance to her Guardian Angel Miglia, who stood by the door, a most graceful smile appeared on the corners of her lips. She turned her full attention to the crowd of eager children.

"Well," she began with focus and deliberate thought. "What a special day this is, and I have decided to devote some time just for you, my newest and youngest fans."

Those words prompted an excited outburst with all of the children wanting to be heard at once. Janee laughed and covered her ears.

"Oh, oh no, my dears, I can only hear one of you at a time, and I do so want to hear you, everyone, but you must speak softly and only one at a time."

"Tell us a story, Auntie Janee, please!" one of the Applegate children blurted out.

Janee laughed warmly and reached over to touch the one requesting a story. "Yes, I shall do that, but first think very hard. You have these moments with me right now. Is there something you would like to tell me, or ask me?"

A little girl sitting near Adam raised her hand. "I do, I do," she said as she bounced up and down.

Janee nodded to her.

"Auntie Janee, what is your favorite color?"

Janee took note of the child's pale yellow top. She thoughtfully rubbed the side of her face. "Well," she answered, "I saw lots of bright lights and colors in my 'before' life, but none could compare to colors I saw in Paradise."

"Were one of those your favorite?" other children asked.

"Tell us," another piped up.

"I think," Janee paused for effect. "I truly believe that today . . . my favorite color is . . ."

The children and adults held their breath.

"Yellow. It absolutely is yellow!"

The little girl's eyes got big and she covered her mouth in excitement. The children went wild and Janee had to calm them to regain order.

"Ok, someone else?" Janee looked around.

An older boy stood up and showed respect in his quiet voice, "I have a question, Miss Stemper."

"Yes?"

"I love horses and I'm wondering if you plan to do anything about them in your programs?"

"I am glad you asked that question because that is exactly what we are about to do. We have planned by Lord Jesus' direction to begin filming a series this winter about the Horses of the World. We are seeking heartwarming stories that we can screen and then record the most outstanding ones. Great question! Yes, we have staff working on pre-production right now, and Praise the Lord, we never have any funding problems." Janee laughed. "It should air in a year or so. Do you think you can wait that long?"

Farmer chuckled from the sofa where he sat. "Thinken' on thet, Janee, I reckon we still got near a thousand years ta do it all."

Everyone laughed and clapped. Janee nodded to her grandpa. "I love you," she whispered, then turning back to the children. "Anyone else?"

An older girl raised her hand.

"Yes dear, what is your question?"

"I don't have a question but want to tell you something." The smile on the girl's face went flat.

"I am a Tribulation Saint and I was old enough to remember how messed up the whole world became with everything dead and destroyed. I remember how I longed to see deer run in the meadow, or find a pretty flower. I can't forget, no matter how . . ." tears trickled down her cheeks.

"I never saw what you did or lived through it as you have," Janee murmured, "but I, too, saw a lot of suffering, misery, and terrible wars. Still, I can tell you this, we will never go through any of it again."

"That's what I meant to tell you." The girl brightened. "Your program every Monday evening called 'Rebirth of Our Planet'? I love it, and haven't missed a one. Thank you so much, Auntie

Janee. It helps me believe that earth once was beautiful and now it's perfect. Thank you."

The girl jumped up, brushed away her tears, and hurried to Janee, giving her a hug and kiss. Then she turned away and retreated shyly back to her spot.

Janee took a deep breath. Looking into solemn, tear-filled eyes, she decided to declare, "I do believe it is time for a story before we have birthday cake and presents." Everyone cheered and clapped.

CHAPTER 18

THE MOTH AND THE LIGHT

"Who can tell me if they have seen a moth?" Janee began. One of the younger girls jumped up. "I have. I saw hundreds this morning in my mommy's flowers."

"Those were butterflies, stupid," Adam mumbled.

The girl dropped her head and plunked back down on the floor.

"Shame on you, Adam," Mark scolded. "We don't tolerate name-calling. I want to hear an apology."

"Sorry." Adam spit the word out.

"Sorry for what?"

"Sorry I called you stupid, but they were butterflies."

"They probably were butterflies," Janee interceded, wanting to get back to her story. "There are some differences between moths and butterflies. Listen carefully, because these differences are part of the story of the Moth and the Light."

"There once was a moth who longed to uncover mysteries about herself. She wanted to understand life and explore the world around her. She watched the beautiful butterflies from the safety of a corner high in the doorway that opened out into a beautiful garden alive with colors from flowers arrayed in a multitude of shapes and sizes. The Moth studied the butterflies as they danced across blossoms, kissing each with a gentle touch, or sampling a taste of sweet nectar with their tongues."

"'If only I were like them,' she thought. 'They have rainbow wings with distinct markings, while I,' she sighed with a lonely and heavy heart, 'have a plain body and wings of dismal gray and markings resembling smudges. They flit and play in the sunshine among the flowers all day, while I must find a dark closet and crawl around on clothes to look for a suitable lunch.'"

The children giggled and laughed.

"'When the sun sets, the butterflies find a place to settle in and sleep. When darkness falls, I come out to play. And fly! I soar in the breeze, my wings glistening in the moonlight. Night is when I go on my quest to discover my life, my purpose, my moment of fame.'

"Well, the moth searched and flew for many a night without finding any answers. Then at the lowest point in her life when her faith and hope had totally caved, it happened!

"It was the darkest of nights. So dark she couldn't find her way and fluttered smack, bam into a wall. She crawled around trying to feel a place in which to hide. That's when she saw it. Too dark to see her own wing in front of her eye, she saw the slight glimmer of a light. Tiny, and far away, but how far? She had no idea. She watched its warm glow, so inviting, drawing her to it; calling her to come, come now; she must; she must go to the light. Whatever it takes, no matter how far away; she must go. The power of the light was hypnotic, enveloping her, exciting her senses until she grew dizzy. Any fear or resistance fell away into the dark. All she could see or think about was that speck of light. She knew she must seek it out. Fly! Fly!

"That she did, leaving the safety of the wall, setting her sights towards that distant light. And, would you believe, to the moth's surprise, forces around about her seemed to hasten the journey. The wind blew from behind to speed her flight. When she drifted off course, was it the brush of a passing crow that jolted the frail moth onward towards the target?

"The closer she got to the light, the stronger its pull became, engulfing her, taking her into itself, like being swept into a whirlpool. Was she no longer flying towards the light, but being sucked into something much stronger than herself?"

"Run away little moth," one little girl blurted out. Other children agreed, then quieted, waiting to hear more.

"Well, by this time, Moth was exhausted when she arrived at the light. It was huge, glowing yellow and orange, bouncing shadows of light and dark. Moth could feel its warmth – so comfortable and inviting, she must get closer. 'Come to me,' the light beckoned. 'Embrace my pleasures!'

"She flew a circle around the light to seek an appropriate spot to land. Stones ringed the glow, which appeared to be shooting out of logs. Grotesque faces appeared in the bouncing light and she heard coarse voices and laughter. A hand came out of the darkness swooshing so close to her that the rush of wind threw her to the ground between two of the rocks. Oh my! The heat was so intense she thought she would die. This light was not warm, but a blazing fire. Her eyes burned, her wings were searing; she must flee! Flee!

"Moth flew blindly into the blackness of the night, more frightened than she had ever been in her life. She dared not look back, just frantically flew, but where? She was lost. Hopelessly lost."

"I was like that once. It was dark, and I was alone and so scared, my stomach hurt. I cried out for help!" one of the Tribulation boys commented.

Janee smiled. "That's exactly what Moth did. She cried for help."

Some of the children sat up straight, intent on the story.

"You know what happened next?"

"What?" Janee heard breathless responses from children and thought she detected a couple of adult voices mixed in.

Janee made her eyes big and jumped to her feet. She gestured with her hands. "Another light shone before Moth. It lit the way for Moth to go. Although Moth did not understand why, this light was different; not the intoxicating, hypnotic pull of the blazing fire. This light seemed—safe! Moth flew quickly towards this new bright beacon. Her little heart beat with excitement. She was not afraid."

Janee walked among the children and adults. She held out her right hand and opened it wide; with her left hand, she made little flapping movements, depicting Moth flying around and around the opened hand. Every eye followed her.

"To Moth's amazement, the light was emitting from a hand." Janee's fingers bid the moth to land. Janee fluttered her other fingers into her open hand, which gently closed.

"Moth was bidden to land in the Hand that was so full of light. There she saw a terrible scar and her little heart broke. She covered that scar with her wings."

"King Jesus!" one girl cried aloud.

"Yes, He ever so gently enfolded Moth in His Hand."

Then Janee, still holding the fingers of her left hand in her right, slowly opened her hand and fluttered her freed fingers upward, higher into the air.

"You see, children, when our Lord Jesus Christ released Moth, He transformed her into a most beautiful creature. Her wings sparkled in the light as she mounted up, up, up. Her body was radiant as pure silver. Her eyes dazzled with the brightness of a glittering starry night. Her heart swelled with joy and a new understanding of life. Her purpose? Realized for the very first time, she was to serve the King and love Him. She was free! Free. Free forever."

"The moth was you, wasn't it?" Adam observed.

Janee was taken back by Adam's insight.

"Not so!" Johanna objected. "I've seen Auntie Janee in some pictures when she was little and played in the movies. She was beautiful! Not some dingy old moth!"

"Yes, Johanna, Adam is right. That was me," Janee confessed. "Beauty is not in a face or the skin or hair. True, I was adored by everyone who met me or saw me on the big screen. They saw a stunning woman, but honestly; inside I was dark, mean and ugly. Lost.

"I helped a Marine once in a war—a dirty, sweat-smeared face, rough man; but his heart . . . beautiful! I observed many others, plain—common, but beautiful from the inside out. God made them that way.

"I thought I was a butterfly, and I flew dead-on into the blazing fire only to crash and burn. It was not until Jesus found me and held me in His arms that I could be transformed. That's the moment I became beautiful. And, when I saw Him face-to-face, I kissed and kissed those nail-scarred hands. Yes, children, I was the Moth in the Light."

CHAPTER 19

FARMER AND EMILE'S GIFT

Watching John and Johanna excitedly opening their birth-day gifts, Farmer's mind wandered back to a conversation with Emile that had been ongoing for weeks. He rubbed his chin and smiled.

'Well, what kinda gift do ya get youngsters liven' in the Millennium?' he remembered posing the question to Emile.

'Oh Farmer, they want for nothing!'

'Cept what we aim ta give!'

'But do you think it wise?'

'Emile, in our 'before' years, I never reckoned ta be given' a birthday gift ta anyone during the Millennium. Fact be, never thought ta much 'bout it atal. Bible didn't say a lot 'cept it be a thousand years and Christ bein' King an' the devil tryen ta take over at the end. Still, never dreamt ta be given a gif ta a set o' twins four generations removed.'

'Well, mister, I hate to break it to you, but it won't stop with these two. Oh Farmer, we haven't even discussed our gift with Mark and Nikki.'

'I reckon them ta be fine with it.' Farmer ran his fingers through his hair.

'Shocked,' might be a better word!'

'Not when they think on the worth o' it.'

Emile shook her head. 'I fear it may frighten the children.'

'We carry no fear in this age, Emile, an' the twins be stronger then ta get scared.'

'Yes, but we must not forget they are Tribulation children. They need air to breathe, food to eat, they get tired, they can suffer, and . . . be frightened—as we once were.'

Farmer thought on what Emile had just said for a few minutes before he replied. Emile searched his face, his eyes, for an answer.

'True. What ya say be true. Yet, as we once was, they be now. They are full o' life; they be eager ta explore an' learn. Thet Johanna is curious as a kitten, an' John be steadfast an' smart; quick to catch on. They surely have feelings; an' one much the stronger then fear be their deep capacity ta love.'

Emile smiled, kissed him and took his hand. 'Like us,' she murmured. I'm just excited and nervous at the same time.'

"Farmer, our gift," Emile whispered, as she tugged on his arm.

Farmer was jolted back to the birthday party. He heard Mark declare, "That's all of the presents, John and Johanna. You both received some wonderful gifts."

"Yes!" Nikki clapped her hands.

"Ya all hold on," Farmer interrupted. "Ya missed one."

"We did?" Mark and Nikki questioned. They began looking around.

"Our gift to the children," Emile announced, excited.

"Where is it, Grandmamma Emile?" Johanna asked in eager anticipation.

"Let me tell ya 'bout it." Farmer motioned for the twins to be quiet and listen.

"Ya both be twelve today, and thet be a special age ta reach. Fer centuries thet were the age when families reckoned the youngens ta be most growed, an' a time ta get something different; a more growed-up type o' present. So, our gift ta ya fer yer birthday, with yer mom and dad's permission o' course, is to take ya ta see King Jesus our Lord in Jerusalem."

A collective 'gasp' rose from the group.

CHAPTER 20

REACTIONS

John was stunned. His mouth parted but was unable to form words. He shook his head slightly as if to be sure he had heard his grandpapa clearly.

"Wow!" he jumped up. "For real? I mean—Wahoo! To Jerusalem? See Jesus! I mean, when, how? Wow!" John held his face between his hands. He began laughing.

Johanna leaped up and jumped into Emile's arms. "Oh Grandmamma. Oh goodness!" She was laughing and crying all at once. She reached over to grasp Farmer's hand. "Dear Grandpapa." she was crying now. "This has been a most wonderful birthday for us. I love each and every one of my presents and am thankful for them, but you and Grandmamma have made this the best birthday ever!"

"Well now, Johanna," Farmer drawled. "Thet be a mighty big thing ta say see'n ya got near a thousand ta go."

Everyone laughed.

"I can't wait to go." John hugged Farmer. "Let's leave first light tomorrow."

"Oh yes. I'm ready! I'll pack a bag tonight," Johanna chimed in.

"Whoa, hold on youngens." Farmer put his arm around John and let go of Johanna's hand. "We got us some plannen' ta do."

"First," Emily paused, looking towards Mark and Nikki. "Mom and Dad must give their OK."

"Oh, Farmer, oh Emily, I don't know." Tears welled up in Nikki's eyes and she covered her mouth. The mood of the party quickly swung from festive to somber. "The children have never been that far away before . . ."

Farmer realized he had placed his great, great-grandkids in an awkward position and wished not to violate their trust.

"Oh please, Mommy and Daddy, please let us go," John and Johanna both pleaded.

"How will they get there?" Mark questioned.

"We can take them to Applegate to the Transporter Station," Emile answered. "Farmer and I will arrive at the Jerusalem Station the same time the children do."

"None of us have transported yet, "Nikki responded. "I get really nervous about that form of travel."

"Didn't you transport to meet Jesus that first time?" Great-grandma Rachel asked.

"I honestly don't remember how we got there. All surviving humans the world over appeared before the Lord. We suddenly were there, but all the Transport Stations had been damaged beyond use or destroyed in the Tribulation. I just remember they weren't reliable. Sometimes luggage made it, but the owners never did; and whatever was lost, was gone. So many disappeared in the malfunctions."

"There have been no mishaps with our Transporter Stations in Alaska, and I'm sure Applegate's system is flawless," Clifton offered.

"Have you ever transported, sir?" one of the Applegate mothers questioned Clifton.

"No," Clifton replied. "They didn't exist when I lived on earth. We flew in airplanes; the companies always told folks, 'It's safer in a plane than driving a car!'"

"True, I remember that," Nikki responded, "but you all, along with the angels, transport all over the universe in a blink of the eye. We can't. We are Tribulation Saints and must transport from Station to Station. That means my children will step into that, that box and be broken into micro pieces, while I'm praying to God they get put back together again, in Jerusalem. Oh God, that scares me so!"

Nikki broke down and covered her face. Mark put his arm around her and held her tight. He spoke slowly, thoughtfully.

"Not long ago I worked to assemble the Transporter Station in Applegate, so it hasn't been in existence long; but there have been no malfunctions or accidents so far."

Another of the Tribulation parents raised her hand. Mark acknowledged her.

"You said 'so far.' What if it shorts or goes bad or there is a power failure?"

Farmer started to answer, but Mark stopped him. "Sorry, Grandpapa. A Tribulation Saint posed the question, so I think I should answer it. We don't live in a fallen world, and the Tribulation is over and done. We live in the Millennial Kingdom; a perfect world, and The King of kings and Lord of lords doesn't make junk, or things that wear out and break. I know for sure He loves us with a greater love than we will ever understand, and I know that I know, He doesn't plan on losing any of us, and that promise includes Nikki's and my children, as well as all of yours."

"Amen and amen," Caleb agreed. "Sarah and I clung to that promise for you those seven years in paradise."

Others around the room murmured their agreement.

"My thought is this," Mark continued. "This is a great honor for John and Johanna to see the King. They were babies when we went before, so they don't remember. But as you said, Farmer, they are at the right age. Now, I hear there are throngs of people all the time around Jesus, so they see Him from afar. Is that how it will be for these two?"

"Well now, thet be right smart thinken, Mark." Farmer grinned. "Emile and I didn't just go off half-cocked a plannen' this here gift. We talked ta Master Jesus 'bout it."

This grabbed everyone's attention.

"He say," Farmer continued, "it be time fer them ta come ta Jerusalem. I will welcome them inta My presence an' speak with them.

The children suppressed the urge to giggle with excitement.

"And Jesus told us the day and time," Emile added. "I am so elated I can barely keep still!"

Stillness enveloped the room. All eyes turned to Mark and Nikki.

"Oh please, Mommy," Johanna whimpered. "Yes, let us go, Daddy. I'll behave and do all my chores without being reminded."

"Please, we want this more than anything," John implored.

Mark held Nikki close and the love and respect he felt for her overflowed. "What do you think, Sweetheart?" he whispered. "Do we need to take time to pray and discuss this?"

Nikki shook her head. The children thought she was saying 'no.' They wailed, broken-hearted.

"No, No!" Nikki protested. "Mark, dear, our children must go to Him at the time He specified."

Mark's face lit up. "It's settled then!" he shouted. "John and Johanna are taking a trip with Grandpapa Farmer and Grandmamma Emile to see our Lord Jesus Christ in Jerusalem!"

Everyone broke into frenzied, excited laughter and chattering. Many came to hug the twins and Farmer and Emile.

Suddenly, Adam yelled, flung down his SAT phone and fled to his bedroom, slamming the door.

CHAPTER 21

ADAM

Darkness was falling and all the guests, save Caleb, Sarah and Esther, had departed, when Mark and Nikki slipped into Adam's bedroom. It was semi-dark, illuminated dimly by the screen on Adam's PC. Mark went over to shut the computer down while Nikki sat gently on the side of the bed. She desperately wanted to talk with him, knew it was needed, yet what would she say? What went through her youngest child's mind during the birthday party? Why was it so hard for Adam to be happy and excited for his older brother and sister? Was he consumed by envy? Was the gift from Grandpapa and Grandmamma the ultimate insult for him?

Adam was different. Nikki expected that. Every child is different; even John and Johanna had differences; yes, major differences. But Adam was a handful from birth. It seemed that even in his infancy Adam was in constant conflict with something or someone. Oddly, his mood swings separated those differences in greater degrees with each passing year. He was explosive to the point of violence; then, he would shift into a sweetness that was adorable and could melt hearts. This behavior concerned and perplexed both his parents, as well as their resurrected family members.

Mark joined her and stood beside the bed. "Should we wake him up and get this over?" Mark grumbled. He was still upset over Adam's reaction and angry retreat to his room.

"I don't know. He is sleeping peacefully," Nikki replied softly. She ruffled Adam's hair and pulled the cover up, tucking it around his neck. Adam didn't move.

John and Patty Probst

"I can tell you that I won't," Mark got louder raising his voice; then checked himself. "I'll be steaming the rest of the night if we don't get this settled."

Nikki took Mark's hand in hers and rubbed her fingers over his. She pressed her head against his side and felt him shift his weight from one leg to the other.

"You are upset, my love, and I am distressed and hurt. Perhaps neither of us are in any condition –."

"No!" Mark reacted, insistently. Nikki squeezed his hand and held tight. She pulled back to look at him. Mark looked into her eyes and his face softened. Nikki knew he was questioning what he should do and trusted him to seek wisdom. He studied Adam's outline in his bed coverings; then pulled Nikki to her feet. He kissed her lips and whispered, "You are right. Tomorrow."

They quietly walked to the door and as they were about to leave, they heard a weak voice.

"Mommy, Daddy?"

"Yes, Son," Mark answered.

"Please stay. I feel sad and alone."

"We are here," Nikki reassured him. She sat on the edge of the bed near Adam's head and began smoothing his hair. Mark joined her at Adam's side.

"Why do John and Johanna get everything?"

"You get things, too, Adam, just as much, just different." Mark tried to remain calm.

"Not so. They got wonderful presents all day long and everyone came to see them. Then, then, they get to go to Jerusalem and see Jesus. I want to go, too. Why can't I? Do Grandpapa and Grandmamma love only them and not me? All I heard today was John and Johanna, Johanna and John! Everyone talked to them and laughed, and gave them hugs and presents, and paid no attention to me. I felt like some, some, ugly, stupid, dumb kid that didn't belong. I hate them all!"

"First of all, Adam, you need to settle down," Nikki instructed.

"I can understand your feeling left out, but this isn't your birthday. It is theirs," Mark added.

78

"So that's it? I should have been born during the Tribulation like them, instead of being born in the Millennium?"

"You aren't any different; it was just a different day you were born," Mark corrected.

Adam sat up and pushed his mother's hand away from his hair. "I am different," he insisted. "There are feelings I have that they don't."

"Like what?" his mother asked.

"They get sad and cry like me, but there is something else none of you can understand. I am angry inside. It fights every day to overcome me. Most of the time I love the night and darkness, more than the day and sunlight. I fight something that attacks back; a monster trying to seize control of my mind."

"Oh Mark!" Nikki cried.

"I see these differences and then I get mad and ugly, feeling this overpowering urge to hurt someone and tear something up, or throw and smash anything I can grab. Then at the worst of it, I hear a voice. A voice I have heard as long as I can remember, telling me how to act and what to do."

"Who does the voice belong to?" Mark asked.

"I think it is King Jesus. Why can't I go see Him with my brother and sister? Why?"

"Because –," Mark raised his voice. Nikki touched Mark's arm.

"Because, Adam, this is not your birthday or your gift today. Believe me, your time will come," Nikki explained.

"I want to go now!" Adam demanded. "I don't want to wait! I want it now! Now!"

Mark took Adam's arm, which he yanked away. "Don't touch me. I want to see King Jesus. No! No, I don't. I hate him!"

It was like Adam's mouth was slammed shut and for a moment the boy went limp. Mark pulled him up and Nikki patted his face. Adam began to cry.

"I'm sorry, I'm sorry, King Jesus. I'm sorry, Mommy and Daddy, so sorry. Please don't be mad; please don't leave me."

"Adam, we will never leave you, never." Nikki held him.

"We aren't angry with you. I was, but I am over that. I am just trying to understand you." Mark put a gentle hand on Adam's shoulder.

"You can't, you can't."

"How do you know that?"

"The voice told me," Adam yelled.

"King Jesus?"

"No! No!" Adam screamed and grabbed his head. "The other voice. The angry one!"

"Adam, Adam!" Nikki was crying and rocking her son.

Mark slumped over and buried his face in his hands. Could it be? In the Millennium, facing a truth so sinister and out of check? No, it was in check, but still present. But, could it be dealt with or even understood? Understood? Something so sinister slipped into an age so perfect and pure? How could it even exist? Yet, he was hearing it and seeing it for himself in Adam, his own son, his Millennium-born child.

To wrap his head around what Adam was going through, he must go to a distant place and time. He tried, but his mind opposed the unwelcome journey. Could he not go beyond the moment he was saved? He held his head, hearing only his wife's soft cooing to their hurting son. Was that a glimmer? In a flash, he experienced out-of-control anger. His body jerked, and he was mercilessly beating his papa. In a blazing fit of rage, he wanted to kill. Then calm overtook him. Next, he was lying on his bed, with his mother stroking his hair, singing softly.

Mark sat up and wiped his face. The truth hit him hard. Extreme, vital truth! For that instant he experienced what Adam was feeling. He knew, maybe even from the moment this child was born, he wasn't different. No, he was the same as every baby born from the beginning to the very last child to take a breath in the Tribulation. And now, a truth so heavy, weighed on Mark's heart and mind. Maybe he had overlooked it, or ignored it; hoping or dreaming it would no longer be necessary. "Dear Father," he whispered. Yes, there was only one hope for Adam and every other millennial child born.

"Adam," Mark took Adam's hand.

"Yes, Daddy?"

"Do you know that King Jesus came to earth thousands of years ago? He didn't come as a King but as a simple man. He lived a perfect life so He could die for all of us, and wash away our sin; the darkness you tell us about. He makes each of us beautiful, and takes away the ugliness. He did this to free us from those feelings and thoughts you speak about. All Jesus asks is that you tell Him you are sorry."

"I did that already, Daddy."

"Do you believe He died on a cross and shed His blood for you?"

"I don't know. He's alive now."

"Yes He is. They took His body off the cross and put Him in a grave. On the third day, He became alive again. Do you believe all this?"

"I don't know. I guess, if you say it's so."

"You asked Jesus to forgive you and you believe in Him. Would you ask Him to save you?"

"Maybe tomorrow . . . I'm really tired."

"He's asleep, Mark."

The couple walked into the main living room. Caleb and Sarah were waiting for them.

"What was that all about?" Nikki questioned Mark.

"I can tell you, Nikki," Caleb answered. "I see what happened written all over your faces. Perhaps you never thought about it before or even considered the possibility until you saw it in Adam."

"You are right, Dad. I had to go back for an instant into my own past to grasp it."

"What? What are you two talking about? " Nikki was trying to understand.

"The truth in a nutshell is that Adam was born with that old sin nature like every other child, and like all the rest of us, he will have to believe on and trust Christ for himself." Mark's expression softened.

"But, but," Nikki sputtered.

81

"Being born in the Millennium didn't change that part. I saw it, Nikki. That old sin inside, just like I had."

"Oh my, what must we do?" Nikki held out her hand to Mark as she reached for a chair.

CHAPTER 22

THE STING OF DISAPPOINTMENT

Mark bid his 'before' life mom and dad goodnight and made his way to the master bedroom. Nikki stood in the open patio door, staring out into the darkness that hid the green meadow beyond their log home. A gentle breeze fluttered Nikki's nightgown, pressing it against her body, revealing her figure. Mark noted how beautiful his wife was; her dark skin glowing in the pale bedroom light; her long black hair hanging down her back.

"Doesn't the forest smell good tonight?" she spoke low, never changing the direction of her gaze.

Mark joined her at the doorway. Distinct odors of pine, fir and cedar filled his senses. How utterly clean and fresh the air was.

"Yes," he said, and placed his hand around her waist to draw her against his side. They both stood silent, taking it all in, but thinking of other things.

"What a wonderful birthday it has been for the children," Nikki reflected. "Everyone took part in the festivities."

"With the exception of Adam." Mark attempted a laugh.

"Yes, although there were moments when he really did get into the party and managed to have a good time," Nikki countered. She stepped outside onto the deck, peering into the darkness as though searching for something or someone. Mark thought he detected a glimpse of sadness in her face.

"Nikki? Are you tired or sad?" Mark was direct.

Nikki turned to face him. Her moist eyes revealed what she felt. Her lip quivered. "My parents didn't come, and we haven't heard from them at all."

"Well, they can't be dead or injured; maybe just super busy."

"Mark! John and Johanna are their grandchildren." Nikki enfolded herself in Mark's arms and buried her face against his chest. Her body shook as she wept tears of disappointment.

"Where are you, Mommy and Daddy?" Nikki cried out. "Why didn't you –?" She couldn't finish. In a few minutes she was asleep in Mark's arms. He gently laid her in bed, covered her with a light blanket, and joined her. But sleep didn't immediately overtake him. His thoughts replayed events of the day: the excitement of the children; the outburst of Adam; the bedroom episode and trauma that emerged from that. Then, his mind drifted to Janee's effects on the whole family; Farmer and Emile's surprise gift; and, finally he relived seeing his own mom and dad. He could full well understand Nikki's hurt and sadness, as he reversed the roles. What if his parents had not shown up for this special day? How would he feel?

But where could the Savages be? This seemed so unlike them. True, it had not been so terribly long since Nikki's parents' last visit; in fact, from the beginning of the Millennium there were always gatherings with family and friends. Even the rebuilding of the whole planet didn't halt the ability of people getting together, especially Resurrection Saints!

Yet, there could be no acceptable excuse for missing this special day. And, each time Nikki questioned her angel on their whereabouts, she got the same answer. "They are far away on the other side of the earth!"

Mark finally admitted that with all the joy and excitement the twins' birthday party generated, the Savage's silence and absence certainly left its sting of disappointment.

CHAPTER 23

A SURPRISE VISIT

"Mark!" Nikki shook Mark out of a heavy sleep. "Someone is coming!"

"Wha?" Mark shot up straight. "Wha? How do you know?" He tried to clear his mind.

"Waaleen woke me."

"Your folks, Nikki?"

"I don't think so. It is a car and my parents would have no reason to drive here."

Mark turned to his angel to ask, "Detrius, who is this?"

"We have instructions not to reveal their identity!"

"This is true," Waaleen smiled. "They wish to surprise you."

Mark and Nikki bounded out of bed and hurriedly dressed. They had no clue who was coming to their house at 11:30 that night. Mark looked at the time projected on the wall. He shook his head as he pulled on a shoe.

"Someone from Applegate? They forgot something?" Nikki asked.

"The car has pulled off of the highway, and is making its way down the lane and approaching your house," Detrius informed them.

Mark and Nikki raced through the house, flipping on lights and hurrying out onto the front porch. Sure enough, lights could be seen moving in the trees that outlined the road to their log home. The car was moving slowly.

Both of them stared, speechless and baffled; their minds spinning with curiosity.

"I think it is a solar car, an older one," Mark muttered.

"How can you tell?"

"Driving slow. Lights dim. I would guess the battery is nearly dead."

"Who do we know?"

"Haven't any idea, Nikki. Maybe people living in Applegate or Springdale; a Tribulation Saint for sure."

"What if they are robbers or killers?"

"Nikki, this isn't the Tribulation any more!"

The car inched up near the house, the headlights shining in their eyes.

Caleb, Sarah and Esther joined them on the porch. "Who is your visitor?" they asked.

"We don't know," Mark answered. "They didn't want their identity revealed. They want to surprise us."

"How exciting!" Esther laughed.

The car jolted to a stop, headlights still on. The clunk of a door opening could be heard, then a loud thud as it was slammed shut.

"Can we help you?" Mark called out.

"Could do with a hug and a cup of coffee, Sonny," a gruff voice answered.

Out of the glare of the car lights appeared an old man with white hair and bushy beard.

"Hello, missy girl," he bellowed.

Nikki grabbed her heart with a scream.

"Dear God, it's Shag! Oh Lord, Shag, it is you!" She bounded down the steps to greet an old friend.

CHAPTER 24

MINI REUNION

S hag held Nikki for the longest time. She was overjoyed and couldn't stop laughing and crying. Shag patted her back and smoothed her hair. He spoke low, his words heavy with emotion.

"Missy, you are as pretty as the last time I saw you; and we did, by God, survive that nasty Tribulation." Shag wiped tears from his eyes and held out his hand to include Mark in his embrace.

"Never forgot the two of you; and oft times when I feared I was gonna get caught by Combats and butchered up, I kept thinking of your words, Mark: 'I just want to survive'; then remembered how you inspired and drove The Global Team on. I drew courage and the will to live from that. You grew into a leader right before my eyes and now I see you have become the man I knew you could be."

"Shag, I have no words to express what my heart feels now," Mark uttered.

The old man held the couple tight, one in each arm.

"An' who would ever have believed you had twins."

"Oh yes, Shag, a handsome son, John, and a beautiful daughter, Johanna." Nikki's voice conveyed both love and pride.

"And this is a special birthday for them, which I missed; guessin' the party's over?" Shag grinned.

Mark and Nikki laughed. Shag became serious.

"So sorry 'bout that. I had best intentions of getting here for their birthdays, but my old car just wouldn't cooperate. So I missed it." Shag released his hug.

"The day's not over yet." Mark smiled.

"Ha!" The old man's beard jiggled and his face broke into an expression so recognized by Mark and Nikki. "Ha! Well, I musta' barely squeezed in."

"Come," Nikki took Shag's hand. "You had your hug. Let us get that cup of coffee."

"Great." Shag pulled his hand away and turned towards his car. "Let me turn the lights out and get the things I need tonight," he paused, "and introduce you to my friend."

Mark and Nikki were stunned but made no comment.

The headlights blinked off revealing Shag's angel standing guard by the car. He was shorter than the other angels, but looked of great strength, and was definitely a fierce warrior. His breastplate shone like polished brass. A helmet was not included in his attire, but he held a solid shield of pure silver in one hand and a gleaming sword, blade upright and positioned against the breastplate, as if ready for action.

"My guardian angel, Ganteous," Shag hollered; then he commenced to dig out a duffle bag and a smaller carryon case. He stepped back and motioned to someone inside.

Mark and Nikki could see someone moving around inside the car. The backseat? 'Were they coming out the driver's side? Oh yes, they were!'

"That doesn't look like a person," Mark whispered. "Does he have a dog?"

"What the –!" Nikki gasped, as a full-sized mountain lion jumped out of the car.

"My friend, Kimuchka." Shag nodded towards the cougar, as they approached the house.

Suddenly, Nikki felt this huge tawny-tan cat circling around her legs, sniffing. For an instant a surge of panic gripped her mind that perhaps this was not OK. All she could think about were the tales of 'before' life on the ranch from Grandpapa Farmer. 'A mountain lion ken take down a growed horse or steer.' And she remembered coming upon the remains of a deer a mountain lion had killed during the Tribulation. Did Shag expect to bring this, this animal into her house? 'But, this is the

Millennium.' She yanked her mind back to the present. 'These beasts now run and play with the deer,' she mused.

"Oh, you are too cute." Esther cooed and knelt down to stroke the cougar's neck and face. The big cat lay down and nestled his head on Esther's knees.

"What is your name again? Kimachuchee?"

"Kimuchka," Shag answered. "She also survived the Tribulation.

Esther looked up at Shag and held out her hand. "Hi, I'm Esther, Mark's sister."

"Good gosh, I am so sorry. In the excitement I neglected to do the introductions," Mark apologized.

Shag took Esther's hand and gently pulled her up. He studied her face intently for a moment. "Not many of your kind where I am from; mostly Tribulation Saints. You were young and not given much of life. For that I am sad." The old man's gruff edge took a softer tone. A tear rolled down his cheek and into his beard. "But," he continued, "I am so glad you were spared all we went through. It turned your brother from a boy to a man."

"Shag," Mark interrupted. "My dad, Caleb, and mom, Sarah. Mom and Dad, this is Shag."

Shag turned from Esther to give his attention to Mark's parents. He took Sarah's hand, made a sweeping bow, lightly kissing her hand. All he knew of Mark, he now attempted to appropriate into what he saw in his mother. "So pleased to meet you." Sarah smiled and brushed her hair from her face. Shag clasped Caleb's hand in a solid handshake and the two men locked eyes.

"The old Viet Nam vet," Caleb acknowledged.

"Yes, I fought in that horrible war; but it didn't hold a candle to the battle we went through in the Great Tribulation. I knew many men and women in both. Some were courageous; some were cowards. Always in the fire of struggle for life or death, leaders were formed. You, sir, and your wife were true pioneer leaders, this I know. Your son, Mark, and daughter-in-law, Nikki, stood with the best of them."

"They accepted the Lord and were saved. For that, we are eternally grateful," Caleb spoke low.

"Truth you speak, and I can tell you both this. They led many others to make that same decision, gave them hope on which to cling, and encouraged them to stand; even in the face of death, and I see another victory won. He called you Dad."

"Oh stop it," Nikki grabbed Shag's arm. "You are making us all cry!"

Everyone laughed and began talking at once.

"Come inside," Mark urged.

"And, and, bring Kimuchka," Nikki offered.

"Missy, she just don't act right in a house. Riding in a car, she is fine, loves it. But inside, she gets nervous and has to roam. She will disappear out into the timber shortly, but I can guarantee she's back here by dawn."

"Does she, er, hunt other animals?" Nikki asked.

"Naw, just plays she's a hunter. If she catches a lamb, I'm guessen' she wrestles with it till the lamb hollers, 'I give up!' Then they both take a nap."

Everyone laughed and made their way inside the house.

"You are such a jokester." Nikki smacked Shag's arm.

CHAPTER 25

SHAG'S INSIGHT

"Let me look in on the children, please," Shag said eagerly. "Do you want me to wake them?" Nikki asked.

"Course not, Missy girl, just want to see them." Shag swallowed hard.

Nikki stopped and looked at Shag. "Are you nervous?" she asked.

"Yes, I am. It will sorta' be like seeing my own grandchildren for the first time."

Nikki smiled, pleased. She proceeded to open John's door. Shag stepped close to peer in at the sleeping boy. After a few minutes, he whispered, "This one is strong and quiet, like his father. I can tell." He glanced at Mark.

"He is," Mark replied. "Strong, with depth when he speaks."

Next was Johanna. Shag watched her for some time. Once he reached out toward her as if wanting to touch her face. He hesitated and withdrew his hand. "She is you all over," the old man ran his fingers through his beard. "Face, hair, nose, forehead."

"Foof," Nikki whispered. "Only thing from me is bed head in the morning, then endless talk, talk, talk."

"Nonetheless, she is beautiful, and no doubt displays your charm, grace and wit."

Next, Mark and Nikki led Shag to Adam's room.

"What's this?" The old man's eyes narrowed. "You have three?"

"Yes," Nikki murmured. "This is Adam."

The old vet took a closer look. "A Millennial child. It is apparent. How is he?"

"Difficult," Mark answered, "but what do you see, after the other two?"

"Hard to explain, more of a sense, but there is a difference. Tribulation left its mark on John and Johanna. Like it tempered them. Adam was born in a perfect world, yet an imperfect child. More rebellion and struggle against purity—still, there is hope for the lot of them, the millions to come. Countless generations . . ." Shag's words trailed off into quiet thought.

"Come," Nikki said and took his arm.

Back in the living room, Chloe served the coffee she had prepared.

"Reminds me of Rona." Shag watched the robot.

"She is a newer Gamma and was invaluable to the Global Team here in Oregon, but you know, Shag, there will never be another Rona nor the friends we had there. Never! They all bought us time."

"'Nuff said." He dropped his head and sipped coffee.

Esther excused herself to check on Kimuchka. Caleb and Sarah bid the rest goodnight to retire to their room.

"We will see all of you tomorrow." Sarah rose from the sofa.

"Yes," Caleb agreed. "There is so much to talk about. I must hear of Stoner. Sleep well."

But the talking that Mark, Nikki and Shag were so excited to jump into could not wait. There would be no sleep for them this night.

CHAPTER 26

LONG OVERDUE TALK

Nikki jumped up and went over to hug and kiss Shag. He was startled. She dropped to her knees and took both his aged hands. Mark also came over and sat next to his old and dear friend.

"Rona, Snap and Curley bought us time with their lives, but you gave us a chance at life, and, and marriage, and our kids—when –," Nikki's tears dropped on the old man's hands, "you took Stoner out."

"That's right." Mark touched Shag's shoulder and lovingly shook it. "Stoner was on our trail and would have followed us to Oregon, but . . . we were hiding in a secret room when we picked up the news broadcast."

"Before that our entire Global Team had just been killed or captured. Those news reports from here alerted Stoner we might be in Oregon instead of Colorado," Nikki added.

"Had he made it to Oregon he would have eventually located us, tortured us and violently taken our lives. Thank you, Shag, for saving us from a sinister death." Mark's voice broke.

"Stoner was a relentless adversary bent on power and revenge. He was so focused on you, Mark, he didn't cover his back. His evil pride rendered him blind. He refused to believe you managed to slip away under his radar. He was so sure you were still in Colorado he let his guard down.

"I hunted him like the dirty animal he was. I learned where he was staying. I took out one of his satanic priests and stole his robe. Stoner thought a Non Com committed the murder so paid it no mind.

"I was scared, not taking Stoner's powers lightly. I prayed to the Good Lord and asked Him to make me invisible, and He did. I put on that black robe, slipped into the room where Stoner and his cohorts slept. Did the deed quick; you know how silent and deadly my knife is. Slipped out and the law blamed one of his black priests. But Stoner, the Enlightened One, was dead and gone."

"Oh, Shag, we can never thank you enough." Nikki stood up and kissed his cheek again. "We lived in fear and dread every day that Stoner would suddenly, unexpectedly grab us and it would all be over. The moment we read that news article, a heavy weight lifted from our hearts and we a found new hope and determination to survive."

"We prayed for this day and have waited a long time to, to, tell you." Mark echoed his wife's gratitude.

"I have fresh coffee," Chloe announced. "Who would like refills?"

"Right here!" Shag bellowed, holding up his cup.

Chloe poured coffee in his cup and scanned his face with a sweep of her eyes. "I do not find you in my database nor do I know your name," the robot said sweetly.

"Just call me Shaggy Bones." His eyes sparkled.

"Thank you, Mr. Shaggy Bones. More coffee, Mr. Boss Man?" Chloe addressed Mark.

Shag blew coffee back in his cup. "Boss Man?"

"It was Master Mark two months ago," Nikki quipped. "The Millennium didn't change that part of my crazy husband."

"Thanks, Chloe." Mark held up his cup and Nikki motioned to fill hers also.

Mark's grin slowly changed and sorrow filled his face. He contemplated, sipped coffee and then spoke slowly, painfully.

"She alerted us of a Combat invasion. We were into a service at the Church in the Woods. Our Global Team, brothers and sisters, children, friends." Mark paused, his eyes dropped. "I gave them a choice. Stay and fight, since we had fortified the log building and were heavily armed, or they could run. I was their leader, a pastor to them. But, I had to consider my wife and our unborn child—children. We fled into the forest. Even now I can hear their screams of panic. Embedded sounds in my mind that resonate with those moments of decision to run; the fear-filled crying of mothers and little children; orders and war commands of those taking positions to fight . . . their last battle."

Mark buried his head in his hands. "Oh God," he sobbed, "All those memories still haunt me! Will we never be free of the bad ones?"

"Someday, Mark," Nikki soothed. "We don't have to repeat this."

"Yes we do! I do," he snapped. Shag sat silent. The old soldier knew it was time to listen.

"I had preprogrammed Chloe to hide in the trees and be a sniper. She took out, I suspect, a lot of combats. She even blew their chopper out of the sky. Next, she was to hide really well before going into sleep mode. When time came for the program to wake her up she was to walk to our old log house, which she did. After that she stood guard 24/7 for us, especially while we were dead-tired and needed sleep. She was our eyes and ears."

"What happened to your team?" Shag asked quietly.

Mark's face filled with sorrow. "Combats set fire to the church. Those inside fought till they, dear God, burned up. Others who fled were hunted down and sliced up by combat lasers. The weaker ones they captured were tortured for information. We heard a few were held for Stoner to question. I'm certain at least one probably gave our names, which surely triggered Stoner's attention. He was making ready to come here when you took him out."

"How did you and Nikki escape?"

"Earlier, we had discovered a hidden secret room," Nikki answered. "It was stocked with food and other provisions. We brought in blankets to survive the cold, and an extra store of water. It was terrible and filthy. We stayed there four weeks, but it kept us alive, Thank God!"

"The night we ran from the church, I killed a man with the handgun you gave me," Mark confessed. " He popped up in front of us. Without hesitation I shot him in the face, a Combat, just a kid. I got sick beyond words; from fear; from taking a life."

"I know the feeling," Shag muttered. "Felt it that night in Kansas when I took out the two Combats that cut up Eric and Dulco. Difference was you killed out of fear; I reacted in rage. But it don't change how you feel afterwards."

"Oh! Poor Eric and Dulco," Nikki cried, covering her mouth.

"After that, world conditions became so horrible we saw little of the Combats; it was pollution, starvation, the heat, boulder hailstones and earthquakes that we feared most. Somewhere in the midst of the Great Tribulation our twins were born, out here, on this day."

"Thank You, God! The one good thing to come out of such rotten tragedy," Shag breathed a prayer.

"What about you?" Nikki brightened. "We want to hear your story."

"Yes, we do." Mark sat up.

"Not much to tell. Played cat and mouse with Combats after I led them on that wild chase from Kettleman's Lodge. They never did figure out if I was alive or dead. After I eliminated Stoner, I went high up into the Rockies. I mean high! The view was priceless, but the winters proved brutal. That first winter, figured I would pack it in. My shelter was barely throwed together, and apart from night, I dared not build a fire for fear the smoke would be spotted.

"Next summer, I ran across a small commune of folks who hadn't taken Christo's mark. One was a believer; the rest were not. That is where I met Shantra. Shantra Kimuchka, a Cheyenne woman out of Wyoming. She was a fighter and a beauty. Never thought I had any chance at love like I seen in you two.

"She stole this ol' vet's heart and became –." Shag rubbed his eyes and beard. Sorrow clouded his face. Then his keen eyes shone. "The love of my life. Yep, that she was; the love of my life."

"She didn't make it." Nikki shared in his sadness.

"She did not. Autumn day, crisp, blue sky, I was away hunting some elk. Kimuchka spotted some Combats lower in the trees. Her and this other brother, Steven Vogel, acted as decoys and led the Combats on a chase down the mountain away from the commune, in order to save the rest of us."

Mark and Nikki instantly recognized their friend, Steven. Excitement stirred their hearts.

"Kimuchka and Steven ran and hid for hours, but the Combats had tracking equipment and eventually trapped them in a box canyon. I know they fought, but in the end . . . I found my Sweetheart . . . buried the pieces of her body, what was left. Never found old Steven's –."

"But he is still alive!" Mark and Nikki shouted in unison.

"What? How can you know that?" The old man bellowed.

"Our guardian angels told us," Mark answered.

"How do they know?"

"They put out a call to other angels. Steven's angel answered them."

Shag looked over his shoulder at his angel. "Why haven't you let me in on this, Ganteous?"

"You have never requested that information," Ganteous responded with respect.

"Hot dawg," Shag muttered. "This be true?"

All three of their angels rose off the floor with a majestic flare of their wings and sang a beautiful chorus from which Shag, Mark nor Nikki could interpret any meaning. In a few moments the angels lowered and folded their wings.

"Steven Vogel's angel has informed him that you are alive and with friends, Mark and Nikki Hillag, in Oregon. He is overjoyed to learn all of you also survived the Tribulation."

"He dwells in a place called Paragon Colorado," Waaleen added.

"He went home," Nikki breathed softly.

"Don't that beat all! You knew Steven?"

"We traded the Air Van for his electric. He never mentioned that or us?" Mark questioned.

"In the commune we made little talk of past friends or experiences. A precaution, if caught by Combats. Enemy couldn't extract info we never had. All Steven ever said was a couple passing through led him to the Lord and he was forever grateful to them."

"That was us," Mark cried. "That was us!"

"Oh dear God." Nikki covered her mouth.

"Well, all I know about it," Shag continued, "is that me and old Steven Vogel helped nearly ever' last one in the commune to believe in the real Lord Jesus Christ, and that included my sweet Shantra."

The old gentleman sat up to look on Mark and Nikki with sharp, penetrating eyes. He spoke low with defining deliberation.

"I remember them all. The ones who died around us, and the ones for us. I was told that all who died during those terrible days are right now in the very presence of our Father. Don't understand any of that, but I know we will see each other again one day, just as we will our Global Teammates; and I will be with Shantra."

"So, you named Kimuchka after your true love?" Nikki spoke thoughtfully, after a reflective silence.

"Yes. She showed up one day and never left. Almost like Kimuchka sent her to keep me company. 'Course, I know it was the Lord's doing. Almost like the cougar sensed the gravity of the earth and that we must stick together to survive. When Christ returned, she changed, and has continued to stay by my side."

"Do you think you may love again someday? Could there be another?" Mark asked. "After all, we have a thousand years."

Shag hung his head in thought and fiddled with his fingers before he answered. "Always saw myself, if I ever fell in love like that, as a one-woman man. I don't believe there will ever be another. Just wish I coulda' married her, legal-like."

"Oh Shag," Nikki jumped and giggled. "We got married!"

With that came the telling of Tamon, led of God, to find them in the mountains and their miracle wedding. That conversation carried the three through the remainder of the night. Weariness set in and they knew they must seek rest. These were the final words as the sun broke the eastern sky.

"Shag," Nikki implored, "you have nothing in Colorado to demand your return. If Lord Jesus allows, you must stay here awhile with us. Be a new grandpa to our children."

"Absolutely," Mark agreed.

The grizzled old friend yawned, scratched his side, and rubbed his nose. A smile was detected hiding in his beard.

"You're right. I could see myself staying with ones I love for a hundred years or more."

CHAPTER 27

TRANSPORTER TRAVEL

10:00 PM in Oregon; 8:00 AM in Jerusalem.

"Farmer, it is 9:45 and they aren't here. They can't be late!" Emile was fidgety.

"Got fifteen minutes. Reckon they will git here jus' fine." Farmer smiled.

"They never, ever are on time! Nikki takes forever to get ready," Emile snapped. "I swear she'll use up her thousand years long before the rest of us, with folks waiting on her. What is it about these Tribulation Saints?"

Farmer rubbed his hand across his nose in thought, then spoke in his familiar drawl. "Emile, right now ya be sounden like a fussen ol' grandma."

Emile glared at him, then softened. She took his hand. "I'm sorry, but if they are late, these people won't wait; it is such a narrow –."

"There they be," Farmer pointed. Headlights spun around a corner to shine in Farmer and Emile's faces. The children's air car slammed to a stop in front of the waiting couple, lights went off and car doors flung open to a flurry of activity as the family climbed out.

Mark yelled, "We made it with five minutes to spare."

"And I nearly had a heart attack, if it were possible," Emile called out. "Hurry, children."

Mark had John and Johanna running, while Nikki was pulling Adam. Farmer noted a white-haired man gathering two small backpacks out of the car.

"Grandpapa, Grandmamma, I am so excited to go; I haven't slept for two nights!" Johanna hugged them both.

John was more serious and reserved. He walked up to them and stood.

Farmer eyed the boy. "Ya be excited too?" he asked.

John dropped his eyes. "I'm scared," he confessed.

"He threw up just before we left," Nikki whispered to Emile.

Mark dropped to one knee and drew both children close. "There is nothing to be afraid of. In just a few minutes you will arrive and Grandpapa and Grandmamma will be there to greet you and take you on a wonderful adventure. Now get your backpacks from Shag, and let's go."

The party entered through big doors under a large sign marked, 'Applegate Transporter Station.' They walked into a large room filled with noisy travelers. Suddenly, a striking black couple grabbed the twins. "Grandfather, Grandmother Savage," they yelled and threw their arms around them.

"We couldn't be at your birthdays but came to help send you off on your trip of a lifetime," Grandmother Savage spoke with deep emotion.

"Yes, now hurry." Grandfather Savage pointed them to the boarding gate. "They have already called for you."

"Run!" Mark and Nikki instructed.

The stewardess checked them in and gave simple instructions. "When you go inside the Transporter, drop your backpacks to your feet, cross your arms over your chest, and stand very still."

"Will this hurt?" John asked. "If it does, I can take it."

"You won't feel a thing." She laughed. "Now, all of you, proceed down this walkway. An attendant will instruct you."

"Come quickly, please." A man motioned for them. "John and Johanna Hillag?" He checked a form.

"Yes," they both replied.

Farmer and Emile took the twin's hands. "When you arrive we will be standing outside the Transporter just like we are here. Now go." With that Farmer, Emile and their angels disappeared.

The attendant opened a very solid door and escorted the children inside a sizeable room. They looked around. A strange fabric covered the walls, ceiling, and inside the door, cloth they had never seen anywhere before.

"Do not touch anything," the attendant instructed. "Place your backpacks at your feet."

"The floor looks like glass," John whispered to Johanna.

"Shhh," she warned.

"Are you both ready to travel?"

"Oh yes," Johanna said. John only nodded.

"Cross your arms and don't move." He closed the door and heavy bolts clanged into place. He smiled at the family waiting nervously outside the Transporter. "First time?" he observed. He programmed information and commands into a panel and it lit up.

"Bam." Everyone jumped.

"They are on their way. Now if you all will make your way through the exit door. Thank you."

Outside in the dark the family discussed the event.

"Can't make myself travel in one o' those contraptions. You think they are safe?" Shag asked.

"Been operating for years now with no mishaps," Mark answered.

"Oh Mom and Dad, I am so excited and pleased to see you," Nikki cried. "I thought you had forgotten!"

"Forgotten? Never!" both parents exclaimed. "We'll explain later." They turned to hug Adam but he backed away.

"Well, I think this is so dumb. Why did they go in the middle of the night?" Adam growled. "Just stupid."

"It isn't the middle of the night," Mark corrected. "The time is 10 PM here, but it is 8 in the morning in Jerusalem. They have the whole day to sightsee."

"And see Jesus, face to face," Nikki breathed softly.

CHAPTER 28

GUIDED TOUR

"Grandmamma, Grandpapa," the twins shouted as they grabbed their backpacks and bounded out of the Jerusalem Transporter room. Running to Farmer and Emile, the twins were jabbering loudly at once. They were ecstatic!

"I closed my eyes for only an instant, and poof, we were here," John exclaimed triumphantly.

"To me, it was like when I first doze off to sleep and suddenly wake up," Johanna exclaimed, laughing.

"Did you feel anything?" Emile asked.

"My body tingled a little." Johanna hugged Emile.

"My stomach leaped like when I rode on that rollercoaster at Applegate," John said seriously, "but I didn't get sick this time."

"Were ya brave or scared?" Farmer chuckled.

"I was brave!" John declared and stood erect before his grandpapa.

"I closed my eyes and braced for something to happen. Next instant the door opened—we were here. Didn't have time to be either." Johanna smiled.

"Reckon ya both be mighty brave jus' ta make the journey." Farmer took their hands. "Come, let us begin a day ya all will never ferget."

The twins could never have been prepared for the sight they beheld as they walked from the Transporter Station out onto the streets of Jerusalem.

"Oh my!" Johanna gasped. Her hand covered her heart and tears filled her wondering eyes.

John stood speechless before Zion, the City of God.

The Transporter Station number 5 was located in the lower city towards the south, not far from the Pool of Siloam. Looking north up the mount was the magnificent Temple. Beams of beautiful light emitted from every opening of the Temple. Reaching out, searching every street, entering every house, illuminating every alleyway, doorway and window; eventually setting every heart ablaze. Johanna felt it first, then John, as a beam from Christ's throne shown on their faces.

Suddenly, a glorious host of angels hovering over the Temple burst into song. It was music like never heard before on the earth, except for the starry night they sang celebrating the Birth of Christ.

The angels' songs of praise had a profound effect on the teeming throngs of people crowding the streets and marketplaces of Jerusalem. As the wondrous anthem rose, the crowds halted from their hurried pace and one by one began dropping to their knees. Farmer and Emile knelt in humble adoration of their King and Lord. John and Johanna felt an overwhelming desire to worship Jesus Christ. So strong were their emotions that they stretched out on their faces before the Lord, little hands reaching towards the Temple. Prayers and words coming forth from Johanna were so powerful she could scarcely breathe. All she could hear from John beside her were his sobs, "Forgive me, Jesus. Forgive me; forgive me; help me!"

The cries of her brother's heart blended with her own and Johanna began begging the Lord to forgive her. These feelings were all new to her. In her young mind she was uncertain what it was exactly she needed forgiveness for. All she knew as she lay face-down before the Son of God was how utterly unworthy and unclean she felt. She had nothing good to offer the King; even her heart seemed tainted. But, how could she clean it? She knew not, only that something dirty inside of her was lurking that must be washed. But with what? Soap and water? No. She bathed everyday. If that was the answer, why did she feel unclean now?

"Wash me, Lord Jesus," Johanna's young heart reached out in a whisper.

The singing stopped, followed by a few minutes of reverent silence. The twins raised their heads to look around. The scene was of an entire metropolis, still before the Lord Christ. Then, a sweeping sense of deep peace and unspeakable joy descended upon the city. People everywhere arose shouting and laughing. Farmer and Emily reached down to help the children stand up.

"How can I feel so happy and guilty at the same time?" Johanna wanted to know.

"I came to Jerusalem to see King Jesus, yet I wanted to run away and hide," John confessed.

"Reckon ya will find the answers ta yer questions afor' the sun be down ta day," Framer drawled.

"Can we go see Jesus now?" John couldn't take his eyes off the resplendent Temple.

"Not yet." Emile laughed. "Your time isn't until 2:30 this afternoon. Until then, we have places to show you.

"Ya both remember all we read ya 'bout Christ's last days, the cross, an' His being resurrected?"

"Yes, Grandpapa," both children answered.

"Well, not far from here be the place o' the upper room where they shared the Lord's Supper. 'Course thet place be no longer here after two thousand year. Jesus an' his disciples left the room an' went out a gate, probably ta the Valley of Kidron an' made their way ta the Mount of Olives."

"That's where the guards captured Jesus," John spoke up.

"Yes, but there be a place on tha Mount of Olives called Gethsemane. That was where Jesus went ta pray. We will go there first."

Farmer led them to a small gate in the Jerusalem wall that took them out into the Valley of the Kidron. A well-marked path followed a small stream through trees and a variety of bushes, plants and colorful flowers. The twins babbled, taking in the sights along the way. They were full of comments and questions.

The walk took about twenty minutes. They arrived at a sign marking the entrance: 'Garden of Gethsemane.' They found the wooded area sizeable, and filled with a sense of peace. Numerous visitors strolled slowly, thoughtfully, most knowing full well what took place on this very ground the night of Christ's betrayal. The twins looked at Farmer and Emile with questioning eyes but spoke not.

As they walked among the trees they came upon a man sitting on a bench. He smiled and greeted them. "Shalom, brothers and sisters. Won't you sit a spell here in the shade and your children rest and cool themselves."

Farmer started to pass on the offer, but felt a check in his spirit. He nodded his head and motioned for Emile and the twins to sit.

"First time for these youngsters to come to Jerusalem?" the stranger asked.

"Yes, and we are going to see King Jesus," Johanna spoke up.

"I see," the man spoke low. He studied the children before turning his gaze on Farmer and Emile.

'Who is this man?' Farmer wondered. He was not overly handsome, with a full beard, thick hair and eyebrows. He was modest and plain of dress, not too tall, maybe 5 foot 7, as best Farmer could judge him. But his smile was disarming; his light grey eyes spoke of many sights seen. His overall looks and demeanor confirmed he was a resurrected saint.

"You say you are going to see King Jesus?" the man murmured, now as if from some other place in his life. "I remember the first time I saw Him. It was a long time ago in a place north of here. A day like any other day, yet a day like no other. One that changed the course and destiny of my life.

"I had traveled with my friend to the Jordan River Wilderness to hear this crazy wild man preach. He called us to repent and be baptized. We did and followed him, this one known as John the Baptist."

"You knew John the Baptist?" Johanna was awestruck.

"Indeed. Followed him for many a day, until that . . ."

"What?" John encouraged the man on.

"A man walked through the crowd I had never seen before. John pointed Him out and declared, 'Behold, the Lamb of God!' And you know what? My friend and I turned and followed

Jesus. We just seemed to have an understanding that was exactly what John wanted."

"Amen," Farmer whispered. "Andrew?" he asked.

The man glanced an acknowledgement to Farmer and went on with his story.

"We followed Jesus until He asked what we were looking for. We didn't have any idea except we needed to know about Him. So we asked to see where He lived and He took us. I tell you the truth. After spending all afternoon with Him, I had no doubt that He was the Son of God.

"Next day I found my brother, Simon, and told him, 'we have found the Christ!' Well, he had to see for himself, right then, so I brought him to Jesus. The first thing Jesus did was give my brother a new name. Peter!" Andrew shook his head and laughed out loud.

"This is the place where the events of the Passover took a turn and Christ would become the Lamb that was slain, Praise His Holy Name. Come with me."

The man led them along a narrow path into a small grove of old gnarled olive trees. He stopped to look around.

"Yes, I am indeed Andrew and I was here that night. Many of the olive trees were destroyed in the Tribulation, but these are special and I believe the hand of Almighty God protected them. Two thousand years is a long time, but the best I can recall, Jesus left us under these trees. He took Peter, James and John over there under that one, then He disappeared into the mist.

"Very early that morning, I was roused out of a deep sleep by the commotion of a large group of Temple Guards led by Judas. They carried torches and swords. Peter was the strong one; he drew his sword and swiftly cut off Malchus' ear. I only wanted to run and hide; to save myself!

"Jesus showed Himself and shone like light in the dark. He told Peter to put away his sword. He placed Malchus' ear back right then and healed it like new. All that, yet that blind crowd didn't see the light or the miracle. They bound Jesus and took Him away.

"Odd thing about me, all of us I suppose, the instant they tied up my Lord, we too felt bound, totally helpless. Times past when we traveled to Jerusalem, we all bore an air of strength. We displayed boldness. We were confident. But that night, my strength turned to liquid. My bold confidence got bound up like my Lord. My faith collapsed, and my blood ran cold in my veins. I fled into the trees—we all did save Peter and John, who only managed to follow at a distance. Later, my brother denied Jesus three times.

"Follow me and I will show you where they took the Christ from here."

Andrew led them back into the City through the Old Sheep Gate and around the north side of the Temple. He stopped.

"Somewhere in these buildings I believe was the hall where Pilot condemned Jesus to be crucified. But before they brought Him here, He was tried before the Sanhedrin, which was on the West side of the Temple. After that He was sent to Herod. His Palace was on that distant hill over there to the west. The Sanhedrin Counsel brought Jesus to Pilot, here, to be tried because they had no authority to render a death sentence."

"Were you here when they tried Jesus?" Johanna asked.

Andrew dropped his head. Sorrow clouded his face. "I was not," he answered slowly. "I was hiding in a house in the lower city with other disciples. We were fearing for our lives."

Andrew walked down stairs onto a narrow street boxed in by high buildings on either side.

"Our Lord was forced to carry His cross on this street, until He fell beneath the load . . ."

"Wish I could have been here to help Him," John muttered.

A little farther, Johanna burst into tears. "Oh this is awful," she cried.

Nothing more was said as they walked the path Jesus walked. Andrew remembered; the others imagined; all touched by the event of that day; each one accepting the truth. It had to happen exactly as it did, all of it.

In a few more blocks, the group came upon a populated area of single-unit houses and wider streets. Andrew stopped again.

"Back then we would pass through the old wall to the outside of the City. They have built a new wall on the other side of that hill." He pointed to a sharp rise in front of them. "This whole area is now inside the city wall. However, as the Scripture says, 'He was crucified outside the city.'"

Andrew led them through the streets, greeting people as they went. Soon they came to a path that took them to the top of the hill.

"Is this where Jesus hung on the cross?" Johanna looked up.

"Up there?" Andrew asked. "Yes."

"Did He carry the cross up this path?" John questioned.

"He probably took this pathway or one near it. But remember, another carried His cross."

The five climbed to the top of the hill. Andrew made his way to a small, level, grassy spot. He stopped and turned his gaze back towards the Temple.

"See that bald, hard rock surface over there by that jagged edge?" he asked.

Yes." They all looked.

"There, over the centuries by tradition, is where they claim He was crucified, and that is permissible. Yet, as I stand here and remember, I recall it was here on this spot where we stand. Here He gave His life and shed His cleansing Blood."

Farmer studied both places; then looked at Andrew. "Reckon I don't understand. How could folks be so amiss?"

"Golgotha means the place of the skull, so over time Christians picked that spot over there because, from below the cliff, the hard surface up here, resembles a skull. But it wasn't called Golgotha because of how it looked, but because what took place there.

"This hill was a place of executions. Skulls of animals sacrificed and human heads were dumped here and sometimes burned over there. Later the Romans chose this hill to crucify their prisoners. Here is where they could dig a hold in the ground. I know. I saw many brothers and sisters hung on crosses. But listen. Through the centuries believers needed a place to come. Somewhere that they could look upon for comfort and inspiration; a spot to see where it happened; an area to proclaim their faith; a place to fall on their knees and thank God for the sacrifice of His Son for the forgiveness of sin.

"And, down that side of the slope is the tomb. Time and Christians have changed that as well. Truth is, the Romans destroyed the tomb Joseph gave. They feared Christians would try to use it as proof of His Resurrection. That action proved folly. He rose from the dead and for forty days was seen by many, including me.

"So it matters little, my friends, if the designated place up here is twenty feet off, or if the tomb down there actually belonged to someone else. What matters to everyone who will ever live, is that Christ was crucified on a cross. He gave His life and Blood here, so we could be free and come back to God the Father as it was in the beginning. To prove His point and stamp His power and victory over sin, hell and the grave, He Rose from the Dead!"

CHAPTER 29

FACE TO FACE

A sea of faces seemed to ripple down the wide steps coming from the Temple Mount. Farmer, Emile and the children were caught in the flow of visitors going up to the Temple.

From what Farmer could determine, he was seeing people from every nation of the world. The multitude was a mixture of race, size, shape, age, male and female, Old Testament Saints, Church Age Saints and Tribulation Saints. Added to these were hosts of angels, many hovering near their human charges. The sight was indeed supernatural.

The crowds were joyful, excited and noisy. Farmer noticed others with children and wondered if they were bringing them to see Christ, as he and Emile were. Would the twins even have any time with the King?

John squeezed Farmer's hand and held tight as they climbed the steps. A glance at both children revealed perplexed expressions. They must be thinking the same as Farmer.

"Oh, Grandmamma, there are so many people. How will we ever be able to see King Jesus?" Johanna cried.

"Have faith, child," Emile encouraged. "Jesus always keeps His promise and He is never late. Have faith and believe."

They emerged into a large area, the Outer Courtyard. Benches cushioned with plush material like velvet lined the entire east and west walls. Many Saints were seated and engaged in conversation. Others mingled in the open courtyard.

"Where shall we go?" Emile asked Farmer.

Farmer turned to his angel Adreen, who motioned them through the crowd to the Temple entrance.

111

Farmer had never seen the Temple up close, nor looked upon such a sight as this, not even in Paradise. No words could measure or describe what his eyes gazed upon here.

The Temple rose high above them. The walls were unlike anything ever observed anywhere. The sun was dropping towards the west, and its light mixed with the glow emitting from inside the Temple made the hues of the walls change. The Temple shone as pure gold, slowly turning to jasper, evolving to sapphire, then a darker shade of emerald brushed across the walls.

"Wow!" John exclaimed.

"Can we go in?" Johanna was eager. "Is it time yet?"

"In a few minutes," Emile said.

Adreen and Froton dropped to the courtyard floor and stood near the Temple entrance.

"We cannot go inside," they declared.

"Why not?" the twins questioned. "We thought angels could all fly right up to Jesus."

"Only if we are bidden," Froton answered.

John and Johanna turned to their angels, Lonsu and Ofinian.

"But you are always with us." Johanna suddenly was on the verge of tears.

"You have no need of a guardian in there," Lonsu smiled. "We will wait here for you."

"Let us go." Farmer took their hands. "Reckon it be time fer ya."

They proceeded into the Temple. The floor was pure gold yet resembled glass. On the left side of the room was an altar of wood and stone. To the right of the altar was a plain table, huge and built sturdy of metal and wood. The tabletop was bare.

Passing between the altar and table they faced an old rugged hewn cross. In front of the cross was placed a small table with pieces of bread and a goblet of wine. Emile dropped to her knees before the table and wept. Farmer held Emile's shoulder as he removed his boots. Tears wet his face. The twins tugged at his sleeve. Looking into their sweet faces he could tell they were frightened.

112

"We be in a most Holy Place and best we take off our shoes and leave 'em here."

"Come Beloved," they heard a gentle voice bidding them to approach His Throne.

Beyond the cross was a much smaller entrance, no doubt into the Holy of Holies. Farmer himself was moved and confused. He had truly expected this room to be packed with people, yet they were alone. Amazingly, as they approached the smaller entrance, everything around them seemed to blur, fading from sight, and the noisy throng outside could no longer be heard. There was a Holy Hush inside the Temple, and they had no idea what to expect next. The children's hearts beat faster and Farmer heard Johanna whimper. He drew her close and smoothed her hair.

"We be safe in His Presence," he reassured.

On the other side of this entrance, the floor changed to glass that sparkled like diamonds. The walls were covered in material of a wealth and color that denoted royalty. Straight ahead hung a veil across the room dividing the Holy Room where they stood, from the Most Holy. A blinding light filled the room from the other side of the veil. The twins groaned in pain and covered their eyes.

"Come, my Beloved," the voice called again, and suddenly the light diminished. They gasped in surprise and wonder. The veil was not closed but pulled completely open. Sitting on a magnificent throne was the Son of God, yet right now He looked more like the Son of Man. He stood to His feet to greet His guests and walked down the few steps to the floor beneath His Throne. Instead of a royal robe, he was dressed more like a humble carpenter.

The Lord's smile was completely disarming and instantly put them all at ease. He approached them and embraced Farmer, who went weak-kneed in Christ's arms.

"My dear friend Farmer. I joyfully greet you. I have longed to see you. And Emile, dear and faithful wife and Kingdom Servant." Jesus hugged Emile, then turned to the twins.

"You had your twelfth birthdays. So was it to your liking?"

The children were so taken back they could only blush. Emile took both their arms. "I declare," she fumed. "You both are forgetting your manners. What did I tell you to do?"

Both children stood straight up in front of Jesus. "We greet you King Jesus," they said in rehearsed fashion. Then John bowed and Johanna did a little curtsy her momma taught her.

Jesus smiled and His eyes twinkled. He motioned for them to follow as He walked back to His Throne. But instead of going up, He sat down on the steps and patted on each side with His hands for them to sit. He looked into each of their eyes, souls and spirits deeply as He studied them. After some time, He spoke softly and slowly.

"I have looked forward to this meeting for such a long, long time. Far longer than either of you can imagine. This is a special time in your lives, as you both hang in the balance of between being a boy and girl and a man and woman. What you decide today is of great importance and you must be honest and open to truth. No hiding, no pretense, only speak from your hearts. Do you understand?" The children nodded.

"You have read about the time and the events of My life when I first came to earth as a baby and grew to be a man?"

"Yes," they responded.

"Did you understand what you saw when you came into the Holy Place?"

"I believe each part had a meaning that I don't understand exactly," John answered.

"What was the bare table?" Johanna asked.

"That table was where lambs were slain and their blood collected. The lamb was sacrificed on the altar. The cross became the table and the altar because I was the Lamb of God. On the cross I took the sins of the whole world and paid for them with My Pure Blood.

"Your grandpapa can tell you about the small table."

"It reminds us thet on the Cross Ya was broken like the bread, and shed Yer blood like the wine."

114

"You both see and understand what the objects are, but now you must see the event with your hearts." Jesus wiped a tear from Johanna's cheek.

"I saw you stretched out on the sidewalk, praying to Me and I heard your prayers. John, you sought forgiveness. My child, I bought your forgiveness as I died on that cross. And Johanna, you wanted to be clean. My precious blood will cleanse you from the inside.

"As you stood on the hill of Golgotha and looked on the spot where My cross was lifted up, you must understand what nailed Me there. It was your sin."

John drew back in horror, and Johanna covered her face.

"Every person ever born has been given a sin nature passed on from Adam and Eve. I was the only human born without it. As you cried out for forgiveness, John, you were sensing that dark nature in your body and mind demanding to take over. And you, Johanna, struggled with uncleanness because that sin nature pollutes your mind and body. Had it dominated, it would eventually destroy both of you."

Jesus took each of their hands. "The first thing your sin did was beat Me. You lashed My back until I openly bled."

"No, no!" John tried to pull his hand away, but Jesus tightened His grip.

"I won't let you go, John. As long as you draw a breath, I won't let you go.

"Next, your sin nailed Me to that cross. With one hand you took a big spike and with the other picked up a hammer. You raised it high, then struck. Over and over you pounded till the nail was driven deep. Then, my feet."

"I didn't mean to." Johanna wiped her nose and eyes.

Jesus let go of their hands and opened His to reveal two large ugly scars. "The sin of the world did this to Me and these scars will never heal or fade. Not ever! Touch them and know they are real."

John turned his head.

"Touch them, John. I did this for you! Touch them and know I did this for you, Johanna. I bought your forgiveness with My life and blood."

John tried to touch without looking.

"Look at Me," Jesus insisted with an indescribable tenderness. "Look at Me."

John made eye contact and his Savior searched the young man's heart. "Do you want forgiveness?"

John broke. "Oh yes," he cried aloud. "Please forgive me!"

"By faith do you believe I am the Son of God and I died for you?"

John buried his head against Christ's chest and sobbed from a broken heart. He surrendered and believed.

Johanna touched His nail-scarred Hand and kissed it. She held it tightly in her little hands. "They should have nailed my hands and feet, not Yours. You didn't do anything."

"Do you believe by faith, Johanna?"

"Yes, oh, please save me and make me clean."

The King that day wrapped His arms around two children and held them close.

"If you remember nothing else of this day, one truth you must never forget. If you precious ones were the only two in the whole world who ever lived, I would still have come down from Glory and died on that cross for you. I love you that much!"

With that, the King of kings and Lord of lords placed His hands on the heads of the two twelve-year-olds.

"Be ye born anew of the Spirit."

Light ran from Christ through His Arms and Hands into John and Johanna. Their faces shone as the noonday sun and weeping turned to shouts of joy and laughter.

CHAPTER 30

FARMER AND EMILE'S REIGN

The sky was cloudless, but a muted blue as it awaited the sun to burst forth over nearby mountains. In the waning shadows of the trees lining a part of Cold Creek, a herd of deer stepped forth, dropping their heads to drink of the clear water. A black bear and her cub ambled up beside the deer. She sniffed and grunted softly, leading her baby into a shallow part of the stream. Waking doves could be heard stirring in the nearby pine trees. A slight breeze made a gentle sigh.

The great log home of Farmer and Emile stood staunchly among the forest giants, well, upcoming giants for the true patriarchs were all but destroyed in the Tribulation. But these young ones would eventually grow to take their place.

The house was quiet, waiting the coming of a new day. Darkness in the Trevor house was barely illuminated by a dim light in the kitchen. Farmer was knocking around making coffee, totally unaware of the scene unfolding outside with the deer, bears and doves. Nor would he have been that intrigued. He had seen such interactions as well as many others during the beginning years of the Millennium. No, his mind was occupied with a multitude of other thoughts this morning, so by the time he stepped onto the porch with a cup of coffee, the deer, bears and doves had long since disappeared into the forest. Only a pair of squawking scissortails remained, rudely establishing their territory and defying Farmer to intrude.

Farmer stood on the porch staring out into the trees and back brush beyond. He loved what he saw and for a moment he grew misty. He fondly remembered the old log house; Walter and Clifton playing down by the creek, Emile near him holding baby

Leah. There was bliss mingled with pain in remembering, and his emotions were much heightened now being a Resurrected Saint. The memories were so vivid and detailed as to sweep him to a mountaintop with joy or break his heart in a deep valley. Must he resign himself to block all recall from his mind? No, that could never be. Not until God Himself performed such an act.

Why was he so melancholy this morning? He lived in a perfect world with no place for sadness! Yet, he could not deny that he felt—sad. Did something inside wish to drive him back a century before to a time and place he felt truly happy? That was unrealistic. That past carried a flawed happiness, not real and perfect as he experienced now.

Maybe it was a longing to recover and hold onto something that was precious, or simply a desire to renew his life? Make unresolved events right somehow, or was it regrets over lost time with his family? Was it about life that went on while he was in Paradise? Or, was it the indescribable sorrow of separation for Emile, me, and the family? That mattered little now. They were all together for a millennium.

Farmer sipped his coffee and walked down to Cold Creek. He understood his thoughts no more than the brooding he felt inside. A century earlier he would have blamed the devil for troubling him, but Satan was locked up. This was his own doing. No one else was responsible, and he must shake it!

"Farmer," Emile called from the porch. "Are you coming back up?"

Farmer wheeled around and made his way back to the house. They kissed when he joined her.

"Thank you, love, for making coffee this morning." Emile rubbed Farmer's arm. Suddenly she looked into his eyes. "What is it, Farmer? I sense you are troubled? No, I see sadness."

"Aye. Was jus' remembering how our life be in Oregon. How happy we felt. Fer an instant I saw the boys an' ya with baby Leah. Then I reckon regret took hold an' I saw so much life lost, me bein' killed." Tears trickled down Farmer's cheek. Emily reached up and wiped them away. She seemed to understand.

She motioned for him to sit with her at the table. She studied his face for some time before she spoke.

"Farmer, those were precious and happy times, but we can't cling to memories that were pleasant and forget not all the other times. We had hurts as deep as any joys." She took Farmer's hand. "We can't allow ourselves to retreat to the past when a whole future lies before us. We are reigning with Christ and that brings responsibilities.

Farmer nodded, smiled and squeezed her hand.

"Later today Donald and Beth Parrigan will be here from the high country to report on the timber cutting on the mountain slopes and about hauling logs to the mills here and at Springdale." Emile continued, "And now they are recruiting young Millennials to plant seedlings in the burn areas. He wants Adam to help."

"I be concerned over thet boy," Farmer remarked.

"As am I, Farmer, and in a few years we will take him to the Jerusalem Temple to see King Jesus. We cannot, just cannot slip into a trap that sees the twins and Adam as the only grandchildren we will ever have in the Millennium. John and Johanna will grow up and no doubt marry other Tribulation Saints or Millennials, just as Adam will. They will have children and those children will have children. Farmer, do you realize how many grandchildren we will have in a thousand years?"

Farmer pondered what Emily was saying.

He smiled and ran his fingers through his hair.

"When we put Great in front o' all their names, I reckon we will have ta use gigabytes, as Mark would say." Farmer laughed.

Emile was somber. "Our future on this earth has just started, Farmer. We have a thousand years of living to do. A thousand years of family, making memories, doing the work the Lord has assigned to us. Let's remember with fondness good times and blessings of the past and discard the bad. Our lives are here, now. Will the Millennium have history? Absolutely! It begins today. We will only go forward."

Just then the rising sun broke through the trees, shining on Farmer and Emile's faces.

SEGMENT TWO

JANEE'S REIGN

CHAPTER 31

JESUS CALLS

"Janee Stemper."

"Yes, Lord," Janee answered, instantly looking up from the papers she was sorting through.

"I'm listening, Lord Jesus," she spoke again. A quick glance at her clock revealed 9:59 AM.

"Come to me in Jerusalem," Jesus instructed.

"Be there in a minute, King Jesus," Janee opened the door of her office and informed her receptionist, "I'll be gone for a while. Not sure how long." She closed the door and was gone.

In a flash, Janee stood before the Temple. Jerusalem shone even in the dark of night and the Temple reflected the brilliance of a starry night. Many Resurrection Saints were out and about on the streets, but Tribulation Saints and Millennials were mostly sleeping.

There was activity around the Temple, which Janee supposed took place non-stop.

"I am here, Lord Jesus," she spoke nervously. "Are you in Your Temple?"

"I am on the Mount of Olives," He answered in thought. "Meet me here."

Janee appeared among the olive trees. In the shadows, she made out a glowing figure. She ran breathlessly and threw herself at the Master's feet. It was so good to see Him again!

"This is the first time Face to face since My return," Jesus posed not a question but stated a fact. He reached down and took a gentle hold of her arm.

"Rise, My daughter, in whom I am well pleased." He enfolded her in His arms. Janee went limp in His embrace and was flooded with the Son of God's deep and peaceful love.

"Come. Let us walk together." He held out His hand.

"You are doing an important work for Me that has far-reaching effects. The series you recently completed, 'The Rebirth of our Planet,' has touched many lives. You encouraged those who survived the Tribulation that all was not lost, but rather to go forth with renewed hope, like the maiden at the Twins' birthday party."

"You saw her?"

"I see and know everything. Your 'Horses of the World' episodes also reached into many hearts, as it was intended. Yet, it wasn't just the horses you projected, but the stories. Those are what reached the viewers. And your children's shows blessed so many precious little ones."

Janee was speechless!

Now Jesus turned to face her. "I have new work for you to do."

Janee bowed in humble submission. Jesus gently lifted her head to look deeply into her eyes and heart.

"Yes, Master," Janee teared up. Her mind was racing.

"My servant Cecil B. DeMille in his before-life did works that exemplified and honored Me. One in particular was My favorite. Cecil was growing in popularity and movie skills, but was hindered by a dishonest studio and an envious business partner. He had a project to accomplish born of Me, but no place to produce it. Secretly for three years in the mid-twenties he rented a place in Culver City and converted it into a studio. There he filmed 'King of Kings.' I want you to acquire that building and remake it into a studio again . . . and re-do 'King of Kings.'"

"Oh my," Janee gasped. She staggered under the enormity of the project. A full-feature film would be a first for her to produce. Her first thought was, 'Shouldn't DeMille do this?'

"Cecil is doing other projects for me," Jesus replied. "It is you I have chosen to re-make King of Kings."

"Lord," she began, overwhelmed, trying to decide where to begin her questions. "It is 59 years into the Millennium. Is that building still there? Did it survive the Tribulation? So much of Hollywood and L.A. were devastated in the Tribulation wars."

"Yes, it is there, but far from being a movie studio. However, I will not tell you where it is," Jesus anticipated her next question.

Janee frowned, not understanding.

"I want you and your staff to enjoy the assignment and experience the excitement of discovery. Then, I have more projects for you to oversee while the construction of the studio takes place.

"Iraq was instrumental in Biblical History. I want you to document and film the most important places to raise awareness among Tribulation Saints and especially the Millennials, of pressing needs there; and to help advance the rebuilding of that country.

"And, as soon as you complete that documentary, I want you to air a one-time world-wide broadcast of a discussion forum comprised of just Millennials, and I want you to invite your nephew, Adam, to be one of the guests."

CHAPTER 32

PAIGE

Early morning, Janee arrived at her office in Burbank. She had been working out of the old Disney Studios, where she did most of her productions. The studio was renamed, 'Hidden Light Studio,' in honor of the embedded believers who fought against Christo's Combats during the Tribulation wars. Many gave their lives; however, some women and children survived by hiding in the secret underground vaults, where film archives were stored.

During the war, all but two of the sound stages were destroyed or so badly damaged they were rendered unusable. Although some work was in progress, those damaged stages were not yet repaired. Janee was using one of the salvaged stages for her ongoing children's shows.

"Paige here to see you," Janee's receptionist called.

"Oh, good! Send her in."

Immediately Paige was in front of Janee's desk. Janee stood to greet her old friend.

"Good morning, Paige. Have a seat. Where are we today?"

"Well, Bernard and Seth are vigorously searching for the old DeMille Studio. County records for Culver City were all obliterated by the war. Non-Coms fought off Combats there and lost. The Combats razed the whole building. Therefore, there are no records of where that studio is located, and they have searched everywhere. Are we sure it still exists?"

"Jesus says it does. How are you coming on getting a film crew for our Iraq project?"

"I have one Tribulation Saint, tough, with some good experience. I wish I could find more like him. The other is a younger Millennial. That one has experience and talent . . ."

"But?"

Paige took a breath. "He is aggressive, bossy and has a smart mouth."

"Which outweighs the other?"

"I'm thinking, experience and talent."

"OK, any others?"

"Not yet. Working on it. A female has to be strong to do Iraq!"

Janee noticed Paige kept shifting back and forth and often avoided eye contact. In fact, she was often like that. Is she uncomfortable because I am her boss? Are we awkward with each other? She decided to deal with the problem, if there was one. She got up out of her chair and walked around her desk. She sat on the edge and faced Paige.

"Paige, we have been the best of friends for a long, long time," Janee murmured.

Paige dropped her eyes, her face scrunched up. She covered her mouth.

"You were there in the beginning when I got my first big break in movies," Janee added.

Paige tried to wipe her eyes. Janee grabbed two tissues. Paige reached out and took Janee's hand. "You were there and helped me through those awful times with Billy, and the terrible divorce," Paige remembered.

"When I lay dying in the hospital and many stopped coming, you were there, Paige; you and my sweet Bernard."

At that Paige took away her hand and covered her face. She broke down in loud sobs and wails. She tried, but couldn't look at Janee.

"What is it?" Janee demanded.

"That's just it!" Page mustered the courage to speak. "I was there when Bernard—was."

"So?"

"I even came to your wedding."

"You were invited."

"Janee! I married my best friend's husband."

"Oh for pity sakes! I was dead."

"But you're alive now. And I started falling in love with Bernard before, before you died. Janee, I'm so sorry. I betrayed you."

Janee was stunned. "I thought we worked all this out in Paradise."

"You did, I didn't, and now being here, the three of us together...."

"Awkward?"

"Yes, awkward."

The two women just sat and stared at each other. Janee sought wisdom and fought for the right words.

"Doesn't it bother you we are both married to the same man, working together?"

Janee laughed. She saw the humor in their situation. "This tells me only one thing, Paige. I made a damn good choice in a man."

Paige broke into a smile as she dabbed at her eyes. "Not so. I just followed you, girl, like I have always done."

"Well, let me be clear on this, sister. We are in the Millennium and we are Resurrected Saints. For us there is no marriage except to our Bridegroom, the Lord Jesus Christ. No marriage apart from that. I am married, you are married, Bernard is married, each one of us to Christ. That puts us on equal ground. No jealousy here, no guilt or shame, just Resurrection Saints in a perfect world."

Janee took Paige's hands in hers and leaned in close. She spoke low.

"Just you and me. Two long-time and dear friends—forever."

CHAPTER 33

THE FORGOTTEN STUDIO

"**B**ernard and Seth have just found the studio," Miglia announced from his post in Janee's office.

At the same time Janee's receptionist buzzed. "Bernard on line 3, says it's urgent," her voice came over the speaker.

"Bernard, you are calling on a phone?"

"Borrowed a Millennial kid's. Janee! We found it, but you will never guess what it looks like. You must come right away. I will tell Paige."

Janee jotted the address on a piece of paper and disappeared. Next minute she was standing in an empty parking lot. Bernard and Seth were facing a run-down building.

"Hi Mom," Seth greeted her. "We found it."

"Can you imagine?" Bernard was excited.

"Have you been inside?" Janee questioned.

"Yes," he replied, "and you won't believe what we found."

Just then Paige appeared. "So this is the missing studio? How did you locate it?"

"We put out word we were looking for any DeMille memorabilia for research. Two Tribulation Saints invited us to their home. They showed us materials collected by their grandparents. We discovered some old notes and ads that indicated this spot."

"But this doesn't look anything like a studio. The sign on the front says it's an indoor shopping mall," Janee observed.

"It is," Seth answered. "It is divided into little shops."

"It is in grave disrepair," Paige observed. "After so long, why isn't it in use?"

"We know that so much of the earth's population was destroyed. Regrowth here has been terribly slow," Bernard explained. "There are Millennials coming along, but not enough for anyone to open a business here yet."

"Then, it is available?" Janee asked.

"That's the good news. Seth and I checked with the county and when we told them it was for a King Jesus Project, they gladly offered to deed it to us."

"Praise the Lord!" Paige shouted.

The building inside was a wreck. There were indeed small shops portioned off. Wide walkways made each shop accessible. Many walls had gaping holes, and some were completely knocked down. Janee observed that none of the shops had ceilings, but the roof of the building towered above. It was then she realized this building was large enough for a smaller sound stage and maybe some offices. She studied the structure, trying to imagine the great director in this very place, filming 'King of Kings.'

"So, what do you think?" Bernard's question snapped her back to the task at hand.

"We need proof. We must know for sure this was DeMille's studio."

"That's the good part," Bernard said, ecstatic.

"You will be so happy, Mom," Seth added. "Follow us."

Seth led the group down stairs into a basement. It was a large space with several rooms off to one side. Seth took them inside one of the rooms. It was dingy and smelled of age and mold. Disgusting stained ancient wallpaper covered one wall.

Bernard walked over to the wallpaper. Part of it appeared to just be hanging loose. Bernard took hold and pulled it back just enough to reveal an old movie poster. It was faded but readable. 'Cecil B DeMille proudly presents: The King of Kings.'

"Sweet Jesus in Jerusalem," Paige breathed. "You are amazing, you knew."

Janee stood in wonder. She was looking at a century and a half-old movie poster. How had it survived? Why was this building still standing when so much around it was blown up?

She came to understand it was the Lord's protection. This was her proof and she must now take action.

"That does it!" she exclaimed. "Bernard, you and Seth get to work right away. Secure the deed for this property. Procure an architect to transform this building into a viable working studio. Hire as many workers needed to proceed with construction. And try and find an old DVD copy of 'King of Kings.' It was filmed in 1925."

"Paige, complete our film crew for the Iraq shoot and obtain someone to make the travel arrangements."

"I'm on it," Paige acknowledged, and was gone.

Janee stood for a moment looking at the poster. "Thank you, Lord," she whispered, and in her mind she could see Jesus smile.

CHAPTER 34

FILM CREW

Seth greeted Janee at the entrance of the old DeMille Studio. "Hi Mom. Work is going quickly. You will be astounded. Come." Seth walked her inside. Janee was surprised to see the interior was stripped and cleared.

"A crew came in and knocked down all the small shop partitions, then hauled off the scraps. We did save some of the reusable lumber and stacked it out back. Do you want to –."

"That's OK, son. I'm meeting Paige here. She is bringing the film crew for the Iraq shoot. I want to look them over."

Seth grew serious. "Do you want me in Iraq with you?"

"Oh, my precious boy." Janee hugged him. "I need you here to help Bernard get this studio in workable condition. But you can visit to see how we are doing."

Seth grinned. He was pleased with that.

"We're here," Paige announced, as she entered through the main door followed by three men and one woman.

"Welcome," Janee greeted them. "So this is our film crew?"

"Yes." Paige gestured towards the group. "Let me introduce them one at a time and tell you a little about their backgrounds."

Janee nodded.

"This is our director, Brandon. He is a Tribulation Saint. Worked on small projects at Paramount before the Rapture. Continued working until they booted him out for not taking Christo's mark."

"This the one you said had some experience?" Janee asked.

"Yes. He was doing odd jobs here in Culver City."

"But not directing a film project, Brandon?" Janee dug deeper.

Brandon held steady eye contact with Janee. He was not strong of build, but neither was he weak. His skin was dark tan with a leathery appearance. His hair was long with slight sun bleach. He was dressed in jeans and a short-sleeved shirt. Janee took note of his hiking boots, marking Brandon with a rugged look.

"No, ma'am. Not much filming going on. I'm grateful for a chance to do what I love," he replied, his voice low and husky.

"Next is our camera man, Trayco," Paige went on. "I found him on the Internet and he is from Florida. His father is from Puerto Rico and his mother is Cuban. His father does camera work for a local newscast in South Florida. Trayco learned from him."

"Are you as good?" Janee asked.

"Does a donkey have a tail?" Trayco smirked.

"He does and he also has a loud, annoying bray," Janee countered. She was riled. "This project must be first-class and that means professional, A-one results. If you don't give that to me, I will hire a local over there and leave your butt in Iraq!"

"You can't do that!" Trayco sputtered.

"Yes, I can and I will. This assignment is ordered by King Jesus, and I am given absolute and complete control. Now, can you do this job, young Millennial? I mean, a job where you reach inside to accomplish something better than you have ever done in all of your short life? Are you able?"

"Yes!" Trayco yelled back.

Janee scowled. She went over and placed her hand on Brandon's shoulder.

"Trayco, this is our director and he called me ma'am. I don't know what manners your mamma failed to teach you, but until you have gone through what this man has, I better hear 'ma'am' tacked onto every time you address me. And that goes for my co-producer, Paige, as well. Now, look at Brandon!"

Trayco reluctantly shifted his defiant glare to fix his eyes on Brandon.

"This is your director. You respect him and do what he tells you. Direct means just that. I don't want to hear any more of your irritating braying. Do we have an understanding? Because if not, you can leave right now. Am I clear?"

Trayco dropped his eyes and shuffled his feet as though contemplating what to do.

Janee waited.

"Sure," he mumbled.

"Sure what?" Janee snapped.

"Yes, ma'am."

"Good! Then we will get along just fine. I take it this young lady will do sound?" Janee turned to a Hispanic Millennial.

"Si, Senora," the woman was eager to answer. "I am Alicia."

"Welcome to our team."

"Alicia is from California. She did sound for a music group, 'Vida Latina,' until they disbanded," Paige explained.

"Excellent." Janee was pleased.

"Nolan will do our grip work." Paige said, to introduce the last man and offered nothing more. Janee looked at her.

"What are his qualifications?"

Paige gave a little laugh. "Well, I guess a strong back and willing heart. He is from South Carolina."

"What did you do there, Nolan?" He seemed an odd choice to Janee.

"Worked a chicken farm, ma'am, an' I have no problem calling you thet. No problem at all!" Nolan was nervous.

"So, I see," Janee murmured. She studied this chicken farmer. He was tall and lanky, fair of skin and displayed a disarming ways and warm smile. His clothes were too big around his waist and the pants were definitely high-water. Janee noted his shoes were scuffed and worn.

"You have a foreman over you?" Janee queried.

"Yes'm."

"Did he fire you?"

"Was a she. No ma'am, I just quit and came to California."

Janee indicated to Paige they needed to talk apart from the crew.

"Where did you find this guy?" Janee whispered.

"He showed up one day and offered to help clear out boards and sheet rock. He just wanted to work and he worked hard. I figured he could lift and carry our equipment."

"You are fine with all of them?" Janee questioned.

"Completely," Paige responded.

"Then I am, too. Anything else before we wrap this up?"

"Yes, I procured a driver. He is an Iraq Tribulation Saint. An older guy named Ali. He will meet us at the Bagdad Transporter Station."

"Perfect! All right team, you are in. Paige will brief you on details. Brandon, make sure you, Trayco and Alicia have all the equipment you need and it must be sturdy, and the best. All of you shop for complete new outfits to go the distance in Iraq. And I mean complete. Check weather conditions and temperatures. Alicia, you help Nolan get outfitted.

"This is it. In two weeks we meet at Burbank Transporter Station #5 to start our journey."

CHAPTER 35

A CHANGE

"A few more kilometers and we will see it!" Ali was excited. The solar van bumped along sending up dense dust clouds behind it. At times the old vehicle bounced over hard dirt-bumps and rocks in the weather-warn, rutted road.

Brandon had been thoughtful and quiet for some time. As they were jostled about, he suddenly seemed to come alive. He leaned forward to speak to the Iraqi driver.

"Ali," Brandon shouted above the noise. "You say you have been here before?"

"Oh, yes, sir. When I was young man, I sometimes drove Western tourists here. They paid good money. I did a very good job."

"Why did you stop?" Alicia asked.

"Business fell away when Americans left. After that, ISIS took over to the north. After they were driven out, well, you know. Poof! Many people disappeared. Then Iraq got itself blown up during the Arab wars. When Christos took control, his thugs executed many, my mama and papa . . . many, many."

"Oh Ali, we are so sorry." Alicia touched his shoulder.

"But everything is better now. Much better." The Iraqi brightened. "I take you today."

Brandon wiped dirt and sweat from his face with a damp rag before handing it on to Nolan. He hesitated in thought before leaning up again near the driver.

"When you took tourists here, did you explain this place we are going? Were you their tour guide or just a driver?"

"Oh yes, Mr. Brandon. I best tour guide driver. I tell them details. I studied very hard for months one winter season. I knew all about it."

Janee sensed Brandon had some idea in mind. "OK, Brandon, where are you going with this? I see your brain gearing up."

Brandon laughed, sat back in his seat and turned to Janee. He nodded his head in agreement and explained.

"For well over a month now, we have been capturing visuals of the Iraqi devastation; showing the rubble from destroyed buildings of several cities. We even shot three smaller towns recently and then one tiny village near Najaf where the scant populace of Tribulation Saints and Millennials live in hovels."

"The place we were just at?" Trayco asked. "That was pathetic."

"Our reason for doing this," Janee affirmed. "King Jesus wants this country rebuilt and their problems corrected. Go on, Brandon."

"This is different; a historical site. Is it not important to restore? It's a piece of Iraq's past. We have monuments and structures stateside to aid Millennials coming along understand who they are and where they came from. Shouldn't Iraqis have that same chance? I know we hadn't planned to shoot this, and depending on what it looks like, but I'm wondering if we ought to rethink it."

"How will we put it together, Brandon? Do you have a plan?" Paige asked.

"I'm thinking that so far, with all our shoots, we have taken turns with narrating both on camera and off, doing voice-overs. If Ali is as good as I think he is, we can roll camera going in and while he takes us on his guided tour."

"I do it! I do it!" Ali yelled, swerving to miss a rock.

"It's different, but I'll use hand-held with the smaller camera. Easy." Trayco sat up.

"I can mic-up Ali with a wireless and carry the lighter recorder," Alicia answered from her front passenger seat.

"Or, I'll lug the big recorder around, if you want," Nolan offered.

Brandon waited for a decision. "What do you think?"

"Let's do it!" Janee and Paige agreed together.

137

CHAPTER 36

UKHAIDIR PALACE

"There it is!" Ali yelled as he pointed. "Ukhaidir Palace." The team was awestruck, and struggled to express their response. Atop small hill, before their eyes, from the barren and desolate desert floor, rose a massive stone fortress.

"Stop," Brandon commanded. "Trayco, fire-up your camera. Alicia, wire Ali. Let's film him driving us in. He can narrate the background."

"Filming is old school, Director. This is the digital age," Trayco mumbled as he dug into his equipment.

"Don't you think he knows that?" Alicia chided, as she bolted out the door to get to the rear of the van. Nolan followed.

"Whatever this is," Paige said, staring at the distant structure, "it's imposing. Shall we check it out?"

"Yes," Janee answered and smiled. "Let's do the tour. Be daring."

It took better than an hour to get ready. Trayco set the camera, then checked sun angles and lighting. "If we follow the road, we won't have the crisp visual we'd get if we work our way over there, Brandon." Trayco pointed.

"Desert too rough there; blow out tires," Ali objected.

"OK, road it is. In your opening shots, Trayco, keep the focus on Ali; then when I touch your arm, pan slowly across the desert to end on the palace. I want the scene to impact viewers as much as it has us. Listen up, Ali, I want you to preface the show by explaining that we are doing a historical documentary on this site. Then give some background on the Palace," Brandon directed.

When they were ready, Brandon gave the word for Ali to drive, followed by camera and sound checks.

"All right, Ali, when I do the countdown and say 'Action,' start talking. Tell us what we are looking at," Brandon gave final instructions. "Nolan, do the slate. Title it Palace."

"Roger. Palace. Take One." Nolan snapped the slate.

"Camera?"

"Rolling," Trayco answered.

"Sound?"

"Hot," Alicia responded.

"Four, three, two, one, action."

Ali coughed. "We are seeing Abassid Palace at Ukider –." He stopped.

"Cut!" Brandon called.

"I'm nervous too much, Boss."

"OK, calm yourself, Ali. You are our tour guide. We are just this team on your tour. Give us our money's worth. Now, remember, the camera starts on you. I want you to preface this project. What are we seeing and what is the significance of this place? "

"To let everyone in world see this beautiful historic palace, and that it is in need of repair."

"And Millennials need too see and know what this is, why it is here and what it means historically," Brandon added.

"Got it."

"Are you ready?"

"I am your tour guide."

"Perfect. Camera and sound still good?"

"Right on," Trayco was intently focused on camera screen.

"Still hot," Alicia came back.

"Palace. Take two." Nolan snapped the slate again.

"Four three, two, one, Action."

"Today we are in the vast desert of Karbala." Suddenly Ali became relaxed. He seemed to slip into a different mindset. Perhaps he is becoming the individual he had longed to be for many years. He merged into that character in which he felt most comfortable. In fact, he loved it. The team immediately sensed the transformation they were witnessing firsthand. Brandon turned to Janee and winked.

"We are in the 60th year of the Millennium. Not very far from its start with many, many years more to go. And yet," Ali glanced into the camera, "numberless generations of Millennials are coming forth. They are born, grow up, get married, have babies, and those babies grow and the cycle keeps going round and round to finally repopulate the whole earth. These Millennials are smart, and catch on quick. But when it comes to the past, where they came from; what took place long before their cries were heard; all history. They have no clue. A fact? None of them, anywhere, know about this place we are about to see.

"The Millennium, Christ's perfect world as it is in many places, has lush green gardens, beautiful plants and trees, clean rivers. We saw places like that in Iraq, especially around Bagdad. But Jesus didn't promise everything would instantly be that perfect. He said there is much work to do, and as it has been told, we can learn from the past; so we will learn very much today.

"Yes, parts of the world changed when Christ returned. Green replaced brown in many areas. Plants that were dead sprang up alive again. But look out my side window. Here we view only dry, rocky desert, spiny shrubs tough enough to survive harsh conditions. This scene has not changed in 1,300 years. It looked the same then when this structure was built as it does today."

Brandon touched Trayco's arm and he slowly panned the camera onto the Palace.

"Rising out of this desert, I give you Iraq's Ukhaidir Palace." Ali paused, then continued. "The palace was built around 778 A.D. by a prince to live out his retirement years. It stands 70 feet high; I learned the measurements in feet for Westerners." Ali grinned into the camera. "It is more than 550 feet wide. It was built with stone and plaster. The huge walls rise like a cliff out of the desert plain. After the Prince passed on, the Palace became a Khan. This Khan was situated along a caravan route called the Silk Road. That route stretched from Turkey, Iraq and Syria, then all the way to China. This Palace served as a hostel for the caravans and other merchants to rest after long desert travel. The mystery and enchantment of spending the night made Ukhaidir a hub for conversation, and the exchanging of goods.

"Looking directly ahead," Ali pointed, "in the center of this gigantic wall is the main entrance to the Ukhaidir Palace. Compared to the greatness of the fortress, the entrance certainly appears very, very tiny. But, not to fear, as we approach, you will see that this opening is quite ample to accommodate our van.

"I am told that in years past this entrance had a heavy, solid wooden gate. This gate was open during the day with armed guards posted constantly watching. It was locked at night or at other times if there was news of bandits in the area. This gate had a small door through which people could come and go when the gate was locked.

"Now we are driving through the entrance into this very large open courtyard."

"Cut," Brandon called. "Everyone out, we will resume the tour on foot. Take a few minutes to reorganize. The temp shows 99 so drink water and keep some with you. Nolan, when we begin, slate this, 'Palace inside, take one'; and I want to view what we have thus far, Trayco."

Gazing at their surroundings, the team was in awe. They were standing in the middle of a football field-sized open courtyard. The four walls surrounding them were all faced with numerous brick pillars topped by arches. There were only two entrances into this vast courtyard: the one they had just driven through and one directly ahead of them.

"Yi, there is no way out of this courtyard without a tall ladder. These walls are so high," Alicia commented.

The second opening at the far end of the courtyard led into a second story, and beyond that was a third level.

"Would you look at that." Nolan whistled.

Janee scanned the tops of the building and walls. The stones making up the entire palace were of a substance similar to sandstone. Countless, they were brick-sized and were laid as modern bricks would appear. Janee took note that the upper bricks were weathered and crumbling. Some places had caved in, contrasted by other areas that appeared brand-new.

"Are we ready, team?" Brandon called.

"Good to go," everyone responded.

Brandon did camera and sound checks, Nolan the slate.

"Four, three, two, one, Action," Brandon gave command, nodding to Ali.

Ali stepped in front of the camera and began speaking.

"Picture this in your mind. Centuries ago, in the afternoon as it is right now, caravans from the East begin to arrive. Through the open gate they come, tired, thirsty and looking for a safe place to rest. Horses, heavy-laden camels and donkeys lumber in behind their masters. Many walking travelers also make their way inside with the caravans. Goods and merchandise are unloaded and stacked in heaps along the walls. Preparations are made for the night's stay.

"Now, take notice of this low circular wall of stones we are walking towards. That is a well, and from it water was drawn to satisfy the thirst of travelers and their animals."

Trayco tried to get a camera shot down into the well, but it was too deep to view the bottom. Ali picked up a stone and threw it in. A moment of silence, followed by a thud.

"Dry well today," Ali commented. "Take note as you view up above us, how the desert winds have worn away the stones and they are crumbling in many places. But might we suspect the deterioration should be worse after 1,300 years?

"Please observe the tall walls that line this courtyard. The pillars built into these walls and the arches above them are called vaults and arches. This design is Persian, but the fortress as a whole is neither Greek nor Persian, but Arab in its style. You can readily see this style in the four rounded corner towers. Yes, Arab.

"Now, this entrance takes you inside the Palace. Remember, this was used as a hostel, so many pleasant accommodations were afforded guests. There were legions of chambers; every room vaulted and majestic. Banquet rooms served delicacies of the richest foods, luxurious baths were an accommodation to wash off desert dust and take away aches and pains of tired bodies. It was safe and comfortable. After a relaxing bath and a fulfilling meal, visiting took place. This was most popular. There were cultural exchanges, trade deals, religious discussions; so many differences and backgrounds, which led to many late-night conversations.

"Now, I, Ali, your tour guide will take you inside this long-ago hostel."

'Ali is promoting a future business for himself. What an opportunist,' Janee thought with a smile to herself. Paige poked her. She noticed, too.

"As we go inside, it is important to stay very close to me for it is most dangerous. The second-story floor is weakened in places, and I do not wish any to break through. Follow me."

Two hours or more were spent exploring. It didn't take much imagination to visualize the grandeur and beauty this Palace once held. They saw large rooms where evidence of antique artwork graced portions of some walls. They walked through a maze of rooms, long corridors, up and down stairs, along dark hallways once filled with noisy guests. They discovered evidence of more wells, and even underground caves. True to his word, Ali led the group around collapsing roofs. The team had fun doing the shoot. Brandon even playfully included some of the team members in a few select scenes.

Tired but pleased, they emerged back outside into the courtyard. "It's a wrap," said a grinning Brandon.

"Amen," Janee confirmed.

CHAPTER 37

CAMPFIRE

As the team made their way towards the van, Janee spoke to Brandon.

"Looks like you got some good shots there," Janee commented.

"Incredible video, Janee. It was relaxed. We had fun and everything fell into line. This will make a fantastic show."

"I think," Janee went on, "we should add a short promo at the end to ask for help to restore this site and make it into a plush resort for all to visit, especially the Millennials. There will be multitudes coming along and they will want to travel."

"Absolutely," Brandon agreed. "Ok team, let's pack up. We are only about twenty miles from Karbala. We can shut down there."

"Oh, no. Please do not leave this place yet. Not now," Ali pleaded.

Everyone was puzzled.

"Why, Ali, aren't we finished here?" Brandon questioned.

"No, the best part is yet to come. We must stay until after dark for the true feeling of this place. No camera, just us under the stars, as it was for travelers many centuries ago. Come, we gather dried twigs from desert bushes. We make good campfire. I am prepared with cooking pot. I make all of you an Iraqi dinner over the fire. You will be so blessed to enjoy it. I will cook for you and you will be happy. What's to lose? After we eat and visit, still time to drive to Karbala. OK? Yes? You will see the true wonder of the Palace."

Everyone looked at Janee. For a few moments she studied all of their faces. She knew the team was hot and tired and ready to find rooms that supplied a cool shower and soft bed. Should she prolong this project a few more hours to gaze into a starry night they had already seen for a lifetime? Janee looked at Paige; she simply shrugged her shoulders.

"I'm game," Nolan spoke up. "There's something kinda special 'bout sitting around a campfire under the stars. I sorely miss it."

Everyone laughed, and started packing equipment into the van. Ali was befuddled.

"Well, don't just stand there, Ali." Brandon tried to be serious; then he chuckled. "Point us to this desert wood and you dig out your cooking pot; this Iraqi supper had better be great."

The team went outside the Palace walls into the desert to bring in anything that would burn. Then they gathered stones fallen from walls to make a fire ring. Ali prepared his meal and placed his pot over the fire as soon as the flames were hot enough.

The sun was dipping below the western horizon when Ali called them to eat. The team brought folding chairs out of the van, and everyone took a seat around the campfire. Ali served up his specialty dish along with Iraqi bread.

The film team ate their fill. They just shook their heads in wonder at Ali's amazing dinner. They ate up every smidgen of the meal, leaving no bread. Even Janee and Paige, who didn't need to eat, were impressed.

After supper, the film crew sat in quiet for some time. They grew misty-eyed in thought, as they watched the dancing flames of the campfire. The moment took on the eerie feel of sitting in a large war-like castle. Did they picture this very same courtyard projected back hundreds of years ago? It suddenly flickered to life in their minds like an Arabian movie of old; perhaps, numerous fires like this one giving light and warmth; herdsmen in charge of caring for the animals and guarding their master's merchandise huddled around the flames. Calm and peace setting over the courtyard while laughter, music, sometimes coarse talk of men could be heard from within the Palace.

"Merciful Father in Heaven," Alicia cried out. The rest of the team followed her upward gaze. They gasped!

The stars were ablaze, numbering in the millions. Janee had never seen a night sky like this. Ali need not speak. They all understood: the mystery, the magic, the wonder of this place settled over them, sinking deep into their very souls to be remembered forever.

"Thank you, Ali, for this," Paige said with deep emotion. The rest voiced their agreement. Ali gave a satisfied smile.

The evening conversation moved between somber and light-hearted. Brandon poised a question after watching Ali.

"Ali," he began. "We are both Tribulation Saints. That means we both came to Christ during that horrific time we thought would never end. I found the Lord through an underground movement of Non Coms. What's your story, Ali? I'm curious to know."

Ali poked more sticks in the fire, but did not answer. Janee spied a trickle of tears on his face glimmer in the firelight. Presently he sat up and began to speak.

"Before the Rapture, an American tourist gave me a CD. After everyone vanished, that was all I had. No Bible; no one ever told me about Jesus Christ. I knew nothing but that I must seek Him. But how to find Him, if He can be found? I had never played the CD before, but then I am driven. I listened to just one song. Over and over I played this song. I memorized it in my head. It became my Bible, never to leave me as long as I should live."

"What was the song?" Nolan asked.

"I sing it for you," Ali spoke low. He looked up, then began a lovely, almost haunting melody. He sang in his native Iraqi tongue, but the team understood because there is no confusion of language in the Millennium.

"Jesus, what a friend for sinners," Ali began, his voice quivering. "Jesus lover of my soul. Friends may fail me, foes assail me; He my Savior makes me whole.

"Jesus, what a strength in weakness. Let me hide myself in Him. Tempted, tried and sometimes failing, He my strength my victory wins.

"Jesus, what a help in sorrow. While the billows o'er me roll, even when my heart is breaking, He, my comfort, helps my soul.

"Jesus, I do now receive Him, more than all in Him I find. He hath granted me forgiveness, I am His and He is mine."

The whole team was in tears.

"That was my Bible and how I came to find my Lord," Ali spoke softly, not his usual loud, brash self. "Strange, I could never sing the final part until I believed on Jesus. I sing it with great joy for you now!

"Hallelujah, what a Savior. Hallelujah, what a friend. Saving, helping, keeping loving, He is with me to the end."

Trayco buried his face in his hands. "I believe, I believe! I want Jesus right now. I believe, Lord Jesus, forgive me," he sobbed.

Alicia put her arm around Trayco to console him. "He is forgiving you, my friend; He is forgiving you and coming to you. He loves you."

Trayco broke down and wept away pent-up battles of anger and pride. Suddenly he stopped, looked up, and began laughing.

"Jesus is here! He is here!" he shouted. "He just came over me in a flood. A flood! In this bone-dry desert, a flood. Oh, glory! I, too, am His."

Nolan began his Southern whoop. Ali gave a loud, warbling yell, while the guardian angels, wings unfurled, sang praises to the King. Alicia jumped up and danced ecstatically around the campfire. Brandon pulled the young millennial to his feet and they rejoiced together, marching about in triumph, singing victory songs. The team fell in line behind them. Had that old Palace ever housed such a sight?

CHAPTER 38

BRANDON'S PROJECT

The excitement of Trayco's conversion finally mellowed out due to sheer exhaustion; still, no one wanted to let the evening go.

It was Paige who made the suggestion, "Should we pack it in and head for Karbala?"

"I suppose." Brandon threw in the last of the firewood. "But before we go, I have something to discuss with all of you. I haven't run this by Janee or Paige, it's just a suggestion."

"Tell us," Janee encouraged.

"I'm thinking about our schedule tomorrow. We have no more shoots to do. I know we are all tired, well, not Janee or Paige, but we are, and ready to go home."

"Yaaah," the team agreed.

"I've been doing some research on my own. North of here on our way to Baghdad, is the ruins of a city named Anbar. It wouldn't be too far off the route into Baghdad and the Transporter Station."

"What is Anbar's significance?" Janee questioned.

"It is located a short distance from the City of Fallujah, near a canal that connects the Tigris River to the Euphrates River where Anbar is located. Anbar became a refuge for the Arab, Christian and Jewish colonies of the region. It carried the reputation as a hiding place for people of faith. It is even older than Baghdad, founded in 350 A.D. The City had a strong Catholic presence there dating back to 480-something A.D. It was the hub of a Chaldean Church for sometime."

"Is there anything remaining now?" Paige asked.

"Entirely deserted. Only mounds of ruins in great number."

"Why do you want to go there, Brandon? It's obvious you wish to do that or we wouldn't be having this conversation," Janee pursued.

"As I said, the town had a history as a place of refuge—a hiding place."

"So?" Janee asked.

"Mounds, yes, but during the Tribulation, believing Non Coms dug in and excavated a small underground city. They grew in numbers until Combats discovered their secret entrance. They were massacred—even the children. They thought they were safe."

"Is it now?" Alicia was unsure.

Janee's mind instantly went to the USO Tour in Viet Nam she had participated in. She remembered reservations part of the group had about going to Khe Sanh for one last concert instead of flying home on the Freedom Bird. She barely heard Brandon's remark. 'Sure it's safe. This is the Millennium!' Janee's mind was conjuring up dark images of the ferocious attack that erupted while the USO group was on the base. Janee shook her head. Her thoughts seemed hell-bent on reviewing the brutal rape scene. 'No! There is no place for those images here. Why are those hideous thoughts still with me? Why, dear Lord, can I even remember such evil? Oh wretched soul I am, even as a Resurrected Saint, to once again wrestle such memories.' She was unsettled.

"Janee?" Paige touched her.

Janee looked at their faces in the firelight, awaiting her approval.

"What's the purpose?" Janee shook her head. "What would we shoot?"

"A lot of Non Coms died there. I thought it could be a tribute to them, and a message to millennials of the price those Tribulation Saints paid. It is our chance to give respect."

"What do all of you feel about this?" Janee inquired.

"Today's shoot was out of our way and turned out better than fantastic," Trayco commented. "I'm a game boy."

"What's an extra day in a thousand years?" Nolan shrugged.

"I like adventures," Alicia piped up.

"I know the way," Ali grinned. "Your Tour Guide gets an extra day to drive."

"Your call, Janee," Page said.

"Just a minute." Janee walked away from the campfire into the shadows of the courtyard. She raised her hands toward Jerusalem and her King.

"Lord, this project was decreed and established by You. You have guided every step of the way, and You blessed our work today. Please tell me what to do about going to Anbar?"

Jesus' answer was immediate, but His response seemed unusual to her.

"Go, my child. Record what you see. Give honor to those who laid down their lives there. And trust your Guardian Angels to keep you safe."

Janee returned to join her team and stood by the fire.

"King Jesus gives His go-ahead to your project, Brandon. Let's do it!"

CHAPTER 39

ANBAR

The team sat in the van staring at the vast mounds of dirt, some covered by growth of stunted desert bushes, while others were bare. Wisps of dust flew up in places blown by a hot Iraqi wind.

Ali dropped his head onto the steering wheel. "Oye—Oye," he sighed a groan. "How can we find a secret entrance in all this?"

"Working on it," Brandon replied, feverishly pulling up data on his tablet.

"You say this city was founded in 350 A.D.?" Janee mused. "Such a vast amount of time. Talk about ancient history! What was America in 350 A.D.? Like, it didn't even exist."

The others laughed.

"Do you think we could find someone in Fallujah who might help us locate this tunnel opening? That city isn't very far away," Paige offered.

"I have a satellite image of this whole area. I've made it larger and am moving it slowly—back and forth. I don't see anything."

"Wait. What is that?" Trayco pointed.

"Where?"

"There. That spot."

"That's just a spec. It might even be something on my screen." Brandon rubbed his tablet's screen. The spot was still there. "I'll zoom in closer."

"Now the image is too grainy," Trayco complained. "It isn't clear. I can't be sure."

The whole team studied the image. They shook their heads.

151

"Whatever that is, we can tell it's small. A scrub? Trash thrown out or blown there?" Janee wondered. Miglia moved up close behind her. Janee caught sight of her angel out of the corner of her eye.

"Miglia, do you see this?"

"Yes."

"Do you now what it is?"

"A 4 x 8 thick sheet of plywood."

"Dang." Nolan laughed. "You spotted a piece of plywood from way up, Trayco."

"Let's keep looking," Brandon mumbled.

"The plywood is what you seek," Miglia continued.

"What? That makes no sense, Miglia. How can a weathered sheet of plywood possibly have anything to do with this project?" Janee questioned.

"It covers the tunnel you seek."

Everyone threw up their hands.

"Heavens, why didn't he just say so?" Alicia wondered aloud.

"Because I didn't ask," Janee muttered.

"Look, Ali. See on the tablet? We are here in this lower corner. I'll pull this image back, OK? There we are and over here is the plywood. It says we are twenty minutes away. Can you get us there?" Brandon asked.

"I will make it in fifteen!" Ali laughed as the van took off.

True to his word, Ali had the crew to the tunnel location in fifteen minutes. Everyone leaped out of the van as Brandon shouted instructions, "Everyone grab a booster light; Trayco, the small camera; Alicia, minimal sound equipment. Nolan, bring two of our floodlights with one of our smaller screens. Hustle, let's set up."

Ali already had the plywood thrown aside. "Hey, Brandon, boss. There are stairs here going down. It's very dark; very, very dark."

"First shot here at the tunnel opening. I will narrate," Brandon directed. "Set camera and sound. Nolan, our slate will be 'Anbar, tunnel entrance, take one.'"

In a few minutes they were positioned to begin. Brandon took his place at the large mound open-hole entrance. After camera and sound checks, Nolan did a slate and Brandon called for action. He held a mic up to speak.

"We are standing in what was once a bustling city. Its name is Anbar, located in the Country of Iraq. This city was founded in 350 A.D. and it sits along the east bank of the Euphrates River. It was once a capital until Baghdad was founded in 762 A.D. After that, Anbar began to fade until 1074. Today, this site is a short distance from Fallujah.

"So what is the significance of Anbar? What interest would a multitude of dirt mounds hold for Millennials? Let's search deeper; but first, some history.

"Anbar was Arabic, of course, but unlike most of the other Iraqi cities, this one became a refuge for not only Arab runaways, but Christian and Jewish people as well. In fact, there was a strong Catholic presence here boasting a long line of fourteen Bishops. During those years, a large Assyrian community developed, claiming Jesus Christ as their Lord and Savior.

"But Anbar went into decline, until finally it became quiet and still. The city deteriorated into piles of rubble covered by desert sand. Its only cry for worth and fame pointed back to its past glory. These mounds represent homes once filled with people: men, women, children who were laughing, loving, crying and living life. Other mounds were thriving businesses and vibrant churches. A refuge.

"But all died. So was it over? Just some historical site holding no interest, not worthy to even visit? It would appear so, until a strange occurrence happened a few years ago.

"During the vicious Tribulation-Arab wars, a launched rocket veered off-course and exploded here. Amazingly, it revealed an underground tunnel. Later in those Tribulation years, believers in the real Christ known as Non-Coms, discovered that the tunnel led into an underground city. They disguised the entrance and hid here. Again, Anbar became a City of Refuge, as multitudes made their way to this secret location. Let's go now and see where they lived, and sadly gave their lives, when Combats stormed in and massacred them all: men, women and children. Come. Follow me."

Brandon led the crew down a flight of stairs. Their lights reflected a hollow walkway ahead. He stopped to let Trayco reset his camera to the boost lights; then went on.

"We very possibly could be the first visitors here since the Tribulation." He turned to face the camera before continuing. "They discovered numerous side rooms like these, probably used by families for their living quarters." Brandon kept talking as they moved deeper into the underground refuge.

One room totally surprised and excited the entire team. It was rather large with a beautiful pool in the center, no doubt fed by the river. The water was cool and looked clean. A place to sit was built all around the pool.

"We are blown away and completely captivated," Brandon shared, speaking of their incredible find. "Absolutely beautiful! This no doubt was their water supply and perhaps a place to bathe. We are amazed it still exists, untouched."

Moving farther still into various caverns, they discovered one area large enough to hold many people at once.

"This, no doubt, was a room to hold group meetings or church," Brandon commented.

Then the film crew happened on a completely out-of-place room. It was not a small sleeping room, and not big enough for group meetings. This room resembled a place that functioned as a hideout. Not the usual dirt floors, square tiles gave the room color. Adding to the intrigue was furniture: tables, chairs, benches, and along one wall, a larger piece filled with drawers. Brandon walked over and pulled out a drawer. It still contained a few items. "Wow!" he exclaimed. "Nolan, this is unbelievable! We must set up floodlights and shoot this room. Alicia, set your equipment over there. Trayco, can we get enough light in here?"

"I think so, with the screen. We will see," he replied, not looking up.

"Hey Boss, what about that little chest against the wall?" Ali pointed. "Two drawers."

"Like a nightstand?" Janee commented. "Pre-Tribulation era, for sure."

"Just leave it," Brandon glanced up. "Let's get this going."

In ten minutes the crew was ready to resume shooting.

"Camera looks good," Trayco called out.

"Sound hot," Alicia added.

"Anbar—underground room, take one." Nolan slated.

Brandon had Trayco pan slowly around the room ending back on him. He described what the viewers were seeing. Next, he called Trayco in closer as he began opening drawers. There were Bibles and books of Arabic, along with crosses and symbols Brandon didn't recognize. "Secret Tribulation jewelry to identify believers," Ali explained.

Other drawers had old clothes, and the rest contained lots of plates, cups and some utensils.

"Perhaps they prepared meals in this room," Brandon said, "hence the tile floor. Now let's check out this little odd chest of drawers." Brandon approached the nightstand from one side to keep the small furniture piece in camera. He opened the top drawer. Nothing. He slid the bottom drawer open.

"Oh, no!" he screamed. "It's a mine! A Tribulation mine! It has Christo's mark on it."

Completely caught off-guard, Brandon stepped straight back from the drawer. A loud click was heard.

"Don't move," Brandon's guardian angel yelled. "Be still. You have activated a mine under the tile of your left foot. Any change of your weight could set it off."

"But,—but,—there is no death in the Millennium," Brandon countered.

"True, but the enemy left ways to change that. You are flesh and blood with a heart. You could die," his angel answered.

Trayco, who was close to Brandon, still had the camera rolling. He took a step back to get out of the way, another, CLICK! He froze.

"Stop," Miglia ordered. "The young Millennial has tripped a mine under his right foot."

"Miglia, are any more mines still here?" Janee's voice was high-pitched and she felt a rush of fear for her team.

155

"I cannot see under the tiles. If I were in here alone, I would look."

"Oh, dear Jesus, dear Jesus," Janee cried out.

Instantly, she heard her Master's voice in her mind. 'Send your team out. Quickly! Then you and Paige rescue Brandon and Trayco.'

"But . . . but," Janee objected.

'Janee, be of strong courage, not afraid! You are a Resurrected Saint. You are their leader and they depend on you. Now lead and rescue,' the Lord was firm in His command.

Janee snapped out of it and looked into the faces of her crew. She saw overwhelming fear and confusion.

"Brandon, you and Trayco do not move," Janee ordered.

"Don't twitch; don't blink."

"Ma'am, sweat's running down my face and is about to drip," Trayco stammered.

"Let it drip and pray it falls on a different tile. Now we have to keep our heads. Think! Be calm and deliberate. We have all walked around most of the room and found no mines. I believe the nightstand was intended to be a booby trap and whoever did this set those mines for whoever looked inside.

"Ali, make your way out into the walkway. Alicia, take your sound equipment and follow. Go slow and listen carefully. Nolan, leave the lights and you go."

The three waited outside the door.

"You have your lights. Now run! Run as fast as you can outside. Do not stop. Nolan, you carry Alicia's stuff—and her, if necessary. Go!"

Paige looked to Janee. They drew close together. Janee took her hand. "Do you remember when we were young and saved those two boys from drowning?" she spoke low. Paige nodded.

"Well, we are going to do that again, girl. These guys are much bigger, but we are Resurrection Saints. Are you ready?"

"We can do it!" Paige declared.

"What's the plan, Janee?" Brandon sounded weak.

"Here is the plan, guys. Paige, get their booster lights. Trayco, is the camera still rolling?"

"Am I a good camera man?"

"The best!"

"Brandon, I am coming up behind you, and Paige behind Trayco. Very carefully, slightly open your arms so we can get our arms around your chests and lock our fingers together. As we do that, we will give you your boost light. If you can turn them on, go ahead. In all of this, keep your weight on your mine foot. When ready, Paige and I will snatch you guys up and whisk you out."

"You gotta be kidding," Brandon snapped. "You are women and we are too heavy."

"No, we are Resurrection Saints, and you are about to get the ride of your lives. Count it down, Director. We go on action!"

"I hope this works," Trayco whimpered.

"No one dies here today," Janee countered. "Ready, Paige? Just like when we were young."

"Let's do it."

"Count, Brandon,"

"Four, three, two, one, Action!"

Janee and Paige in perfect sync slipped their arms around the men's chests and locked their fingers. In a flash, they took them out the door and flew down the tunnel. Deafening explosions erupted behind them. Smoke blew through the doorway followed by flame. Red-hot fire followed them at breakneck speed. Janee could feel the heat over her back. "Faster, Paige," Janee urged. "Faster!"

Shortly, they left the danger behind. She sensed their guardian angels were impeding the destruction racing behind them. Janee glanced behind her at Miglia. Her angel was magnificent with wings spread wide and gleaming sword in hand. She smiled. He nodded.

The two Resurrection Saints set the men down at the base of the stairs to let them walk out. The rest of the team cheered and clapped when Brandon and Trayco emerged from the tunnel.

Trayco's legs grew wobbly and he collapsed. Alicia ran to help him. She patted his face.

Janee and Paige walked out into the sunlight, looking and feeling triumphant.

Brandon gave Janee and Paige an enthusiastic hug.

"Thank you both for saving us; and yes, for giving us the ride of our lives!" Brandon's voice was husky.

He turned and walked over to Trayco, who was sitting up. He picked up the camera, looked at it, and shut it off. Janee watched him.

"Well, Mr. Director. You got us one heck of a show!" She smiled.

CHAPTER 40

PREPARATIONS

Janee was signing papers in her Hidden Light Studio office when Bernard suddenly appeared before her. Janee jumped.

"Bernard, you startled me!"

"Sorry. I didn't think I needed to go through your receptionist."

"You don't, Bernard."

"Just payback for all those times you called me or rang my doorbell in the middle of the night," he teased.

Janee smiled, remembering. "How are we doing on the Millennial Show?" she asked.

"As you know, the post-production on the Iraq specials took longer than we wanted. We just can't find enough Millennials with the skills to produce a quality piece of property."

"But aren't their skills improving?"

"Yes, the ones coming up are better but still slow. Anyway, we have used up Millennium 60 and are into 61, just finishing the Iraq series, plus the Palace and Anbar specials. Setbacks in the reconstruction of the DeMille Studio have us six months or more out before building a set there."

"Have we had new problems?" Janee inquired.

"No, it's just the size of the expansion. The old studio was 1920's vintage and too small for a major production today. We've had to move all four walls out and then go higher on the roof. Plumbing was difficult, and now we are contending with electrical and lighting. Of course, you know, we are solar on the roof."

"Yes," Janee acknowledged. "What do you propose?"

"I made the decision to clear the sound stage we've been using at Hidden Light and do the Millennial Discussion Show here."

"Ok. Let's proceed."

"Good, now on to present business. A young set designer will meet us at our sound stage in a few minutes. Let's head over there now." Bernard held out his hand.

The morning was stunning, the sun filling a clear blue sky. The air was crisp, as winter still lingered; however, the sun gave just a hint of warmth with spring was announcing its presence. The pair strolled down a street lined with trees, green grass and office buildings. There was no indication of destruction from the years of Tribulation left to taint their scene.

"I love this time of year," Janee murmured.

"Yes," Bernard replied. "In the 'before' life, Academy Awards would be coming soon."

"Ha! With all the stress and drama." Janee laughed.

"Do you miss those times?" Bernard asked.

"Sometimes," Janee confessed, "especially since I wasn't present to receive mine when I finally won."

Both were silent until they turned onto the street where the large stage buildings were located.

"Is Hidden Light Studio making plans to repair these damaged Sound Stages and make them operational again?" Bernard ventured.

"There are discussions going on."

Janee and Bernard walked up to one of the large buildings. It towered over them. High above, huge black letters faced a sign identifying, 'Stage Two.' Standing near a small entrance was a young millennial. He held an electronic tablet in his hand.

"Good morning, Parker," Bernard greeted.

"Perfect day, Mr. Swift." He shook Bernard's hand.

"Janee, meet Parker Martin. He is the set designer I told you about. Parker, Janee Stemper, our Executive Producer."

"Pleased, Ms. Stemper." Parker held out his hand. Janee shook it lightly.

"How old are you, Parker?" she asked.

"Twenty-seven," he answered brightly.

"Humm, you are second generation and your parents were young and were also quite young when they married?"

"Yes." Parker dropped his eyes.

"Not much experience all the way around," she quietly deduced. "Let's go inside and see what you have."

Bernard opened the small entrance door to let the three inside. It was pitch-dark until Bernard switched on the overhead lights. To the right was a wall lined with miles of heavy cable, much of it black and others in a variety of colors. Standing tall were myriads of lights, their bulbs of varying sizes. In a far corner stood four large camera units, dark and silent. Apart from scattered pieces of equipment and scraps of boards, the huge stage was empty and cold.

"The set will be built in this general location," Janee indicated, gesturing to the area where they were standing. She went on to describe what she had in mind for a set.

Parker listened and thought before responding.

"No offence, Ms. Stemper, you really do not know anything about set design, but I understand that. All you have ever done was acting, some directing and producing. Now let me show you concepts I have drawn up. I'm certain you will find one of them perfect for your show." Parker handed her his tablet. "Just watch, it will give an automatic presentation."

Janee carefully studied Parker's set designs before she commented. "Parker, how old do you think the Millennials are on this Discussion Show?"

"I don't know. Various ages?"

"There will be four Millennials on the program. They will be thirty to fifty years in age. What you are showing me looks like a children's set."

"That's what you have been doing, Ms. Stemper."

"Bernard, didn't you explain our project to young Parker here?" Janee was irritated.

"I did." Bernard shook his head in disbelief.

Janee picked up a piece of wood from the floor. "Don't know anything about set design," she mumbled. With her finger she quickly drew on the wood. Her finger glowed with heat until the wood smoked, as she burned the design into it. Parker was awestruck.

Janee handed the wood to Parker. As soon as it touched his hand, it developed from the black outline into a perfect photograph. Parker jumped.

"How?" he stammered.

"Because I lived life, died, and have been given a resurrection body that can do wondrous things. Now, can you give me—this?" Tapping the photo with her finger. "You can create your own design but do not waste my time with anything like what you just showed me."

Parker's face flushed. "Give me three days. I'll do you one better, Ms. Stemper," he called back as he ran out the door with Janee's piece of wood.

Before Janee and Bernard could further discuss Parker, Paige walked through the door. "Who was that?" she asked.

"Set designer," Bernard answered. "Did not go well."

"I gathered our old crew. Are you ready for them?"

"Yes, bring them in," Janee answered. She was anxious to see her friends again.

Paige ushered Brandon, Trayco, Alicia and Nolan into the Sound Stage. When they saw Janee they rushed to hug her. She was overjoyed to see her Iraqi crew.

After they visited a few minutes, Janee got down to business. "I haven't seen you in nearly a year. Have you all found work since our Iraqi trip?"

"Just some educational films," Brandon said.

"Shot some weddings, but no long gigs," Trayco added.

"Sadly, no good sound work, but steady." Alicia smiled.

"I'm cooking chicken." Nolan grinned. "Can't get the heck away from chickens."

Everyone laughed.

"Well, we have two projects coming up: one for a broadcast, the other a movie. We want to offer you jobs on both of these. The TV-style broadcast will take several months; the movie a few years. Of course, these will be more extensive than what we did in Iraq. Do you think you can handle them?" Janee asked.

Brandon glanced around the large stage. He was hesitant. "Not sure on the broadcast. Never directed one: three cameras, an ISO, calling shots fast? I wouldn't want to mess it up."

"What if you found a sharp AD to assist you and fill in the blanks," Bernard suggested.

"I think that would work for me. As for the movie project— let me at it!"

"I can handle anything you throw at me, Ma'am." Trayco seemed excited over the prospect.

"I will do it," Alicia said with confidence.

"Always got stuff to carry around and move, and I ain't gotten any weaker," Nolan was ready.

"Good, it's settled. You are hired and you start now." Janee was pleased to have their crew back. "Go with Paige and get to work on this first project.

The crew made an excited and noisy exit with Paige. Janee turned to Bernard. He flashed that old familiar smirk at her.

"What?" she questioned.

Bernard laughed and shook his head. "Just you. Some things never change."

"They certainly didn't, Bernard. So, do we have a moderator for the Discussion Show yet?"

"We do. Jason Finn."

"What? A Resurrection Saint? Do you think that is wise?"

"Actually, our Lord suggested it."

"He did? Well, Jason would be good, no doubt. Will his 'before' life wife be there?"

"Probably. Is that a problem for you, Janee?"

Janee had to look deep within. She knew she once adored Jason. Still did, in a different way. Lover? Husband? No. That dream never materialized in her former life. What was wished for then could never be realized in resurrection as she was today. He was a dear friend now, whom she loved and respected only in that way. Nothing more. Any hint or glimmer of anything else was put away in that instant. Besides, she stood facing her 'before'-life true love.

"Not at all, Bernard. Make sure she has an invite. What is Seth doing?"

"He has been aiding Paige and her staff to secure commitments for the Discussion guests."

"Do we have Adam?"

"Yes."

CHAPTER 41

MILLENNIAL DISCUSSIONS

Sound Stage Two was a buzz of activity at Hidden Lights Studio, getting ready for an evening live broadcast in Millennium Year 61. It occurred on a Monday in early May. The night sky was mostly cloudy and stars shown only occasionally through open patches. The night air was pleasant, a little cool, yet such to make people want to be out on the town. Weeks of preparation culminated tonight.

A sizable, boisterous crowd of Millennials was lined up outside the stage door. They all had been randomly picked to make up the show's live audience. Inside, three long rows of bleachers were situated to face the set: one directly in front, and the other two angled slightly on either side. Bernard estimated they could comfortably seat 325. However, they could possibly add 50 more, if everyone squeezed closely together, or stood.

In the sound booth, Brandon was positioned before a wall of monitors. He intently checked each view from four different cameras. Trayco stood by Camera A, which fed close-ups of the guests who would be speaking. Camera B covered the moderator, Jason Finn. Camera C could pan the set as well as capture audience reactions. Camera D was ISO, which rolled constantly on the entire set.

Brandon busied his staff of assistants hovering around him as he issued orders.

Alicia, also assisted by her own crew, set up sound. Mics were placed on guests and moderator. In addition, directors and camera people, plus any other behind-the-camera personnel, needed their own closed lines of communication.

Bernard was engaged up front with Parker Martin, to ensure the entire set was in perfect order, every item in its place, every detail covered.

Janee stood behind Trayco looking on. She did have to admire Parker's set design. Not too flashy to distract from the guests and moderator, but with its own distinct look, which seemed to embrace all the show was meant to be. It held an appeal able to beckon all who walked into its lights to instantly feel most comfortable. Even though it was not exactly like the one Janee designed that day on a broken board, she was compelled to admit it was far superior. There was no question; Parker would work on the movie later.

A young, pretty aid approached. "Ms. Janee, Ms. Paige wants you to meet our guests in the green room before they go on the show."

Janee immediately joined Paige.

"Janee, let me introduce you to our special guests." Paige nodded to four Millennials, who rose from sofas and easy chairs to greet her.

"Welcome. Thank you for coming," she warmly greeted her guest discussion participants.

"Of course, you know Adam Hillag," Paige began the introductions. She touched his arm, but Adam walked apart from her.

"Thank you for giving me my platform tonight," he spoke boldly. Janee peered deep into his eyes and soul in a fleeting attempt to discern Adam's meaning. She could find nothing concrete.

"Adam represents America," Paige went on.

"Do it honorably, Adam," Janee admonished. He threw himself into a chair.

"Devin Sully is representing Australia." Devin displayed a rough cut, like he just came in from the Australian Outback, but his smile was infectious.

"Jocie Falvo comes to us from the Philippines." Page walked over to a petite, dark-haired young woman.

"Are you nervous?" Janee inquired.

166

"I am fearless," she declared.

"My kind of girl!" Adam shouted from his chair, kicking up his feet. Janee stared expressionless at the boisterous millennial until he averted his eyes.

"Rebecca Otterman is from Israel," Paige said as she presented the fourth guest. Rebecca was plain of face and sturdy of build. If military existed in the Millennium anywhere, she would surely be in it.

"Well?" Rebecca waited. "You did not ask if I was nervous."

"Didn't need to," Janee responded, in a matter-of-fact voice. "I am anticipating a great show tonight. We are on countdown of 30 minutes. May our Lord Jesus Christ bless and guide your discussions."

CHAPTER 42

DEBATE

The Broadcast began. Jason Finn was introduced and welcomed on stage amidst wild cheers and applause from the audience.

"Thank you. Thank you," he said as he waved, his eyes going to the front row of the audience. Janee followed his gaze to see his 'before' life mate, Molly Dugan. 'Who cares if she beat me out of a husband and an Academy Award. This is tonight and this show is real. Right now, we are in homes all over the world. I'm just glad Molly is here and Jason looks great,' Janee mused, joining in the applause.

Jason took his seat. "Good evening, or morning, depending on which part of our planet you are on when viewing this broadcast. Welcome to stream cast coming live from Hidden Light Studios in Burbank, California. Thank you for watching Millennial Discussions, a special time given to four millennials from different parts of the globe to share their views, feelings, and yes, struggles, if that were possible in a perfect world.

"Let me give our eager audience in our studio a few guide lines. First, while we are shooting live, no one can leave this building. Since most of you are millennials, restrooms are through the exit on your right. If you must go, be quiet. Let me re-emphasize to our audience, no talking during panel discussions. Save your applause until breaks or end of show. Also, during the guests' discussions, we want no audience response. Please keep silent. These mics are very sensitive. And of course, this necessary last thing. Make sure all electronic devices and SAT phones are off. Thank you, and thank you for your participation.

"Now, to you in our audience, here in our Studio and viewers all over the world, let's give a mighty welcome to our guests."

The live audience went crazy with excitement.

"Rebecca Otterman, all the way from Israel."

"Devin Sully from down under, Australia."

"Jocie Falvo, joining us from the Philippines."

"Adam Hillag, representing America."

The four millennials made their way onto the set stage amid a thunderous standing ovation. The audience energy gave a sense that these four represented them, and would be their voice. The guests took their places, and the applause subsided as the audience sat down.

"Welcome to the four of you," Jason began. "We are honored you have joined us for this discussion. It is the first of its kind and designed for our growing populace of Millennials all around the world. This is in reality your show.

"So, to get started, let me share the discussion rules. I have four questions, and all of you will be allotted five minutes per question to give your answers. I will rotate the speaking order for every round so each of you can have a first turn to answer a question. Are you ready?"

The panel acknowledged they were.

"OK, our first question. Did you meet King Jesus in the Temple in Jerusalem, and what was your reaction? We will start with you, Rebecca."

"That is easy." Rebecca brightened and glowed. "Since I live not far from Jerusalem, I could not wait since I had already believed. He was dressed as a King in a beautiful robe and wore a crown. I ran to Him and fell at His feet. Jesus gently lifted me up. I felt so loved and knew I belonged to Him, the King of kings, my Lord, Messiah." Tears wet Rebecca's cheeks.

"Devin." Jason nodded.

"I was a scared Aussie and felt out of place coming to a sight I'd never laid my eyes on in Australia. Like when I saw Jerusalem and stood before the Temple. Little me? What was I thinkin', coming here? I shook as I entered, and thought to pass out comin' into the presence of a King, as Rebecca said. But He wasn't like that at all. He looked like a Shepherd, and I know shepherds 'cause in Australia, we have sheep. He beckoned me to come and we just walked, all about the Temple. He explained a draft o' stuff, and finally when we were back at His throne, He asked, 'Do you know Me? Really, with your whole heart?'"

"Suddenly, I wanted that very thing. I realized my heart wasn't merely thumpen' in my chest, happy. It was achen'. I felt guilty, lost; I really didn't know Jesus. I cried out! Then it happened. I can't explain what it was exactly, but love flooded my heart and soul, like an Australian Monsoon. I left a different Millennial."

"Jocie." Jason moved on.

"I have no story of that," she began. "I live far from cities, deep in the jungle of a remote Philippine Island, so I have never ventured to the Temple. But, Jesus has come to me often in dreams. One time, we walked among the banana trees. Whether a dream, a vision, or real, I do not know, but this I know. It was then, on a moonlit night among the banana trees, I believed. I asked for His forgiveness and to open my heart."

"Now, Adam."

"You sure something else didn't happen amongst the banana trees? Humm, Jocie girl?" Adam began.

There was an audience reaction. It was obvious Jocie bristled, but remained silent.

"No comments on each others' discussions," Jason reprimanded.

"Don't correct me on something Devin did on Rebecca."

Suddenly, Janee fought off the impulse to slap Adam's mouth. "What is wrong with him?" she muttered.

"Yes, I went to the Temple. My grandpapa and grandmamma took me. I was impressed with Jerusalem, disappointed with Jesus. I expected a King, but He was dressed in rags. He showed me the scars and the wound in His side. I held no sympathy for a man who wouldn't speak up and brought about His own execution. I felt no love, and realized that I was as good as He is. Then when He told me my attempts to be righteous were as filthy rags—that angered me, and I wanted to leave. Would you

170

believe Jesus wept? Our King? Crying like a baby. I ran to my grandpapa Farmer and grandmamma Emile and told them to take me home."

Total silence hung over the stage until Jason gave the next question.

"What do you think the future holds for Millennials? Devin, you are first."

"Well, I have read about pollution, hunger, sickness, death. Don't know these things, and suppose never will. That is our future in a perfect world, absent of those bad things. Only filled with good things."

"Jocie."

"Our islands will rebuild and repopulate. We will have beautiful families. I will experience no fear of murderous, crazed rebels killing my babies as Tribulation Saints have told about."

"Adam."

"Future? Nothing but hard, never-ending work. We do the work, while Resurrected Saints like you, Jason, sit in your comfy chairs and order us around. You already tipped your hand, declaring to the world what you think of us. 'Growing populace of Millennials,' you called us. Populace by definition means common. Common people. You Resurrected Saints boss everybody around; we do the hard stuff."

"Adam is commenting on you, Mr. Moderator," Rebecca objected.

"And you on me," Adam shot back.

"Cease!" Jason raised his voice. "Rebecca, your answer."

"One thousand years in a perfect Kingdom under Christ's rule. What better future is there?"

"Thank you, Rebecca. Your answer actually moves us on to the third question. What do you like best about Christ's Millennium Kingdom? Jocie, you start."

"Tribulation Saints have told me how it was in 'before' times. Now, we are free."

"Adam."

"Nothing," Adam declared in anger.

171

"Rebecca."

"With Transporter Stations and nothing to fear, Millennials can travel anywhere in the world. What a thrill. I have so many adventures I want to take and places to see," Rebecca gushed. This brought a response from the audience. Jason held up his hand.

"Hold your applause until the end of our show, please. It's time for our fourth and final question. Do you see areas that need improvement? Adam, you are first."

Adam's eyes narrowed with a glare. His face grew red. He clinched one fist as if to strike. His eyes went from the moderator to the throng of millennials facing him, and into the cameras to a viewing world. He began.

"You speak of freedom. Ha! You joke. When I visited Christ, I saw no King but a dictator. Even ancient Scripture foretold He would rule with an iron fist. He has always been power hungry –."

"Stop. I am calling for a short break." Jason stood up.

"You are cutting me off? Running to Janee for instruction?" Adam challenged.

"Hold your tongue," Jason ordered. He came back stage.

'Lord Jesus, what shall I do? Stop Adam's blasphemy?' Janee quickly asked Lord Jesus.

'Let him have his say,' Jesus whispered in her mind. 'It is part of my plan, just as this show is.'

"What shall we do, Janee? He is defiant and rebellious." Jason asked Janee.

"Lord Jesus instructed to let him have his say, Jason. Then finish out the show."

Jason went back on the set and took his seat. "Resume, Adam," Jason instructed. Adam appeared surprised and pleased.

"There was a war in heaven between two great angels; Jesus and Lucifer."

"Jesus Christ is not an angel," Jocie yelled. "He is the Son of God!"

"Not all people believe that," Adam countered.

Jason held up his hand. He motioned to Jocie to be quiet. He nodded to Adam to continue.

"Lucifer and all the angels who followed him were sent to earth to live. This earth was his and he took on a new name, Satan. But then God created humans and gave them the earth to live in. Now humans lived in Satan's Kingdom and it was great. No rules, everyone could do their own thing. Talk about freedom? That was perfect freedom. But they began to love Satan more than God and that made the old man angry, so He flooded the earth and killed them all. Talk about abuse of power. Anyway, eight survived, but they still lived in and repopulated Satan's Kingdom. Again, they loved Satan more than—Him; so He decided to take it away and give it to His Son."

"You are a babblin', blind fool, mate," Devin exclaimed.

Jason held up his hand.

"Sure, God sent His Son, but the world rejected Him even then and killed Him on a cross. It was still Satan's Kingdom, but a struggle developed between his followers and the followers of Jesus. Yet, history proves that as the years wore on, more and more humans followed Satan and less and less were true to Christ. Finally, God gave up and called home what few followers were left to Him. Again Satan had free reign."

"That reign of seven hears was the most hideous, horrific in all of history. Ask any Tribulation Saint. Ask your mom and dad." Rebecca could stand no more. "We all came from Tribulations Saints."

"Shut up and let me finish," Adam retorted. "God couldn't stand Satan's perfect Kingdom. He wanted it for His own favorite Son, so at the end of the seven years, Jesus came and took it by force. Was it fair to take Satan's kingdom and throw him and all his followers in chains into a deep abyss? Was it?

"Let me pose a 'what if' question. What if Hitler would have been allowed to rid the world of every undesirable and develop his perfect race? What if we came out of that perfection? What would I be now? Perfect!

"Or what if Satan is loosed to restore his Kingdom. What could that be like? I can tell you—Freedom? No rules. Do whatever you want. Power? I understand my dad's Uncle Stoner became an Enlightened One. He had power by his voice to knock whole armies on their backs. He could move objects and mold and throw power balls like missiles. Jesus has never given any of us that kind of power. Wealth? All of Satan's followers amassed and relished great riches."

The audience reacted with angry shouts. "That will never be!" someone shouted.

"It will. Satan will come back, and if all Millennials will turn to him, his Kingdom can once more be restored."

That statement brought the bleacher crowd to their feet with angry shouts of insults, rejection and a few muffled cheers. Jason demanded quiet and everyone to be seated.

"Rebecca, your answer." Jason moved the show on.

"I had my say. Adam misses the big picture. God's plan is set in stone. His Word declares it."

"No!" Adam retorted. "It can be changed. We must change it."

"Stop interrupting." Jason took authority. "I won't tell you again."

"And what? Kick me out? Beat me up? Kill me?"

"Shut up," the audience demanded.

"Devin." Jason went on.

"Had my say as well. What you blabbered, bloke, has as many ding holes shot in it as our old, old time road signs there in the outback, an' your idea's just as old. Believe me, Mate, your theology will last about as long as a dipper of water poured out on a hot noon sand."

"Wait and see." Adam folded his hands in triumph.

"Jocie."

"I have seen some of your kind and belief. They hide even now in the jungle. I have told them, and I tell you now. We Millennials have beautiful color in our world. But your underground world is grey. You are one step away from blackness."

"We close our discussion broadcast with that. Let's hear it for our guests. Thank you for a robust discussion. Thank you to our audience and all our worldwide viewers. Goodnight." Jason folded up his notes, while Paige escorted the guests back to the green room for interviews.

Jason caught Janee before she went to check with Brandon.

"Great job, Jason," she congratulated him.

"Adam has a lot of you in him." Jason took her hand and smiled.

"Too much! Far too much, dear friend," she admitted.

"Well, tonight wasn't a discussion," he concluded. "It turned into an 'old days' kind of debate."

CHAPTER 43

JANEE'S REIGN

Five brilliant beams of light shot straight up into the California sky. They held steady for a few seconds, then broke into circular motions, sweeping, crossing, catching the attention of everyone for miles, finally taking a rest in the steady hold, only to break away again and repeat the cycle. The lights were to accomplish just one thing. Draw people to their source, and that it did.

The sky over Hollywood lit up, its bright shafts of ice white lights circling, crossing, making wide sweeps, dancing upwards, was reminiscent of the glitz and glamor days of old. Only better! And this could only mean one thing. A movie premier! And, that's exactly where the lights led.

Throngs of spectators lined the sidewalks of Hollywood Boulevard on both sides of the Historic Egyptian Theatre. The crowds spread out for blocks, even spilling into the streets making passage of luxurious air limos difficult in reaching the theatre.

The old Egyptian Theatre was one of the few to survive the destructive wars of the Tribulation. Now, the theatre had been restored to its stunning glory that took the moviegoers into a magnificent Egyptian Palace.

A rich deep red push carpet ran from curbside all the way down a Palm-lined courtyard to the entrance of the theatre. The long walkway resembled an ancient desert garden.

The interior of the Egyptian was huge. Elegant seats filled the floor as well as the balcony above. Velvet covered the walls and gold trim was in abundance. The theatre displayed the feel of luxury and wealth when one passed through the ornate doors.

To watch a movie here was not entertainment, it was an experience meant only for the Millennium. The enormous flat screen with stellar technology and surround sound of matching quality transported the audience from watching to being in it. Tonight, this theatre would be filled with some of the elite millennium moviemakers.

Outside, the crowds anxiously awaited the arrival of the heads of production, their cast and crew, and the VIP list of people who would be the first to see this special project. Above this crowd angels were hovering, watching, and shimmering.

A group of fans inside the courtyard stood lined along the red carpet. These people were given or earned special passes to be closest when the premier individuals walked through.

Traffic was clogged, making Janee late. "I'm sorry, Ms. Stemper, but what can I do. Everyone is moving so slow." Her driver motioned toward the line of solar and air cars ahead of them.

"Do not fret," Janee admonished with a smile. "They can't start without me." But the thought had occurred to her several times how easy it would be to just forget the traffic and appear at the theatre. But what fun is that? It would only diminish the excitement of the evening. Do it like it used to be, stepping out of a limo at the premier.

"We're almost here," her driver announced. He pulled in behind three other limos, each in turn letting their passengers out.

Janee was thrilled and amazed at the mass of people. What a sight! They were running in all directions, screaming, laughing, totally caught up in the excitement of the moment. What an event! Several young Millennials broke away from the crowd to walk alongside Janee's limo. They touched the windows, attempting to peer inside.

"It's Janee Stemper!" one of them yelled, and the crowd instantly reacted. They surrounded her limo with shouts, loud talking, wanting to welcome her, show their love. The noise was deafening. They chanted, "Janee-Janee-Janee!"

"You have arrived, Ms. Stemper." Her driver came around to open her door. "You are the star tonight," he said, as Janee stepped out of her gold-colored air limo. She smiled. "The actors are the stars, my dear."

A mass of hands and faces pressed towards her, crushing each other to get near. This bunch had suddenly become overzealous. Miglia set down in front of Janee, wings spread open, making it clear without speaking, they give his charge space to walk the red carpet. Janee began waving, touching hands, throwing kisses; tears welled up in her eyes. A dream lost in life was in this moment coming true. "I love you. Thank you," she cried out, as much to her Father God as to the crowd.

A newscaster greeted her at the courtyard entrance.

"Here she is. The one everyone has been waiting to see. Janee Stemper!" The crowd of people cheered and clapped.

"Janee Stemper, would you tell all our viewers around the world what this premier means to you?"

"I would love to, because this night is so very special and dear to me. It is September 30, Millennium 67, yet this theatre holds great significance, and I will tell you why. In the 1950s a great man of film, Cecil B. DeMille screened his greatest work, a masterful production, Ben Hur, in this very theatre. Today, I realize my time in Christ's Kingdom is just getting started. So there is much work to do: innumerable shows and projects, more than I dare to count, and all of great worth. But none like tonight. This is my greatest work, my triumph, my dream come true. Nothing will compare, not in my 'before' life, nor in my future. There will never be another like this one." As she walked through the courtyard, fans reached out to touch her. Many were in tears.

"I'm a tribulation Saint, Janee. I watched you on the screen of the theatre in my small town as a child. I loved your movies," a man said as he reached out his hand.

"Me, too. Words you spoke when you and Bernard were traveling, gave me hope and helped me believe during the Tribulation. Thank you," a woman on the other side said.

There were so many, Janee was overwhelmed. But, a very old woman near the theatre doors spoke what Janee was really feeling tonight. Janee felt compelled to stop and take both of the woman's hands. This lady's eyes glistened, as she looked deep into Janee's soul.

"Janee Stemper," she spoke low with deep emotion. "You finally made it, didn't you?"

Janee emotions broke, and she hurried into the theatre, dabbing at her eyes. An usher escorted Janee to her seat. A low roar arose in the theatre as she was greeted.

Her son Seth rose to greet her with a hug. There was Bernard on the other side of her, and Paige next to him. She nodded to her cast and crew and mouthed, 'I love you. You are the greatest.'

As she looked around, she spotted her mama and daddy, then so many of her family, going back generations.

Suddenly a flood of joy came upon her. Happiness abounded throughout her very being. She was in a place she loved, about to watch the labor of a lifetime, surrounded by all the people she loved the most and who loved her. She sat down and took Seth's hand.

'Thank you, Lord Jesus,' she breathed a prayer, 'for all of this.' She looked around and teared up again. 'I am truly blessed.'

'I am pleased with you, Janee Stemper, and the work you have accomplished,' Jesus whispered in her mind. 'You see tonight not all dreams are fulfilled in life.'

"Amen," Janee spoke softly.

The lights dimmed, and the curtain opened. The theatre grew dark and the audience hushed.

The screen lit up as the movie started with the title in bold letters.

" KING OF KINGS "

SEGMENT THREE

CALEB AND SARAH'S REIGN

CHAPTER 44

THE TIME HAS COME

Caleb was restless. Unsettled in his spirit, and disturbed, wondering why. In Christ's perfect world it seemed odd; out of place to feel like this. Was it the slow progress in the restoration of Lugar de Paraiso?

"A Place of Paradise?" he quipped, thinking of where Sarah and he had resided before the Tribulation. 'Not even close,' he mused. 'That was indeed Paradise.'

Looking up, he realized he had wandered from his house through several blocks of a residential part of the town and all the way down Azure Drive. He was facing the waterfront. He turned to admire the night-lights of Lugar de Paraiso. The long gradual incline sparkled from homes and businesses. His gaze swept across the many lights upward to the base of Vera Cielo mountain rising like a blackened giant against a starlit sky. Vera Cielo seemed indifferent to the small resort village spread out beneath its feet.

To his right, he saw the Paradise Resort Hotel. It was ablaze and alive, its laughter and music beckoned, 'come to a resplendent building and surrounding grounds.'

"Do you remember how that looked when we first arrived?" Caleb addressed Herculon, his Guardian Angel, who stood nearby. Herculon did not respond.

"Nothing left of the old Golden Sands Casino but the foundation covered with piles of rubble. The whole town had been completely obliterated by Hurricane Chantal. Boards, scraps and litter everywhere." Caleb paused. "And more dead bodies than I could count." He glanced over at his angel.

"I remember, but not as you," Herculon answered his prior question.

"What do you mean?" Caleb asked.

"I recall all things as they were, but you feel things in ways I do not understand. Even now you harbor sorrow, and going back to that time gives you pain. I have never experienced what you do now, but I see it."

"Then why am I feeling like this tonight? I have watched the rebuilding and restoration of this town, even been a part of all of it; yet I am restless and sad. Why? Is it because the process remains unfinished or flawed? It's now Millennium 134, and we still have no Transporter." Caleb took in the view of a long pier jutting far out into the water. "Cruise ships or smaller vessels are the only transportation to our Gulf resort, except for Resurrection Saints, but few of them come; mostly for family or close friends," he muttered.

"A cruise ship is due tomorrow with tourists; then a cargo ship docks next Thursday with supplies. Lugar de Paraiso is so remote I wonder if Lord Jesus has forgotten we are here or has just placed His attention on more interesting or important places. I saw the shows Janee did in Iraq to boost that country's reconstruction. I've requested such help over and over from the Lord—received only silence. I wonder, have I angered Him? Or done a lousy job? I fear I am wasting time. I simply don't understand and Sarah has no clue either . . . but she is visibly troubled."

Azure Drive intersected Beach Row, which Caleb crossed now. It was late with very little traffic. He descended a small slope onto the sand and walked along the beach away from the pier landing.

This was Caleb's favorite place. He thought of Jesus and His disciples walking the shore of Galilee; yet he was reminded of when he spent seven years with Jesus in Paradise. Can't top that! He squatted to scoop a handful of sand. The Gulf was tranquil.

The waves broke one by one, coming in succession against the beach. The white foam of the cresting breakers gleamed florescent in the reflection light from the hotel. The low roar gave a sense of peace and serenity, its calming effect filling Caleb's spirit.

"Good evening," he acknowledged a passing millennial couple.

As he continued walking, overcast slowly drifted onshore, blotting out the stars. A cool mist blew against his face. A thousand vivid memories filled his mind. Herculon was right. He could not remember without feeling. He was dreadfully incapable of blotting out the past and never thinking of it again. Too much of his life happened here. There was too much embedded in his mind, always to be triggered by who knew what. Suddenly, the outline of a man appeared in the dim light walking toward him.

'I don't recognize this fellow,' he thought. 'I know most of the locals. It's probably a vacationer.'

As Caleb drew closer to the stranger, out of the corner of his eye he saw Herculon glow brighter, wings slightly open, head bowed. Then Caleb recognized his Lord, Jesus Christ. He ran, dropping to his knees before his King. He immediately was convicted of his comments to Herculon.

"Oh, forgive me, Lord. You said you would never leave us or forsake us—ever. I spoke foolishly."

Jesus placed a hand on Caleb's head. "My child," He spoke with love and tenderness. "I have not forgotten you and Sarah, or your labor here. I am well pleased with the progress you have made." He aided Caleb to his feet.

"But Lord, it has taken so long," Caleb blurted out. "One hundred thirty-four. That's two lifetimes."

"Do not fret, my son. Do you not remember in my Word where it says, 'A thousand years is as a day?' You haven't even used a fraction of a day," Jesus smiled. "Come, let us walk. I am here to tell you, the time has come; time for Lugar de Paraiso to have its own Transporter. I am sending Mark and Nikki to build it."

CHAPTER 45

TELLING GOOD NEWS

As soon as Jesus left him, Caleb appeared before Sarah. He could hardly wait to tell her Mark and Nikki were coming.

"Jesus just met me on the beach and we talked," Caleb shouted. "He is sending Mark and Nikki to construct a Transporter here in Lugar de Paraiso!"

"What?" Sarah jumped up from her chair, reaching for Caleb. She couldn't believe what she was hearing. "Oh, Caleb, I have dreamed of such a day as this, but so much time passed and He has been so quiet. I was giving up hope!" She looked into Caleb's eyes for confirmation. "Can this be true? They are really coming?"

"Jesus promised. Two weeks."

They held each other tight and rejoiced. This simple assignment held answers going far beyond the need of a Transporter; but affirmed awareness of Christ's approval of the work already accomplished. Just knowing their Lord was pleased gave them assurance they were exactly placed in the Kingdom's work. Then, the added blessing of having their kids with them, gave the reminder that although time is timeless, the Lord still keeps His promises.

"Caleb, do you realize Mark, Nikki nor any of their family have ever visited us here in 134 years? We have gone there, but never—Oh, Caleb, think what it means. They will all be able to make trips here anytime they please. They will absolutely love our resort. I am so excited; we must tell everyone the good news."

CHAPTER 46

LUGAR DE PARAISO

At dawn the next morning Caleb and Sarah tracked down Chris Fowler at Paradise Resort. He was supervising three Millennials in remodeling projects on the second floor. They were startled by the couple's sudden appearance.

"Dang," one of them blurted out. "Why do you Resurrection Saints do that?"

"Keeps you guys awake and working." Chris grinned. He turned his attention to Caleb and Sarah. He sensed something was up. He stepped apart into the hallway to talk.

"Good morning, dear friends; what brings you to Paradise this early?"

"Oh, Chris, we have the most wonderful news!" Sarah could not hold back.

"Jesus came to walk with me on the beach last night," Caleb went on with the story. "We are finally getting our own Transporter and He is sending Mark and Nikki to construct it."

"No, you say? Wow! Really?"

"True, Chris. They will arrive in two weeks." Caleb took Chris's arm. "Think of what it means."

"My mind is boggled!"

"Can Paradise Resort handle the influx of visitors?"

"No. We'll have to expand; more rooms, more personnel. We must let Maybeline know, since she oversees the whole Resort operation. But first we have to tell Kay. She will be so excited. Gosh, the last time I saw Mark was in a Mexican jail." Chris's mind was spinning.

"Where is Kay?" Sarah asked.

"She is assigning staff to clean and reset rooms. Maybe in her office."

"Want to come with us?" Caleb asked.

"You go. I need to check on these millennial contractors; but I will inform Maybeline to gear up. Wow!"

Caleb and Sarah appeared in Kay's office. She wasn't there. Both looked to their angels.

"Herculon, where is Kay Fowler?" Caleb asked.

"In a third-floor room with a female millennial," the angel answered.

"Wait, Caleb." Sarah took his hand. "Portus, will you get word to Esther that her brother and sister-in-law will be here in two weeks to build us a Transporter?"

"Of course." Her angel immediately communicated with Esther's angel. "She is overjoyed and will also come here soon," Portus informed them.

Next they flew to the third floor. Kay saw them from down the long hallway and came to them. Sarah rushed to hug her closest friend.

"Kay, you won't believe this. Our Lord Jesus is sending Mark and Nikki to build us a Transporter."

"Oh Glory!" Kay cried aloud. "Thank you, Jesus. When will they arrive? Will they stay here?" Kay was speaking so fast. "Yes, they are Tribulation Saints and will need to eat, of course, and sleep—yes, shower." Kay's face scrunched up; she became teary-eyed and held Sarah tight. "Do you know what I am remembering right now?" Kay whispered.

Sarah shook her head 'no.'

"That night at Casa de Amor. Chris and Mark were in jail and you and I . . ."

"Shhh, Kay. That night is gone forever, and here we are today. All together again."

"I'm so happy," Kay cried, and wiped her eyes. "How soon?"

"Two weeks."

"Two weeks! Sarah, we must get busy."

"And, that we shall," Sarah laughed.

The rest of the morning Caleb and Sarah broke the news to the remaining old Global Missions Church. Then they went to the mountain village of Vera Cielo and located Junto Angeles, the old priest.

"Greetings, my friends," Junto greeted them. "Are you faring well?"

"Very well, brother. We have news. Words you will rejoice to hear. Our Lord came to me on the beach last night. We will have our own Transporter and He has assigned our son, Mark, and his wife to construct it."

The old man began waving his arms, unable to speak. He cupped his hands in prayer, as tears streaked his weathered cheeks. He moved his head from side to side; a smile graced his face as he looked up.

"Thank you, Father," he spoke in a low husky voice, "for answering our prayers, for your grace and mercy to bring Caleb and Sarah's children here to us. Thank you. Thank you." He bowed his head.

"I truly rejoice over your words," Junto spoke in a reverent hush. "My heart feels overflowing, if I had one." He looked up with a smile. His face beamed as he took both of their hands. "Bless you, my friends."

Caleb knew the conversation was over. Junto could say no more.

"Will you tell Hank and Tulipan?" he asked'

Junto nodded and released their hands.

Instead of vanishing to appear below, Caleb and Sarah walked through the village, speaking to residents on the way. It just seemed a fitting thing to do. In passing, they came upon the ruins of Saint Marco's Church. They studied the remains of the caved-in roof and rumbled walls.

"I feared we might die here, Sarah."

"Me, too. Chantal's winds were so strong."

"But the church held, just as it did for two thousand years. The winds of hell could not prevail against it."

"We saw the end," Sarah murmured, "and have come full circle."

They walked hand in hand to where the road started down the mountain. From there they could see all of Lugar de Paraiso spread out before them.

"Look at that," Caleb spread his arms exuberantly. "Just like it was when we first came, only better. One hundred thirty years old and just starting."

"Like we did," Sarah put her arm around his waist, "and our children were young."

CHAPTER 47

CRUISE SHIP ARRIVAL

"I see it!" someone in the crowd shouted.

All eyes scanned the Gulf horizon. "Where?" another asked. "I cannot see anything," a woman cried as she searched the sea. "Nor I," a man added.

"Not there. Far left to the North. I saw a sun glint."

Soon everyone spied the vessel and excitement swelled. Paradise Resort had electric carts lined along the pier to receive passengers who would soon disembark the ship. Two air trucks waited their turn to pick up luggage.

A crowd was gathering to greet the ship, but more importantly, Mark and Nikki's celebrity status had preceded them. For two weeks they were the talk of the town. They were coming to build a Transporter. That very event would open new doors for the small resort town.

Chris and Kay Fowler joined Caleb and Sarah.

"I feel like a teenager," Kay giggled.

"If I were still in my 'before' life body I fear I would pee my pants." Sarah laughed.

"Come on, ladies," Caleb and Chris responded.

Rubin came alongside Caleb. "I will keep everyone safe in Lugar de Paraiso," he assured.

"And in Paradise Resort," Plomo said as he joined them.

Sarah caught a glimpse of Espolita and her girls. Fina and Carmen were also in the crowd. "She must have turned the school out early," she remarked.

Maybeline Collier came up behind Kay. "Are you excited?" she asked Kay.

"I haven't slept in days." She caught herself. "Silly, I don't need to."

Everyone laughed.

Millennials began pouring in, curious.

Junto Angeles waved to Caleb from the crowd. Hank, Tulipan and their angels suddenly appeared in front of Caleb and Chris. Hank smacked Caleb solidly on his shoulder.

"Just like old times, huh preacher?" Hank bellowed.

"Sure is, Hank, surely is."

The crowd moved out along the pier, covering every inch of the way to where the docking took place. Rubin and Plomo had to clear a space around the electric carts. They moved the Millennials back towards Beach Row to prevent their being shoved off the pier into the water.

As passengers began filing down the gangway, noisy cheers arose. The tourists were puzzled to receive such an enormous enthusiastic welcome. Most of the townspeople and millennials had no inkling whom they were looking for.

In about twenty minutes, the vacationing tourists were off the ship and being carted to the hotel. A few of them made their way into the crowd and found loved ones.

Caleb and Sarah's excitement took a hard hit. Had Mark and Nikki missed their ship? Changed their minds?

"They are there." Portus motioned upward.

Sarah screamed and frantically waved. Caleb along with their friends joined in, shouting and waving. In a moment Mark saw them and pointed. Nikki waved excitedly and the couple ran down to the pier, pushing their way through the throng of town folk, eager to welcome this special pair. Mark and Nikki broke through with shouts and laughs of joy into Caleb and Sarah's arms.

CHAPTER 48

PARADISE RESORT HOTEL

"Nikki, are you awake?" Mark whispered.

"Umph? What Mark?"

"Do you hear that?" Nikki stirred and listened. "No."

"The waves on the beach. Doesn't it remind you of La Pasada in Manzanillo, where we first met?"

"Yes, of course," Nikki grew dreamy. "We must go there, someday . . ."

Nikki's heavy breathing told him she was back asleep. Mark got up to get a drink of water and use the bathroom. Standing in the dim light by the sink, Mark's thoughts rehearsed events of their arrival in Lugar de Paraiso. It was a little weird that his parents put them in the resort hotel instead of letting them stay in their home. 'We have a walk-in shower to rinse dust off, but no toilet or sinks. We don't need them,' his mom had explained. Mark shook his head and laughed to himself. 'If we are going to be here ten years or more, we must change that situation. I'll contact a couple of millennial carpenters I heard Chris mention to build a bathroom and kitchen in Mom and Dad's place.'

Mark reverted back to his old Global Missions days when he would be up late at night. He wasn't sleepy; no, he was still charged up by the trip and the excitement of seeing his parents and old friends. He was thrilled to be able to show Nikki the place where he lived for eight turbulent years. He had a fleeting impulse to shake his wife and drag her out of bed to get going! No, he shoved that thought aside and pulled on his jogging outfit instead.

It wasn't that he was restless. Curious, would be the better description. He felt compelled to roam around the resort. He wondered if it really did resemble the old Golden Sands, or was it just his imagination. He grabbed the room key, nodded to Nikki's angel, Waaleen, that he was going, and slipped quietly out the door.

The lobby downstairs was quiet and empty except for two young millennials at the reception counter. They both acknowledged him by looking up. They went back to their work when Mark walked into a large plush lounge. It brought back memories of sitting in similar chairs, feet propped up on an expensive coffee table, laughing and cutting up with beautiful, rich tourist girls.

This lounge had numerous soft easy chairs and expensive-looking couches spread about. Low tables with glass tops were easily accessible no matter where you sat. Along one side was a baby grand piano.

'This is different,' Mark thought, as he walked over to it and commenced to run his fingers over the keys, playing a simple little tune. The place had the feel of a nightclub after the show was over. Light jazz gave smooth, slow life ambience to the resort. Mark sunk into one of the plush chairs. Looking around, memories flooded his mind. They would not be denied and insisted on their emotional partners. A bevy of women he had met there paraded in front of him. The thought of their faces, skin, figures, and sleek tan legs excited him. Those thoughts moved in natural progression to rooms upstairs and what went on behind closed doors. All of those encounters were one-nighters and he never saw the girls again. Mark felt shame. But there was a different one, Kim. He fell in love with her. Those old feelings surfaced only for a moment until the nightmare night of Hurricane Chantal invaded his very heart and soul. Surges from the Gulf storm-driven waves, blew out their rooms windows, washing Kim's friend Terri out into the icy black water. Mark caught his breath remembering how he and Kim struggled in the water and fought to stay alive. Grief flooded his heart; then he remembered Kim in Colorado. He coughed and choked on disgust at what she had become. The love he felt for her was frivolous; nothing like what he had with Nikki. He wiped his eyes and started to get up when he heard his name. He turned to see Maybeline Collier behind him. He stood to greet her.

"I am surprised to see you here. It is so late. Is your room satisfactory? Are you and Nikki comfortable?"

"Couldn't sleep, but that's me. Nikki is out. I just wanted to look around, remember. This seems so, familiar." Mark gestured, looking around.

"Like the Golden Sands? As it should; it was reconstructed on the Sand's foundation, so it has the same dimensions. Millennials coming in to rebuild didn't have much imagination, so they used a few old photos we managed to find. Just duplicated, they did. Do you like it?"

"Amazing, Maybeline."

She looked him over carefully. "You look much as you did then," she spoke softly. "Young, wild; and you gave your mother, dad and sister fits, you know. Look at you. Everyone ages so slowly in the Millennium, and here you are with your wife; and you have kids and they have, oh, you know what I mean."

"Rad, huh?" Mark grinned.

"Don't you turn that old charm on me, young man; but I, all of us cannot express our eagerness and gratitude to finally have our own Transporter. It will change our resort town. Anything you need let me know."

"I'll need workers," Mark commented.

"Chris can help you."

"Where can I find him tomorrow?"

"You can probably catch him out on the veranda. He and Kay were there with visitors earlier. They all left and Kay just went home. I believe Chris is still there, if you hurry."

Mark took off. He knew full well where the Veranda was located. Plomo caught up with him. "Senior Mark, are you OK?" He grabbed his arm.

"I'm great, Plomo. I'm trying to catch Chris."

"Si, he is through that door and outside. Anything you need, I am here to help."

"Thanks, I'll remember that." Mark hurried onto the Veranda. It was dark. He saw no one.

"Hello, Mark," came a familiar voice from the shadows of an end table. "Come sit a bit."

Mark joined Chris at his table. Chris was genuinely glad to see him. "What can I do for you?" He went right to the point.

Mark started to blurt out his request, but checked himself. He sat a moment collecting his thoughts. There was so much more to say, then ask for help. He swallowed hard and began.

"Chris, I have never had a chance until now to thank you for saving my life at the Concert Crusade."

"Did get a tad hairy that night. Yeah, what a night it turned out to be. Stoner, the satanic priests, fire-ball fight. Did you know Sierra was the stranger who took on Stoner?"

"Dad told me," Mark replied.

Chris grew sad. "Rubin and Plomo gave their lives that night trying to save the rest of us."

"I found out, after the Tribulation."

"As I remember, we both landed in jail." Chris sat up.

"I did, you escaped." Mark laughed. "Man, you freaked me and the guard out. But I have to tell you, he stole your wedding ring."

"Oh?"

"Yeah, and I took your blue solar. Drove it to Manzanillo, before it got confiscated."

"Humm. Often wondered what happened to that old car. Lots of memories for Kay and me." Chris smiled.

Both men fell silent and Mark sensed it was time to end the visit. Tiredness hit him now, but he covered a yawn before he spoke.

"Chris, I need a crew to build the Transporter housing, and a bathroom and kitchen in my parents' house.

Chris gave a knowing laugh. "Meet me here early morning two days from now. I will have your crew."

CHAPTER 49

MILLENNIAL LABOR

Mark found his millennial crew eager to learn and work, but also became frustrated with them. Afraid of their making mistakes made him cautious and that amounted to slow-going. He was observing work on the Transporter when Nikki approached him.

"Hi Sweetie," she greeted him, with a kiss. "How goes the project today?"

"Turtles move faster," Mark replied dryly.

Nikki watched the work a few moments before she replied, "I know, Mark. These millennials are way beyond us in concepts, but in practical skills? Things we knew and could accomplish in Junior High, we are teaching thirty-year-olds, especially here. Lugar de Paraiso is so remote. Yet, on their tablets and SAT phones, you would think they are wizards."

"Doesn't teach them how to hammer a nail or saw a true line. They know how to solve complex games but can't measure sixteen and one-eighth inches."

"Well, my dear, don't be too hard on them." Nikki grinned.

Mark laughed. "I gave up on that two months ago."

"I came to tell you that we finally received confirmation on the Z-complex battery units and the high amp solar panels. We have a promise of shipment on either the next cargo ship or the one after."

"Excellent."

"Also, to let you know, Fina wants to bring her second/third grade students on a field trip here to see the Transporter and hopes you will explain how it will work," Nikki continued.

"When?" Mark questioned.

"They can walk over here in thirty minutes, or I can schedule another day," Nikki offered.

Mark studied the Transporter structure. 'Not too much to see, but maybe if they see it like this, it won't be scary later,' he pondered.

"OK, give Fina the go-ahead."

"Will do." Nikki turned to her angel. "Waaleen, would you tell Fina's angel that it's ok to bring the children?"

"Hey, crew, listen up. In about thirty minutes, we will have a pack of school kids here to see the Transporter," Mark shouted as he approached the structure. "Take the time to show them what you are doing and make them feel special."

"And lay off teasing your old teacher," Nikki added, as she came alongside him. "Mark, Fina and her students will leave after math. Maybe an hour before they get here."

"That's good. Thanks, Nikki." Mark squeezed her hand.

"I see Tyrome and Erma coming in their solar," one of the Millennials on top of the Transporter building called out.

"Oh no," Mark groaned. "What can they want? I pray there are no further problems with mom and dad's bathroom."

Soon a dark green car pulled into the large open area that would later accommodate parking for the Transporter Station. Two young Millennials climbed out and ran to Mark and Nikki.

"All finished," the woman excitedly announced.

"Wow! Erma," Nikki exclaimed. "That's great." She hugged her.

"It's a good job, Senior Mark," the man proudly proclaimed.

"Would Caleb and Sarah be pleased?" Mark asked. He knew they were gone for two weeks, so had not seen the finished job.

"Si, they would be most pleased."

"Nikki, will you stay here in case Fina shows up before I get back?" Mark asked.

Nikki nodded.

"Let's take a look, Tyrome. You and Erma drive me over there."

Tyrome's solar car was new. He found it online and had it shipped from a Texas Dealer. Mark thought of the contrast to his 'before' years. The struggle to gain money to purchase a car, and often the workmanship was shoddy and unreliable. The solars in those days were short-ranged. This car on the other hand displayed superb quality and never ran out of a charge. Above that, there was no money system in the Millennium. No buying, no credit, no banks, nothing to prevent anyone from making a purchase. Everyone had a job to do and did their best unto the Lord Jesus, and all things needed were provided. Tyrome had need of a car and Jesus agreed.

"We have been so blessed with this work." Erma looked back at Mark. He simply nodded.

As soon as they arrived, the Millennials ushered Mark into Caleb and Sarah's home. The house was quite large with lots of rooms to accommodate guests. Now, there would be a bathroom facility for toilet use and cleanup, and a complete kitchen for cooking.

"You like?" Erma opened the door to the bathroom. Mark was impressed. The change over the last month was incredible. The finishing touches made this bathroom one better than those at the resort, which Mark considered plush.

"I do like," Mark nodded as he looked around.

"Wait until you see the kitchen." Tyrome hurried his boss along.

Mark was flabbergasted. He knew the room had been expanded, but now he walked into a full-blown, completely stocked kitchen. There were beautiful sets of pots and pans, stunning silverware and place settings. A walk into the pantry showed rows of food goods, cooking oils and seasonings. Mark was amazed.

"Great job," he uttered. "Perfect."

Both millennials beamed, then grew solemn. Their sudden mood shift was obvious.

"What?" Mark questioned.

The two millennials crowded close to Mark like children. "Are we finished?" they both asked.

"Yes," Mark said, hesitating.

"But Senior Mark, we don't want to be." Erma teared up.

"We don't want to leave you," Tyrome added. He hung his head and spoke with emotion deeper than Mark seldom observed in most millennials.

"Please, let us stay." Erma cupped her hands in prayer.

"I don't know," Mark was touched. "I will talk to King Jesus."

CHAPTER 50

FIELD TRIP

Mark arrived back at the Transporter site in time to greet Fina and the children.

"Welcome," Nikki said as she hugged the teacher.

Fina stopped the children in front of Mark and turned to address her class.

"Children, this is Mr. Mark Hillag. Mr. Hillag lived here once in the 'before' years. He was a teenager and I have to tell you, he was most handsome, and I had," Fina looked back at Mark and Nikki to wink. "I had a terrible crush on him."

With that revelation, the children began tittering and a few giggled.

"You're rad, handsome." Nikki nudged Mark.

"Mr. Mark and Ms. Nikki have come to Lugar de Paraiso to build us a Transporter," Fina went on. "They are going to show us the work of building, and tell us what it will do when completed." She turned to face Mark and Nikki.

"Thank you, Fina. We will certainly be happy to show the Transporter under construction and explain the amazing transport it will afford. Come, follow us." Marked motioned to the class to lead them across the large field.

"This will be a parking lot for travelers' cars," he explained.

"And right ahead of us will be the reception area where people departing check in and are briefed on this trip. For arrivals, there will be an area to meet family or friends, or picked up," Nikki pointed out.

"Straight ahead is the transporter site," Mark pointed out.

The children gasped and grew excited. They wanted to run to the building, but Fina stopped some of them and made them walk.

At the Transporter building, Mark continued, "The very first thing we will do is introduce you to our construction crew and let each of them tell what they are doing."

"They are Millennials just like you, only older. As you can see the building is only partly finished. What you see here is the framework. Mickey and Josh are responsible for erecting this building. This is Mickey and up top is Josh!"

"Hello," they both greeted. The children waved and returned their greetings.

"We first built a frame out of these wood studs. Next, we wall in the back and sides. This big opening is where the transporter door will be," Mickey explained.

"And I am boarding in the roof," Josh spoke up. "When the walls are complete, Mickey and I will coat them with a very durable and thick coating. This sealer doesn't just protect the building but prevents electrons from emitting through the back and sides. The door will also block those electrons."

"But the roof is most special. You see, all those blocked electrons can't stay trapped inside, so where must they go?" Mickey asked.

"Straight up out the roof," a little third-grader answered.

"Correct. Right through the roof."

"That means the roof coating must be different," Josh elaborated from up above. "Tough to withstand the sun and weather, but it has to do what?"

"Let the electrons escape," the class shouted.

"You got it," Josh finished.

"Looking inside," Nikki pointed, "that guy in the funny outfit is Audio. Audio, what are you doing?"

"Stringing cable and coax inside the frame to make this thing light up and do its job," Audio answered, with only a glance.

"And Rosaretto, what are you working on at those tables?" Nikki asked.

"I am preparing the intricate and special fabric to line the inside of the Transporter." Rosaretta smiled, holding up part of the material.

"Can you explain what this Transporter will do?" Fina asked.

"I can." Mark started to describe how the Transporter breaks a person down into tiny particles and sends them in a lump to another station. 'I can't frighten them with that disturbing mental image,' Mark thought. He shifted his presentation. "When people come here to travel, this Transporter will make it possible for you to see the world. They will only have to choose the place, step inside, close the door, cross their arms like this, and poof! They are in their chosen location. Where would you like to go?" Mark pointed to a young girl.

"Ireland. We saw pictures in class."

"I want to go to America to see the desert," a boy piped up.

"I saw a place in Africa with multitudes of animals. Can I go there?" another student asked.

"Wherever there is a Transporter."

"How long to travel."

Mark clapped his hands loudly, which startled the kids.

"That fast," Mark exclaimed.

"Does it hurt?"

"Not a bit."

"Will my whole family fit together?"

"Up to ten."

"I have a question," a millennial girl spoke. "My Bible speaks of a horrible time on the earth before Jesus came back. What was that like? Resurrection Saints can't answer and I have never met a Tribulation Saint until you. What was it like to live then?"

Nikki rushed to hold the girl. "Oh child," she cried. "You know not what you ask. Thank the Lord Jesus you will never face what we did. Just believe in Him and give Him your heart, and you will be safe forever."

Now the class buzzed with questions, but Fina stepped in.

"Children, say thank you and good-bye to the Hillags and their workers. This concludes our field trip.

CHAPTER 51

EQUINOX

Caleb was sitting at the table in his remodeled kitchen, when Mark stumbled in.

"Hey, Dad," he muttered.

"Good morning, Son. I made you some coffee," Caleb greeted. "When did you start drinking it?"

"'Bout the same time you refused to touch it." Mark poured a cup and came and sat down by his dad.

"My mango juice does me fine."

Mark studied his dad for a moment. With a slight shake of his head, he had to laugh. "I reckon I got too much o' my Grandpapa Farmer in me," he joked.

Caleb laughed. "You sleep well, Son? You and Nikki pleased with your room? Your mother and I are so glad you are here."

"I slept too well." Mark yawned. "Our room is great. We are so glad to be out of the resort; too noisy for me. You know how quiet it is at our log home."

"You miss it?"

"Of course. We miss our kids and all the grandkids. I wonder how many have been added to our family since coming here."

"I'm losing count," Caleb reflected. "I see the Transporter is coming along fine."

"But maddeningly slow." Mark sipped his coffee. "Look how long it took to do your bathroom and kitchen."

"I know that feeling. But the Lord reminded me I haven't even used a part of one day. Ha!"

"Morning, guys." Sarah brightened the room.

"Hey, Mom."

"Nikki awake?"

"Are you kidding? She's a sleep-in gal."

"Does she ever rise early?" Sarah asked.

"She did a lot when we were running for our lives." Mark got up to refill his coffee. "Where are you taking this, Mom?"

"Caleb, have you told them about the Equinox?" Sarah took Caleb's hand.

"No, I have not."

"I've heard that term. I think it has something to do with the sun, moon, or planets." Mark returned to the table.

"It comes twice a year. It is the time when the sun crosses the equator, making night and day of equal length in all parts of our earth. All of the people in this area gather on the beach to welcome the sunrise," Caleb explained.

"You and Nikki must come and take part. It is deemed sacred by all of us," Sarah explained. "But I must warn you. The Equinox makes sunrise very, very early."

CHAPTER 52

GREETING THE SUN

"**A**re they going to make the trip to the beach?" Caleb paced the kitchen floor. "Are they even awake?"

"They are." Sarah sighed. "I saw their light shining under the bedroom door."

"The Millennium still has alarms on clocks," Caleb reminded her. "By the time Mark has his coffee and they eat, we will be late."

"For goodness sakes, Caleb." Sarah jumped off her bar stool and walked to him. "Don't be so loud. They can hear you."

"At least wake them up." Caleb stopped his pacing. "You know I detest being late."

"Amen, amen. When you weren't the first at church, your whole day was messed up. I'm surprised you weren't first Raptured before the dead could get out of their graves."

Caleb stared at Sarah. Deep love welled up in him. He had to admit the humor in what Sarah spoke. A smile spread across his face. He chuckled. "Just might drive me to drink coffee," he admitted.

"That'll be the day!"

"Whoa, you just said you were gonna drink some coffee." Mark and Nikki joined them in the kitchen. "This must be some beach party for you to drink coffee."

"Your father is afraid he will be late," Sarah said as she hugged them.

"How far is it?" Nikki asked. "It is two hours before dawn."

"About 2K to a small inlet. Mom and I can be there in an instant, but you have to walk."

"Oh, what fun!" Nikki was delighted. "I am so excited. Please walk with us. We can run some if you want. I can't wait to see the sunrise."

Caleb studied his daughter-in-law a moment. He realized once again how perfect she was for his son.

"I thought you said she didn't like to get up early," Caleb commented straight-faced.

"She doesn't. But once up, she is a ball of energy," Mark said dryly.

"Oh stop it, you two. I'm ready to go."

"Probably no bananas to pick." Caleb gave Mark and Nikki beam lights. "But mangos should be good."

The four of them talked as they walked down Azure Drive. As they neared the beach, they joined streams of people coming from all directions of the city. It quickly became a parade of lights marching to their own music and vastly uneven cadence.

"This is incredible," Nikki burst out. "The town must be empty. There are even resort tourists mixed in."

"Many journey down the mountain from Vera Cielo."

"Just to watch the sun come up?" Mark questioned.

"Oh, it is more than that," Sarah added. "You will see."

Suddenly, Mark was aware that many around him carried musical instruments of various sorts. He saw many drums of various sizes; a few traditional bongos, while one fellow carried a small polished piece of log and a stick. As he watched more closely, he noticed timbres, tambourines, flutes, Guitars, base boxes and wood pipes. "Is this a concert?" he blurted out.

"Not like you have ever heard," Caleb answered.

Farther down the beach, light from huge bonfires could be seen emitting above the cove inlet. As they got closer, music could be detected.

"I hear drum beats." Nikki strained to see and hear. She wanted to hurry.

They flowed with the crowd into a small cove. Bonfires lit up the area and the beach was alive as people found places to stand or sit on the sand. Behind the crowd, those with instruments were gathering on small dunes that divided the beach from the trees and vegetation, where dark shadows from the firelights danced.

"Watch the ones on the dunes. They are beating out a rhythm and as musicians arrive they pick up the beat," Caleb explained. "Now, notice the tall man, bright shirt, cutoffs and white hat? He has a large richly finished wooden drum. His is the deep mystic sound you hear. He sets the rhythm and the rest pick it up. This is totally unrehearsed. Since it is early, the beat now is more deliberate and slow; however, as sunrise nears, it will pick up and become feverish."

Mark tuned out the conversation between his mom, dad and Nikki to focus on this strange, almost weird musical gathering. At times, he could pick up the distinct sounds of flutes, pipes and guitars. He watched the players with fascination. The rhythm droned on, sometimes broken by a brief pause, only to pick up a new beat or tempo. Mark studied their faces, especially the ones with small bongo drums. They seemed transported into another dimension or in a trance, their fingers tapping out a pattern over and over. Then, his eye caught sight of numerous women shaking tambourines or tinkling cymbals. They were swaying to the music, eyes closed. Mark knew many of them would soon be dancing.

Nikki slipped her hand inside his arm, and looked into his eyes. She voiced what Mark was thinking.

"This is hypnotic," she purred.

"Crazy," Mark said.

As the dawn drew nearer, little by little, slowly mounting, the intensity and speed of the tempo increased. Different members of the group began singing out notes in loud voices. No words, just a quick melodic note; perfectly in time to the beat and in harmony with the instruments.

By the time the sun was to come up, everyone was captured by the moment. This was no longer simply watching a sunrise, but a celebration of it. The rhythm was fever-pitch now! The crowd was on up on their feet, yelling, clapping, singing, energized to a point of hysteria by the rapid throbbing beat of the drums.

Suddenly someone screamed out, "Here it comes!"

A hush fell over the cove. They waited. Then it happened. A bright sliver of golden light slowly rose out of the dark waters of the Gulf. Stars began to fade. Mark thought the crowd and the musicians at this point would have gone wild. But no, there was silence. Only the breeze and the lapping of the waves broke it. The entire crowd was mesmerized.

"Today," the rhythm leader shouted loudly.

"Today, this day the night and day become even. Equal in time all over the world. This reminds us that when God created the world, first there was darkness. Then God created light. Darkness came first, then came the dawning of the first day. This morning we celebrate the victory of light over darkness. Today we greet the sunrise."

Instantly, the drums exploded into an insane, frenzied beat. People shouted praises to God. Clapping, singing and joyous dancing broke out. Caleb shouted, "Glory!" to the beauty of God's creation and His incredible plan for mankind.

By and by as the sun rose higher in the sky, people wound down and began to disperse.

"I'm hungry," Nikki confessed. "That papaya I picked didn't last."

"We can go, Sweetheart." Mark took her hand.

As they began walking Plomo joined up with Caleb.

"That was something, eh?" Plomo commented.

"Never gets old, does it?" Caleb responded.

"Si, Caleb, but today I hear word of something new and troubling."

Caleb stopped to face his friend. He motioned the others to go on. He waited for Plomo to share what he knew.

"You remember when Senior Mark went missing for days?"

"Yes. We feared he went into the jungle. I even checked with Junto."

"Si. Again I am hearing of bad things, wicked things happening there."

"Millennials are migrating deep into the jungle. It is rumored they gathered yesterday evening at sundown to welcome the darkness."

"How can this be, Plomo?" Caleb was aghast.

"They are turning against Christ. They want Satan and his darkness to return."

"How may?"

"That I do not know. I asked my angel and he said firmly, 'Do not go there!'"

"Have you told King Jesus?"

"Yes, He knows."

"He knows?"

"Si, He knows everything. He said this is foretold."

CHAPTER 53

BIG TEST

Caleb glanced out on their tropical patio as he passed by on his way to the kitchen. He stopped and went back to peer out the sliding glass door. The patio was empty.

"Humph?" he muttered. He had grown accustomed to seeing Mark out there early before Nikki or any guests staying in their house arose. This had been a routine for several years now. He started down the hallway to make sure the couple was all right, when he encountered Sarah. She shooed him back into the kitchen.

"What is going on?" Caleb questioned, as he looked around. Coffee wasn't made. "Mark always has coffee going long before now."

Sarah drew close to him, speaking low, "They were talking all night. I couldn't understand everything said, but their discussion sounded pretty heated."

"They were arguing?"

"I don't know. Maybe." Sarah walked to a counter to make coffee.

"Do you think the dedication and big Transporter test today has any bearing?" Caleb queried.

"They have seemed stressed. I'll get your juice, honey." Sarah opened the refrigerator.

"Thanks, Sarah. Have they talked about it?"

"They both appear excited for the project to be complete."

"Humm," Caleb said thoughtfully. While Sarah began preparing breakfast, he took his glass of juice out on the patio and sat at a table. Mark's Bible lay on the other side, so Caleb reached across, opened it and read some passages. It was

211

difficult to concentrate because his mind was distracted with concerns for Mark and Nikki. Finally, he just closed the book and held it to his chest. His mind wandered to his old Bible, to the moment of the Rapture. They were all gathered in the meeting room of Casa de Amor. 'Where was my Bible?' he tried to remember. 'Our bedroom? On the pulpit? Was I holding it?'

"Good morning, Dad." Mark slipped through the sliding door, coffee in hand. He looked tired.

"Morning, Son." Caleb eyed him.

"I see you found my Bible." He sipped his coffee."

"Yes. There is much to talk about and catch up. Have we ever discussed my old Bible?"

Mark smiled. "Now that's a story.

Caleb drank his juice and waited to hear.

"When I got out of jail, I went back to Casa de Amor in the church van. The meeting hall was full of clothes, shoes and jewelry. Only one there was Tazada."

"Yes, Tazada. So sad."

"I can't remember for sure, Dad. On the floor? No, I believe it was on the pulpit. Your Bible helped me believe and hold to faith when everything was falling apart. I needed it in those moments when I dealt with the death of friends; and especially when Nikki and I both struggled to survive. Then I became Pastor of a rag-tag group of Non Coms at the Church in the Woods—your notes aided me in forming my messages. As I found it on a pulpit, I left it on the Church pulpit when Nikki and I fled from Combats attacking the church. It burned up in the fire . . ." Mark's voice trail off.

"I could not be more proud of you both, Son," Caleb spoke with emotion.

There was silence as Mark finished his coffee. In a minute, he set his cup down.

"I'm scared!" Mark went on. "We will test the Transporter today. I have been under a lot of pressure to use a millennial to do the test, and I have several volunteers."

"You are frightened for them?"

"Me."

"You?

"Dad, I can't send someone to test a unit whose construction I have supervised."

"What will you do?"

"I will send myself to Applegate."

Caleb studied Mark thoughtfully. "Son, you have successfully erected a number of Transporters. All have worked without any accidents, so why the nervousness?"

"Not all the equipment we needed was received, so we improvised. These millennials are not well trained."

Caleb's perception didn't agree. "Mark, I don't think you are scared. You are bothered."

Mark looked away. He wiped his eyes.

"How is Nikki taking your decision?"

"She's freaking out. We butted heads all night. It was hard on her when our kids traveled. She went once and was uncomfortable, a wreck."

"Is it that bad?"

"Heck no. A tingle, a heat rush and you are there. It is the idea that frightens her. Taking apart and putting together."

"What does Nikki want?"

"For us to use a millennial. But Dad, I could not let them send someone else, and they—I can't."

Caleb rubbed his face with his hands, as if to clear his mind, before he spoke. He chose his worlds carefully. "My Son, even in your youth you were never one to just sit by while others took action. Do you recall what you did at the Concert Crusade in Mexico City?"

"You mean being Stoner's pawn?"

"Before that."

Mark thought. "I was shuttling the shanty folks in the church van, load after load to the concert."

"Exactly. You did what you had to do by your own decision. Today you will do the same. The big test is to have faith that in the Millennium, Jesus makes no mistakes and won't allow you to either."

CHAPTER 54

WILL IT WORK

Sarah was in their large meeting room seated in a comfortable chair when she heard Nikki come out of their bedroom. She shuffled down the hall and slid open the patio door.

"Hello?' Nikki called.

"I'm in the meeting room, dear."

Nikki entered the room and slumped down in a sofa. She was unkempt with tousled hair, no makeup. Her face was drawn and her eyes red.

"Where's Mark?" she mumbled.

"He and his dad went to the Transporter Station to get ready for the big test today," Sarah replied.

Nikki tried to hold back, but couldn't. She began to sob.

"Oh no, Nikki," Sarah said to her distraught daughter-in-law. She sat down and held her tight.

"I am so upset and frightened," Nikki blurted out.

"What is it?"

"Mark refuses to use a millennial for the test. He is going to do it himself."

"But thousands are transported every day without –."

"Those thousands are not my husband," Nikki objected. "When our children and grandchildren took trips, I was a bundle of nerves. Why is Mark so headstrong and stubborn?"

"I can tell you, Nikki, because I know exactly how you feel. When Hurricane Chantal was bearing down on us, I saw my Caleb stand up in a meeting on top of a table and urge the people to go up the mountain. People came against him in a rage, but he stood his ground. They tried to kill him, and Nikki?

I was so scared my chest hurt. I couldn't breathe for fear." Sarah squeezed Nikki closer.

"You must understand the men you and I have. They see something that needs to be done; they strive do it. They are solid and brave. But believe me, they both would lay down their lives for us. Mark is deeply troubled knowing he is hurting you. Still, there is something born deep inside him demanding he be courageous; to go beyond himself and do what he knows to be right. It is unselfish, and not born of pride."

"Yes, I saw it that horrible night we fled from the Combats. He didn't want to run and abandon our friends. He put me and our baby, babies, first, and held us out of the freezing water of Cold Creek; and, and he took a life without hesitation to save us. It was a nightmare, but through it all he stayed strong."

Sarah smoothed Nikki's hair tenderly.

"If the situation were reversed, I know exactly what Caleb would do."

"He would do the test," Nikki sniffed. "Thank you, mom."

"Nikki, how that warms my heart to hear you say 'mom.' Speaking of that, we must hurry and go. Mom and Dad Savage are coming and will be here with us for a while. How exciting."

"Yes." Nikki jumped up. "I will be ready soon."

The dedication was brief and held before a very excited and energetic crowd. Several city leaders spoke and Caleb blessed the Station and all who would use it. Everyone was aware of the tremendous changes the Transporter Station would have on Lugar de Paraiso. Then Mark stood to acknowledge his crew and thank all who helped on the project. Everyone hushed awaiting his announcement of who would do the test. Nikki held Sarah's hand on one side and Mother Savage's on the other.

Mark held a long moment of eye contact with them before mouthing, 'I love you, I love you.'

"I could never send anyone on a journey that might endanger them or, at the worst, bring death. So, I am testing this station today myself."

There was a collective gasp across the crowd. Someone yelled out, "What if it takes you apart and fails to put you back together?"

"Then I guess I'll get my Resurrection Body way ahead of time," Mark quipped.

The crowd laughed.

"Not funny," Nikki said, wanting to cry.

"You wonder, will this work?" Mark went on. "The proof will be when I send word through my angel to Nikki's, 'I am safe and well in Applegate, Oregon.'"

Mark turned to the Station. He nodded for Audio to set the program. He then shook hands with his crew and stepped inside the Transporter.

Audio started the program sequence. The heavy door closed, and the locks could be heard slamming into place. A slow whine slowly began and revved into a high pitch intense enough to cause millennials to cover their ears. A loud crack sounded and it was over. The door opened to an empty Transporter. The astonished crowd milled about nervously.

Minutes passed, before Portus loudly announced, "Mark's arrived in Applegate, Oregon, safe and sound. He says the Transporter worked."

CHAPTER 55

SURPRISE

One week had passed since Mark's departure to Applegate and their home at Douglas Landing. He was scheduled to return this morning so the population of Lugar de Paraiso was gathering to welcome him back.

The Superintendent of the School, Espolita, her teachers, and their students were formed in noisy lines to wait. Rubin and Plomo stood to one side ready to keep order. Maybeline, Chris, Kay Fowler and other support staff of the Paradise Resort were present.

Of course, in the very front stood Caleb and Sarah, Mark's wife Nikki and her parents, the Savages. Caleb looked around at the crowd. His gaze stopped at Esther, who had arrived from her work in Tennessee. She grinned when they made eye contact.

Junto Angeles, Hank and Tulipan, and several others were present from the Village Vera Cielo. Caleb didn't know if they would come, but because Mark would leave before long, he invited others of The Global Mission Church.

Suddenly, Bomba appeared. She ran to Plomo, her dear friend, hugged him, took his hand and stood proudly at his side. Caleb immediately teared up. A love, unconfessed, unfulfilled in the before-life, could now be expressed as a dear friendship in the Millennium.

Caleb knew Sarah saw and was feeling the same. A tug on Sarah's arm turned her attention to someone behind her.

"Oh, my goodness! Blanca? Yes, it is you."

"I would not miss this welcome for Mark, or to see you, Sarah. You were my mother in our 'before' life."

"Look at you," Sarah went on. "Grown up and so beautiful."

Caleb hardly recognized this woman who had been a teenager in the old church. He hugged her and expressed how excited he was to see her.

"You came from Mexico City?" He asked.

"Si. When my assignment there is done, I am hoping King Jesus will let me come home, here."

"Oh, yes," Sarah agreed.

"Have you seen Arcy?" Caleb continued.

"Two years ago. She also was in Mexico City but no, not since."

Caleb nodded that question to Herculon. The Angel lifted up.

"She is in Hawaii doing an important assignment and cannot leave," Herculon informed them then folded his wings.

Nikki could stand no more. "Audio, the Transporter door is open. What if Mark tries to come back now?"

Audio stepped out of the control room and squinted in the bright sunlight to see who was asking the question.

"Do you need to shut the Transporter door now? What if he is trying to return?" Nikki repeated.

"That is the genius of these stations, Ms. Hillag. When Mark is ready to Transport from Applegate, the unit there will close this door as well and the two stations lock into each other. He has to Transport here and no other station in the world can interfere," Audio explained.

"It has only been a week," Nikki turned to her parents, "but I have missed him terribly. Since we married in the Tribulation, he has seldom left my side. I am so excited to see him."

"What has he been doing there?" Mrs. Savage asked. "You have not heard from him at all."

"Of course I have. We chat online. We talk on SAT phones. He has been checking on the kids, grandkids and great-grandkids. That takes a while." Nikki laughed. "They are all happy and active. Shag takes care of the house and mediates any squabbles. Mark told me they miss us and want us home. It has been eight years." Nikki sighed.

"Eight years in a tropical beach resort can't be all that bad," her dad teased.

"And what a blessing for us," Caleb and Sarah agreed.

"Here he comes!" Josh shouted from the audio control room.

The heavy door slowly closed and locked with a thud. The whirling sound started up, then revved faster and faster. Instead of a sharp crack at the point of transmission, there was a loud suction of air. There arose an anxious clamor from the crowd to hurry.

The door disengaged, slowly opened, and out stepped –.

"Adam?" the family gasped in unison.

Adam walked away from the Station a few paces and surveyed the crowd. He was dressed in a faded camp shirt, ragged jeans, and flip flips. A black duffle bag hung from one shoulder, which he stopped to hoist up. Cocked to one side of his head was a dingy ballcap. He stood there a minute, then a smirk of smile spread across his face.

"I'm impressed," he declared loudly, spreading both arms wide. "My mother, two sets of grandparents, even my Auntie Esther. Wow! And will you look at this. Such a crowd of admirers I don't even know. Thank you, one and all."

"Adam, where is your father?" Nikki asked.

"Father? Oh yes. He is still in the Transporter," Adam now raised his voice. "Unloading all the crap we had to bring. I said to myself, 'I should help him?' Then I said, 'No, I shan't because I don't feel like doing any work today.' Humm, surely you have dumb millennials somewhere to do it."

The crowd began to bristle at Adam's obnoxious behavior. Caleb approached his grandson.

"Adam, we are excited you came and we look forward to you staying with us." Caleb opened his arms to welcome the young man.

Adam held up his hand. "No hugs!"

"Adam!" Nikki was aghast.

"Nix." Adam glared.

"Don't you –."

"Nix," Adam interrupted her.

"Cut it!" Mark emerged from the Transporter.

When the crowd saw Mark, they clapped and cheered. Nikki ran to him, threw her arms around his neck and kissed him. The town went wild.

"Humph!" Adam was sour. He looked around and spied a few nearby resort carts. He ambled off towards one, but Chris stopped him.

"You shouldn't talk that way to your parents."

"Who are you?" Adam scowled.

"I was in jail with your dad when the Rapture hit. He is a good man."

Adam looked hard at Chris before he answered.

"Should'da—Would'da. You both should'da stayed there and I would'da been so much happier today."

Chris moved to retaliate, but Kay stopped him.

Adam continued to the solar cart. Plomo met him and stood with folded arms.

"You work here?" Adam questioned.

"I am in charge of resort safety."

"Ah, hired help," Adam spoke with disdain. "Take me to the resort."

"Sorry," Plomo growled. "These are not for your use. You will walk. That way." He pointed.

"Just my use or anybody's use?" Adam challenged.

"You will walk. That way," Plomo repeated his order, more firmly. "Perhaps they will have a room for you. Perhaps not."

Adam gave Plomo a dirty look, hoisted his bag up on his shoulder and took off walking in the direction of Paradise Resort.

"You will love Lugar de Paraiso. The resort town is a tropical paradise. The people are loving and friendly, Dad told me. Ha! Surprise! Bad joke. Lie. It's hot and stinks. The people are cold and clannish," Adam declared, loud enough for those nearby to hear.

He heard his dad shouting from the Transporter Station. "Espolita, bring your teachers and students close. Adam and I brought a surprise; supplies from Beverly Ann and the school in Douglas Landing. Come. Nikki, help me hand them out. Where's Adam?"

CHAPTER 56

ONGOING INVESTIGATION

Weeks went by with no word from Adam. He never came to Caleb and Sarah's house. They discussed the possibility that he had a problem with them. However, Mark and Nikki felt certain the rift was with them.

"He's just weird," Esther concluded.

Nevertheless, Adam's behavior was troubling for it seemed wherever he went, strife followed. Caleb even tried his angel Herculon, but he had difficulty tracking the millennial, because Adam didn't have an angel. Herculon did report that other angels would see Adam out late at night.

"What can that boy be doing at night?" Sarah was deeply concerned. "Mark and Nikki must be worried sick."

"They are. Remember how we were when Mark went missing?" Caleb felt that old uncertainty and fear for a child. He shook it off.

In desperation, Caleb called a meeting with Chris, Rubin and Plomo. They arrived at the house very late one night. He took them out on the patio and asked Sarah to get Mark. The five men sat in the patio shadows for hours, discussing the situation. Caleb called on the Lord Jesus Christ. "Ask for wisdom and I will give it," Jesus instructed.

In the early morning darkness, they hatched a plan. Chris and Rubin would follow Adam's activities at the Resort. Mark would monitor the pulse of the Millennials to learn what they had seen or heard.

Caleb and Plomo would spend more time patrolling the dark streets and walkways of the city since they didn't sleep anyway.

Two more months went by without any real contact with Adam. There were fleeting sights of Adam in the resort. Chris even used the excuse of maintenance checks to go into Adam's room. It was always empty, even late at night. Yet, the shower was used and the bed slept in. However, the frequency of use was unknown.

Mark pried some disturbing news out of the Millennials. 'We see Adam Hillag going up the mountain to Vera Cielo.' This prompted Caleb to pay a visit to Junto Angeles soon after Mark shared that news.

"I have seen your boy with some of the Vera Cielo millennials," Junto reported.

"What are they doing?" Caleb asked.

"Mostly gaming on their tablets, talking, laughing." Junto shrugged his shoulders.

"Good kids, these ones."

Caleb picked up on Junto's uncertainty. "What else?" he asked.

Junto's face darkened. He dropped his eyes, and shifted his body stance. He shrugged again.

"Come on, brother. What are you not telling me? You are thinking something. Tell me."

"There are growing . . ." Junto hesitated.

"What? Don't hold anything back that might involve my grandson."

"I hear growing concerns, no fears, that millennials are slipping off into the jungle to do evil things in the darkness. Their numbers are growing."

"Adam?"

"I have no proof of that, of any of them. Rumors only."

Caleb shook his head. "Jesus knows about this?"

"Si. He says to live in His Light and to beware of the darkness only."

The situation did come to a head on a rainy night in the coming winter months. Caleb encountered Adam in the downpour coming out of a park walkway on the street. Both men froze and stared.

"Adam, where have you been? What are you doing?"

"Hanging out," Adam sputtered, and blew the rain from his mouth.

"Why haven't you been to our house? Why are you avoiding your family?" Caleb demanded.

"My family?" Adam wiped his face. "I have family? I will come to your house when I feel like it."

"Months? What do you do everyday? Who are you hanging out with? Where do you go? Answer me!"

Adam clinched his fist and shook it in Caleb's face. Caleb thrust his open hand towards Adam and the force threw Adam down. He leaped back to his feet. He lunged at Caleb but Herculon stepped between them.

"Yeah, sure, big man. Use your Resurrection power and your stupid angel against me. Get one thing straight. I don't have to answer to you or anybody. I am One Hundred Thirty-one Millennium years old. Back off. Take your 'Perfect World, Glorious Future' crap and chuck it. Leave me alone. Get it?" He disappeared into the darkness.

In the morning, Sarah found Caleb at the kitchen table crying uncontrollably.

"Caleb, Honey, what is it?" She rubbed his back and patted his face. She held him and kissed his cheek but he would not be consoled. His body shook in convulsions. Emotions and expressions felt in the mortal body were discovered to be so much more intense, sensitive and eruptive in the Resurrection body. Caleb wished to die, were it possible. Could God have never intended for the Resurrected to experience such hurt or grief?

Caleb simply held his head in his hands until he finally became spent and crying ceased. When he looked up, Sarah's tear-drenched face told that she felt his pain even though she didn't understand. She wiped his face, then hers and waited.

"Sarah," he began. "It was just like that day with Mark, when he beat me so badly; the biting words, the hate, yes, hate coming from him. Adam tried to attack me. I had to use force to throw him down. He came back again. Herculon stopped him.

223

Adam was vicious like an animal. He has become someone I don't know; still, it was like fighting Mark all over again. Sarah, if I had a heart, it would be broken."

"But look at Mark now. See and appreciate what he has become. We must have the same hope for Adam. We must tell Mark and Nikki –."

"No, Sarah. They must never know."

"But, Honey, Adam is their son."

"They must never hear of it. The pain would stab deeper than they could bear. Yes, they do need hope. Adam said he would come to our house when he is ready. That is the hope we shall give them."

CHAPTER 57

MEE ANTRA

More time passed. The family returned to their assigned tasks. The Savages went to their work on the other side of the globe. Esther was back in Tennessee. Caleb and Sarah oversaw the workings of Lugar de Paraiso, all the while keeping their eyes open for some sighting of Adam. However, he proved as allusive as a fleeting shadow at dawn.

Mark and Nikki put finishing touches on the Transporter Station. The reception building was constructed allowing for a flux of arrivals and departures. The final work of the parking lot and landscaping was near completion, and Nikki had supervised the training of the millennial crew to take over the operation of the Lugar de Paraiso Transporter.

What happened next took place one evening. It was a clear night. Galaxies of stars were brilliant, lighting up a moonless sky. The family had just shared a scrumptious dinner and retired to the meeting room. The conversation was lighthearted for Mark and Nikki. Caleb and Sarah cherished the time with their children. There had been a lot of laughter. For Mark and Nikki it was a sort of mini-celebration over the final phases of the Transporter Station.

The doorbell rang. Caleb rose to answer.

He had no idea who it could be, but there were so many people in and out of their home, it could be anyone. He pulled the door open to face Adam and a pretty millennial woman.

"Hi, Grandpa," Adam spoke like the little boy Caleb remembered. "I wanted to see you and Grandma." He pulled the woman forward towards Caleb. "This is Mee Antra, my fri—er—girlfriend."

Caleb was in such shock he just stood there staring. Suddenly, he was jolted back to the present.

"Of course, come in, come in." Caleb did what seemed so natural, so longed for. He took Adam in his arms and just held him. He felt Adam's weight collapse into him and his grandson just held on. Next, he hugged Mee Antra. He could feel the young woman tremble and heard her softly sob.

Caleb stepped back to look at them. "You have no idea how happy I am to see you," he whispered. "Come." He ushered the pair into the meeting room.

Sarah, Nikki and Mark jumped to their feet when they saw Adam. Sarah and Nikki shouted, Mark came directly to Adam and took him in a bear hug. Nikki was next, then Sarah. Mee Antra stood quietly back with downcast eyes.

"This is Adam's girlfriend, Mee Antra," Caleb introduced her. Mark eyed her while Nikki and Sarah welcomed her in.

As Caleb studied the pair, he realized just how unkempt they were; dirty feet, mud splotches on their legs and arms. Adam's shorts and shirt were filthy, and his hair matted. He had grown a beard. Mee Antra's top was ripped; her shorts had holes, one on her back exposing her underwear. She had a beautiful face with striking brown eyes. Her hair was long and stringy. Caleb wondered if her brown hair was just a dirty tan.

"Are you still at the Resort?" Mark asked.

"No, Dad. Been gone months. They needed the room."

"Oh my, Adam, where have you been staying?" Nikki took his hand.

"Different places," he murmured. "At Mee Antra's for a while. Friends' homes, 'till we wore out our welcome."

"Oh you poor dears," Sarah reached out to Mee Antra. "Are you hungry?"

"Oh yes," the woman broke down. "We haven't eaten for days."

"Thank you," Adam murmured. "Thank you, Grandma."

Sarah took them into the kitchen and sat them down at the breakfast table. She and Nikki began pulling out dinner leftovers to heat up. Sarah kept talking as she prepared a meal.

"You both listen to me. You will stay here as long as you like. After you eat, you can shower and clean up. Soap's in the shower, and I'll put out fresh towels in the bathroom."

"That sounds wonderful. It has been—days—no, over two weeks." Mee Antra was embarrassed. "We weren't near water, I mean."

"Where were you?" Mark questioned.

"I don't know." Mee Antra could barely be heard.

"Remote," Adam said. It was clear the couple did not want to discuss this.

Caleb had a multitude of questions and he was pretty sure the others did as well. He ventured with one he thought a start.

"Where did you two meet?"

"In Vera Cielo," Adam answered. He was shoveling his food so fast he could hardly speak.

The couple cleaned up every scrap of food. They ate food and drank water so fast Caleb feared they would sicken themselves. When the meal was over, Mee Antra hurried off to the bathroom. Sarah used the opportunity to speak with Adam.

"We have separate rooms for you and Mee Antra."

"That is so old school, Grandma. We have been together for months."

"Are you married?"

"No."

"Do you want to marry her?"

"What's the use? We have already been together."

"Doesn't make it right. Sleeping together?"

"I didn't say that, Grandma."

"As hard as it was, your mother and father waited until they got married."

"Time changes things, old rules, habits, all change."

"Not in the Millennium. God's laws are more real and adhered to than ever."

Sarah looked long and hard into Adam's eyes, peering into the very heart of his soul.

"Adam, are you still a virgin?" she questioned bluntly.

Adam answered without hesitation. "Is there darkness yet in the night? It's fine, Grandma. I'll sleep in the separate bedroom. That way everyone can rest easier."

Later, after Adam and Mee Antra were asleep in their rooms, the family met in the kitchen. They posed a hundred questions, fueled by the pair's sudden appearance at the door: the mysterious, vague answers, both filthy and unkempt—no spare clothes? What happened to Adam to humble him, change his personality? Was it Mee Antra? Who was this Mee Antra?

CHAPTER 58

A REVELATION

Adam and Mee Antra slept well past noon the next day. The family quietly let them catch up on much-needed rest.

While Mark and Caleb sat out on the patio trying to figure out answers to a hundred questions, Nikki and Sarah slipped out and obtained several new complete outfits for the couple.

"I'm going up the mountain to Vera Cielo and see if Junto can shed any light on Mee Antra or Adam," Caleb said. "How can two people disappear for such large blocks of time and no one see them? It's like they became invisible. Look, Mark, all we know about them right now is that Adam has turned 132 and Mee Antra is 87 millennium years old."

"In our 'before' lives, that would be impossible. Crazy," Mark laughed. "Shall I go with you?"

"Let me go. I can be there quickly and won't have to use a car."

Mark agreed and instantly Caleb was gone. He located Junto and told him of the events the night before.

"I know nothing of this woman or your grandson." Junto stroked his beard in thought. "To learn, we must dig deeper. Let us talk with a millennial, one who knows many secret things. I know not this woman, her name, nor have I looked upon her face. However, she may know something to aid in your quest. Come."

The two men appeared outside a house, partially hidden in a grove of thick trees and under brush. Junto led Caleb around to the back wall to a small window. Junto stretched to tap on the glass. Three taps, pause, then four.

"If she is here she will open the window and speak." Junto glanced at Caleb.

By and by the window slid open. Caleb could hear shuffling inside and rose slightly off the ground to see the woman. It was totally dark in the room. Junto motioned Caleb down.

"What brings you, Junto, and who is your curious friend?" the voice was kind, yet deliberate.

"My friend is Caleb Hillag. He oversees Lugar de Paraiso."

"I know of you, and what you did here 'before.' I also know you have questions."

Caleb felt strongly impressed to ask an all-important question. "Are you a believer in the Lord Jesus Christ?"

"I like your boldness and your question. Yes, I am."

"Then why are we meeting in secret?"

"I hear many things from our Lord and I speak only what He tells me. Already, works of darkness vie for the hearts and minds of millennials everywhere. Some will choose to come into the Light while others willfully seek darkness. As time progresses, the expansion and power of wickedness will escalate. There are strong forces here even now which, if I am found out, will move to silence my voice."

Caleb shook his head. This was the Millennium, a Perfect World. How can evil still exist? Was Satan's power even now emitting from the pit? 'Lord Jesus,' Caleb cried out in his mind. 'What am I to believe?'

'Listen to her,' the gentle voice of Christ responded.

"Are you satisfied with my answer?" the woman asked.

"Yes. My grandson Adam has met a girl, Mee Antra. Do you know of them?"

"Mee Antra, I understand, is not from here. Her parents are Tribulation Saints who came out of the great influx of Syrian refugees before the Rapture. Her relatives settled in Corpus Christi. She rebelled against her mother and father, as has Adam against his."

"Have they ventured into the jungle?" Junta asked.

"Unsure. They speak of it and desire so. It is possible, but I can say this. They will not speak of it to you, even if you question them. They both have built walls."

"Are they beyond hope?" Caleb struggled to form the words.

There was a long pause before the woman answered.

"As long as they yet live there is hope. But remember the grey at sunset. It precedes the darkness. When there is less and less light, darkness takes over. The hope is, the darkness in all its might cannot snuff out the smallest light. The answer to your unvoiced question is this. The reason they came to you in such a desperate condition is that because of stubborn pride, they exhausted places to stay and food to eat. King Jesus in His great love and mercy drove them to you."

CHAPTER 59

PERVERSE ACTIVITY

Conditions in Caleb and Sarah's home were peaceful and pleasant the next two weeks. It appeared that Adam and Mee Antra were in love, which fostered the hope there might be a permanent change in both of them, especially Adam.

But now the equinox was again approaching. Three days before the event Caleb brought it up to Adam and Mee Antra. They both revealed they knew of it, but their reaction to attend the sunrise gathering garnered little interest.

"Well, not tomorrow, but before the following day, we will gather on the beach to greet the rising of the sun. You both are welcome to go with us," Caleb invited.

The next morning at breakfast, Caleb, Sarah, Mark and Nikki laughed and talked. They discussed the equinox meeting that would occur tomorrow morning. Mark and Nikki joked they could each take a pot and spoon to bang upon.

"We have pretty good rhythm," Nikki joked.

"Sure, why not? Is there any rule that the instruments have to be professional?" Mark chimed in.

"Have Adam and Mee Antra said if they are going?" Sarah asked.

"They didn't appear to be interested," Caleb answered.

Looking around, the group realized the young couple had not joined them for breakfast. That was unusual and prompted Nikki to go check on them. She knocked, waited and then opened the doors. Their rooms were empty.

"Mark! They're gone!" Nikki yelled.

A closer examination revealed Adam and Mee Antra took all of their belongings.

"What the heck?" Mark questioned.

"Something is going on," Sarah remarked, going back into the kitchen.

"Yes, but what?" Mark refilled his coffee cup.

While the others explored possibilities to explain this completely unexpected disappearance, Caleb sat deep in thought, trying to piece together any clues that might indicate the couple's whereabouts.

His mind kept going back to the strange reaction to his sunrise greeting invitation, but why? Did that have any bearing on their leaving? Wham! A conversation from a prior equinox gathering popped into his head. Plomo said it.

"Millennials are migrating deep into the jungle. It is rumored, they gathered yesterday evening at sundown to welcome the darkness."

It hit Caleb like a thunderbolt. 'The evening before would be tonight. It wasn't disinterest in the equinox meeting for Adam and Mee Antra. I invited them to the wrong one!' His mind was racing. 'What do they know that I don't?' He jumped up.

"I'll be back in a few minutes. I have to check something," he declared, and in an instant he was beside the secluded house in Vera Cielo.

He proceeded stealthily along the side of the house to the back. He reached up and tapped on the window glass. Three taps, a pause, then four. He waited for what seemed a long time before the window slid open.

"Hello, Caleb, what brings you to my window once more? Ah, you are troubled."

"I need to know, is there a gathering in the jungle tonight?"

"Caleb Hillag, you have years of experience in your 'before' life, and now you are a Resurrected Saint. Your guardian is ever by your side. I know of none of this because I am a young millennial. I can only tell you of what I hear and what our King and Master Jesus Christ tells me. I believe Jesus has already revealed to you the answer. But, He is faithful to confirm what He impresses on us. I give confirmation to what He has already revealed."

233

Caleb fell to his knees, crying out. "Lord Jesus, what am I to do? Is Adam and Mee Antra attending this gathering? Oh, what wickedness are they embracing? Shall the rest of us stay away from this rebellion? Do nothing? Help me!"

The Lord halted Caleb's feverish thoughts with His command.

"Gather all the Resurrection Saints to Vera Cielo. You will lead them into the jungle in the power force and light with which I have anointed you. Confront the millennials; make the proclamation I tell you; then call forth those who will believe in me and disperse the rest into darkness. This defiant, perverse activity will be broken up tonight."

CHAPTER 60

WARFARE

Caleb arrived back at the house and apprised the family of the night gathering, the possibility of Adam and Mee Antra being present, and the Lord's stern command. Caleb went immediately into decisive action.

"Herculon, contact all of the Guardians of Resurrection Saints in Lugar de Paraiso and Vera Cielo. Tell them to meet at the old mission ruins at sundown. Tell them to be prepared for battle."

"Sarah, you and Portus will be by my side as we go in."

"We are going with you," Mark and Nikki both insisted.

"Too dangerous, and slow," Caleb objected.

"We both have angels, too," Mark argued.

Caleb turned to face Detrius and Waaleen. "What say you?" he asked.

"You are both Resurrected Saints. You cannot die. Mark and Nikki are Tribulation Saints with flesh and blood. They can be wounded or killed. We cannot protect them there," both angels answered.

"We are going, dad—mom, if we have to start walking now. I think we can beat any millennial in a fight," Mark countered.

"I am not afraid of a fight or death. We have faced both before." Nikki moved close to Mark's side.

"No," Sarah spoke up. "I once feared losing you to whatever was lurking in that horrible jungle. I won't chance it again."

"Adam is our son," Nikki raised her voice.

"Mom, when you thought I was lost in that jungle, weren't you ready to go in and search for me?" Mark stood their ground.

"Dad, would you have been afraid? Or remained home while others searched?"

Caleb decided to make the tough choice. He was ready to forbid the couple to go into battle when the Lord Jesus intervened with His Presence. All four angels knelt and the adults fell to the floor.

"Stand before me, my children." Jesus reached out his hands and the four huddled close. "I call you to a difficult work. You are going into warfare. This is one of the first in my Reign, but not the last.

"Caleb, I have commissioned you to lead. Sarah, you faithfully stay by his side. Mark and Nikki, my brave ones. I know your hearts. I give my permission to go, but not on the front line. Take my light into darkness." Jesus was gone.

The four swung into action.

"Let's go to Vera Cielo to meet the Resurrection Saints, Sarah," Caleb ordered. "Mark, you and Nikki come up the mountain as quickly as you can. We will wait."

"But what about going into the jungle? The battle will be long over before –."

"Son," Caleb interrupted. "We will all march."

The Resurrected Saints and their angels formed a formidable army. The Saints stood together in strength and valor; the angels with shining swords and shield. Caleb knew as they drew closer to the battle lines, the angels would become brilliant and the Saints would glow intensely.

"We have been ordered by King Jesus to disrupt this meeting. These millennials will be there to greet and give allegiance to the darkness. We will challenge with the Lord's proclamation and provide opportunity for them to believe in Christ. Next, we are to disperse the rebellious ones into the jungle. Mark and Nikki have the permission of our Lord to be with us. They are Tribulation Saints; that means we will all march to the meeting site. I will lead the way. Sarah will be with me, Mark and Nikki follow. Junto and his Saints march behind them and the rest of you fall in to take up the rear guard. The Lord be with us."

The last parting rays of the sun were shooting over Vera Cielo mountain casting blazing colors of deep yellow, gold and dark rose, indicating that night was pushing ever inward, upward to take over and envelop the world in blackness. Now Caleb and his army pushed into the jungle.

Herculon and Portus led the way through dense growth, lighting the path for the army to follow. Some places the undergrowth was so thick the army had to walk single-file, pushing limbs and vines out of the way. They had no idea when the path split or another one crossed, or which direction to take. They had to trust the angels to keep them on track to reach this evil meeting.

"Mark, in this heat and humidity, I am exhausted." Nikki tugged on his arm.

"I'll carry you." He picked Nikki up and carried her for about twenty minutes. Suddenly his knees wobbled and buckled. Nikki jumped out of his arms and attempted to help him up. Sarah halted Caleb and motioned to stop. "We stop and rest. Give them more water," she ordered.

"How much farther?" Caleb asked Herculon.

"We have been climbing, making heavy exertion for our Tribulation Saints. However, soon we crest a pass that will lead down into a short, narrow valley. The descent there will be quicker and easier."

"Mark?" Caleb asked.

"Good to go," He gave a thumbs up as he got to his feet.

"Nikki?"

"I can walk now."

Another fifteen minutes, the army reached the floor of the valley. Herculon and Portus halted the army.

"We must become Glimmers and difficult to spot, if we are to surprise the millennials," they communicated the order as the angels' lights faded. The Resurrected Saints scooped up moist dirt to cover hands and faces.

"Well, we have one advantage," Mark joked. "No light."

"Shhh," Nikki smacked him.

The army began spreading out among the trees and undergrowth as they neared the meeting. Ahead, the light of a huge bonfire could be seen. Quietly, slowly, blending into the jungle the army surrounded the millennials. Closer they all crept, slipping up to the trees that lined a large open area. Caleb was shocked by the multitude of millennials gathered here. Caleb noticed makeshift tables lined with plentiful food and drinks. His eyes focused on the millennials themselves. They were in groups, some milling around the fire; others dancing; some making out with lewd passion. Nakedness was prevalent throughout, and sex openly performed.

"How awful," Sarah gasped. "This is an orgy."

"Please tell us Adam and Mee Antra aren't willing partakers of this," Nikki whispered.

The four of them strained to catch a glimpse of Adam or Mee Antra, but with the shadows dancing in the firelight and bodies moving in all directions, they couldn't be sure.

"Time to do this!" And with shouts of battle, the army rushed out of the woods to wall in the Millennials. The angels grew in size and shone with brilliant light. Their swords and shields burned white-hot.

The Millennials screamed in fear and panic. They shrieked in pain from the light attempting to cover their eyes. Others scrambled to find clothing and cover themselves. Sneers and angry cursing could be heard. Others were shouting, "Go away! Leave us. You have no place or authority here."

Caleb and all the Resurrection Saints stepped in front of their angels. Mark and Nikki and their angels stayed back.

Caleb walked closer. "Silence," he shouted, and the power issuing from his voice shook the ground. There was an instant hush.

"I am making this proclamation to you tonight. Give heed and take warning to the Word of God. It can give you freedom or it can condemn you.

"There is no judgment awaiting those who trust God. But those who do not trust Him have already been judged for not believing in the only Son of God. Their judgment is based on this fact," Caleb yelled.

"The light from heaven came into the world, but they loved the darkness more than the light, for their actions were evil. They hated the light because they wanted to sin in the darkness. They stay away from the light for fear their sins will be exposed and they will be punished. But those who do what is right come to the light gladly. Choose you this night whom you will serve."

"We have made our choice, slaves of the King, and we have a surprise for you," came brash shouts from the jungle. Millennials emerged from the underbrush. They had weapons.

"They have Tribulation lasers," Resurrection Saints shouted.

Instantly the angels were ready for battle. Laser pulses began flying, angels deflecting the blasts with their swords and shields.

Before Waaleen could reposition to protect his charge, Nikki took a hit in her back. She dropped to the ground. Mark came to her side and Detrius and Waaleen covered the exposed couple.

The angels sounded a battle cry like one never heard before on earth. Their swords were flaming now as they advanced on the armed millennials.

Seeing the angels go into battle, Caleb gave the order, "Attack in the Name of the Lord!" And the Resurrection Saints rushed into the throng of millennials. The battle was intense. The noise deafening as Saints and Millennials fought. They kicked, punched, threw rocks. The Resurrection Saints moved swiftly about, throwing defiant millennials to the ground, blocking punches, locking arms and hands, throwing groups backwards to the ground with just their sheer power.

By the time the warfare was ended, the fire was dying. The angelic beings lit up the area. They marched the captured, armed leaders into the circle to face their followers. One by one the lasers were cast into the fire, building it up again. All must observe the objects they had placed their trust and hopes in burn up.

While this was going on, Kay rushed to Caleb. "Come quickly." she grabbed his arm to pull him. "Nikki is wounded."

Caleb dropped beside Sarah and Mark. Nikki lay motionless on the ground. Her back was blood-soaked. Mark had his shirt off attempting to stop the bleeding.

239

"I can't—I can't, Dad. She keeps bleeding!" Mark cried.

Sarah sought Caleb's guidance for direction. Caleb stood and peered into the heavens. His mind was churning. He had always been able to think clearly in a crisis situation, making swift, accurate decisions. But this was his daughter-in-law, and time was running out.

He took this prayer to the Father. 'What am I to do? Is there to be a death in the Millennium?' Without understanding, instincts kicked in and he took action.

"I need Chris and Kay. Bring me Junto Angeles right now," he ordered. In a moment they were gathered around him.

"Listen, we are Resurrection Saints and the Resurrection Power flows in us. Mark, keep your hand pressing on Nikki's back. Sarah, your hand on his, mine on yours, Chris, Kay, come. Junto, put both your hands on ours. The scripture says, 'by my stripes you were healed.' Do you believe that is still true right now?"

They affirmed their faith.

"Then, all that is written for us, send that power and healing into Nikki."

They began to groan as if something was draining from them. Mark cried out, "My hand is burning."

"Lift your free hands to God and plead for Nikki's life!" Caleb cried.

A sound as a mighty rushing wind blew across them. Mark grabbed his hand away. "Ow!" he rubbed his hand.

"Look," Sarah exclaimed. "Her bleeding has stopped."

"Not only stopped, but the blood on her clothes and Mark's shirt is completely gone. An act of God!" Junto declared jubilant.

"Sarah, you must carry Nikki home," Caleb instructed. "Can you do it?"

"Yes." Sarah gently gathered Nikki in her arms and vanished.

Plomo and Rubin came to Caleb. They directed his attention to a sizeable group of millennials who stood broken, weeping, yet with the appearance of joy in their faces.

"These are the ones who believed tonight in Jesus Christ. They came to His Light."

"Praise the Lord," Caleb breathed a prayer from a grateful heart, not only for these saved but for Nikki's healing. He quickly scanned this group for Adam and Mee Antra. They weren't with these new believers.

"And the others?" he asked.

"We sent them fleeing into the jungle, as you ordered," Rubin said.

"Were Adam and Mee Antra among them?" Caleb feared the response.

"No," Plomo answered. "We searched carefully."

"Sorrow flooded Caleb's spirit for those who choose the darkness, but hope sprang up. His grandson and Mee Antra weren't seen with them.

"Take these new believers with us and find where they belong. The warfare is over," Caleb proclaimed to the army.

CHAPTER 61

WHERE IS ADAM

A week passed with no word from Adam and Mee Antra. Life continued in Lugar de Paraiso. The battle in the jungle was victorious for King Jesus' champions and news quickly spread among the millennials to cast away even a fleeting consideration of joining any rebel movement. Peace again settled in the resort town and the village of Vera Cielo.

Caleb and Mark left the house for the Civic Center to check on a teaching class with the new millennial believers. Both of the men were to speak to the group; then they would go to the transporter Station. Mark needed to finish up a few minor tasks.

Sarah and Nikki decided to stay indoors instead of braving the rising heat out on the open patio. The women took cold drinks and found a comfortable sofa. Conversation was mostly adrift, centered on inconsequential topics, because they both wished to avoid discussion of the one issue that dominated every thought. There was no putting it out of their minds; it barged right back in. Rest had been stripped from them; a snarling wolf hunted them every waking moment. A resolution eluded them because the answer was not there. They came in the meeting room to relax, but that wasn't happening. Nikki could take no more.

"Sarah, where can Adam and Mee Antra possibly be hiding?" Nikki blurted out. "It has been seven days since the battle."

"I don't know, Nikki. One moment I fear the worst and my mind caves in. The next, I hope and pray for a miracle. I have comfort from the Lord, but no answers." Sarah spoke softly. "I have rehearsed every possible scenario over and over in my head until I think my mind will explode. Nothing connects."

"There have been moments I get so angry at both of them," Nikki vented. "Why can't they call? Send a text or come home? When Adam was little, I could send him to his room. The difference then was that he was home. He was safe. I knew where he was. Now he is grown and it seems I have no influence or control over him. Is it right for me to be afraid for him and Mee Antra? Are we allowed to worry in the Millennium? I have cried so much this week; I've run out of tears, but not heartache. Sarah, I have no clue what I am supposed to do with all of this. Mark approaches it by saying they are adults and have to fend for themselves, yet my heart and mind reject that. I feel so helpless."

Sarah did not speak. She was void of answers. Both women stared silently into space, thoughts racing, pushing at their minds, brute images demanding dominance. In the jumbled mix, suddenly a seemingly out of place poignant memory emerged in Sarah's.

"I thought we had lost Mark twice," she began slowly. "The first was ugly and so unsettling. Mark and his father had a horrible fight. Mark beat Caleb with merciless force. Mark ran away and I was sick at heart. Caleb was angry and lost. I felt caught in the middle of two warring men. To complicate matters, even back then were whispers of evil people and activities deep in the jungle. I lived on the verge of panic for days. I rejoiced the day he came home. All the bad disappeared and I was mom again. No anger, no hurt, love overflowed and he was my little boy. I sang to him as he slept."

Nikki sat silent. A tear trickled down her cheek. She brushed it away.

"The second time was terrifying. The furry of Hurricane Chantal was coming down on us. Caleb begged people to go up to Vera Cielo mission as God had instructed him. Most of the people in Lugar de Paraiso rejected Caleb's plea, including Mark. While the violent tempest raged against the mission, and as I felt its force and saw the fears of the people around me, my heart grew faint with fear for my son. Where was he? Was he safe? I cried out to God over and over for him, and for all of us.

"But the real horror began when we came back down the mountain. Dead bodies were strewn everywhere like castaway driftwood. I went with Caleb for a while to try and identify the dead. I died a thousand deaths over every body we came upon. I have never known such utter fear. When I would turn over, O dear Lord, the remains, and the hollow lifeless eyes looked up at me? Each time I feared it would be my child, and my heart stopped. I could take no more and retreated to the shelter that had been set up. Bless his heart, Caleb kept searching for both of us."

Both women sat quietly for a long time. What else could they do? Just wait? Wonder? Hope? It ground on their nerves. Nikki curled up in a ball on the sofa and tried to sleep. An hour or more passed.

Noise from the patio door sliding open startled them.

"Is someone there?" Sarah called out. Nikki sat up.

"It's me," a very weak voice answered. Mee Antra walked into the meeting room. She was badly bruised on her face, arms and legs. She stumbled, but caught hold of the back of a chair.

Sarah and Nikki leaped up and steadied her. Slowly they helped her to sit down. They were full of questions.

"Merciful God, what happened?" Sarah asked.

"He beat me!"

"Adam?" Nikki grabbed the distraught woman's hands.

"Yes," Mee Antra began weeping. "Over and over. He hit me with his fist; he slapped me on the head, punched me and kicked me when I fell. I have never seen him so angry. He is violent and cruel." Mee Antra could not go on. She was shaking uncontrollably.

Sarah and Nikki held her and waited until she settled down. Nikki questioned her softly when she thought the time appropriate.

"Do you know where Adam is now?" she asked.

"No," Mee Antra whimpered.

"Why did Adam do this to you?" Sarah questioned.

Mee Antra covered her face and groaned.

"Do you know?" Sarah pressed.

"Yes," Mee Antra sobbed.

"Can you share what it is?"

244

Mee Antra shook her head back and forth. She pulled away from Nikki and held her hands up in protest. Sarah kept her tightly encircled in her arms and her voice softened.

"How can we help you, if we don't know?" Sarah spoke low. "Please, Mee Antra. Tell us. What happened?"

Mee Antra was silent, downcast.

"Please, Mee Antra. We are here for you. We love you."

With that, the woman broke down again. 'What happened to cause such pain for Mee Antra and ignite such cruel anger from Adam?' Sarah wondered. They waited until the weeping ceased and Mee Antra grew limp in Sarah's arms.

"Please, Mee Antra," Sarah urged.

Mee Antra swallowed hard. "I told Adam I was pregnant with his baby," she could barely be heard, but sat up to face them. Sarah and Nikki were stunned. Mee Antra continued.

"He flew into such a fit, I ran away for fear he would kill me or hurt the baby." Her face scrunched up. "I didn't know what to do. I felt rejected and abandoned. I truly thought Adam would be happy, not curse me, not beat me and drive me and our baby away."

"Are you sure?" Nikki asked.

"Yes. I'm starting to show and missed two periods."

"Will you go to your family in Texas?" Sarah asked.

"I have no family there. They disowned me already. My sin disgraces them. They cast me out when I –."

Nikki, who had been closely studying Mee Antra, dropped on her knees in front of this young woman and took her hands.

"Then we will be your family." Nikki peered intently into Mee Antra's moist eyes. "But there is something you must do first.

"I, too, felt abandoned when my parents disappeared. I just knew they would come back, but they didn't. Mark found me and rescued me. We were scared and alone, but we found a Father who would never, never, abandon us.

"There on the beach near the ocean, we believed in Jesus and the sacrifice He made for us. We felt our separation from Him and knew *our* sin, not anyone else's, kept us apart. We asked Him to forgive us and believed He died on the cross,

245

shedding His blood just for us, to make us free. Suddenly, we felt His love and forgiveness. He drew us to Himself and made us His children. Would you like to have a Father like that and be His child?"

"Will He have me?" Mee Antra doubted. "I am not married."

"No mistake you can make is too enormous that God won't forgive, nor stain too deep He can't wash clean. Not even in the Millennium."

"I feel so alone. I do want Him. I believe all the things I've heard about Jesus. I never went to the Temple, but there were times I thought I heard Him calling me. I call out to Jesus now. I believe; oh, save me Jesus!"

Mee Antra wept out her confession of sin and declaration of faith, and she was transformed into a believing millennial. She cried for a long time, not in pain or sorrow, but of joy in newfound forgiveness and acceptance. Sarah and Nikki held her for the longest time, sharing in her excitement.

The three women were now engaged in chatter, bubbling over with jubilant discussion about what God had just done. That is what they were doing when Caleb and Mark burst into the house. The men stopped in shock.

"Mee Antra?" both echoed. "What happened to you?" Caleb gasped, seeing her cuts and bruises.

"I'll tell you later, but Mee Antra just became a believer," Sarah said, thrilled.

"Wow! That's tremendous, Mee Antra. We, too, are thrilled," Caleb responded. "What an important step of faith you have taken."

"We don't know where Adam is," Nikki added sadly.

"We do." Mark went to Nikki and sat down next to her. He reached for her hand. "We just came from the Transporter Station. Rosaretta told us. A group of tourists came to transport and she was sure Adam was among them. She checked the register as they left. Adam listed his name as Mee Antra."

"What?" Mee Antra couldn't believe this.

"Where, Mark?" Nikki turned to him in shock.

"Chicago," Caleb answered.

CHAPTER 62

GOING HOME

The family gathered at the Transporter Station, and many others came to say goodbye to Mark and Nikki.

And where do goodbyes begin? Start first with the least-known, then closer friends, and finally family? Or should the whole group just wave and blow kisses? Had anyone thought farewells would be easier in the Millennium? Even now an element of sadness followed every goodbye. Caleb remembered a statement his Grandpa Farmer said: "Reckon one of the things folks fear most is separation." Caleb had dreaded this day and he knew Sarah did also. But, here it was and people began coming to Mark, Nikki and Mee Antra.

Erma and Tyrone, Mark's workers came first. Erma hugged her bosses, but was so emotional she couldn't speak. Tyrone thanked them both and shyly whispered to Mee Antra, "If that Adam don't come around, you remember, I'll take care of you and your baby."

The old Global Missions church gathered around Mark and Nikki with tender thank you's and goodbyes. Chris grabbed Mark by the shoulder and gave a gentle shake as he spoke. "Last time we were together, I was whisked away. This time, you are whisked away. I love you as my own."

"Nikki, don't you wait a hundred years to come back, you hear?" Kay joked through tears.

Junto Angeles' eyes sparkled as the old man took Mark and Nikki's hands and held them. Nothing was voiced but a bond of what the three had come through was deeply sensed. Junto turned to Mee Antra, gently touched her tummy and looked deeply into her eyes.

"You are a precious child of the Lord Jesus," he said.

A leading spokesman for the city stepped forward to make a declaration.

"Mark and Nikki, the City of Lugar de Paraiso wishes to express their deepest gratitude for the work you have done here. The construction and completion of this Transporter Station has been a work of art, a labor of love and nothing short of a miracle. Your project is changing the face of our resort town and the village of Vera Cielo."

"Hear, hear!" the crowd clapped and shouted.

"Our population is growing, and we are seeing new homes and distribution outlets. Soon we will have our own marina and a second hotel. We stand in agreement. Thank you, Mark and Nikki Hillag."

Caleb felt a deep sense of love and pride as he and Sarah stepped close to say goodbye to their kids and newfound granddaughter.

"I'm missing you already," Sarah cried as she hugged Mee Antra, Nikki and Mark. She patted the young woman's face. "You will have a beautiful baby and we will be there with you. I promise." She held her son and daughter-in-law. "You can come here any time you want now, and just as fast." They laughed.

Caleb held Mee Antra. "Adam will turn. It may take a thousand years, but he will turn. Trust me. He is a Hillag."

Next was Nikki. He looked into her face. "Nikki," his voice was husky. "I have thanked God over and over again for saving you for my son."

"Me, too," she whimpered.

"Son, I am so proud of the man you have become." Caleb drew Mark close.

"Thank you, Dad," Mark responded in love.

It was time to depart. Audio, Rosaretta, Mickey and Josh escorted Mark, Nikki and Mee Antra to the Station and said their goodbyes. Then, the three travelers, reluctant to leave, yet eager to return home, walked inside the Transporter with their luggage. The door locked shut and they were gone.

CHAPTER 63

CALEB AND SARAH'S REIGN

Caleb and Sarah didn't immediately return home, but decided to walk the streets of the city they knew as their Millennium home.

"I can't believe ten years have passed so quickly," Sarah murmured.

"Nor I." Caleb took her hand. The couple strolled along in thoughtful silence. A thousand memories raced across the threshold of their minds. Each scene of the past cast its vision, hoping to be the one captured by its owner and held precious, lingering for a moment.

The pair stopped in passing a building marked with a sign, 'Food Center.'

"This is where the church once stood," Caleb remarked.

Sarah let go of Caleb's hand and came close to him. "Do you remember the first time you preached here?" She looked up at him.

"Vaguely. I mostly see their faces. All of them."

"I was so proud of you. There was strength in your message, confidence in your voice. You were my man then as you still are now." Sarah squeezed his arm.

Caleb kissed and held her awhile before they resumed walking.

"I do miss preaching," Caleb continued. "Teaching Millennials is not the same.

"True." Sarah smiled. "But what was it you did with them in the jungle?"

Caleb stopped with the realization. "That was preaching!"

Sarah laughed. "No, I call it thunder!"

As they continued, both slipped into a serious, melancholy mood.

"What's going to happen?" Sarah turned to search Caleb's eyes. "Here? Our family? The future?"

Caleb gazed towards Vera Cielo Mountain, as though trying to peer ahead eight hundred and fifty-six years. "Lugar de Paraiso will fill in and expand all the way up this slope to the base of the mountain. Coastal jungle will be cleared to make room for more homes and services. I predict our inlet will become a marina with fancy hotels to accommodate the influx of tourists. It will change, Sarah, as we will change."

"How can we change, Caleb? We are resurrected."

Caleb thought for a minute before he answered. "It will be by our family. Families are in constant change. Ever-moving, expanding, each new member presents a different set of challenges. Each with their own story."

"What will happen to Adam?" Sarah spoke low. "Mee Antra will present us with a new grandchild?"

"Yes." Caleb led Sarah to a bench. They sat a long time without talking. The sun behind them made the water of the Gulf come alive with yellow light. The waves seemed to be engaged in a playful dance with the white beach sand every time it washed ashore; a scene Caleb and Sarah had viewed over and over, yet each time held its own uniqueness; a significance that would blend with the moment's mood. It did that just now.

"The water is peaceful." Sarah nodded towards the beach. "How different it is in the Millennium. As God promised never to flood the earth again, we have had no horrible hurricanes. The whole world is still, yet ever in motion. Caleb, necessity will dictate we travel a lot."

"How so?"

"By the end, can you imagine how huge our family will be? We would need a millennium number of Grands just to name them and a millennium just to make the rounds."

Caleb laughed and hugged his sweetheart. "Our reign becomes a legacy," he declared.

SEGMENT FOUR

TIME OF UNREST

CHAPTER 64

SHADES OF DARKNESS

The year 666 seemed to hold significance for millennial dissenters; however, they were not exactly sure what it would be. Was it revenge Satan wanted over the loss of the monster antichrist he had created? Was it the devil's attempt to hold onto this unholy mark he had viciously imposed on mankind? Would it be his way of influence over his growing number of followers from the darkness of the deep pit where he sat in chains? Or could it be the rising hope of the rebel millennials that this was the year their master would burst forth from his prison and lead in battle to a victorious overthrow of the Millennial Kingdom of Christ?

Regardless, Adam was keenly aware of the year when he stepped forth from the Transporter Station in Albany, New York. This had been paramount in his thoughts for months, but for now he needed to focus on the task at hand.

It was a balmy June afternoon. Adam had dressed light but rugged for hiking. Travelers filled the Station and forced Adam to push his way along as he searched for his contact. There would be no sign held up and the few Tribulation Saints in the crowd with their angels made him nervous. His presence here must not be disclosed.

Through the maze of people, Adam caught sight of a young millennial by the walkway wall. The young man was searching faces as travelers hurried by. Adam approached the millennial and halted before him.

"Are—are—you Adam Hillag?" the millennial gulped. Adam nodded.

"Hi, I'm Temblar, your escort to the meeting location. Was your trip from Chicago pleasant?"

Adam spoke not a word but followed his escort down the long walk and into a broad parking area. They stopped by a green AWD double cab pickup. Temblar took Adam's duffle bag, threw it in the rear seat and opened the passenger door for Adam to climb in. He took note of the mud caked on the sides of the vehicle. It was obvious the meeting was not downtown Albany.

"Where are we going?" Adam asked bluntly.

Temblar turned the air pickup on. Adam waited for an answer, leveling a steely cold stare on his escort.

"I. I." Temblar shuffled his body in the seat and avoided eye contact. He started to move the shift lever to back out when Adam grabbed his hand and held it in a tight grip.

"Where are we going?" Adam demanded.

Temblar grew red-faced and his eyes appeared to bulge with fear.

"I was instructed not to divulge our destination."

Adam's jaw dropped. He felt the hair on his neck stand up.

"They also wanted me to blindfold you as soon as we are out of the City."

"What? Why?" Adam snarled.

Temblar swallowed hard before crying out, "They don't trust you. Oh, I'm sorry, but they don't trust you."

"Then why the heck did they invite me?" Adam muttered as he released Temblar's hand. "Look at me," Adam ordered. "And you? What about you?"

"I have heard about you for several years." Temblar faced Adam. "You are notorious among millennials. How you arrived in Chicago from nowhere. Unknown, yet you gathered millennials who wanted to run away, forsake and leave Christ's Kingdom. You inspired your followers to rebel. You rose to power and I have heard it spoken, 'you have become an emissary of our Master Lucifer.' I fear you more than I trust you." His voice had diminished to a squeak.

Adam sat back. "Temblar, drive. There will be no blindfold and you will tell me everything you know about this meeting." Adam's tone made it clear he wasn't fooling.

The two men drove on in silence. Temblar was nervous to the degree of being sick. He was trapped between the orders of his peers and objections to the contrary of a powerful Millennial from Chicago.

A few miles out of Albany, Temblar left the freeway and took secondary roads, narrow and less-traveled.

"Where are we going?" Adam asked again. Temblar dared not evade the question a third time.

"We are going high into the Catskill Mountains to a campground. It is one of the oldest in the state.

"Why this campground?"

"Remote. It is named Devil's Tombstone Camp. It gives access to the twenty-one mile Devil's Path Trail. It is on a freshwater stream."

"Why this campground?" Adam sensed interest besides what Temblar had voiced.

"There is a giant-sized natural granite formation on the campground that resembles a tombstone. We believe Satan will rise from the grave at the Devil's Tombstone. Uh, well, when he returns in power."

Adam digested that information for a few miles before he spoke again. "How long before we arrive?"

"An hour, maybe more. We will climb into the mountains and the road is curvy."

"How many millennials will show up for this meeting?" Adam asked.

"We are a strong band with powerful leaders. Over a thousand will gather, easy."

No more was said. Adam had no desire to engage in frivolous conversation. His only wish for Temblar was that he get him to this meeting and return him to the Transporter in Albany. He forced his mind onto the speech he was to give and rehearsed his words until he fell asleep.

CHAPTER 65

CAMPGROUND MEET

"Wake up, Mr. Hillag. We are here." Temblar tugged on Adam's arm.

Adam blinked, trying to connect to where he was. He sat up to be greeted by dozens of curious millennial's faces trying to catch a glimpse of this famous Chicago visitor through the truck windows. He climbed out of the pickup, retrieved his duffle bag and slammed the truck doors. He followed Temblar into the noisy multitude. The meeting attendance was massive. Millennials were everywhere; some were armed with knives, clubs and a few ancient weapons.

The campground was crowded, and rebels filled in spaces among the trees. Adam knew he would have to shout to be heard. Suddenly, the crowd stepped back, revealing a strange man Adam perceived to be their leader. He was dressed in a long black robe with hoodie pulled over his head. He stood firm with feet planted apart and his hands on his hips. The expression on his face spelled defiance.

'You've got to be kidding!' Adam shook his head. He strode up to the man and held unflinching eye contact.

"I am Droid Millennial Xeno, the powerful leader of this activist band," he growled, raising his arms and turning for all his admirers to see. There were claps and cheers. Adam stepped close to Xeno and promptly slapped his face with a smarting blow, then yanked his hood off his head. The crowd gasped and started to close in. Adam with a sweep of his hands waved them back and demanded silence.

Adam got in Xeno's face and screamed, "Power? Power? Where do you think you can get power? Our Master Satan sits in chains in a deep abyss. Do you think he can dispense power from there? No! As long as he is chained, he has no power, unless you all get busy and smart. You egotistical idiot, I would think your power would have come with brains. Unless, and I repeat, unless, our leader is not returning. So, Xeno, I want your mouth shut—totally, and I will instruct all of you what must be done."

"Temblar, move your pickup here so I can stand in the back and be seen. Xeno, get rid of your ridiculous outfit. We need to blend in, not stand out, and I mean now. Burn them."

Adam waited while Temblar positioned his truck. Xeno disappeared in humility. The crowd could see why Adam had whipped together such a fighting force of millennials in Chicago, and they instantly respected this 'take charge' guy, hanging on his every word. He climbed onto the bed of the truck and stood upright with strong resolve.

"Eons ago the greatest rebellion of all times took place," Adam began. "Lucifer was fed up with the way God ran heaven. He wanted to rule his own kingdom, so he built his own army of angels. Sadly, they lost, but not completely. God granted him a kingdom on earth. All went well for a while and Lucifer ruled as he wished. But then, God created a man and woman and gave them dominion, and gave Lucifer a new name, one of contempt: Satan.

"So, the question arose, 'Whose world is this anyway? God's or Satan's?' Hence the battle began again; but listen, we can learn from what we know."

"As the world populated, more and more humans followed Satan. They wanted him to rule, but what did a loving God do? He killed them all and gave the kingdom to eight humans. Eight! So let us learn. How to defeat God? Everyone rebel and make His Kingdom unfit.

"So the earth repopulates again and over time everyone wanted to follow Satan. What did God do this time? He said he wouldn't destroy mankind by water, but what did He do? He gave the Kingdom to His Son, Jesus Christ. Well, conditions deteriorated to the point where Jesus just took all His followers away to heaven.

"Satan took over and everyone was giving allegiance to him their new king. What did God do? Wiped them all out and gave the Kingdom back to His favorite Son, Jesus Christ—and that is where we are today. Today! Yes! Now! This Year of 666; our coming out year; our year of release."

Adam stopped to study his listeners' faces before he continued.

"Think on these possibilities," Adam screamed to the mass of millennials. "Here is what must be done—here—all over the world.

"Recruit, recruit, recruit. What if all Millennials turned away and against Christ? He would have nobody. Or, what if there is such a vast number of rebels demanding their own country, or kingdom? There is strength in numbers. Multiply our army.

"And, speaking of army, you must arm yourselves with effective modern weapons. Be smart. I was with a group of rebels once. Saw them raided. It wasn't the millennials that defeated the rebels. It was the Resurrection Saints and their angels. They can't be killed, but we can. Those millennials had Tribulation lasers, and they lost. Our weapons must be the darkness. Every night, somewhere, sabotage city infrastructures. Strike and disappear. Strike and disappear.

"One last thing. Remember, if only one of God's promises is broken, His Kingdom will collapse. It has been tried before, unsuccessfully.

"God said Christ would be born a tiny baby. Herod had all the babies in Bethlehem murdered.

"He said Christ would not die but give His life as a sacrifice on the cross. Men tried over and over to kill Him.

"God proclaimed His chosen people would always be on the earth. Hitler tried in vain to eliminate every Jew from the face of the earth.

"So, what broken promise would end Christ's Kingdom forever? There is no death in the Millennium. So what if just one—just one millennial was killed? One life sacrificed so that our glorious master would rise and usher in his kingdom?"

Adam raised both arms high with clenched fists; the millennial sign of revolt in the very face of the Living God.

CHAPTER 66

HOME FRONT

Mark stormed through the front door of his log home. Anger clouded his face. He slammed the door behind him.

"Mark?" Nikki called from the large family room.

The instant Nikki and Mee Antra saw Mark, they knew something was wrong.

"What happened?" Nikki sat up.

"I am deeply vexed in mind and soul." Mark fell into a chair.

"Was it the meeting?"

"Yes! If you could call what went on that. Long ago they ceased from productive discussions for improvement of our communities to senseless debates and arguments. At times, like today, fights break out."

"Goodness." Mee Antra was alarmed. "Was my son there? Any of his family?"

"Yes, Abel was there but none of his boys or grandkids. John came in late with Ezra and Joel," Mark answered.

"Were any of our family involved?" Nikki asked, knowing her son's brash responses.

"Some of the Hinkleman boys started it." Mark related the story of what happened. "They have been growing adversaries to the Kingdom's work and even our Lord's rules. The split between believing millennials and non-believers is the deepest I have ever seen it. The Hinklemans attempted to rally support for their cause even among the believers. They came down hard on Abel."

"How? Is he unharmed?" Fear gripped Mee Antra.

"Abel is tough. Gavin Hinkleman was nose-to-nose with Abel demanding to know, with his dad Adam such an advocate for rebellion against the system, why wasn't he joining them in the cause? Abel steadfastly stood his ground and declared his faith in the Lord Jesus Christ. At the mention of that Name a brawl broke out. One of the millennials rushed Abel to strike a blow; John intercepted the attacker and knocked him flat. Oh, Nikki, this is becoming like it was before the Rapture."

Mee Antra stood in sullen silence, staring at the floor.

"The meeting quickly escalated out of control. Tribulation Saints and their angels used force to bring order and demand silence. There were but ten of us present, and the unbelieving millennials don't respect us. It is our angels they fear and detest. It came to me today as I studied their faces and watched the angry ones' reactions to the angels. They have something to hide. What was done in secret in the dark jungle years ago, must be far more wicked today."

"How can this be, in a perfect world, Mark?" Nikki cried out. "It contradicts the very meaning of the term 'perfect world.' I can't wrap my head around this."

"It is a perfect world, Nikki, in spite of appearances. No pollution, sickness, death, we age so slowly, our bodies will last one thousand years. Everyone has work to do, food is abundant, beautiful clothes to wear, solar and air cars or we can transport anywhere in the world. The problems and dissention only occurs within the millennials. Today, I was rudely confronted by how bold and outspoken they have become, especially the younger generations."

"What's all the hullabaloo about?" Shag walked into the room.

"Dissention broke out in the Applegate men's meeting and erupted into a fight. I can't understand this anger and rebellion in a perfect world," Nikki related.

Shag stroked his beard in thought before he spoke. "Ye can't ignore what the Scriptures say. In Revelation Chapter twenty it says, 'When the thousand years end, Satan will be let out of his prison. He will go out to deceive the nations, and gather them together for battle. A mighty host; and this next part we must pay attention to, for it is what is foretold." Shag's eyes blazed. The old Viet Nam Vet's face was grave, and the three adults saw it and immediately sensed Shad had something of utmost importance to share, which they needed to hear.

"A mighty host, as numberless as the sands along the shore," Shag continued. "What did that say? Numbers like the sands on the beach? Well now, just think, missy girl, Millennium year seven hundred twenty-two with a world population at four billion, and most of those are millennials, Mee Antra, like you. Consider, Mark and Nikki, the size your family has grown to from just your three children. You could fill Cloverdale time and time again."

Mark and Nikki laughed and had to agree.

"So." Shag hitched up his pants and took a deep breath. "I ask you a question, and Mee Antra, girl, you won't understand this but don't fret. In our 'before' years we were familiar with this passage, so how did we think on it? Would the world populate and when Satan is released would millions and millions like the seashore sands instantly be fooled and follow the devil, or would a process of insurrection take place over years. Which would it be and why?"

"You're right," Mark was catching on, "and Mee Antra holds the key."

"I do?" she questioned.

"I'm confused," Nikki voiced. "Why would Christ allow this to happen? Millennials everywhere are rising up against Him."

"Your daddy knew, Mark, and told it at John and Johanna's birthday party."

"Yes, he did. I remember and had forgotten. He said of all people who have ever been born and lived, all have had to have faith in Christ and believe in what He did on the cross. All had to come to repentance, accept and believe."

"It would be totally unfair to all of them, to us, if the Millennials were exempt," Nikki spoke thoughtfully.

"All of them was done born of Tribulation Saints and the sin nature passed on, so they are capable of sinning," Shag added.

"Christ is giving them the freedom to choose," Nikki murmured.

"Like I had to do." Mee Antra smiled. "I'm so glad I did."

"To answer my question," Shag concluded, "it can't be millennials living a perfect life, because in our perfect world, they are the only group that lives and breeds imperfection. Sin can't exist a thousand years and not sin. Freedom would not permit that to happen. The number of years holds no sway on decisions to be made, but freedom to choose allows it, by God's love and grace in a perfect world."

After Shag went outdoors, the three sat in silence with racing minds. Mee Antra was the first to speak.

"Gavin Hinkleman spoke of Adam to Abel. Where could Adam be? I have waited five hundred and seventy-eight years for Adam to come back to me. Yes, I count, and those times I thought to forget him and our love, it grows ever stronger. My heart won't let me give up on love or let it die."

"An unbearable truth, Mee Antra." Mark grew sad. "It has been that long since we heard anything on Adam. All the times I transported to Chicago to find him I came away empty."

"Do you think these rebel millennials know of him and are not telling us?" Mee Antra wondered.

"I could swear to it," Mark replied.

"There is one hope I cling to that Grandpa Caleb said to me when we left Lugar de Paraiso. 'Adam will turn. It may take a thousand years, but he will turn. He is a Hillag.'"

CHAPTER 67

MILLENNIAL SUBCULTURE

A dam stepped out of a newly installed Transporter Station, one of fifteen, in the reconstructed former Greyhound Bus Station of Detroit, Michigan. The night was stormy. Adam looked up into a starless sky and a brush of rain pelted his face. He pulled the hood of his long black overcoat over his head. Winter was here and the air bit his hands and face.

Adam walked through the Transporter gateway and spotted an expensive air car limo parked curbside. The limo driver climbed out of the car, pulled his coat close across his chest, opened the rear door and stood at attention.

"Hillag?" The man greeted him in a deep gruff voice.

Adam nodded and got into the plush air car. Inside were drinks and an assortment of delicacies. To his shock, a young, beautiful millennial woman was seated provocatively in the seat facing him. Adam bristled!

"Hello, my name is –." She smiled.

"Don't tell me your name," Adam barked.

"I, I was sent to entertain you," the woman continued.

"I don't need entertainment. Get out!" Adam was threatening.

"But, but, my boss will be upset if I –."

"I care nothing about what your boss thinks or where you will go. Get out! Driver, I want this woman gone."

By now the driver was next to Adam. "Please, don't make this difficult."

"I didn't send for her."

"I'm trying to find a solution," the driver stammered. "Would it be permissible for the young lady to sit up front with me?"

"Does this limo have a barrier wall?"

"Yes."

"Is it opaque?"

"You mean no see-through? Yes."

"Thank you. Close it up and let her in." Adam motioned them away.

When they were underway, Adam stared out the window at a rain-drenched scene. However, he was fully cognizant of the route they were taking and his surroundings.

The limo left the Station and took side streets a short distance until entering the 10 express way. A few miles later the road veered off on an exit lane to the '94.' Adam saw an overhead road sign, Edsel-Ford Freeway. Before long, they passed a sign that read Dearborn. Now Adam knew they must be close to his destination. Soon the limo took an exit and drove onto highly maintained two-lane roads to enter an Auto Industrial Park. The factories were gigantic and first-class. It was obvious this was the birthplace of many of the world's trucks, solar and air cars.

Into this vast maze of parking lots and huge manufacturing plants, the limo drove. Without warning, the air car turned onto a smaller street running alongside one of the plants. It inched along as if searching; then turned a short distance and stopped beside an alley that was as dark as a cave. The driver came around to let Adam out of the limo.

"You are here." The driver attempted a smile.

"Where?"

"In there." The driver pointed into the pitch-black.

The limo drove away, leaving Adam to ponder his next move. He perceived the driver was either off \-point or had clear instructions to drop him at this location. If that were true, someone knew he had arrived and was now monitoring his movements. He cautiously walked into the blackness, feeling his way along, moving his hands back and forth in front of him.

"Welcome to Detroit, Michigan," a creepy voice came from the dark alley ahead of him.

"This is Dearborn?" Adam countered.

"Dearborn, Dearborn Heights, Inkster, River Rouge, one and the same to us bums. All Detroit."

A light flashed on, shining at Adam's feet.

"Walk behind the light so you don't fall down, Hillag. Follow me."

Adam walked down the alley keeping close to the lighted spot. The flashlight was fairly directional, so he could not make out much of his surroundings or his host who carried it. Soon Adam was relieved to see a door swing open to reveal a lighted hallway. His host switched the light off and motioned Adam into the hallway.

"So, you are the mighty feared and fearless Adam Hillag." The man held out his hand. "My name is Monte Mole. The last part is not a nickname. My vengeful parents named me that because I look like one. Oh, and I grew up in the dark."

Adam slowly shook Mole's hand, all the while taking stock of the person with whom he was to conduct future business and act as liaison.

Monte Mole was a wiry, shriveled-up millennial. His skin was pale, yet his hands and the sides of his face were dark and hairy. He wore boots, jeans with a tee shirt, covered by a warm black leather jacket. Adam was soon to find out, although small of frame, Mole was strong. His movements were quick and agile, especially in the dark. Monte was as fast with his tongue and carried an air of being tough, and street-smart.

The two proceeded down the long hall to doublewide doors. There was a small window on each side, which Monte proceeded to glance through. He checked his watch.

"It is between shifts and the plant is down and empty for one hour. We have this open window four times a day," Monet explained.

"To do what?"

"You'll see. Come with me now. Quickly!"

Monte and Adam burst onto the plant's floor and ran along an air car assembly line. The whole factory was lit up so completely it illuminated every part and corner; there were no shadows. The brightness appeared to be painful to Mole, as he shielded his eyes.

Far into the manufacturing assembly plant, Monte crossed a parts line and dropped to his knees. Adam could see a small door with a heavy-looking floor level lock. Monte pulled out a key and unlocked the door, pulling it up and open. "Hurry," he invited.

Adam looked. They were at the top of a long-forgotten ladder leading down into the underbelly of the plant. Adam began his descent and Mole came after him, locking the heavy plate door.

When Adam stepped onto the floor, he turned to look around. He was amazed. This was an area as large as the plant above and equally well-lit. Cars were everywhere; some in stalls, others on hoists, many in pieces, and some in mint classic condition. Monte joined him.

"What is this?" Adam questioned. "Who are you?"

"We are rebel underground millennial racers." Monte scrunched up his face in a grin.

"All I see are solars, the turtles of the car industry."

"Not these. They are modified." The two began walking "I'll show you."

"Why here?"

"No one would ever look here. This is just an empty, worthless basement to the jerks upstairs. Not even Jesus knows about us, unless someone tells him." Mole gave Adam a long, hard stare.

"We aren't on speaking terms." Adam turned his attention to the racers and their cars.

"We use their power. They have never suspected; they just believe they use lots of wattage. Ha!"

"You race these cars? Where? I hear of no millennial races anywhere."

"Rather boring, wouldn't you say? We street race, late at night, in the back streets and off roads. We have a secret ramp to sneak our cars out onto. Pow, and we are gone."

Monte led Adam into one of the stalls and interrupted a millennial mechanic.

"This is Oliver Knor, one of our rebuilders. Oliver, this is Adam Hillag, an emissary of our Master."

The millennial was cautious, but eager to make a good impression.

"Hillag says solars are slow," Mole added.

"Not these puppies." Oliver laughed. "We steal high torque industrial electric motors whenever we can find them. We match them with sophisticated gear ratio bands to the wheels. With no transmission, this motor just winds up and can blow the tires off these babies."

"How fast?" Adam was skeptical.

"This one when I finish, will clock a quarter mile at 155 in 7 seconds. High end will probably be around 250 MPH—and the batteries last all night."

"Impossible!" Adam gasped.

"It's true. Nothing on earth can touch them." Oliver grinned with pride.

"But I'm not here about cars," Adam reminded him. "You have a sub-culture of your own. How extensive is it?"

"Racing chapters are in many major cities all over the world, but mostly in this country," Monte answered. "All concealed, but growing. We can mobilize an army."

"That's what I am pleased to hear. Is there a way to bring them all together for a rally?"

"Glad you asked that." Mole wiped his mouth. "We have plans for a Grand Prix race. We only have to wait for the right time, when we can come out in the open."

CHAPTER 68

MERITY

Adam's SAT alarm went off. Squinting at the alarm light to see the time, he sat up on the side of the bed. His room was dark. He switched on a bedside lamp, making note of the time. '3:10 AM July 16, year 890.' He clicked his alarm off, rubbed his face and combed his dark hair with his fingers. He looked around, torn between wanting more sleep and being pressed for time to ready himself for one of his crowning achievements.

His motel room was plain in an older part of Mesa, Arizona. On a king-size bed, not the best sleep, but OK. Forty-inch flat screen mounted on one wall, two off-center desert-scene pictures on another wall, which Adam promptly straightened the first thing he walked into the room. There was also one desk and one dresser, both worn on the edges.

"Umph," Adam grunted. Not the plush style he was used to, but he picked this motel so as not to draw any attention to himself.

He took a quick cold shower, combed his hair and trimmed his beard much closer than usual to combat the day's 118-degree heat. Last, he brushed his teeth. As he checked himself in the mirror, he saw a tired millennial staring back at him. Were his eight hundred-eighty-eight years catching up to him? He smiled, thinking 'never understood my dad's and grandpapa's love of coffee, but today I might just figure it out.'

He dressed in a faded camp shirt, matching shorts, old and comfortable walking shoes, suited for the desert. He pulled out a crumpled-up hat from his duffle bag and tried to smooth its wrinkles.

He walked over to the window and peeked through tacky curtains. The night was dark. He turned to gather all his belongings into his duffle. As soon as his ride arrived, he would step out into the darkness and not return here. He sat on the bed to wait.

Exactly at 4:00 AM a light knock sounded on his door. He crammed his hat onto his head, grabbed his bag and pulled open the door. A young female millennial faced him. Adam eyed her with one swift glance; long, sandy hair in a ponytail, a round tan face, stout arms and legs, slightly overweight. She wore a pale pink tank top, denim shorts and lightweight, tan hiking boots.

"Hello," she smiled warmly. "I'm Merity." She held out her hand to Adam. He slowly responded and quickly realized Merity had a solid grip, which he was glad to have released.

"Are you ready?" she whispered, not taking her eyes off his.

He nodded, stepped outside of his room and closed the door behind him. He followed Merity to her car. She had the door open for him. He stopped in shock. This was not an air limo or cab—not even a passenger car. It was a two-seat race solar. The sky was turning grey in the east, allowing just enough light for Adam to study and admire some of the car's features. The workmanship was superb; with paint in rich, pale yellows and greens so thick he felt he could scoop it up in his hand. Headlights and top lights were covered with protective wire mesh, and enlarged taillights were mounted in the rear. The body was long and sleek with a low roofline. Solar panels filled the deck.

Adam stuffed his duffle bag in the small space behind his seat and slid in. The seats were made of fine leather. There was no headliner, but a padded roll bar ran only a few inches above his head. The dash and steering wheel were of a material new to Adam.

Merity climbed into the driver's seat and pulled on racing gloves. She studied Adam's face.

"You are surprised?" she asked.

"Yes, I am."

"Is it me or my car?"

"Both. They usually send a man and a limo, not a race solar," he muttered.

"Well, I'm it for today; and, solar, why not? We're going to a race," Merity commented, not looking at him. She flipped a switch and the dash and outside lights blasted to life. She pulled out of the motel and onto the Mesa surface streets. The car ran with a low but hefty hum. When Merity merged onto the freeway and accelerated, Adam could hear the electric motor start to whine. He had no doubt this car wanted to run.

The Interstate turned in an easterly direction. Rugged ridges that topped the mountains ahead were glowing in golden hues. Adam knew in a short time the sun would be shining in their eyes.

"Where are we going?" he asked.

"We are in Mesa on the Interstate that ends at Apache Junction. From there, we pick up Old Route 60. Twenty miles more and we take an off-road to King's Valley. The town was abandoned, so us racers took it over as our staging site. Lots of flat desert, little vegetation, all the racers will be there."

"How many?"

"Four hundred eighteen."

"Won't they be all over each other on a two-lane highway?"

"Sure, starting, but believe me, we will thin out."

"Are you racing? In this?" Adam was shocked.

"You got it! Is it a revelation that Millennial women race?"

Adam made no comment. He was over talking. He stared at the passing desert and its abundance of saguaro and yucca. 'What different and complex forests these make,' he mused.

"It's amazing, we organized this race in three short years." Merity smiled.

Adam frowned at her. "You speak from ignorance. This project started ninety-five years ago in Detroit."

"You don't like women, do you Mr. Hillag? And may I call you Adam?"

"No! And no, most of them I don't. I find them frivolous, superficial and giddy, like yourself."

Merity whipped over to the side of the freeway and screeched to a stop. "You pompous pig!" she yelled, and raised her hand to slap him.

Adam instantly threw up his open hand smacking her head against the window.

"Ow!" she cried.

"That was stupid. You have no idea of my powers."

"Get out," she demanded.

"I will not. You will drive me to the staging site at King's Valley as agreed," Adam growled.

Merity burst into tears.

"Is that what you do when it gets rough? How will you handle a real battle when that starts? And it will."

Merity wiped her eyes and then tightly gripped the steering wheel. She burned with anger.

"Drive," Adam ordered.

Merity turned to him, her eyes blazing. "I volunteered to drive you because no one else would and I wanted to meet you. I am using up precious battery charge that I need in this race; so if you want me to haul your butt to King's Valley, you'd better be nice to me. Nice, Mister! Not silent, but I will talk. I'm going to talk all the way there. You can listen or have civil conversation. No other options. Be considerate and talk to me. Comprende?"

Adam glared at his millennial driver. He saw the fire in her expression and determined in that instant she meant business. He decided not to war with her and softened his stance. He motioned for her to drive.

Merity accelerated into freeway traffic.

"How old are you?" she asked.

Adam was silent.

"Oh, come on, Adam—enough of the silent treatment. It is so juvenile. Are you twenty? Talk to me. Don't withdraw. Are you a leader or a coward?"

That tore a raw nerve in Adam. For the first time in decades, he teared up and stared out his window. "Eight hundred eighty-eight," he mumbled.

"Oh my gosh, you are a firstborn, Adam Hillag."

"Millennium year two," he answered. "And you?"

271

"I am one hundred forty-four. A mere child compared to you. I have seen so little, while you have experienced everything. The whole millennium!"

Merity was quiet as they drove into Apache Junction. Coming to a sign that denoted Route 60, Merity turned right onto a much older road that was weathered and worn. As homes were left behind and replaced with open desert, she picked up the conversation.

"Well, in all your eight hundred eighty-eight years, did you ever fall in love? Know a woman? Really? You know what I mean."

Adam turned and looked at her. "That's very personal."

Merity looked from the road to his face to the road. "The manner in which you answered tells me you did. What was her name?"

Adam was uncomfortable at digging in his past. He resisted any discussion of personal things, yet something compelled him to empty the baggage he had hidden for centuries. Yet, he was afraid if he once started, where would he stop; could he stop?

"You still love her, don't you? After all these years! She has your heart and no other woman can have it."

That did it! Adam broke. How could a young millennial get to him like this?

"Her name is Mee Antra," Adam spoke slowly. "We met in a Mexican resort town. Her parents were in Texas."

"You still love her?" Merity asked gently.

"Yes . . ."

"Did she leave you"

"No, I left her. We fought; I beat her."

"What would upset you so that you beat her and left? Was she cheating on you?"

"She was pregnant."

Merity was stunned. "What! What did you have?"

"I don't know."

"I can't understand, Adam. Why?"

"I didn't have time for that."

"What did you have time for?"

272

"I have only one mission. Preparing millennials for battle against Christ. Organizing, instructing, preparing an army for war. The rally after this race is our 'coming out in the open—showing our strength' movement. It is my crown and total focus.

CHAPTER 69

THE GREAT RACE

A simple, plain sign standing by a badly weathered narrow, paved road pointed to King's Valley. Merity pulled off of Route 60 onto this side road. Adam saw no evidence of any traffic going into King's Valley. He was about to ask if they were on the road leading to where four hundred-eighteen racing solars were supposed to be gathered, when Merity glanced at him and smiled. He would wait and see.

The sides of the pavement were deeply eroded from extreme temperatures. Broken holes pitted the road, making a rough ride. However, two miles into barren desert the paved road abruptly ended and a gravel, mainly graded dirt road took off into the desert. Adam was amazed to see at this juncture tire tracks going in all directions, hundreds of them.

"We are careful to make no tracks at the main highway, but out here, we cut loose."

Merity floored her solar! Adam's head snapped back and he was crushed against his seat.

"Wahoo!" she yelled.

The landscape on Adam's side instantly blurred as Merity swerved from side to side kicking up a massive dust cloud behind them. Small desert scrubs and cactus were flying towards the front faster than Adam could stand to see. His mind and emotion refused to comprehend this ferocity of sights and sounds, threatening to shut down, or even think, demanding he close his eyes.

The solar was shaking violently; then suddenly the ride became smooth as the car sailed through open air. Adam held on for his life, while Merity was having the time of hers. He studied her face a moment. She was quick and intent, watching for rocks, gullies, dodging cactus. His eyes went to the dash speedometer. It was climbing. One seventy; one eighty; one ninety.

'This crazed millennial is going to hit two hundred miles per hour,' Adam gasped. 'This insane bitch will kill us both.'

Topping a rise, Merity spun in several drift spins, bouncing to a swift halt overlooking a long, low valley spread out before them.

"There's part of your crown, big shot," she laughed. Her eyes danced with excitement.

The valley was crawling with movement, like when you stir up a major anthill. Solar cars crowded every available open space, their brilliant colors lighting the whole valley with spectacular life in contrast to the dull desert scene.

"Will I ever see you again?" Merity's demeanor changed from exhilaration of the race to a strange, unexpected sadness.

"Probably not. Some paths cross for a moment and it's over."

"I think it's depressing. Don't you ever wish for lasting relationships?"

Adam looked hard into her eyes. "Are you hitting on me?"

"You've got to be kidding! You are way too old for me. You could be my grand pappy, or great, great, great. You get the idea."

"Then what do you want?"

"Will you cheer for me? I know you will transport to the break points. When I come through will you be there for me . . . like family?"

Adam was taken aback.

"I am a rebel outcast and have never had anyone come to see me race."

Adam thought for a moment, while Merity waited in hopes for an affirmative answer.

"Will Monte Mole be racing here?"

"Monte is at every race and always wins. He never places less than third."

"Have you raced him before?"

"Only one time and he whipped my rear."

"Can you beat him today?"

"I don't know. He drives hard and fast."

"So do you. Where does he do the best and worst?"

"Unbeatable on the open desert, but he doesn't like the miles of tight mountain curves."

"That's where you have to beat him for speed and distance," Adam advised. "Can your car and you make the run non-stop?"

"I could try. What would I need?"

"Snacks and lots of water to drink. Plan to make a quick roadside stop, find a cactus. How about your solar?"

"The sun is going to be intense for a good steady charge, but hours of climbing and high speeds can be brutal on my batteries. I could be pushing it across the finish line."

"So if Monte gets tied up in break towns and you go non-stop?"

Merity looked puzzled.

"Do you want to beat him and win this race?"

"With everything I have."

"Then I will root and cheer for you, quietly."

Merity was thrilled and attempted to throw her arms around him in a hug. Adam blocked her. She sat back.

"I just wanted to hug you." She was hurt.

"Merity, I'll make you a deal. You beat Monte and I'll hug you, and believe me, that will be a first."

In a few minutes Adam was let out into a sea of millennial racers. He went off to find Monte Mole, while Merity connected with her pit crew.

Adam spied Monte by his car and walked quickly towards him. When Monte saw him, he opened his arms and his face broke out in his snarly grin.

"We did it!" he greeted Adam. "What do you think?"

"I'm impressed. What is the full extent of this group?" Adam asked.

"At least one racer from all fifty states and twelve internationals who brought their cars piece-by-piece through Transporter Stations. Some states have multiple entries. Each racer has a pit crew and their families and friends here, who will follow to the rest and break cities. But the wild part is that each of the racers' chapters is huge in cars and numbers and growing every week. Adam Hillag, we have formed a mobile army." Monte was ecstatic.

"Excellent, excellent." Adam was pleased.

"I must get back to my solar and crew. We are getting ready to move cars and drivers to the starting line. Stay close, Oliver will go with you on the Transporters."

Soon a general convergence of the racecars and drivers to the start line began. There was order and each team appeared to have knowledge of their position. Adam followed along with Mole's crew, keeping tabs on Oliver. For an instant, Adam spotted Merity and her team, and then she disappeared into the crowd.

The sun had now topped the mountain ridges and excitement in King's Valley was at a fevered pitch. Cars and drivers settled in their places and crews and all others were ordered to hillsides that lined the valley floor. A restrained hush fell over the throngs of people as they awaited final instructions. Clicking and tapping sounds emerged from the huge sound system. People milled about in anxious anticipation. Suddenly, a voice boomed across the valley.

"Welcome to our first ever Millennial Grand Prix Race. Listen carefully to the rules.

"This race will be run and completed today only. Each driver can stop at will, but there will be only two designated official stops. Those are: Springerville and Fort Sumner. Pit crews can only service cars there, but no other towns along the way. If there is car trouble or loss of a tire along the route, and the driver can locate, fix the problem with locals and get back in the race, that will be permitted. Otherwise you are out of the race. Remember, each driver can stop and start at will. It is your time."

"Now, let me reiterate the route map, which you each have. You are seeing this for the first time, so follow along with me and don't get impatient. Your batteries are charging."

Laughter followed his statement.

"Do not veer from this course. I repeat: do not deviate from this route. You will be disqualified. We are monitoring each racer.

"From this starting point, go towards the far end of this valley. There you will connect with Route 60. Do not fear being noticed. This is our 'coming out' time. Rebel Millennial Racers."

A roar arose from the crowds. Adam's heart swelled with pride.

"Your course takes you through Globe. From there, narrow winding roads follow along the Salt River Canyon, then you will climb high into the mountains, at times to elevations in excess of 4,000 feet. Route 60 will go through Show Low. Keep safety in mind always, as no one knows you are coming. Watch out for other cars and people in the streets.

"Proceed on to Springerville for your first rest break. At that point, you are close to the New Mexico border.

"In New Mexico, you will experience a difficult climb into the Gallo Mountains. Next, you cross the Continental Divide at Pie Town. Later you may take a brief rest and eat stop in Socarro, but there will be no pit crews there.

"Make note on your maps, stay off short segments of I-25, and remain on Old 60. It gets tricky there, so be alert. Proceed to Los Nutris, then head due east into the Los Pinas mountains. Remember, in the valleys and low places the heat will be excruciating, but the mountain air cool.

"Next comes one hundred-ninety miles of dangerous curves and blistering heat to test both car and driver to limits beyond their ability. There are only four towns you can stop in; but only Fort Sumner will allow your pit crew.

"The finish line is located at an abandoned Air Base from Tribulation days. Ten miles past St. Vrain, go south on an unmaintained road for sixteen miles. Watch carefully for this cutoff.

"Now, are you ready to race?"

The crowds roared with exuberance.

"Drivers, prepare your cars." There was a long pause. "Go!"

There was no roar of engines, but one could feel the ground vibrate with the power emitting from these solar racers. Dust and dirt roiled up as they tore out across the desert floor.

CHAPTER 70

DIFFERENT OPINION

Oliver had a rental air car for himself and Adam. The rest of the pit crew would haul equipment in their solar pickup to the finish line. They would arrive early tomorrow morning.

Oliver tried the Transporter Station in Apache Junction, but it was swamped with millennials from the race attempting to get to the rest points. Mesa was just as crowded, and Tempe Station was even worse. To beat the lines, Oliver took Adam fifteen miles west into Glendale. There, they turned in the Air Car and had a three-hour wait. He checked to see where they were on the schedule, and then came to where Adam was sitting.

"The Transporter Station in Springerville is small and overwhelmed with racers. We still are two hours away on the list." Oliver sat down. "But I thought of another problem: getting out of Springerville. So I checked on Fort Sumner and for an extra thirty minutes, we can transport there."

"What if Monte needs some repair when he comes through Springerville?" Adam questioned.

"He's on his own." Oliver laughed. "Hey, Mole is very resourceful and knows how to get things done. Believe me, we have the best solar in this race. Right now he is far in the lead, while half of the four hundred eighteen have blown tires, crashed, missed curves, went in the trees or over a cliff. He knows the racer and how to drive it to win. I'll text him we are waiting at Fort Sumner."

The town of Fort Sumner stood in stark contrast to its former condition in pre-Tribulation days. Back then it was a small town, rundown and struggling just to stay alive. Empty ghost shops, boarded-up, or with broken windows lined the main street that now bustled with lively activity. They got news of the race headed their way and cars were clearing sidewalk parking spaces making more room for the racers. Shops on the main road and even businesses on side streets were making ready for the influx of the pit crews, families, friends and the ever-growing gathering of on-lookers.

While Oliver walked away from the Transporter Station to explore, Adam found a quaint little café on one of the streets near the main highway. It boasted several tables and chairs on the sidewalk. Adam glanced behind him, noting he could watch for racers to pass by on the highway.

He chose a table and sat down, positioning himself to see the main street. An older millennial took his order, a light salad and vegetable drink. As he ate, a melancholy mood he was unfamiliar with settled into his thoughts. He tried to shake it off and mentally prepare for the rally that would take place in the morning. Yet this weird, annoying sadness persisted. If he entertained these feelings for even a moment, his mind wandered to the events of the morning and Merity. Was it interest in where she was in this race? Concern for her safety? No, why should he care? He didn't know her or a thing about her. That made him even sadder. Nothing, where she came from, lived now, what about her family? Family! That word fed his blue mood. That was crazy. That had nothing to do with anything!

"Yes, it does," he muttered. He suddenly realized he was strangely warming to the idea of a daughter, no granddaughter. Something foreign stirred inside him, making him uncomfortable; still, he liked it. No, it wasn't just Merity. She triggered something deeper, buried, forgotten.

Mee Antra! He teared up. Somewhere he had a son or daughter, and how many after that he knew nothing about or had even seen? Maybe a great, great-granddaughter, even someone like Merity. That thought opened a gaping hole in his heart, which birthed a longing he had never known before. It grew unbearable and he hated it.

"Hello, Adam Hillag."

Adam jumped, snapping out of his dream, looking into the face of an unknown millennial woman. She had striking blue eyes, dark tan skin. Her black hair was in a long braid that fell over her shoulder. Her shirt was of a lightweight western-style coarse cloth. Her worn leather pants were tucked into dusty cowboy boots. She sat down, facing Adam.

"I don't know you and don't recall inviting you to my table," Adam snarled.

"You didn't. I invited myself," she said and grinned.

Adam felt anger heating up, wondering why he should have any woman bothering him today. He was ready to get ugly!

"You can dismiss me, Adam, with a wave of your hand and I'll leave you alone. However, should you make that choice, you will never know who I am, why I am here, or who sent me, and you will always wonder . . ."

Adam stared at her a long time. The woman didn't blink, but matched his stare. Finally, Adam averted his eyes, and motioned her to proceed.

"My name is Fema. My people are Hopi, and I am a believer in the true Savior, The Lord Jesus Christ. He sent me."

"Bull crap, I don't believe you," Adam growled.

"Then how would I know your name?" Fema asked.

"I'm well-known. You could have researched my background."

"Not me. I live out in the desert and have little contact with the outside world. Besides, you take big steps to remain in secrecy and do your deeds in darkness."

"How do you know that?" Adam demanded.

"Jesus told me."

"He doesn't know where I am or what I do!" Adam thumped the table in anger.

"Then how could I know your name and find you here?" Fema remained calm.

"I don't talk to Him. I don't know Him. He is only a tyrant King to me." Adam sat back in his chair and glared at this Indian Millennial.

"Jesus knows all things, Adam: who you are, where you are, what you are doing, even in the blackest night. He longs for you to know Him; really know Him with your whole heart and being, not just know of Him."

"He is tyrannical, with endless rules. I hate him!"

"He loves you. He died on the cross for you."

"You will change your narrow mind when Master Satan returns and defeats Christ and we take over the world."

"Yes, Satan will be released from prison, but didn't you read the rest of the story? With just a thought or word by His power, Father God will cast Satan and all who follow him in the lake of fire, forever, with no end."

"Purely ancient fiction," Adam raised his voice. "We will be strong enough with our massive, united army led by our Master, to defeat Christ and all the weak millennials."

"You are delusional, Adam. Do you really think you can defeat the Creator of the Universe with good intentions? Overwhelm Christ with a driving passion for your cause? You and your blind army bringing down God Almighty's Son with sticks, throwing little bombs, and shooting your toy guns? You haven't a chance." Fema faced off with him.

"Adam," Fema made her last appeal. "Why would you choose forever in hell with evil Satan when you can choose life, heaven and forever with your family, with Christ?"

Adam jumped to his feet and raised his fist to strike. Fema covered her face.

"Get away!" he raged. "Disappear to where you came from. If I see you again anywhere around here, even a glimpse of you, I'll have racers drag you into the desert and rape you unconscious." He kicked his chair aside. "Get out of my way, you psychotic, ignorant, demented Indian!"

CHAPTER 71

RACES END

It was still dark, yet Adam could not sleep. He gave up seeking additional rest, threw on some clothes and walked outside his motel room. He looked into a brilliant starry sky and scanned the universe. Was there really a heaven out there as Fema alluded to? How dare she even use the word in his presence? He searched for the moon; ah, there it was, a slight sliver of its former self some days ago.

He walked the motel grounds several times before stopping at the pool. He tried the gate, opened it and wandered around the turquoise depths. The water mirrored the sky above it and the motion of the rivulets made the starlight dance.

'Is there a heaven?' The thought persisted. 'If so, could there be a hell? Rubbish. Lies.' His anger flared. He picked up a pool toy and flung it into the water. He paced around the pool trying to clear his head. Finally, he dropped into one of the chairs at the deep end of the pool.

He sat for a few minutes trying to force every unwelcome, troubling thought from his head, but his mind fought back. He shook his head and decided to retreat to a review of yesterday's events.

He began with Merity and the race into King's Valley. He lingered there. 'She wanted me to be there and cheer for her,' Adam mused. He honored that request, not at Springerville, but Fort Sumner. And he had a plan.

'A perfect plan,' Adam thought as he smiled to himself. He located a café near the entrance on the main highway. He was positioned at a table to see the road. Suddenly, Fema barged into his memory with her stinging question, 'Why would you choose hell, when you can choose heaven?' Rage exploded inside Adam and he cursed. He lay hold of that memory and cast it away into the New Mexico desert.

He calmed down and pressed his mind to remember after that. Oliver found him at that table.

"How is Monte?" Adam inquired.

"Very well. He has widened his lead."

"Do you think he will join us for a quick lunch?"

"I'll find out." Oliver was texting. "I'll give our location in case."

The response was swift. "Mole said yes." Oliver grinned.

It wasn't long before Adam saw Monte's racer slow at the opening and slide into curbside parking. Onlookers gathered around to see a famous racer and his solar car. He broke through the clamoring crowd.

Adam remembered Monte Mole's striking figure running towards them. His helmet was off and he was tearing at his racing gloves. He was grimy and sweat-soaked patches covered his suit. He threw himself into a chair.

"Water! Lots! Ice cold. Hurry!" Monte bellowed.

The next sequence of events both amused and filled Adam with a sense of attainment.

First, Adam engaged Monte and Oliver in a lively conversation concerning details of the race so far.

Second, while talking, Adam noticed the next lead racer come through, then another. Adam became louder and more intense, all the while mindful of the highway. Monte paid little mind to the cheering and applause of the crowd of onlookers. One more racer came through, then Merity, who was driving harder than the rest. Adam smiled.

Now, he shifted into an even more engaging discussion with Monte, concerning the rally, the impending conflict with Christ and the future.

Suddenly, Monte grabbed up his water, gulped it down and ran for his racer. Leaving at the same time, Adam and Oliver ran to the Transporter Station. An hour's wait and they transported to Clovis, New Mexico, and were met by a driver who took them to this motel.

Later that afternoon, the crowd assembled at the old Air Base finish line to welcome and congratulate the racecars as they came in. Monte, of course, was first and the center of attention. The second car was a few minutes behind and came roaring in. There followed several more chasing across the finish. Coming slower was Merity to clinch tenth place. Adam was surprised at himself how excited and proud he was. He sought Merity out.

"You are here," she cried through tears.

Adam hugged her.

"I didn't win," she said and laughed.

"Tough race, stiff competition." He quickly wiped away a tear, then pulled back, shocked at himself. What was happening to him? He walked away into the crowd.

Adam recalled what Monte told him late last night when he stopped by his motel room.

"Would you believe, Adam?" Monte snarled. "I was almost beat by a fool crazy millennial female. She was dogging me most of the race, but I distanced her in the desert. Then she got ahead of me outside Fort Sumner. I swear, that bitchy woman was outdriving me and I couldn't pass her."

"What happened?" Adam asked.

"Her battery conked out, I guess. She just tanked it the last stretch." Monte shrugged his shoulders.

Adam felt a surge of pride for Merity that confused and scared him.

CHAPTER 72

MILLENNIAL RALLY

A nice solar convertible picked up Adam from his motel room. As soon as the car turned off the main highway from Clovis, the driver stopped and got out to open the trunk.

"What are we doing?" Adam questioned.

"Giving you the recognition you have earned and deserve," his driver replied as he saluted him. He pulled out two magnetic signs and stuck them on each door panel. They read in bold letters:

OUR MASTER'S EMISSARY—ADAM HILLAG

Millennials lined the road leading up to a huge plane hanger. Just as they neared the crowds, Adam sat up on the top of the rear seat. Throngs were waving and cheering. Many pressed close to the car calling his name, reaching out to touch him. The driver went slowly as in a processional. Adam stood up in the floor of the rear seat. He stood erect and displayed strength as a military leader or king. Many began bowing before him as he passed by.

As they reached the hanger entrance, horns blared announcing his arrival. The army legion inside made way to clear a path straight to the speaker's platform. Everywhere people bowed in homage to one they acknowledged as their leader. The army came to attention and saluted the one they hailed as their General

The car stopped in front of the platform and the driver jumped out to open the door. Adam stepped out into the throng of racers, who began a slow chant: "Hillag, Hillag, Hillag, Hillag."

Adam climbed the steps and walked onto the platform's floor. He was met by Monte, who escorted him to be seated beside three other Millennial Racer leaders. Adam greeted all three before he sat down. Monte went to the podium to introduce Adam. He cleared his throat and held up his hand to quiet the assembled multitude.

"I first met Adam Hillag in Millennium Year 795 when he came to our Mod shop in Detroit. That night, a friendship was formed and this project was born. Now, here we are in Millennium Year 890, almost a century later, and look how far we have come. Let me say to you today, most of all our accomplishments are due to the persistent and astounding leadership of Adam Hillag. I give him to you now."

A low rumble that soon swelled to a roar emerged from inside and outside the hanger. Adam shook Monte's hand and took his place at the podium.

"I offer my congratulations to all of you," Adam began. "For each of your organizations, your amazing mechanical enhancements of all the solar vehicles, maintenance by your crews, the expertise of your drivers, and dedicated support of families and friends. I am pleased and applaud what has been accomplished. I hasten to add; I doubt few of us recognize the bigger picture of what lies ahead. Yesterday was so much more than just about racing; it is a preparation for war!

"I ask of you boldly with authority from our Master, what do your Chapters have to offer our cause? Let me be perfectly clear, I need to be more than impressed." Adam stood by silently, looking out at countless millennial faces.

Minutes passed, until by some unspoken command the racers formed a large opening in the center of the hanger. Several trucks drove in and stopped. Millennial men and women jumped out and unloaded sizeable crates. When finished, a racer came forth. Looking up at Adam, he declared, "We are racing Chapter 19 from Oakland. We have amassed food supplies to sustain millennials in combat."

"Very good," Adam complimented him.

Those trucks left and more drove in to take their place. A mass of crates were unloaded and stacked high. Their leader stepped forth. "Racing Chapter 81 from Pittsburg. We have rebuilt an old factory and tooled it to manufacture weapons to arm ourselves."

"Excellent!" Adam exclaimed with glee.

Another leader came forward. "Racing Chapter 32. We are making ammunition for those weapons"

"Perfect. Perfect." Adam was exuberant.

More trucks drove in and crates unloaded and stacked. "Racing Chapter 47, Tampa. We found a way to duplicate the manufacture of old combat lasers. We are in full production."

Adam clapped his hands in excitement.

As those trucks drove away, one lone truck, larger than the rest, drove in. It nosed in facing Adam, then turned to its side. Suddenly, the sides dropped revealing armed millennials inside. Monte Mole dropped down from the truck and faced Adam. He held out his arms.

"Yours truly, Detroit Chapter. Our assembly line puts out one per week. Fifty-two a year, ten years running; 520 Transport trucks ready for war."

"Wow! Monte, I am speechless." Adam saluted his old friend.

Other chapters came with their offerings. Adam waited until he was certain all participating Racer Chapters had come forth before he made his final speech.

"I couldn't be more pleased and proud of what has taken place here. I am completely taken back by your accomplishments and creative methods to build and enforce our cause. Your dedication and devotion will not go without notice and reward. What you have done today is of monumental consequence that will shape the earth's future.

"The return of Satan is eminent and will take place soon. We will no longer hide in secret and remain quiet. We will be united and ready at a moment's notice to go to war for our Master.

"I declare to you all today," Adam shouted with authority. "We can hasten our Master's return. Not passively but with determined aggression. Listen to me. We can no longer be a movement simmering. We must bring our cause to a boil!"

SEGMENT FIVE

LOOSING OF SATAN

CHAPTER 73

RESURRECTION SAINT ALERT

Farmer was sitting in the den of his log house reading. He glanced out the window. The dying glimmer of the sun was setting in the west and darkness was falling. His eye caught the jerk of Adreen's angel wings; then, before he could react, a terrifying announcement filled his mind.

"A great angel with the key has descended into the bottomless pit, broken the seal and loosed Satan out of his prison, that he may go forth to deceive the nations. Resurrection Saints beware and be alert."

"Who thet be who spoke into my head so clear?" Farmer was stunned.

"Michael, the archangel of war in the spirit realm," Adreen answered. "He spoke on the authority of the Lord of Hosts."

"Farmer! Did you hear that?" Emile was yelling from the bedroom.

"Reckon I surely heard thet most dreaded news," he replied. He stood up to go to her, but Emile came running into the den. Fright covered her face. Farmer held her close and smoothed her hair.

"Dear Lord, is this happening so soon? Not now. It is only Millennium Year 966," Emile cried. "What are we to do? Oh Farmer, we have faced this moment for centuries and I thought to be brave in trusting our Lord, but, but, I am frightened."

"Reckon this be in Lord Jesus' timetable, an' it do seem a mite soon." Farmer attempted to pull back and look at her.

"No! Please. Just hold me tight and don't let me go. Fear grips me. Does this mean we must have thirty-four years of war? That possibility paralyzes my very being."

"Satan can't harm us, Emile."

"Oh my, Farmer," Emily began to cry. "I fear not for me. It is our millennial family I cry out for. Not all are believers, and in those instances I allow myself to consider the end and future of those who follow Satan. I, I . . ."

"Shh, perhaps we can yet warn them." Farmer tightened his hug.

"But there are so many and scattered—everywhere."

Suddenly, Joe and Sally Baltman and their angels appeared. They saw the couple holding each other. In his brash fashion Joe started to speak, but Sally stopped him. They instead waited.

Farmer released Emile and the two faced their friends.

"I surmise you heard that?" Joe was concerned.

"We surely did. Any response from your family?" Farmer asked.

"Not yet," Sally answered.

Emile turned to her angel. "Froton, any word from the kids' angels?"

Fronton rose slightly off the floor making contact with Mark and Nikki's angels. Settling to the floor, he spoke. "Their angels heard, but were instructed not to tell. Same with Shag's Ganteous."

"Does that mean Tribulation Saints didn't hear that announcement?" Emile deducted.

"That is the word we are getting." Donald and Beth Parrigan joined them.

"I'm puzzled," Beth said, overwhelmed. "I wasn't ready for this yet; and why haven't the Tribulations Saints heard? They have angels."

Farmer pondered Beth's questions. She was right. He made no sense of it, until. Wait. It hit him: so simple, yet a horrifying conclusion.

"I thought on this and reckon the good Lord struck me with the idea," Farmer added and paused. "It be so simple I missed it, but where it took me is troublesome. The Tribulation Saints be as the Millennials: flesh and blood. They can be killed."

Emile sank into a chair and Sally covered her face.

"But Tribulation Saints be saved," Donald argued. "For them to get killed and die would mean a resurrection. Where does that fit in Scripture?"

"It doesn't," Farmer agreed. "We do know from God's Word there will be a war; we just don't know who will fit into it, and how?"

"Who will tell our Mark and Nikki and others like them?" Emile questioned. "If their angels can't, we dare not."

"Until instructions are given," Beth added.

"Did you hear that announcement?" Gordon and Ella May Brooks joined them.

"Does that mean war in Douglas Landing? What of the children?" Ella May was fearful.

Everyone in the group looked to Farmer. After all, he and Emile were overseers of the Douglas Landing operation and populace. Farmer ran his hand through his hair, not knowing how to answer. Facts were not complete, so he decided to only take what he knew and run with that for now.

"This terrible news done took us all by surprise. Scripture tells us thet the ending o' Satan be at the end of the Kingdom's thousand years. Seeing thet, and this announcement hitting hard now, must mean thirty-four years the ol' devil gets his way once again."

"Lord have mercy on us," Ella May cried out.

"What must we do?" Gordon asked.

"Not counting the angels," Farmer continued, "we hev three groups: us, the Tribulation Saints, and the Millennials. This be too soon at best to know much o' anything. We will hev to wait fer King Jesus to sort it all out an' make plain instructions fer us all. Tonight, this be only a Resurrection Saint Alert."

295

CHAPTER 74

FAMILY MEETING

Families all over the world were called to meetings as King Jesus instructed. His orders would be given out at each of these meetings. Farmer and Emile had decided to make theirs as enjoyable as possible by hosting a giant BBQ.

Family millennials began transporting in to Applegate days in advance, so the Trevor's log home as well as Mark and Nikki's were filling up to capacity. The few Tribulation Saints came in the day before, and Resurrection Saints began appearing the day of the meeting. This was exciting because some of the family had never met before.

Farmer and Emile's children, Walter, Clifton and Leah with all their family arrived early. Janee showed up mid-day.

Caleb, Sarah and the Savages appeared at Mark and Nikki's around dawn. Esther came in later. All of the family there would walk over to Farmer and Emile's. As arrivals kept coming in, the look of it resembled an army rather than a family.

It was a mild autumn day. Serious-sized barbecues were lined up along the rear of the house. Smoke steamed its varied aromas from each cooker. In the open meadow beyond, a multitude of tables and benches were set up. Plates, napkins and utensils were provided at each table's end. Single chairs were clumped in groups ready to seat the many family members gathered to visit and await instruction.

Shag was barking orders at millennials manning the barbecues, since all the cooking was primarily for theirs and the Tribulation Saints' benefit. The Resurrection Saints would eat mainly for the joy of sharing a meal, not because of necessity.

To accommodate such a crowd, the rest of the cooking was done on open fire pits blazing in the meadow. Pots were simmering over fires tended by scores of families. Mark watched this scene for some time. At one point he caught Nikki's eye as she hurried by with loaves of bread. She paused to look at him and followed his gaze. She teared up and without a word knew what he was remembering. She ran to place bread on the tables.

Mark sought out Farmer, and found him sitting with several family members. He waited until one next to his Great-grandpapa got up to go check on activities. Mark sat down. Farmer eyed his great, great, great-grandson.

"I reckon ya be thinken out loud," he drawled.

Mark had to laugh. "Does it show that much?"

"Aye, but what I see be more sad then laughter."

"I was watching the meal preparation in the meadow, Grandpapa. You remember I told you how we grew a congregation of Non Coms at the Church in the Woods?"

"I do and am right proud o' it."

"We had a Thanksgiving pot luck once."

"And this has the same looks an' feel?" Farmer's question was perceptive.

"In more ways than one. Did you ever do anything that was meaningful and exciting, yet a dark cloud hung over it that you couldn't get rid of?"

"More times then I care ta count. What be yer joy and excitement back then?"

"There was so much. A deep satisfaction to preach the Word; see people saved. Behold a family emerge out of scared, desperate people; to experience a depth of friendship born of courage and the willingness to fight; to see them happy in the face of terrible oppression."

"An' what be the dark cloud?"

"Evil Christos and his Combats; always in the shadows, knowing we could be attacked any minute."

"Thet moment came, didn't it?"

"Yes," Mark dropped his head. "We, lost them all."

"Do you feel thet same joy watchen our family?"

"In a different way. These are actual family, and I can rejoice and bask in God's love and blessings. The love I feel here is greater still than what I felt then."

"What be yer dark cloud now?"

"Satan has been released. It is like Christos all over again, but ten times worse. Will there be war?"

"It is foretold, Mark. Would ya fight if need be?"

Mark sat quiet for some time as if in a battle within himself. Finally, he straightened up and looked at Farmer with solid resolve. "In a heartbeat."

A group of young giggly millennial girls rushed up to Farmer almost falling into him. "Great-grandfather Farmer, they are ready to eat. Will you come thank King Jesus?" they breathlessly requested.

CHAPTER 75

GREAT ROOM GATHERING

The meal was festive. The conversations lively and even animated at times. Walter could still charm with his homespun humor, Janee's stories captivated everyone, while Caleb was ever able to stand and inspire. Farmer thought it to be refreshing to watch and listen to the millennial reactions, especially the younger ones. Even nearing the close of the thousand years, babies were still being born.

Through the entire meal, Farmer remained quiet except for an occasional conversation with those seated around him, and the occasional smile and wink at Emile. 'What a legacy the Lord has given Emile and I,' he thought, as he watched the family. 'We met, fell in love, married, and look at this—and not all of them are here.' He had to smile.

Now the family crowded into the log house great room. Farmer stood in front of the rock fireplace and waited while everyone assembled. 'What a sight,' he thought.

Members filled all available sofas and couches, chairs were brought in, and younger ones filled out the floor. Many positioned themselves along walls and stood. Others filled up the stairs and the open loft above. Angels hovered overhead. Family that couldn't squeeze into the great room packed hallways, the dining room and kitchen that could be seen from Farmer's view. Farmer's eyes scanned the family, taking in different ones. He stopped with eye contact to Emile. She nodded. Farmer raised his hand for all their attention and silence. Parents quieted their little ones. He began.

"This be a most exciting time as our family has come together. There be great joy an' meaning fer us ta all be here.

I saw much love and closeness, an' thet most certainly would warm my heart ifen I still had one."

There was laughter.

"What I did feel was even more so than I ever remembered, an' made me right proud. An' the meal we enjoyed be amazing an' one to be most thankful fer. To God who gave it, an' ta those who prepared it.

"Excitement can create laughter an' fun fellowship an we mostly all experienced lots o' thet today. Still, we be knowen fer sure we air gathered fer a most sobering reason, so I reckon we best git ta it.

"A month ago, we received the dreaded news thet Satan be released from his prison pit. I say dreaded 'cause I recall a conversation near a thousand years ago at the twins' birthday, yes, a most distressing conversation. Aware o' what the Scripture predicted, even back then thet shadow done hung over our heads. Did we hope or even dare pray all these years this horrible event never happen? Well, it did, an we be in the midst o' it.

"Since the announcement Master Jesus has give instruction o' what we gotta do, an' I aim ta share it with ya.

"There are three groups involved, not counting our angels. There be Resurrection Saints, Tribulation Saints and Millennials. Resurrection Saints have bodies thet cannot be hurt or killed, never. Tribulation Saints are saved believers, but still have flesh and blood bodies thet can feel pain, be injured, or even killed. Ya must be protected at all cost. Then, we have a mass population o' millennials, an' thet be where the final war takes place, but let me make it most clear. This war be not fought where many think on it ta be. Not on a battle ground with weapons, an' killen, but just as deadly. This battlefield will be waged in the minds o' millennials.

"The Lord Jesus has instructed us Resurrection Saints and the Tribulation Saints ta stand down. Our battles be over. This war be amongst the millennials. 'How can thet be?' Ya ask.

"Well, this be what the Lord Jesus Christ done tol' me an' it comes with a warning at the end. The Word says that Satan will go out to deceive the nations. Thet be the people. Look at the devil's history.

"Lucifer was the most beautiful an' powerful o' the cherub angels. He hovered over the very throne o' God. Pride took hold o' him and he deceived his self. Then he convinced millions o' angels ta follow him in rebellion against God Almighty Himself. Thet battle didn't last long I reckon, an' Lucifer became Satan, the most hated of all creatures an' God cast him an' his fallen demons ta the earth.

"When the Lord created man and woman, Satan be right there to –?"

"Deceive," the millennial children echoed.

"Of truth," Farmer went on. "An' how do he deceive? In two areas, an' we saw this throughout the 'before' years, an' now amongst millennials. First is with their 'cause.' They are deceived ta lay hold on ta a passionate, obsessed belief thet their 'cause' be right; when in reality, they be wrong. Dead wrong!

"Second deception be about the outcome. They air sorely driven ta believe they will win. The truth be, however, they cannot win. As sure as the sunrises each morning, they will lose. As sure as God created the heavens and earth, they will lose."

"Why are they so stupid?" A millennial girl was incredulous.

"The blind following a blind guide," an older boy answered.

"And where does this battle take place?" Farmer became more intense. "As it always has, in your mind. An' how can this be? Why is it this way? What makes the mind a place o' battle? Listen well, 'cause what I say now could most surely determine yer destiny.

"Like the rest o' us, all millennials air also born with the ol' sin nature. As we had ta battle it, so must each millennial. Ya kin feel it pull, hear a dark whisper even as I speak, a suggestion ta reject all thet I say. Yer only hope ta win this fight is ta believe thet Father God loved ya so much thet He sent His Son, His only Son, ta die in yer place, that ya can be forgiven o' thet sin an be washed clean in the shed blood o' Christ an' live. The deceiver will whisper in yer thoughts ta turn against Christ an' make him your new god. Now thet Satan be loosed, thet attack in yer mind will be more powerful then it has ever been. Some o' ya millennials have believed by faith in Christ as yer Savior an' been redeemed. Yer future in heaven is secure. Hold tight ta King Jesus.

"A decision must be made today by other millennials. Ya stand at a crossroad. One points ta darkness, evil, death an' hell. The other calls ya ta light, righteousness an' life. Why would ya chose forever in a lake o' fire an' eternal pain where mental torment never goes away. Not in millions o' years will it change. Never, with no hope. It will never end. Or, by faith believe He died on a cross jus' fer ya, ask His fergiveness, an open yer heart ta Jesus today, an' live forever in heaven with Him an' yer family. Today ya must choose.

"We face Satan on the loose. He will be relentless in bending the minds and wills o' any who be undecided. We declare war here and now. I want ever' Resurrected Saint an' Tribulation Saint ta make sure ever' millennial in our family has the opportunity ta decide ta be a believer in the Lord Jesus Christ. Then we spread out ta the rest o' our family who be not here today an' beyond ta every millennial we meet. Only then do our family win this war."

CHAPTER 76

DEEP SORROW

The fall morning air was crisp; still, the sun provided a hint of warmth on Mee Antra's face when she stepped out of the house. The sky was blue with a few clouds. Everywhere she looked smelled clean and fresh after last night's refreshing rain. She breathed deep and looked around. Splashes of reds, yellows, browns and orange were scattered among the dark greens of the pine and fir trees. Down the path from the house was Cold Creek, flowing fast and clear as it had ever since she arrived. She loved the home the Lord Jesus had placed her in, the family that had taken her in as their own, and the life she was blessed with. She walked toward the Creek.

This morning she awoke feeling alone, anxious and strangely sad. Should she be worried that the loosing of Satan would take all she held dear away? After all, she was a millennial. This would be their battle, her battle. Mark and Nikki reassured the war would not come to her. Would it affect Able or the family, which had grown from him? Somehow she doubted they would all remain untouched by a conflict she sensed would come.

She walked slowly over the bridge Shag had built across Cold Creek. She lingered a moment above the water to watch it tumble beneath her, but it only managed to feed her dispirited mood. Farther on the path past the bridge was a peaceful place Mee Antra loved to go, and she sought it out now. In a grove of lodge pole pine, sat four wooden benches Shag crafted many years ago. He meant it for a quiet retreat, somewhere to go for prayer, or sit alone with one's thoughts, or just quiet reflection. He built it for the family he had grown to love, and Mee Antra was grateful to be here now.

As she moved among the trees, she was startled to come upon Shag's pet mountain lion. The big cat rolled on its side as though waiting for her attention.

"Hello, Kimuchka, you big baby. Let me scratch your ears and chin. You like that? What are you doing out here?"

Mee Antra continued slowly towards a bench and Kimuchka stood up and followed her. She sat still, watching the fall leaves flutter occasionally to the ground, yet not really seeing anything at all. First her mind wandered aimlessly, jumping from one thought to another. She reflected on the Great Room gathering a week ago; different families present, some new, some old; images of the meal preparation, then the feast itself. She tried to recapture the joy and excitement she felt then. She grasped to hold onto those feelings for a moment, but all was fleeting. The house once more was quiet. Family one by one dispersed to their homes and duties, only Caleb and Sarah remained.

Then, she attempted to reenact Grandpapa Farmer's passionate speech. In her spirit, she knew it carried a message of great significance. But try as she might, a recreation of his exact words eluded her, and she settled to recapture only those thoughts that had so deeply impacted her.

How, in a perfect world with Christ as Ruler and King, could so many engage in a stupid rebellion? It seemed equally simple to her just to love and follow Jesus, yet she knew, deep in her heart, she knew. They didn't really love Christ in their hearts, so they fell for Satan's lies. Lies Satan believed himself: a blind devil leading blind, fallen angels and a horde of Millennials.

She heard voices. As she peered into the trees, by and by, she caught sight of Emile and Sarah walking from the direction of the Trevor log house.

'Odd,' Mee Antra thought. 'These Resurrection Saints can transport anywhere in the universe in seconds, and still they prefer walking.'

The women caught sight of Mee Antra and waved; then, choosing to make their way through the trees, they came to her.

Emile and Sarah studied the young Millennial a moment before sitting down.

"I see you found Kimuchka, or did she find you?" Emily asked with a smile, making small talk.

"She was here when I came. She loves me to pet her. Such a big baby."

The women sat in silence for a while. Sarah sensed Mee Antra might wish to be left alone. "Would you rather we leave?" she offered.

"Yes . . . perhaps . . . No, don't go."

"What is troubling you, sweetheart?" Emile took her hand.

"I've been thinking about the meeting and the loosing of Satan. I get so confused, scared, uncertain."

"I know you keep saying this war will not come here, yet I am not sure it won't. Doubts take over and that brings feelings I can't control. The very thought of many Millennials following Satan to their destruction makes me sad. I am so weepy. Some of those could be our family."

"Why don't you admit the one you are afraid for?" Sarah was gentle.

Mee Antra burst into tears, tried to look at them, but buried her face against Sarah.

"Oh where is he? Is he safe? What has become of him? Why did he just disappear without a word? He has a son, a family, me. Oh Adam, Adam, Adam, please, please! Don't let pride and anger control you. Accept Jesus as your God and King before it's too late. Don't end up with those lost forever. I could not . . . . could not bear that."

Mee Antra wept uncontrollably for some time; then grew still.

"You still love him, don't you?" Emile murmured.

"I never stopped," she sniffed. "When I fell in love, I knew it would be forever."

Nikki found them. "Good morning. I wondered where you all had gotten off to." She took one look a Mee Antra's tear-drenched face and sat down with them.

"What's going on?" Nikki asked, reaching out to touch Mee Antra.

"She's crying for Adam. Wondering where he is, what he's doing, afraid he will follow Satan," Sarah said.

305

"We all fear that," Emile added. "We all love and miss him, wondering."

"I hurt for him." Nikki dropped her head. "At times in the dark of night, I sense things happening. It's like I can almost see him, know what he's doing, where he's at, yet not sure."

"Me, too," Mee Antra sat up. "I love him so much. I thought love would be like a flame; growing smaller with time and absence. Finally, unable to burn any more, it would flicker and die out. But my love hasn't flickered and died. In fact, it has drawn from some source beyond myself, burning brighter, growing, becoming strong as a beacon. Oh, that Adam can see it, wherever he is."

Nikki was deeply moved. A new strength was forged within her.

"I, too, have feared Adam would sell out to Satan based on his past actions. But there is one hope I cling to that will not be denied. I met Mark, an angry and rebellious young man, then a miraculous change began when he believed. I watched him grow into a leader, even against his will. Over and over in the midst of danger and fear of death, he stepped up to take charge. I know the key to Adam's safety is that he believes in Christ. But beyond that, Mark always stood up and spoke. He gave direction, order and hope. What I know is this. Adam has a lot of Mark in him and his Grandpa Caleb before that. I know without a doubt, Adam is somewhere leading, speaking, taking charge, directing. Somewhere in all of that I have to believe he will follow in his daddy's footsteps and be saved. That is the hope I cling to."

CHAPTER 77

CHINA LAKE MISSION

Adam stepped out of the Tehachapi, California Transporter Station in the middle of the night. The sky was dark, moonless, even the stars appeared to withhold their light. No wisp of breeze, a dead calm enveloped the area. The Station was quiet and void of any travelers apart from himself.

A camo-covered air van awaited his arrival in the pick-up area. The side door slid open and Adam hoisted himself into the vehicle, which quickly sped him off into the night.

Both men before him were also dressed in camos and wore military caps. These Millennials looked to be very young, no more than three centuries old, Adam guessed. Two laser weapons were racked between the front seats, within easy reach. This van was not designed for pick-up, but for war.

The passenger turned to Adam. "Emissary Hillag?" His voice was stern and rough.

"Yes," Adam answered. He felt empowered and confident. "Where are we going exactly?"

"The less you know the better. Forces watch our every move."

"What forces?"

"Millennial believers who give allegiance to the Christ," the driver answered.

Adam shook his head in disbelief. "Those are cowering, trembling, insipid wimps, who are clueless to what we are doing and frankly could care less. The two of you could take out hundreds with your lasers."

"No, we can't," the driver argued.

"We have tried to kill some of them with both conventional weapons or our lasers," the passenger added.

"And?" Adam insisted on an answer.

"Some unseen shield seems to protects them. We have wounded some, even fatal shots, but they recover. They are protected, somehow."

"Impossible," Adam argued.

"It's true," both millennials insisted.

They drove east out of the Tehachapi Mountains down to the California desert. The driver turned north on State Highway 14 and proceeded for what seemed hours. Little could be seen of the passing landscape, aside from the barely visible ridge of mountains on his left and flat desert spreading out on his right. Adam was confined to watch only what the van's headlights illuminated in front of him.

Reaching a highway junction, they headed north on Highway 395. Adam had become aware of how desolate this place was. No town in over fifty miles, not even a sign telling of one. After twenty more minutes of driving they passed through a spot on the road named Little Lake.

"Where is the lake?" Adam was amused.

"You're in it," the driver joked. "Dried up."

A half-mile beyond the ghost-like town, the driver turned off the main highway onto a narrow paved road. Adam could tell by asphalt patches, someone maintained this stretch of road. Four miles in, they came to a fence that disappeared from view in both directions. The paved road followed the fence line another three miles and ended at a gate. Looking up, the header read 'China Lake Millennial Camp.' Six armed millennial guards approached them. They acknowledged their two comrades, glanced inside at Adam, stepped back, came to attention and held a salute as the van passed inside.

As they proceeded into the compound, Adam was shocked by its magnitude. This wasn't just a camp, but indeed a major city.

Adam was escorted into the Camp's Headquarters as the eastern sky was turning grey. Already there was a buzz of millennial activity getting ready for the day.

An officer and six lower-ranking millennials were waiting street-side when his van pulled up and stopped. The soldiers came to attention, weapons ready, as Adam's door opened. The officer saluted when Adam stepped out. He returned the salute. The officer extended his hand.

"I'm Major Herbert Dean. Welcome to China Lake Millennial Camp." He was polite but curt. Adam shook his hand.

"Follow me," Major Dean instructed. The enlisted soldiers formed a protective guard. Three preceded the Major and Adam; the other three formed the rear.

Inside, the Major led Adam through long corridors with numerous doors to a spacious boardroom. Five officers rose from their seats at a large table to salute Adam. He returned the salute.

"Emissary of Lord Satan, Adam Hillag," the Major introduced the dignitary.

The officers greeted Adam and introduced themselves.

"Colonel Sebastien Edward. Compound one."

"Colonel Rafael Humberto. Compound two."

"Colonel Odette Bonnie. Compound three."

"Colonel Hermine Ernesto. Compound four.

"Colonel Karl Gaston. Compound five. Do you have orders from High Command for us?"

"I do," Adam motioned for the group to sit. "But first I require your reports to take to our Master."

"Of course," Colonel Ernesto replied. The young millennial female officer proceeded to pull a wall map down for the group to observe.

"China Lake was a naval weapons and training center before the Tribulation. Christos disbanded the base and it was deserted for centuries until we took it over," she began.

"We did extensive reconstruction," Colonel Humberto explained. "We converted ammo bunkers into living spaces, training center offices and barracks became small apartments.

"In open areas, we built additional housing and mess halls. We have become self-contained cities," Colonel Gaston added.

"Don't forget we revamped the broken water and sewer systems, then constructed plenty of service centers with latrines, bath and laundry facilities," Colonel Bonnie proclaimed, "which was my favorite project."

"On the map, here is where you entered our territory at Little Lake," Colonel Ernesto pointed. "And this is our location," She tapped the location on the map. "This large area on the north side where we are now was a weapons center. Lots of bunkers are now populated. Even the large open areas used for gunnery practice are completely filled with housing. This area is divided into Compounds one and two.

"The area here to the southeast is Compound three, Colonel Bonnie's city, and this large area east of Compound three is the old fort and training center. It comprises Compounds four and five."

"How many millennials in each Compound?" Adam asked.

"One million," Colonel Edward answered flatly.

"How can you be sure?" Adam challenged.

"We keep accurate count," Edward countered.

"How many families, children?" Adam queried.

"None," Colonel Bonnie answered. "If they marry or have babies, we transfer them. We cannot tolerate any distraction from our mission."

"So what is our new mission?" Colonel Gaston stood up. "Five million millennial troops fully armed. We are ready to fight. I am eager for war."

Adam stood and motioned Gaston to sit. "It is Millennial Year 985. Here are your orders from Lord Satan. For the next ten years, you are to transmit your army and their weapons. There are no checks into luggage, you can even use fake names. The kingdom millennials are stupid and blind to our movements.

"You are to regroup in your assigned countries undercover and be ready for war in ten years. Compound one will migrate to Saudi Arabia. Compound two relocate to Jordon and Lebanon. Compound three move into Syria and overflow in Turkey. Compound four, you infiltrate Egypt. And Compound five, Colonel Gaston: your army is to fill Iraq and Iran.

"Move slowly, but China Lake is to empty itself in ten years. Any questions?"

"Yes, Sir, just one," Colonel Gaston asked. "What is our target?"

"I thought you all astute enough to figure out this top secret mission. We will march on Jerusalem from all sides to seize control and capture the King."

CHAPTER 78

THE ASSIGNMENT

Millennial officers from Compound four held a party mixer in honor of Adam. The whole room snapped to attention upon Adam's entry. Colonel Hermine Ernesto, the leader of Compound four stepped forth to greet him. She smartly saluted, followed by the rest of the officers. When Adam returned her salute, the gathering broke into shouts and clapping.

"We are honored to welcome Adam Hillag to China Lake Millennial Camp. He has brought secret orders from Lord Satan, which will be disbursed at the appropriate times.

"Emissary Hillag's reputation precedes him, so make sure he is comfortable while our guest and his every need taken care of. That is an order. Now, cut loose, have fun tonight and enjoy yourselves."

Drinks plus a variety of delicacies in abundance were constantly offered. Adam first conversed with the Colonel, taking note of her as they talked. Her soft green eyes complimented her sandy hair. Her skin was tan, no doubt from time in the desert sun. She knew protocol and Adam was intrigued how these millennials had such strong militarism in a kingdom that discouraged and abhorred any kind of military. Was it instinct? Had they found and studied old manuals?

"Where did you study?" Adam casually asked.

"We developed our own boot camp and training."

"How did you know what to instruct?"

"We found Navy files and books. We improvised on what we weren't sure about. But tell me of you, Adam Hillag? How did you get where you are today?"

"I was favored, devoted, and nasty." Adam stared the Colonel down. She dropped her eyes when saying, "So I've heard."

Adam turned to accept an hors d'oevre and walked away to mingle. A Captain came to him with questions.

"You brought orders from Lord Satan?"

"I did, and don't ask what they were." Adam was straight-faced.

"Of course, Sir, I know better, but I wondered, have you heard his voice?"

"I have."

"Does he sound kind? Authoritative? Mean?"

"He doesn't sound. What you hear is sheer power. He talks, you don't."

"Wow!" the Captain exclaimed. "Have you ever seen him?"

"No one has seen Satan . . . and lived," Adam turned to a young female Second Lieutenant. She took his empty glass and offered her full one. Adam accepted it as she came closer.

"Are you married?" she whispered.

"How old are you, Lieutenant?"

"One Hundred twenty-seven Millennium years."

"A baby. I don't date babies. Are you looking for a transfer off this base, because if you are, I can arrange that." Adam didn't wait for a reply but spun away.

Officers gathered around him mostly, engaging him in small talk of little substance. Adam quickly tired of that. A millennial servant walked by carrying a platter of mini sandwiches. Adam selected one.

"So you are the famous Adam Hillag I have heard so much about," a voice came from behind.

Adam turned to face an older Major.

"And what have you heard?" he asked as he took a bite of sandwich. He eyed the Major as he chewed.

"You are mean. You never mince words. You are cold and your stare can cut through steel. And, you get a job done without a lot of crap."

"You are pretty much right on, Major," Adam growled. "So what's your point?"

"Point being, Sir, that makes you an honest man."

"Try me," Adam finished his sandwich.

"I've read the Bible, how it says this ends. Can we achieve Victory? What if those words are true? Would the price we pay be worth all this?"

"Major, do you believe for truth a book so old and filled with contradictions?" Adam's eyes narrowed.

"I don't know." The Major dropped his eyes. "I saw Jesus in the Temple when I was young. I never forgot."

"So did I. He was dressed like a beggar. I never forgot what a disappointment our King was."

"He was dressed like, like a friend to me."

"Then, why didn't you believe in him? Why haven't you now?" Adam snarled.

"I just followed my friends."

Adam studied this officer a minute, shaking his head. He handed him his empty glass.

"Major," Adam's voice was blunt and gruff. "I would surely question going into battle following a leader who didn't know if he could win or not. If you cannot figure it out, I certainly can't educate or convince you. Get your head on straight or transfer out." Adam walked away.

Adam tired of socializing quickly, but managed to stay in the room engaged in conversations. At times he felt he was talking to children. He discovered to his delight a few men and women very engaging, creative, passionate and confident concerning the upcoming war. Finally, he sought out the Colonel to thank her for the evening and excused himself from the party.

He retired to his room, analyzing the events of the day. He was tired so he undressed for bed and pulled on his pajamas. Wham! A force hit him so strong it threw him on the floor.

"Adam? Adam Hillag?" A voice so powerful it filled his brain with pulsating pain.

"Yes. Yes," Adam choked. He held his head for fear it would explode. He knew it was Satan.

"You have done well and accomplished much for my kingdom. I have an assignment for you that will be the greatest of your life."

"I'm ready, Master," Adam moaned, writhing from intense head pressure.

"I disclose nothing to you now, only the magnitude and importance of the task I command of you. You, Adam Hillag, will use my power to usher in the downfall of this malicious Kingdom. The reign of this weak King must topple and end. Adam Hillag, you will push that collapse."

By now, Adam was squirming on the floor, jerking his body and legs.

"From this moment on you must be ready for my call. To answer, then go wherever I send you and quickly carry out my assignment."

A power surge cut to the core of his soul and spirit. He cried out before going limp.

"Do you understand?"

"Yes," Adam could barely speak.

"Are you ready to start this war?"

"Yes, Master, yes!" Adam screamed as his body twisted with intense pain.

SEGMENT SIX

THE FINAL BATTLE

CHAPTER 79

AN URGENT REQUEST

Mee Antra was breathless when she ran into Mark and Nikki's bedroom. Both were startled.

"What is it?" Nikki threw a robe around herself. Mark sat up in bed.

"I just got the strangest private message on my SAT. It reads, 'Come quickly. Urgent. I have information on Adam. Meet me in Applegate at the Transporter parking lot.' Look at it! See. Could it be possible?" Mee Antra was shaking.

"The message also says that I am to come by myself and bring Abel."

"But Abel is in Springdale," Mark reminded.

"He can transport down. Maybe it's Adam wanting to see me and his son."

"Oh, Mee Antra, don't let your imagination send you after a wild and unsubstantiated possibility," Nikki warned.

"Any idea of who could have sent this message?" Mark took her phone to study the text. "What number did it come from?"

"Unlisted," Mee Antra answered. "If I don't meet whoever this person is, I will never know. What shall I do?"

"Humm," Mark was thinking. "I guess we will have to play this out." He sent a text reply on Mee Antra's SAT phone. 'When can I meet you?'

In seconds, the phone lit up. 'Tomorrow night at exactly ten minutes to midnight. I will only speak with you concerning Adam if you come alone and bring your son Abel.'

'What if I refuse and ask you to come to my home. Abel could be here and the house empty,' Mark texted.

319

'Then you are reading my last message. Be smart, not stupid. I have vital information concerning Adam Hillag that you and your son will want to hear. Confirm our meeting or I'm gone.'

Mee Antra was in tears. Nikki tried to console the distraught millennial, but Mee Antra pushed her away.

"Maybe, some of us go earlier and hide to keep you safe," Mark offered. Mee Antra threw her hands up, crying out. She paced the floor, torn, sobbing one minute, beating her head with her fist the next. Suddenly, she stopped, looked at Mark and Nikki with desperate eyes. She walked sternly to Mark, grabbing her SAT. 'Confirming visit,' she texted. 'Ten minutes to midnight, tomorrow night, Transporter Station parking lot. I'll be alone with Abel.'

She locked herself in her bedroom to make arrangements for Abel to join her.

Early the next morning, Grandpapa tried to talk with Mee Antra. "I can't believe this ta be on the up-an'-up. In my spirit, I reckon it ta be some evil plot ta harm ya an' Abel," Farmer warned.

Mee Antra teared up, crossed her arms, shook her head in defiance, and retreated to her bedroom.

Grandmamma tried in vain to talk to Mee Antra later that morning to no avail. Mee Antra isolated herself the rest of the day and didn't emerge until it was time to leave. She walked into the kitchen where Mark and Nikki sat at the bar-counter.

She held up one hand. "I've made up my mind. I'm determined to make this meeting, so don't try and stop me," Mee Antra declared.

"Oh Sweetheart, " Nikki cried. "We are worried sick."

"But we won't stop you, but promise this. Keep your phone on you and text us when you arrive. Tell us that Abel is there, and message when you see your contact. Will you do that?" Mark asked lovingly.

"Yes, thank you," Mee Antra agreed. She grabbed her purse, walked out the door and soon Mark and Nikki watched the taillights of her solar disappear down the lane.

Mark picked up the tracker on her SAT. It traced her movement when she turned onto the Applegate Highway. He followed her into the city. True to her word, she texted she was in the Transporter parking lot. A few minutes later, she confirmed that Abel was with her. They were by her car and walked about short distances. At precisely ten minutes to midnight, Mee Antra texted, 'I see someone walking towards us. I think it's a woman.'

Mark monitored Mee Antra's movements. She seemed to stay by her car a few minutes, then walked a short distance away and was at that location until midnight, then went back to her car.

"Does this mean the meeting's over?" Nikki watched Mark's phone.

Ten minutes slipped by, then thirty. A sickening dread filled both of their stomachs.

"Not good," Mark muttered. He called. It rang and went to voicemail. He tried again and again. No answer.

"It shows she's still at her car." Nikki was near panic.

"No! Her phone's at the car," Mark yelled as he bolted down the hall to bang on Shag's door.

In an instant, Shag threw the door open.

"Something has happened to Mee Antra."

"You telling me her meeting went south?" the old Vet growled. He dressed, grabbed his knife and ran to the kitchen.

Soon their air car was racing towards Applegate. Nikki laid her head against the window and wept quietly. Shag, behind them, smoothed his knife on his pants-leg while muttering to himself. Mark couldn't tell if it was prayer or anger. For the first time in years, he experienced that icy clutch at his heart and mind; so heavy that his whole body was enveloped in an ugly kind of pain. So out of place for a perfect millennial kingdom, more at home in a bag of terrible Tribulation emotions. He wiped his eyes and cried out to King Jesus. His mind was so distressed by now he couldn't hear any answer.

It seemed another century before they raced into the Transporter Station parking lot.

"Over there!" Nikki pointed. "Oh, dear God, let them be safe."

All three of them jumped out of their car and surrounded Mee Antra's solar. The car was empty with the driver's door ajar. On the ground by her car lay Mee Antra's SAT.

CHAPTER 80

THE CALL

The long-awaited call from Lord Satan that would herald the greatest war the earth would ever experience came nearly ten years after Adam's Assignment was given. He was with Monte Mole in Detroit, coordinating their battle plans with other units in America.

Detroit millennials had been secretly moving their military trucks to numerous Millennial Divisions across the United States for years; however, Detroit kept enough for their own ranks.

War orders directed all millennial groups to sweep inward declaring war in America. They would converge to finally join fighters in Mid-America. The conquest would be swift and decisive. All they needed was Master Satan's directive.

"You will be our great leader," Mole commented to Adam with his shriveled smile.

"Yes. We have completed the years-long preparation. All we can do now, Monte, is wait for Lord Satan's orders to advance. When that comes Millennials all over the world will attack."

"Where do we go from here?" Monte inquired.

"Not sure. I need to make certain all of the China Lake Camp has disbursed their troops."

"Well, let me know."

Four nights later as Adam made preparation to leave Detroit for California, Satan's call came. It was 1 PM on January 26, Millennium Year 993. The power of Satan's voice smashed Adam face-down on the floor of his room.

"Your time has come. Are you ready?"

"Yes, Lord Satan," Adam gasped. "Yes."

"Listen carefully as I won't repeat my orders. Transport tonight to the Transporter Station in the old Visitor's Center in Richmond, Virginia. Take a private shuttle to Jt. John's Church. Your arrival time at the church must be exactly 11:00 PM, but do not go inside the church. Walk in the church cemetery. There my associate will meet you with your instructions. When I send you into the church, I will give you your mission. Now go and obey all I command you." Satan's voice and power left in a clap of thunder that shook his room.

Adam jumped up and made haste to leave that night for a Detroit Transporter Station. The January winter chill was brutal. Adam wore heavy boots, pants and an overcoat, yet the bitter cold went through all of these. A wool scarf covered his nose and mouth. He hurried from the drop off into the Station where he requested the programmer to send him to the Visitor Center, Richmond, Virginia Transporter.

It was cold and dark in Virginia also, when Adam grabbed his duffle bag and walked out into the well-lit Richmond Station. He looked outside to see wind-driven snow. He pulled on his gloves, and wrapped his scarf around his neck and face. The night air took his breath.

"Woof!" he shuddered.

He motioned for a private shuttle when one came around. He hurried to jump in. "St. John's Church," he instructed.

The driver turned to stare at Adam in disbelief. "You sure? On a night like this?" he questioned.

"I believe I was clear," Adam snapped. "St. John's Church."

"Sure, but it be closed. Been empty and boarded-up for centuries. The steeple toppled over, the rest of the building has not changed much except it be in gross disrepair. It's the old part of Richmond and folks don't go there, just passersby, and I'm certain no one's there tonight, only dead people in the cemetery."

"That's where I want to go. The cemetery," Adam spoke gruffly.

The driver glanced back at Adam to make sure he heard right. He frowned and shook his head. "That church is really old. First church in Richmond, built before the war," he tried, in an attempt to make conversation. "Lot of famous people met in that church in the 'before' years. Some of them are buried in the cemetery. You can see their markers; well, not so easy tonight in the dark."

Adam let the driver talk on. He was caught up in the strangeness of the mission. Go to a church cemetery in a snowstorm. Well, Satan surely knows what he is doing.

The drive to the church was short and the driver let Adam out. "There's the church and on that side is the cemetery," the driver pointed out.

Adam hurried among the gravestones, peering through the snow for a sign of his contact. He glanced at his SAT. Two minutes early. Then, out of the shadows, he saw a dark figure moving slowly across the cemetery grounds. As this creepy contact drew closer, Adam saw a person clothed in a long black shroud, which covered his head in a hood. No sign of hands or arms; whoever it was certainly fit the setting as the death angel himself.

"Adam Hillag," the voice was deep and foreboding. Adam could not see a face, but this was definitely the voice of a man. The contact came even closer and Adam could make out two eyes that glowed blood-red.

"Adam Hillag," the man spoke again.

"I am he," Adam answered.

"You must understand the significance of why you are here."

"I'm listening, but can we please hurry?" Adam's teeth chattered.

"Silence, foolish Millennial." Adam was hit with a force easily able to knock him over.

"Lord Satan?" Adam gasped.

"Do not flatter yourself, Adam Hillag. Lord Satan would never appear to you. Now listen well to me. Forget whether you are cold. Indeed, forget yourself; and think only of your mission. Multiple centuries ago a revolution was birthed in this building; a revolution that brought change. Tonight a new revolution will be born; a revolution that will bring Lord Satan's change and dominion over the whole world. Religion was preached here. Now Satan's religion will be preached, starting here. He will be worshipped and obeyed as supreme ruler of this world. That worship in this church starts tonight. The cry that resounded inside these walls, 'Give me liberty or give me death,' will become the war cry of Satan's vast army. Now, proceed to the church door, Adam Hillag, and Master Satan will instruct you. But do not go inside."

Adam ran to the front door of St. John's Church. The door appeared locked, and the church itself was dark.

Instantly Satan's voice filled his head.

"Adam Hillag, there is only one way that this corrupt King can be made to topple from His Throne. One of His promises must be broken. Hitler, my servant attempted to break God's promise that there would always exist a remnant of His chosen people. Adolph drove his followers to kill, kill, kill, kill, but failed in his mission rid the world of every Jew.

"In the Millennium, the promise of no death has been made. For one thousand years not one human has died; but tonight that promise will be broken. You, Adam Hillag, must break it. Inside this church, a sacrifice has been prepared. Three millennials are on the altar. You will see a dagger. Pick it up and plunge it deep into their hearts, starting with the oldest. Now go, and obey me!"

The door opened for Adam and he went inside, dropping his duffle bag.

No pews, the church was bare. Candles gave off light and smoke. Adam choked. As he stepped inside, the door closed behind him.

He took note the windows were sealed shut. No light could come in, and none could be seen from outside. The candles formed a circle on the floor. Against each wall, north, south, east and west stood a coven satanic priest. Adam had heard of them, but had never seen one. These were covered like the man he encountered among the gravestones. He questioned they were even human.

In the center of the candles was a raised flat altar. It was about waist-high and tied down on this altar were three naked millennials: one female, one male and an infant. The baby was attempting to move and fussing.

Adam stepped inside the candle circle and walked to the altar. He saw the large knife and without hesitation grabbed it up. He made his way slowly to the side where the victim's heads were positioned. He determined he would not look at their faces. He wanted never to know who they were, nor see their death expressions.

"Oh Adam, please don't do this," the woman pleaded.

Adam stopped. He stared in disbelief. "Mee Antra?" he gasped.

"Please, Adam, this is your son, Abel. Our son. And the baby boy is far removed, but still in your lineage."

Adam dropped the knife to the floor, and fell to his knees. "I can't do this. Not these. Give me others and I will kill them," Adam appealed to Satan in his mind.

'Others will not give me the power to overcome. It must be linage from a missionary, a preacher before you, then you. When you joined with your wife, you became one. She takes your place.'

'We never married,' Adam challenged.

'Marriage is a union.

'And the most power comes to me from the sacrifice of an infant in your lineage. Now, pick up your dagger, and obey me. Kill them now.'

Adam reached over and grasped the knife. He stood up, blinded by his tears. He raised the death weapon high over his head.

Mee Antra began trembling and pleading. "No, Adam, don't! I love you! I never stopped loving you. All these centuries I loved you. I will even now love you, even if you take my life."

"Don't take mom's life," Abel cried out. "Take mine."

Adam stumbled to Abel and raised the razor-edged knife.

"It's alright, dad. Take my life, but spare mom and the baby."

Adam shrieked in unimagined torment. He passed on to the infant, stopped, raised the knife, but hesitated and looked in the baby's face. The little one quieted, laughed, trying to hold up its hands to Adam.

"Oh, no," Adam groaned. He felt along the edge going back to Mee Antra. He raised the dagger high with quivering hands.

'Do it,' Satan roared in his mind. 'Plunge the dagger deep into her heart. In seconds it will be over. I will give you power and fame you never dreamed possible. You will have no boundaries. We will rule together. Now obey, Adam Hillag. Do it! KILL THEM!'

Suddenly, thoughts rushed into Adam's mind. He heard Fema, 'Why would you choose death and hell, when you could have life forever with Christ?'

'What if the Bible is true about the end? Satan and all the millennial rebels would be destroyed,' the Major had questioned.

Dozens of conversation bites with family surfaced. Each one focused on the Son of God, King Jesus. Adam dropped again to his knees and held the knife to his chest, ready to sacrifice himself.

"Adam, please believe. Please open your heart," he heard Mee Antra call softly. "He loves you."

Suddenly in his mind, he was a youth in the Temple. He had a glimpse of Jesus dying on a cross—for him. Then he saw Christ once again as he did that day long ago, not a King in beggar's rags, but a crucified King. He saw the wound in His side, the nail-scarred hands and feet. 'I did this for you,' Jesus whispered.

'Don't be a fool, Hillag. You would throw a thousand years of prestige and position away in a moment of emotional weakness?' the devil thundered.

Adam grabbed his head. He wanted to call out but the very thoughts were snatched from his brain. He raised the knifepoint to his chest. He moaned.

'Then kill yourself, Hillag. Give me victory. It only takes one death.' Satan's power warped Adam's mind.

"I offer forgiveness and eternal life, not death,' the voice of Christ broke in. 'Will you believe?'

Adam threw the knife down. He bowed his head to the floor, sobbing. "I have sinned and fought you for so long, Lord Jesus. If you have any mercy left for me, please forgive me, a sinner. I believe you died for me. You are my King, if you will have me."

There was a sound as of a mighty wind in the church. The Satanic priests, who were chanting kill, kill, kill, were silenced and knocked over like chess pieces in a hurricane. Some of the candles blew out as the wind swept over Adam. He felt the immediate change and presence of the Holy Spirit wash over him. It was real! He was forgiven, cleansed of sin, a saved, believing millennial.

CHAPTER 81

FLIGHT

A dam jumped up, a man entirely different than the one who walked into church an hour before. He snatched up the knife and cut Mee Antra's hands and feet loose. She threw herself into his arms. He kissed her quick and pulled off his heavy coat to put around her.

"Listen," he ordered. "The building is shaking. Satan is raging. I can't hear him but I feel him and his burning heat. He intends to destroy us. Hurry. Grab my duffle bag over there and pull out clothes for Abel. Carry the baby inside your coat to keep him warm."

Adam cut Abel's ropes before releasing the baby. Mee Antra came to him.

"Adam, I can't open the door. There is a force holding it. Adam, we have no shoes."

"There are socks in the duffle. Put all of them on, both you and Abel. Hurry. I can feel Satan's rage glowing red-hot. Mee Antra, put those jogging pants on. Abel, you get the slacks, tee shirt and shirt. Let me hold the baby. Quickly, good, here's the baby back. Let's hit that door."

The lock was open but they couldn't budge the door. They threw themselves against it to no avail. They even kicked it.

"What will we do? I'm burning up—oh! Adam, the walls are smoking," Mee Antra cried out.

Abel studied the door, and then ran back to the altar to retrieve the knife. His face was pebbled in sweat when he returned. He started prying the old pins up on the door hinges. The top two came out but the bottom hinge was rusted in place.

"Adam," Mee Antra took his arm. "That wall has caught fire."

Abel and Adam pried with all their might to gain an opening at the top of the door. It moved enough to give the two men a handhold. They yanked at it over and over until the door broke. The cold air gave a sudden jolt to the millennials. It also ignited a second wall on fire. The Satanic priests were stirring and cursing.

"They will burn up," Abel observed, as they ran out onto the drive.

"No, they won't. They are demons and might as well get used to the flames," Adam sneered.

They followed the main highway a short distance, and then veered off into a residential district. There was street after street, row upon row of older houses. Soon they were lost.

"Why did we come here?" Abel questioned.

"Because by now Satan has alerted every millennial in this area to cut us off, capture us."

"Kill us," Abel added.

"He can't," Adam answered, shaking his son's shoulder. "Right now, we have to find shelter."

Adam was freezing as ice cut his hands and face. He looked at Mee Antra's and Abel's stocking feet and knew they were wet and cold. Mee Antra looked to him to lead them and he realized she would follow him unto death, if need be. That placed a heavy weight of responsibility on him for all their lives, not to take them with a dagger, but to save them.

They came to the corner of a long street. 'East Grace,' the street sign read. Homes lined both sides of the street, mostly two-story and old. All had front porches, and once in a while a whole porch appeared to be made of iron.

"Abel, run ahead and look for any house with a light on," Adam instructed.

"Lord Jesus, please lead us to the right home. One with believers, not rebels. I ask in Jesus Christ's name," Mee Antra prayed, in trust.

That struck Adam as odd. 'Praying? In a crucial moment such as this could God really help? Would God even care? Did He even hear that prayer?'

Abel came running back. "I found one," he cried, excited; his breath puffed vapor in the cold air. "It has one of those metal porches."

Abel led them to the house. A faint light was shining through a side window. The millennials joined up together on the porch, and Adam pounded on the door. He was persistent.

There was a long pause before someone cautiously opened the door.

"We are looking for believing millennials. We need help." Adam was loud. "We've got to get to a Transporter."

"Come." A young millennial welcomed them in.

"Thank you," Adam clasped the young man's hand. "We are freezing."

Just then, a millennial woman joined them from upstairs. "Doug, who is it?" She too was cautious.

"I am Adam, this is my wife Mee Antra, and our son, Abel."

"I have a baby." Mee Antra exposed the infant's face. He began to cry. "He hasn't eaten in at least two days. Do you have milk?"

"Oh, you poor dears," the woman exclaimed. "My name is Charity. Come with me."

"Stand by the fire. Let me build it up with more wood. I'm Doug. We are believing millennials." He eyed Adam and Abel, wondering what happened to them.

Adam sensed his curiosity, but before he could explain, Doug grew suspicious. "You said your name was Adam. I've heard tales of an Adam Hillag."

Abel, standing near the fire, stiffened.

"I was an emissary for the devil," Adam admitted. "I was ordered to kill three millennials to break a promise to God. I didn't know it would be my wife, son and great grandbaby. I couldn't do it. A ferocious battle of the mind took place. I broke and believed in Christ. Satan's rage set the building on fire."

"Where was that?" Doug insisted; he was concerned.

"St John's Church."

"No way! That's been abandoned for centuries."

He ran upstairs to return a few minutes later. "You are right. I see the glow of the fire. Dude, what was going on in there?"

"It was to be a satanic coven ritual sacrifice. The goal was to kill millennials and topple the Kingdom of Christ. Satan wanted to burn us alive in the church. We escaped and fled.

Mee Antra came in dressed in Charity's clothes.

"Mee Antra told me everything. They had no clothes, poor dears. We must help them escape, Doug," Charity said to her husband.

Adam sensed movement behind him. He spun around to face an older Resurrection Saint and his angel. Adam was startled.

"I call him my grand uncle," Doug introduced. "Reginold Sullens."

"Captain Reginold Sullens of the Confederate Army, Suh. I fought in a battle near here, and got myself kilt by a Yankee bullet."

"Captain had no family, so we took him in," Doug explained.

"I heard you tell of goings on in St. John's Church. Pity. History happened there. However, if evil works being done, best it be purged to the ground," Captain Sullens shared.

"Captain, sir, can you help us get them to a Transporter?" Doug queried.

"Son, you know my orders. I cannot interfere in the millennial fight, though it do me proud."

"How about this?" Adam had an idea. "Would you ask your angel to tell my dad's angel Detrius and my mom's Waaleen that we are safe and coming home to Applegate?"

The old Captain considered the task a moment before turning to his angel. "Has little to do with the war. Suppose we can grant your request."

His angel lifted into the air to relay Adam's message.

Doug threw on his coat. "We must hurry. By now, rebels are everywhere in this area, searching for you. Our Solar is in the garage and charged. Come. Charity, you go with me."

They hurried to the car and climbed in.

As Doug pulled out of his garage, he muttered out loud, "Rebel Millennials will be spreading out from the church to find you. By now, their range has enlarged. They will be covering Route 60, so we must slip a few blocks south to State Highway 5. That is an old road with little traffic. It will be slower but safer."

"There is a large group of Millennial racers up around Mechanicsville. I'm sure they will be out in force, if Satan is mad enough in his rage to burn down a church," Doug said.

'Those racers would give anything to get ahold of me now," Adam thought. Fear churned his stomach as he recalled the speed they could attain. 'There would be no outrunning any of them.'

"We can't risk a Transporter anywhere in Richmond tonight. Much too dangerous. We will stay on Highway 5 into Williamsburg. I know of a small Transport Station on the outskirts of town. It's little used but big enough for you all to fit inside."

The highway was indeed deserted and poorly lit. They passed only one small town. Adam listened to the two women chatter behind him for a few miles until his mind drifted. His whole life was turning upside down, from willing to obey Satan and kill for him, to salvation and allegiance to Jesus Christ. Regret swallowed him alive. He felt the depressing pain of wasted years; too many of them. Mee Antra who never stopped loving him. He raised the dagger above her ready to plunge it deep into her heart. Still, how many times had he already stabbed her by his silent absence?'

'And Abel, whose knowledge of him was only an ominous name and fragmented vicious rumors. Centuries of years that the lad lived without his father were lost. Lost forever.

'And the baby. Who did this infant belong to, who was kidnapped by evil millennials? Those parents must be overcome with worry. I must find them. But where is any comfort, anything redemptive for me? All I face are mistakes, decisions made in ignorance. Dear Father, I am undone.'

Then, for the first time, Adam heard the tender voice of the Lord Jesus.

'Adam, I forgave you and saved you. Your life is a slate wiped clean of sin and mistakes. Wasted time? You have all of eternity to catch up, starting now.'

Doug pulled into a parking area of a small Transporter Station. Wet snow fell heavy as they all trudged to the main entrance.

"We made it safe, dear friends," Doug said, relieved and happy. "No one's here."

Adam made his way to the Programmer.

"Applegate, Oregon" he requested. "Adam and family."

He returned to the group to say goodbye. There were hugs and tears. The two women cried.

"We hardly know each other; why are we crying?" Mee Antra blotted her eyes.

"There is only one family in God's Kingdom and we are all in it." Charity hugged Mee Antra goodbye. She squeezed the baby and patted Abel on his cheek.

Adam faced Doug and for the first time in many, many cold-hearted centuries, a tear trickled down his cheek. "I owe you and Charity for rescuing us. I will not forget you, my friend, and what you have done."

"Ready?" The Programmer ushered them into the Transporter.

The heavy door bolted shut. Adam was nervous. He had no idea what to expect when they arrived. What would his family do? Would they even be there? Would his dad be angry with him?

Only a moment later they were in the Applegate Transporter. The door opened and they hurried into a clamoring station, filled with family and friends. They were cheering!

Adam saw his grandpa Caleb and Grandma Sarah. He saw John and Johanna and so many people he didn't even know. He saw Shag standing to one side. Then, his eye caught sight of his momma and daddy. He broke and ran, falling at Mark's feet. Weeping, he muttered words that sounded unintelligible. He couldn't even lift his head.

Mark and Nikki gently helped him up and held him. Their boy had come home.

CHAPTER 82

TWO LOOSE ENDS

After the excitement of Adam's conversion and subsequent return to Douglas Landing calmed down, he requested a meeting with just Mee Antra and his mom and dad. He determined there would be no more secrets, no disappearing without any word. He would lay out exactly what he proposed to do.

Mark and Nikki were sitting in the den near the fireplace. This was Adam's favorite room in the log house. It held fond memories when he was very young. Snowy, freezing days like today, he would seek the warmth of the fire. As a youngster he was fascinated over the growing numbers of books his folks were collecting, and he devoured each new one as soon as it was placed on a shelf. This inviting study would truly make it easier to discuss his plans with the ones he loved dearly, and hopefully make those plans more accepting for them.

His parents showed their uneasiness when Adam and Mee Antra entered the den and took a seat across from them. They waited for Adam to relay his reason for this meeting.

"I always get right to the point." Adam remarked.

"Yes, the Lord didn't change that part when He saved you," Nikki spoke lovingly.

"Got it from my dad," Adam smiled.

"Should Abel hear what you have to say?" Mark was serious. He sensed gravity in his son's demeanor. "What about Shag?"

"Abel is in Springdale and Mee Antra will tell him later, and you can tell Shag."

"Do you know what this is about?" Nikki addressed Mee Antra.

Mee Antra shook her head no.

"The great war is about to explode. I wasn't privy to the exact date. All I knew was that the sacrifice would supposedly begin the process. My refusal to kill was a thwart to Satan's plan, but not a deterrent. His orders to attack will be issued soon because he is out of time. And, so am I. I have two things I must do before war breaks out."

"I met a millennial racer in Detroit." Adam choked up. His voice became husky. "We worked off and on for a century to build and co-ordinate all the racers and their crews to prepare for this war. His name is Monte Mole. At the time, he was simply a means to get the job done and garner the Devil's reward. But now my heart grieves for a man who became a friend.

"By this time, Satan has sent out a curse and a death wish on me, so Monte may not even take a SAT call from a defunct satanic emissary. Or, if he does, his anger may tear away his ability to hear what I have to say to him. While Monte's heart may burn with anger, mine burns with the longing and love to lead an old friend to belief in Jesus Christ."

Adam paused to get his family's reaction.

"You are wanting to call this Monte? Contact him from here in our home? Not go see him?" Mee Antra asked nervously.

"Yes. It's too dangerous to go to Detroit, or wherever Monte is."

"Well, the devil's curse or death wish has no hold on you or any of us," Mark commented.

"What is the second matter you spoke of, dear?" Nikki asked softly.

"The second," Adam cleared his throat, "depends on the first. I was to speak at the closing rally of the millennial Grand Prix. Racers from all fifty states and a few international entries gathered in Arizona to race to an old Air Base outside Clovis, New Mexico. I was picked up and driven from my hotel to the starting point by a young millennial woman named Merity. She was spunky, intelligent, and could drive her car like no one I have ever seen. She touched me in a way I can only describe as an awakening inside of something that died and was dormant for centuries; the stirring of a longing for a family, my family.

337

I found myself cheering for her in the race; wanting to see her win as I would a granddaughter or great-great-granddaughter. The thought of her following Satan and being destroyed in this war tears me apart. I wish to find her if Monte will assist me. I will go to her, lead her to Christ, and since she has no family, bring Merity to be part of ours."

"You will go to her?" Mee Antra wiped her eyes.

"If I can locate her." Adam held his wife. "I have no feelings for her as lover or wife, simply as one of our family; a granddaughter."

"Then you must go and bring her home." Mee Antra gave her permission with a kiss.

"I'm frightened, Adam, but proud. Do what you must," Nikki spoke in a low tone.

Mark stood up. "I sense, Son, you wish to be alone to begin your tying up of these two loose ends."

CHAPTER 83

MISSION INITIATED

The family left Adam alone in the den. He sat for a long time staring at the fireplace. With a sigh and prayer, he brought up Monte Mole's number on his SAT. He tapped call and waited. On the fourth ring Monte answered. Adam could see his snarly face before he even spoke.

"How dare you call me, you traitor? I curse you," Monte said, bitterly sardonic.

"Don't hang up, Monte. Hear me out. Please!"

"We are forbidden to have anything to do with you. Master Satan has even issued kill orders on you and your family, which I never knew about."

"Monte, you were always one to break rules, same as me. Let me tell you my side of the story."

There was a long silence. Adam broke it. "Monte, we have been friends a long time."

"Not anymore," Monte growled. "Traitor."

"But we were. We, er, served together a century."

"What possible reason could you have to turn?"

"Satan commanded me to kill my wife, my son, and my great-grandbaby. I have never been in a fight as severe as that night. Satan screaming commands to kill. All the while, my wife is pleading with me for her life. Then my son was begging me to kill him instead of his mother. Satan's demand for my total obedience to kill keeps blowing up in my head. Suddenly, King Jesus calls me to come to Him. When I raised that knife above my great-grandbaby, Satan's power gripped my mind and hands, pressing hard to force me to plunge the knife. Monte, my baby looked in my face. He trusted me, Monte, he trusted me and laughed, trying to hold his little hands up for me to take him. He reached out to me with the heart that I was about to drive a knife into. I couldn't do it, Monte, I couldn't. I broke and fell to my knees. Would you believe that Satan then commanded me to kill myself? He wanted a sacrifice."

Monte was silent.

"Then in my mind I saw Jesus, not as King, but a condemned man hanging on a cross. Jesus Christ was the Sacrifice. Satan drove men to kill Him there, and Satan thought he would have the power of the universe. But in truth, Monte, Christ died so that you and I could live. I drove the spikes in His hands and feet. My knife became the spear that pierced His side. His death bought my freedom and I found it that night. I experienced His forgiveness, love and power. Not power like Satan has that tears at my body and makes my brain pound like it's ready to explode, throwing me to the ground to twitch and jerk in pain. Not like that; but a lifting up as when you reach your hand out to a fallen comrade to help him stand. Yes, there was power, a gentle power born in light and love, a power that conquers fear and gives faith. Power to love, even in the face of hate. Yes, the incredible power of even a single tiny light that no degree of darkness can ever obliterate. I embraced that light and became a millennial believer that night."

Monte did not say a word, but Adam could hear him breathing. So he continued.

"I believe what the Bible predicts, Monte. This war will start and rebel millennials will indeed attempt to take control of the world and make Satan ruler." Adam paused and pondered what next to say.

"Monte, do you remember that café in Fort Sumner where you made a pit stop to eat?"

"Of course," Monte grunted.

"Before you arrived, a millennial Indian woman, Fema, came to my table. I didn't know her but she knew me. She had a message from King Jesus. She questioned my ideals as delusional. She challenged me with, 'Do you really think you can defeat the Creator of the Universe with good intentions? Or because you possess a driving passion for your cause? You and your blind army bring down God Almighty's Son with sticks, throwing rocks and shooting your toy guns? You haven't a chance.'

"Monte, her words have troubled my mind ever since the race. The Bible says that in an instant, God will send fire from heaven and destroy Satan and all who follow him."

"Lies!" Monte bellowed.

"What if it is true? I don't want you to end like that. Believe with me. Open your heart and mind to Jesus Christ. Come be a part of my family."

"This is my life, Adam. I am in too deep, and I don't believe in you or your Christ. My allegiance is to Lord Satan. I once admired you as a strong man and leader. I only see you as pitiful. Don't call me again."

"Wait, Monte, then will you please do this for me? Before the race, I was picked up from my hotel and driven to King's Valley by a millennial driver. Her name was Merity. I need to repay a favor. I know you have contacts and records. Spelled M-e-r-i-t-y. Will you give me her location? Please. It's very important."

"Why should I? So you can preach to her?"

"I ask because we were once friends. I ask this one thing and no other. Please, Monte. My heart grieves that you won't believe in Christ, but He never forces belief on any person, nor can I. But please, as your friend, no matter what you think of me, please do this one last request? Find Merity."

"I'll see what I can do." Click.

Adam sat by the fireplace in silence a long time. In all his life, he had never known a love to make his heart so tender. Before, he would have just written them all off as losers and good riddance, but that was no longer acceptable. The thought of millennials he met over the centuries being sent to hell broke his heart. Why should he care? They can believe on their own or perish. No! He loved them all with this strange new indescribable powerful love. He glanced at his SAT. No message from Monte.

Finally, weariness took over and Adam went to bed. Around 8 AM Adam was deep in sleep when his phone went off. It was a text from Monte. It read: 'Merity is with a racer unit in Durango, Colorado.'

CHAPTER 84

THE MISSION

Mee Antra dropped Adam off at the Applegate Transporter Station. She was uneasy, but supportive.

"Be careful and come back to me." She kissed him. "Bring our great-granddaughter back with you."

Adam held his wife an extended moment before stepping inside the Transporter. He waved as the door clamped shut. In a matter of seconds, he was in Durango, Colorado.

The frost-laden air stung his face and hands. An abundance of snow was piled on road edges and against the shops and buildings. He walked hurriedly for several blocks seeking a restaurant that served hot coffee.

'How do I find Merity?' he wondered. 'Where do I start? Just ask around? This isn't just some dinky mountain village.'

The waitress returned with his coffee. "Anything else?" she asked.

"I'm looking for an old solar racer friend named Merity. Would you know her?" Adam ventured.

She shook her head. "I can tell you this. No racer is out in this weather."

Adam noticed another patron in a booth wearing a racing-type outfit. Adam left his table to inquire of the fellow.

"Hello. I'm looking for a solar racer named Merity. Are you a racer?"

"Naw, buddy. Just like the shirt. Hope you find her."

"A lot of racers hang out at Vingo Sports," a voice came from the adjoining booth.

Adam stepped aside to face an older Millennial. "How far is that?" Adam asked.

343

"Other side o' town," the man mumbled. "Take the shuttle."

Adam returned to his table. 'Lord Jesus,' he silently prayed. 'I'm just getting used to this praying business so I don't even know if you hear me, but I need help and direction to find Merity. Should I go to Vingos?'

Adam was shocked and almost dropped his coffee cup to hear a gentle voice whisper, 'Keep on three more blocks, turn right and go five.'

Adam waited near the front door until he saw a shuttle coming. He ran out to wave it down. "Three blocks, turn right, then five blocks," he instructed the driver.

When they reached the fifth block, Adam was watching. "What's in this block, for a visitor?"

"Visitor Center?" the driver suggested.

"Perfect. Let me out." Adam scrambled out of the shuttle and raced inside the Center. A rather plain-looking receptionist greeted him. She wore no makeup, her hair hung straight. The marker on the counter listed her as Jean. She smiled warmly and asked, "What brings you out on such a cold day?"

"I'm looking for a Solar Racer named Merity. I'm an old friend. Can you help me locate her, um, Jean?"

"Merity is well-known among racers here as she has won top places numerous times. But I can't give out personal information."

Adam rubbed his chin in thought and paced back and forth a couple of times. "Could you give her a message?" Adam asked.

"Can't guarantee, Mr.?"

"Adam."

"I cannot guarantee she will even receive a message from me, or that she will answer."

"Gosh." Adam ran his hand through his hair. "I have traveled from Oregon. We are old friends and I want to return a favor. I wish her no harm."

"Sorry, I can't be more helpful." Jean was kind.

"Let me ask this. Can you send me to a restaurant, a public place, a reasonable distance from her home, if you have her address, and message I am wanting to see her?"

Jean studied his face and looked him over, trying to decide if he could be trustworthy. She appeared to soften. "Yes, I will do that for you." She picked up a SAT. "What is the message?"

"Adam is waiting where?"

"The Mountaineer."

"Adam is waiting at the Mountaineer today and wants to talk. Please come."

Jean typed the message then opened a file to get Merity's number. "It's done," she said, and smiled.

Adam caught another shuttle. The drive to the Mountaineer took forty minutes. Adam chose a semi-private booth from which he could observe those who came in the restaurant. His mind was torn as he waited.

'What if she is out of town or in another state? Racing in Arizona where it's warmer? Or, she could message back and I would never get it. I didn't leave my SAT number with Jean. How stupid! No, maybe my number shouldn't be out here, in public.'

Adam ordered coffee, juices, water and stretched out lunch for two hours. No Merity. A sick disappointment settled in his head and made its way to his stomach. He began wondering if he should just figure this meeting a wash and go home? No, perhaps he should get a room for the night and not cave in so easily. Or, should he return to the Visitor Center and start over? Then, there was still Vingo Sports.

He decided he had worn out his welcome at the Mountaineer and was about to leave, when he recognized Merity coming into the restaurant and begin looking around. She spotted Adam and hurried to his booth, sliding in the seat. She was catching her breath.

"Adam Hillag, I got your message and knew it was you. What are you doing here?"

"I came to see you."

"But why? You are condemned among the rebels. There is a kill order on you. Racers see you as a traitor. Why, Adam? What happened to you?"

"During that brief ride-race in Arizona you awakened something in me that should have been there not just years but centuries ago. I missed and longed for my family, my wife, to know a child I had never seen. I began feeling towards you as a granddaughter, and I still do. Thank you for your words that day. You touched my heart more than you can know."

Merity looked away and brushed away a tear. She half-laughed. "Well, you don't look like Grandpa, and I don't know if I fit a granddaughter mold, but, hell, huh, here we are. Did you manage to find your family? Your wife and child?"

"Yes, Merity, I did." Adam took her hand and began to relay the same story he told Monte Mole. Adam posed the same questions and challenges he gave Monte and explained that his old friend rejected him, but researched Merity's location.

The two of them talked for a long time. Adam told of the change in him, his spiritual birth, and his reunion in Oregon. Merity listened, and teared up. She was attempting to analyze and understand everything Adam was telling her. The conclusion was reached and she pulled her hand from his and looked away. Adam feared she was turning away from him as Monte did.

"Is this all it's about?" Merity spoke softly. "To thank me for setting your life on a different course? You're welcome. I'm glad I did that for you. You shared your story. Was this just to do that, Adam?"

"No," Adam whispered.

"What do you want from me then?" She took hold of his hand again.

"Open your heart and ask Jesus in; become a believing millennial as I did."

Merity stared intently into Adam's eyes. "You have changed; from the harsh, blunt, cold leader of Satan's rebels to a man who can love again? Is that possible? Adam, I don't know if I can do as you ask. I'm not sure I understand. Can I think about it?"

"Merity, you don't have time. War is about to be declared by the devil. Once it is, you will be sucked into it and destroyed with millions of others. Merity, I don't want to see my granddaughter end up in eternal darkness and torment. You are my family."

With that word, Merity buried her face in her arms and wept quietly in gentle convulsions. Adam waited prayerfully for her to work out her salvation with Jesus.

Suddenly she jerked, sat up, beginning to laugh. She wiped her wet face with a napkin.

"Adam! It happened!" she exclaimed. "Just like you said. I feel it. I am a believer. My mind is free, my heart and soul are free. Oh, thank you, Adam. Thank you, Jesus. I feel I can soar."

Adam was moved beyond words. All he could do was laugh and squeeze her hands.

"Merity," he burst out. "You are truly my family. Adopted yes, but every bit my family; and they are all waiting for you to come home."

Merity grew serious. "I don't know," she responded.

"You can't stay here, Merity. Not now."

"I won't leave my racer."

"We'll take it. There is family and mountain roads in Oregon."

"But how?" She was unsure.

"Come on, Granddaughter. I knew you would never live in a city that your racer couldn't fit in a Transporter. Springdale has one. I checked. We'll go there and drive; we'll race the hour to Douglas Landing. You will be loved and safe there."

Merity dropped her eyes and bit her lip. She was letting go of her past rejections, hurts, and fears. Her head doubted but her heart told her, 'Go!' She looked up.

"When do we leave?"

"Right now. Pack what you can in your racer and we'll dash to the Transporter Station. Are you ready?"

"You bet." She stood up.

The rest of the late afternoon was spent in a crazy dash to her apartment. She bagged up only the necessities. There would be no contacts to say goodbye. She was a new Merity and would disappear from the old and drive into a new.

They raced to the Transporter and Adam instructed the programmer to enter in their destination Springdale, Oregon. In a whirl, they were in Oregon and racing madly to Douglas

Landing. Pulling into Mark and Nikki's log home was dream-like for Merity. A huge banner reading, 'Welcome Home, Merity,' hung along the porch. As the racer pulled up, family poured out of the house to welcome their newest member.

CHAPTER 85

THE FINAL BATTLE

The dreaded day, awaited for a thousand years, began without announcement or any fanfare. There was no Global order, or at least none revealed to the world. It was shouted out by Satan, heard only by his troops and followers, and a total surprise attack.

Hordes of millennial rebels appeared from every possible source. They marched or drove military-style vehicles. The armies were united, armed and rose out of the mountains, jungles, deserts, urban cities and aggressively advanced to take over.

The believing millennials fell as easy prey to the rebel hostiles. Any resistance was met with force. There were instances of weapons used, but invariably the bullets or laser beams were deflected or simply missed the target. To their utter frustration, the angry millennials' rifles jammed or their laser charges died, leaving them to hold useless weapons.

For the most part, the believing millennials simply gave up and obeyed the orders of their captors.

Massive millennial armies were rapidly moving towards Jerusalem. Satan was confused as to why King Jesus didn't order His millennial troops to come against his massive armies. He wrongly supposed Jesus' lack of leadership to fight was born of disorganization or fear. 'The King is cowering before my might,' he mused.

Meanwhile, the Trevor family hovered around live news streams non-stop to monitor events of war not only in areas surrounding the Holy Land, but other parts of the world. America was not exempt. Satan's army had prepared and existed for this very hour. They were mean, well-organized and disciplined.

One day, Monte Mole was seen in a news brief as he led a charge of his racers to take over six small villages in Iowa. A few days later, Merity recognized some of her friends in an Arizona land-and-town grab.

Adam, Mee Antra, Abel and Merity were all heartsick because they understood where this war was headed and how it would end.

"Well, at least it looks doubtful the war will extend its ugly arm into Douglas Landing," Mee Antra murmured.

However, her prediction proved to be only wishing thinking. At dawn, three weeks into the war, rebel millennials surrounded the Hillag log home. Looking out strategic windows, Shag estimated at least fifty troops. Mark went out the front door with Detrius to confront them.

Millennials leveled their weapons as Mark stepped out on the porch.

The officer in charge marched briskly up to face Mark. "Adam Hillag?" he barked. "Are you Adam Hillag?"

"No."

"Is he inside?"

"None of your business, rebel."

"I will not tolerate your insolence, nor a lie," the officer raised his voice. "I will order my soldiers to shoot."

"Go ahead. My angel will protect me and you know it."

The officer stepped back an instant to consider the next move, while his army stood firm. "Bring Adam Hillag out or we will burn your house down with all in it."

Mark started to answer when Adam stepped through the door. "It's all right, Dad. Let me handle these blind eyes." He walked to the top of the steps.

"I am Adam Hillag," he said as he addressed the officer.

"You are charged with high treason by Master Satan. We have orders to hold you under house arrest until our leader gains total victory. When ready, we will transport you to his high court where you will stand trial."

"That isn't going to happen. Give up while you have the chance. Surrender your hearts and believe on the Lord Jesus Christ."

"Silence," the officer screamed. "Do not speak that Name in my presence, you imbecile."

Mark and Adam turned and walked into the house.

Mee Antra ran to Adam. She was proud of her man for standing up to the rebels, yet deathly afraid for him. "I was so scared they would shoot you," she gasped.

"Today I held the same feelings as when we challenged the millennial rebels out in the jungle," Mark added.

"It was a lot worse." Adam shook his head. "Mean, better armed, but this time I was on the opposite side of the cause. I offered them a last chance to convert and choose life."

The troops set up bivouac around the house. The tents were course fabric to ward off the wind and snow. Each shelter held two men and was supplied with a heater. Hot meals were brought in daily, probably provided by some captured millennial restaurants. Guards stood posts day and night allowing no one to exit the house or any outsider to have access to the family.

The second day of captivity Farmer and Emile approached the house. A guard blocked them.

"You are forbidden to enter the house. Leave."

Farmer walked close to the guard. He spoke low but direct. "Youngen, I don't reckon ya ta be ignorant, so why ya be acten' so? Ta be clear, me an' my Emile air gon'a walk right in thet house and when done, we will walk right back out."

"What makes you think you can defy us all?" the guard snapped, leveling his rifle.

"First there be these two angels with us," Farmer said, indicated Adreen and Froton. "You touch me or my misses, they will take ya all out. An' second, in case ya ain't figured it out, ya can't kill us. We be Resurrection Saints. SO MOVE!" Farmer thundered.

The guard stepped aside and Farmer and Emile passed through. "We could have just appeared inside," Emile chuckled to Farmer.

By the fourth day Shag had enough. "I'm sick of these snot-nosed, wet-diaper, babies holding us hostage in our own house. Besides, even as cold as it is, Kimuchka needs her outdoors time."

Shag donned a heavy coat and stuck his knife in his belt. He whistled for Kimuchka and they left to go out the door into the cold.

The millennial guards drew back when Shag emerged with his pet mountain lion and his angel Ganteous. Several guards intercepted him.

"Go back in the house, old man," they ordered.

Shag kept walking until he was face-to-face with four guards.

"Turn around! Go back in the house!" the lead officer shouted. "Or we will shoot."

"With what?" Shag smirked. "These BB guns?"

"These are weapons, fool. I can kill you," one guard challenged.

Shag stepped closer and in a flash military move snatched the guard's rifle and turned it on him.

"Now I've got your weapon." Shag's eyes blazed. "What think yee to do about it?"

"We'll kill you dead!" The officer yelled.

"Not today, Sonny," Shag shoved the rifle barrel into the guard's belly. "Don't be stupid."

Ganteous rose up in battle mode. He opened his wings and drew his sword, which immediately turned red-hot, bursting into flame. The guards fell back, petrified.

"And one more thing. Any of you yokels harm my pet mountain lion, there will be hell to pay before your time."

As Shag moved on towards Cold Creek, the officer stood down. "Let him pass. Our fight is not with him."

For the next ten days, war news totally captivated the families' attention. Each day brought Satan's armies ever closer to Jerusalem, yet no word or action from King Jesus. Still, the family sensed the end approaching. They speculated on how the final battle might take place.

"Will we see it? Hear anything?" They asked each other. None had any idea what to expect. They just knew how it would end.

By the twelfth day, millennial rebels had conquered most of the populated world. Satan's army had Jerusalem totally surrounded. The devil now declared himself new ruler of the earth, appearing as a figure of light. He demanded that Jesus concede His Kingship to him. That's when it happened.

The ground began to shake. Not the kind to cause damage, but more of a quiver that kept growing in intensity. The family felt they were in a huge globe with someone's giant hands shaking it. This quake was not in isolated areas. No, the whole planet shook as though attempting to shed itself of a disgusting evil that had pervaded all of nature and humankind since the Garden of Eden.

As the family members struggled to hold on and gain footing, there was a blinding flash of light, so piercing they all shrieked from the pain.

Suddenly, the temperature rose dramatically. The air was stifling, stinging the lungs with every breath. "Mercy, Lord," some cried out.

"I can't breathe," Abel gasped, clutching his throat.

"Oh, God!" Merity cried out. "Were we wrong? Has destruction come to us?"

"No! Have faith! Grab on to faith. Believe! Hold on!" Mark shouted the command.

Bam! There was a clap of thunder so strong and loud it knocked them flat on the floor. The house groaned and rattled as if to come apart. Shelves emptied, furniture toppled. Then silence. The family slowly picked themselves up, ensuring no one was injured before checking for damage.

"Look!" Abel shouted from a window. "The guards are all gone. But their weapons and clothes are covering the ground."

The family ran outside. True, their weapons, clothes, boots and personal belongings were strewn over the ground, but there were no visible sign of the guards.

"It's like the rapture was," Nikki gasped, observing the scene.

Adam reached down to pick up a rifle. It burned his hand. "Yow!" he cried. "This thing is hot."

"It's also melted, like these over here," Shag said.

Merity squatted down to touch one of the uniforms. "Their uniforms are scorched. Oh God, dear Lord, to think these could have been my clothes, somewhere.

"This wasn't a 'calling up' Rapture, it was a 'fire raining down' destruction," Mark deducted.

Farmer and Emile arrived. "Reckon it ta be all over," Farmer announced. "Satan got captured an' all his evil, his demons, his army an' followers were soundly defeated. Thet be the final battle o' the ages. There will never be another, ever."

SEGMENT SEVEN

THE GREAT WHITE THRONE JUDGMENT

CHAPTER 86

WHAT'S NEXT

The Thousand Year Reign was now complete. The final battle was over, and now an unspeakable, rich peace settled over the whole earth. Sin and its evil presence were eradicated and the world and everything in it returned to the perfect state once again, as it was when God first formed it.

Families began to gather in clumps around the planet. These groupings were perhaps prompted by the uncertainty of what they were to do next. There was no measurement of time, seconds, minutes and hours. Everyone lost track of which day it was. What measurement could be used? Days, months, years after the Millennium? That hardly seemed appropriate.

The Temple in Jerusalem had been closed and silent since the final battle. All work and related projects ceased, so it seemed the obvious thing to do was to gather together in groups of family or friends and wait on their King.

Walter, Clifton and his people joined Harold, Leah and Janee in California. Mark, Nikki and all of their local family, went to Farmer and Emile's log home. Esther came from Back East, and Caleb and Sarah left Lugar de Paraiso to join them. After everyone took time to join together in Farmer and Emile's Great Room. There was so much to discuss.

"What I don't understand," Merity got right to a nagging question, "is when God's fire destruction fell, we heard it and felt the effects. The soldiers' weapons were melted, their clothes were singed; we even saw burn holes in the tents. Yet nothing else was touched. Why didn't we see the fire, or hear the soldiers scream?"

"Yeah," Mee Antra agreed. "Seems so weird."

"One thing we gotta reckon. We be so far away from the main battle. Maybe it was bigger there an' more seen," Farmer suggested.

"If fire fell from heaven, wouldn't it burn up all the earth?" Emile asked.

"God's judgment in the Tribulation scorched the plants and trees. We've all seen newscasts from around the world. Nothing is burned, not even in Jerusalem," Mark said.

"Do you think God's wrath came on Satan's army in the spiritual realm? That it was real, and destroyed; we just couldn't see it?" Sarah wondered.

"Reckon we just hev ta take it on faith thet our Lord protected all o' nature, an' ever' living thing, meaning us, from His terrible destruction. An' thet He spared us from seeing the tragic, horrible end o' all those rebel millennials."

"Amen," the whole family agreed. It was a sobering thought to even try and imagine what those millennials saw as doom came upon them.

"But it isn't over for them," Caleb, who had been quiet, spoke up.

"What do you mean?" Adam questioned. "They are all dead and gone."

"Dead, but not gone," Caleb answered.

This statement created a host of frenzied conversations from the family. Farmer attempted to calm them.

"Explain, Poppy Caleb, I'm confused," Abel blurted out.

"I'll be glad to." Caleb stood as if to preach. "I think the answer will also give insight into what is really on all our minds right now.

"In Scripture, two resurrections are mentioned, the First and the Second. The First resurrection must be complete before the Second one can occur. We Resurrection Saints are all a part of the First Resurrection, but that spiritual work is not done."

"You are right, Dad," Mark caught on. "Me, Nikki, our kids, grandkids, Shag, we are still flesh and blood. Tribulation Saints and believing Millennials; we will be part of the First Resurrection."

"You are correct, Mark," Caleb continued. "The Second Resurrection comes after the First is complete. Those are all the lost. The rebels were killed, but will be resurrected. Think about the magnitude of it. Every person who has ever been conceived and born will be resurrected. The Bible says the earth and the sea will give up their dead.

"We understand from Scripture that after the Millennium, will be the Great White Throne Judgment and all will stand before that throne. The First Resurrection Saints to observe, and the Second Resurrected to be judged."

"Why can't we who are flesh and blood go as we are?" Adam questioned.

"I don't think I could take it," Nikki replied.

"My heart would surely stop." Mee Antra covered her chest with her hand.

"Reckon it ta be like throwen' our bodies in a tornado ta jus' get ripped up." Farmer spoke solemnly.

"You all answered your own question. No flesh and blood human could go before that White Throne and live," Caleb concluded. "So, I think this is how it will play out. First must be the finalization of all Tribulations Saints' and Millennials' Resurrections. Next comes the Second Resurrection of all the lost, including the Millennial rebels. All must stand before the White Throne Judgment. Only the Anti-Christ and the False Prophet were immediately cast into the Lake of Fire."

Nikki turned pale and held her stomach.

"What's wrong, Nikki?" Sarah noticed the change in her demeanor.

Nikki swallowed hard. "Does that mean Stoner? I don't think I can face him."

Caleb was silent. "Nor I," Sarah whispered.

The family sat in reflective thought, each seeing images of family or people they knew in their lives.

"Well, after the Second Resurrection comes the Judgment. With that, we have the answer to the question we've all been wondering. What comes next?" Caleb sat down next to Sarah and held her.

CHAPTER 87

FIRST RESURRECTION

The last plague, which liberated the Children of Israel from Egypt's bondage, was the death angel sweeping over the land killing all first-born, including Pharaoh's own son.

All Israelite first-born were spared if they remained in the house where the blood of a sacrificial lamb was sprinkled on the sides and tops of the doors. The death angel passed over them in the dark of night.

Now another spirit will pass over the land. Not just one country, but the whole of earth. This spirit will reach into every cave, forest, desert, house and building, from the highest mountain to the deepest canyon, searching out each living Tribulation Saint and Millennial.

This miraculous event that will sweep across the whole planet will not take place in the dark, but in the light of breaking day. When the sun rises in the east and its rays of sunlight spread before it, the warm gentle breeze of the Holy Spirit will follow the dawning of a brand-new day from east to west. It will search out every Tribulation Saint and Millennial to be able to breathe His Resurrection Life and Power into their very beings.

The family gathered at Farmer and Emile's house indeed felt it; a warm breeze where there should not be a breeze; a soft whisper when no one was there; a strong touch by an invisible hand.

Mark felt it happen as he was in the kitchen having coffee. Whoa! 'What was that?' he thought. Then he looked at his hands, felt his face. He was different! He rose and walked to his bedroom to awaken Nikki. He was astounded by what he saw. Her beauty radiated from her face. Her skin, her hair was immaculate. He hesitated to touch her; she looked angelic.

"Nikki, sweetheart." He shook her tenderly.

She stirred, squinting at him, and then her eyes flashed wide open. She gasped!

"Mark? What happened to you?" She sat up in bed. Mark leaned down to place his ear against her chest. She giggled. "What are you doing?"

"Shh," Mark listened for a long time. He took her hand. "Nikki." He was astounded. "You have no heartbeat, yet you live. Don't you feel the strength? The enormous energy? My mind seems super-fast and clear, and you are absolutely beautiful."

"Yes, I feel—amazing. You are the most handsome thirty-year-old man I have ever seen. Let me take your pulse." Nikki placed fingers on his wrist, then his neck.

"Mark, I can't find a pulse," Nikki declared.

Merity screamed from a bathroom. Mark and Nikki jumped up and ran to her. She was trembling. "Can this be real?" she muttered over and over. When she looked at them, she was shocked. "You both are, so, bright," she struggled to find words to describe their looks.

"Can it be? Is it?" Merity wanted affirmation.

"Yes!" Mark and Nikki chimed in. "We have been resurrected, Praise God! We've waited for this a thousand years."

"We have no hearts, no blood. Our bodies are glorified!" Nikki shouted.

Shag wandered down the hall. "What's all the dang noise?" he mumbled.

"Oh my gosh!" Mark, Nikki and Merity exclaimed.

"Look at you, Shag." Nikki laughed and pulled him to the bathroom mirror. "You are the best-looking silver-haired warrior I've ever seen."

"We've been resurrected!" Mark hugged him.

"By thunder, you are right. My hands ain't been this spotless since I was born, an' I feel like a teenager again."

"Did I hear you speak of a resurrection?" Emile poked her head in the bathroom door and took one look. "Oh my, it's true. Farmer, Farmer, it's happened!" She ran, yelling out through the great room, "Where are you?"

Mee Antra squeezed into the bathroom as Merity left out. Then Adam joined his wife. They were both speechless and in awe of their new bodies. Soon everyone was awake and the excitement was high-pitched. They eventually moved out of the bathroom and into the Great Room. Emile had gone out to fetch Farmer, who was walking along Cold Creek. They appeared in the room with the rest. Farmer glanced at each of their faces and bodies.

"Well, I declare. The Resurrection done took place and Emile an' I be right proud an' pleased. My, an' what a pretty picture y'all make. Do Caleb, Sarah an' Esther be back?"

"Not yet," Mark answered, "but they only went down to Lugar de Paraiso for a short time to check on friends and conditions there. I'll have Detrius inform their angels."

Instantly Merity appeared in their presence. Everyone assumed she was still in her room.

"Wow! Wow! What a rush!" She was flushed. "You know I have that racer spirit, so I just had to try it for myself."

"What?" They all wanted to know.

"I got to thinking about the big Racer Chapter that built up in King's Valley, Arizona and wondered about their solar racers. Then, as I sat on my bed, I got this notion to go see. I just put the thought and place in my head. Wham, I was there!"

"What did you find?" Adam was intrigued.

"Hot and desolate. No living souls. The cars were twisted, melted, like they were tossed about. Some piled on top of others. Only dirt devils whipping up sand as they spun across the valley floor. I came promptly home."

"Aye, an' thet be wise. None be gone long as we wait fer King Jesus ta call," Farmer said.

"Adam, how about you and Mee Antra? Some place? What a thrill. No more transporters." Merity was ecstatic.

"I'm afraid a trip like that, just in the open, would take my breath completely away," Mee Antra objected. "I'll have a heart attack for sure."

Everyone laughed but Mee Antra was serious. Emile came over and sat by her and took her hand. "My dear Mee Antra, this is all so new to you," Emily spoke lovingly. "First of all, you won't know fear; you have no heart to be attacked; and although it feels like you are breathing, you actually are not. Last, and greatest, you will never die. You have been given the gift of eternal life in a perfect body."

Abel jumped up. "I'm going to Springdale to see friends."

Adam and Mee Antra started to tell him not to be gone long, but he had disappeared.

"Come on, Adam," Merity urged. "You and Mee Antra have got to try it."

Adam leaned over and whispered in Mee Antra's ear and took her hand from Emile. He grinned, she nodded, and they were gone.

"Well now," Farmer said as he ran his fingers through his hair. "This be plumb astounding, everbody getten a hankeren ta take a trip. Mark, ya an' Nikki best go somewhere since the family got travelen' in their heads."

Mark looked at Nikki. "Let's go see the twins and their families at the Lake House in Georgia." She was ready. They held hands and were gone.

"Dang." Shag stood up, not to be outdone. "Never could get into one of those Transporter contraptions, but now this seems to be the real deal. I'll go look up my bud Steven Vogal in Colorado. How I do this? Just think about the place?" He vanished.

"Reckon they found their wings," Farmer laughed.

Later that evening, Farmer and Emile were watching a gorgeous sunset. "Never tire of a sight liken this, do ya, Emile?"

"Not as long as I'm with you, dear."

Adam and Mee Antra walked out on the porch.

""Oh, you are back. Where did you two go?" Emile asked.

363

"To Jerusalem and it was wondrous," Mee Antra answered. "I have long dreamed to go, but . . ." her voice trailed off.

"Ya see King Jesus?" was Farmer's question.

"No, it was dark and the Temple blocked off."

"But I could tell it is beautiful," Mee Antra quickly added. "And the town and people were incredible. There was a celebration going on."

"What gave ya the idea ta go there, Adam?" Farmer inquired. "Ya reckon Jesus would even be in the Temple?"

"I don't think so. My dad told me recently that after this is all over, everything will be destroyed and a new heaven and earth will be made. I just wanted Mee Antra to see it, before it is gone, that's all."

"Thank you," Mee Antra murmured. "It was wonderful."

By next morning, all but Shag were back home. There was a lot of discussion over the first resurrection, as they continually realized differences and new things about their glorified bodies.

"I don't get hungry," Abel mentioned casually. "Strange for me, as I had a ferocious appetite."

"All our Transporter Stations will be trashed," Mark mused.

"Potties and beds gone, gone, gone," Merity sang.

Shag arrived back around noon. He spoke not a word, but took Kimuchka and headed into the forest.

"He misses his love," Nikki whispered to Mark.

Mark dropped his head. "We too, miss our old friends, martyred precious ones. Maybe soon, Nikki."

Later in the afternoon, Mark took Nikki by the hand and they walked down to the creek and stood over the place where they sat in the water to keep cool during the heat blast.

"I was ready to give up," Nikki remembered. "I hurt so bad, and our poor little Chesterfield. Will we remember this always?"

"I don't know, but there is a place I would like us to go, one last time."

Without a word, both knew. She held him tight and in an instant they stood in the beach area of Hotel La Posada. Lisa Martinez was walking from a room to the sala. She jumped when the couple appeared. She eyed them carefully, started to walk, then looked again.

"Mark? Nikki?" She couldn't believe her eyes.

"Yes," they shouted and ran to her with hugs.

"Come. Come into the sala. I'll get Juan. Come. Oh, I am overjoyed to see you."

Mark and Nikki looked around. They were amazed by how little the Bed and Breakfast had actually changed in a Millennium. The pool had been redone several times, and board repairs were evident. They could see the rooms extending out on both sides from the large openings in the sala.

"I was in that room over there, and you were on this side," Mark said as he grew misty. "I remember it as if it was yesterday."

"I fell in love with you that day. My hero."

Juan and Lisa came running in.

"Where do we start? Welcome. How exciting to see you both. We often wondered," Juan stopped, just to look at them.

"You are here because of the resurrection, aren't you?" Lisa asked softly. "I always knew you would come back, someday."

"We had to thank you for all you did here. Both of us never forgot." Mark spoke from deep feelings of gratitude. "We could have both died in this place."

"But you didn't," Juan interjected. "We owe you our lives. You shared and helped us believe in the true Christ. What you don't realize, you started a movement that took hold and others ran with it. We owe you, my friends. We could easily have been deceived and taken Christo's mark. Instead, we survived the Tribulation as you did. Here we are, thanks to you both."

"We are married and have a huge family. Twins and a millennial son," Nikki blurted out.

With that, the two couples attempted to condense a thousand years of history and memories into two hours of conversation. There were tears, lots and lots of laughter. Quiet moments occurred, only to shift to jovial joking and teasing, only to drift back to tender topics. The time passed all too quickly. By and by, La Posada guests wandered in for a supper meal. They came more in habit or just from joy in sitting around a table in a beautiful setting. Juan and Lisa rose from the table to tend to their guests. Mark and Nikki said their goodbyes.

"Will we see you again?" Lisa wiped a tear.

"Why not? We have forever." Mark smiled.

The couple walked a path of long ago along the beach. They sat down in the sand to watch a blazing sunset. They remembered how the harbor lights would begin to announce the coming dusk. There are moments you spend with someone you love that are so deep with emotion, so rich with memories, so precious to savor, words don't come easily nor are needed. In their minds, they went back to this very spot where they were given their freedom in Christ. Then came a blur of images, events, family, friends, struggles, pain, joy, and victories, all mingled together. Nikki snuggled closer and slipped her hand inside Mark's arm. The sun was sinking into the Pacific.

"Would you change anything, Nikki? Less pain or struggles? No deaths?"

Nikki pondered Mark's question silently for a long time. "No," she answered. "Not that I would want to, but to change any of it would alter our lives, who we are. It would not only affect us, but our kids and all who came after. Events meant to happen could have altered friends' lives, Global Missions. Perhaps many of those would never have believed. No, I wouldn't change any of it, but there is one thing I would hope and long for."

"What is that?" Mark looked into her eyes.

"I read in history books of certain couples. It was said of them, 'they never left each other's side.' That would be my wish for our forever."

CHAPTER 88

THE JUDGE TAKES HIS THRONE

The summons came to all believers in every part of the world, via countless numbers of angels. Orders were given to assemble in the vast Valley of Destruction located to the east of Mount Sinai. The Valley was so named because of its harsh and deadly weather conditions. On their journey millenniums ago to Mount Sinai, the Israelites camped on the cooler west side of the mountain. When they departed, travel across the Destructive Valley was as hurried as possible. Many believers wondered the Lord's reason for this location.

Arriving in the Valley of Destruction, Resurrection Saints were greeted by a huge White Throne at the far south end of the valley. The Throne rose high above the floor of the plain. Looking the opposite direction to the north, black columns of smoke spiraled high into the sky.

The valley was indeed hot. So high was the temperature, any flesh and blood would perish in a matter of hours. However, the Resurrected were unfazed by the heat. There most certainly was a protective cover over all believers. But what of the lost who would stand in their own righteousness, which was as filthy rags in the Lord's sight?

Resurrected Saints were directed by angels to form masses on either side of the valley even up into the mountains. Their numbers looked as vast as the grains of desert sand. Every human who ever lived and believed in the Lord Jesus Christ, from Adam and Eve to the last millennial right up to the collapse of the devil's kingdom at the final battle, was present. The center of the valley was left open from the south end way up into distant mountains towards the north. A lower range of peaks lined the east side of the long plain, and Mount Sinai towered above the Valley of Destruction on the west.

Saints who came from Paradise recalled and relished the sight of millions of angels and their singing. But this was new to the recently Resurrected Saints and they were quite overwhelmed.

As soon as the last arriving Saints took their places, trumpets began to peal loudly to fully engulf the entire extent of the valley. At some point the sound was as bells, then horns, but in majestic harmony, announcing the arrival of the King of kings and Lord of lords.

As the trumpets blared, there arose a roar that swelled ever increasingly in strength, like waves washing ashore, each larger than the one before. These were resurrected voices cheering, singing praises, welcoming their beloved King. Each wave added more and more voices, louder, bolder, shaking the very ground. Then, in perfect harmony, the angels joined. Voices in that valley reached out to fill the universe with praises to the Lord on High.

Then Jesus descended out of the sky. Immediately angels folded their wings and bowed before the Lord of Hosts. Saints quickly followed their example.

The Son of God slowly dropped. His countenance radiated light brighter than the noonday sun. There would be no night in His Presence. He came not as a simple carpenter, nor a shepherd. He was not as a lamb slain, or the Son crucified. He was King, resplendent in His regal robe, a King's crown on His head. His feet touched the ground in front of the White Throne.

He motioned His Saints to stand and opened wide His arms. Christ's face was kind and loving as a Savior, not harsh and stern as a judge. His keen eyes took in every one of His Resurrected Saints and each felt their Lord look directly at them and into the depths of their souls.

"My children," He addressed them. "This time will be the most difficult of your lives. Regret and anguish will tear at every mind, body and soul. There will be weeping and gnashing of teeth. You will not be shielded from what is about to take place. Only by thankfulness that you are not condemned but forgiven will you be able to pass through the pain and sorrow.

"If you come to accuse and present evidence of condemnation, rid yourselves of it. Books will be opened and deeds read. Those deeds will present condemning evidence enough.

"If you harbor anger, cast it away now. The only anger in this court comes from me. Beware you fall not under my wrath, as the condemned.

"Thoughts of revenge, no matter how sweet you entertain them, strike from your minds. Vengeance is mine and no one shall take pleasure in seeing even the most wicked cast into eternal damnation."

Jesus turned towards the throne. He removed His robe and crown and handed them to ministering archangels. He was brought a Judge's Robe. He put that on and mounted the steps of the White Throne. When He turned to take His seat, his face changed from loving and gentle to frightful. As Scripture says: *'Him that sat on it, from whose face the earth and the heaven fled away.'* His face was horrible and the Saints could not look upon Him. They wanted to run away but could not.

Christ took His seat on The Great White Throne.

CHAPTER 89

ASSEMBLY OF LOST SOULS

A most unusual change took place in the face of Christ. His expression remained judicial; still none of His Saints could look upon Him without intense fear.

"Only by His mercy ta us," Farmer whispered to Emile.

A host of Angelic Trumpeters flew in to line up in front of the Throne. They blew a regal but solemn march. The sound that captured respect.

"The procession of Tribulation Martyrs," a high-ranking angel loudly proclaimed.

Slowly, these martyred saints who had refused the Anti-Christo's unholy mark and gave up their lives, walked the center of the valley to take a place of honor on either side of the White Throne.

As these martyrs passed by, angels and Resurrected Saints bowed their heads in humble respect.

"Our dear Tribulation brothers and sisters," Mark and Nikki cried. They stretched to catch a glimpse of any of their friends.

"Aye," Shag grabbed Mark's arm. "I thought I saw Dulco and Eric, for a second."

When this favored group was assembled, the Trumpet Angels flew away.

"Bring forth all those of the Second Resurrection," the angel's command filled the whole valley and reverberated off the mountains.

Next legions of angels walled in the Resurrected Saints on both sides of the valley. They stood shoulder-to-shoulder, swords drawn and ready to guard. There would be no crossing the angelic barrier by lost or saved

The immense throng waited. Murmurings were heard among the Saints as they speculated the coming judgment. A low rumble from the north end of the valley began to seep into the Resurrected Saints' consciousness. A deathly eerie silence took over except for a far away sound that offered no clear distinction as to its source. They could only assume it was the lost of the ages.

"It appears that we are closer to the north end of the valley." Caleb kept trying to see off in the distance. "I think the Old Testament Saints start at the Throne. If I were willing to wager, I would say Adam and Eve are there. After them is the church and since we came along last, we are at this far end."

"True," Sarah smiled, "but we get to see them pass first."

"Except for the Tribulation and Millennial Saints, which are gathered farther beyond us," Emile noted.

"Where Mark, Nikki an' the rest be." Farmer's eyes were trained on the north entrance to the Valley of Destruction.

The noise that the saints first heard as a low rumble turned to a distant roar, which became a more audible clamor. Now cries and screams began to divide the noise into diverse sounds. These were torments and fears of the lost as they came to impending judgment.

A reactive wave swept among the Tribulation and Millennial Saints.

"There," Nikki pointed. "I see them."

Millions of the lost became visible as they emerged in the distant entrance to the enormous Valley of Destruction. Wave upon wave moved closer to the Saints, but not waves of a gentle sea. This was chaos, waves churning and whipped to froth by violent winds. They appeared they would dash themselves to pieces if that were possible.

As distance closed, hosts of warrior angels could be made out policing the lost and moving this vast multitude along. All at once a deafening, collective shriek of such intensity as to cause the Saints to cover their ears, erupted among the lost and was passed on into this enormous mass.

"What happened?" Mee Antra tried to see.

Word rippled through the Saints that the lost had just seen their Judge Jesus Christ and they were struggling to hide their faces and run away.

Soon, the first wave of the lost was visible enough to make out what they were doing, even to see the expressions on their faces. The scene was unlike anything the Saints had ever observed in their lives, far worse than any disaster, war, destruction; nothing could compare.

The lost had the appearance of tattered and worn refugees. Torn clothes hung in limp strips loosely on their bodies. Even outfits that were once expensive and refined were now rags.

Screams of fright and horror were nonstop as they struggled to escape and fight the angels. Some were bound in chains. Others collapsed to the ground; many were begging, falling on their knees and faces. Many attempted to turn and flee but were blocked by an angel.

The Resurrected Saints could not watch such a nightmare happening. They turned their heads.

Then the unexpected took the Saints by surprise. As the first line of the lost that reached across the valley floor approached where the beginning of the Resurrected Saints were waiting, all the lost were halted.

"What are they doing?" Adam questioned. "Why were they stopped? The whole valley floor is empty."

"Something is going on," Mark observed. "Watch the angels."

"Looks like setting up for some kinda' operation," Shag commented as he watched with keen eyes.

A chant started among the lost. It quickly grew in numbers as voices added to it.

"What are they saying?" Nikki asked.

"Don't know," Mark answered, "but it is not a chant of protest, no, more of a plea."

"They are pleading for mercy," Adam spoke low.

"Silence!" the voice of Christ thundered.

The lost were blown backwards like dominos, falling back, back, back as far as the eye could see.

"There is no more mercy. Now stand before Me and observe."

CHAPTER 90

GREAT CONFESSION

Saints were anxious as they waited in silence. All angels faced Christ awaiting His command.

"It is time. Bring them here." The Judge gave the order.

Swiftly angels brought in millennials who in their lives had followed Satan or just as condemning, rejected Christ by unbelief or disinterest. These millennials filled in a portion of the valley floor back away from the Throne. They stood close to where Mark and his family were located, behind the line of defense angels. They studied the millennial faces. No longer were they the proud, rebellious and arrogant, but rather a sad, hopeless lot who were facing eternal sentences.

Adam gasped. Right in front of him on the other side of an angel Adam caught sight of Monte Mole. The resurrection had not done him well. No radiant beauty, the change only amplified Monte's deformities and twisted ugly face. Adam could only stare when Monte looked over and they made eye contact with each other. Such sadness unspoken went between them; Monte realizing the folly of his rejection; and Adam, knowing what could have been, was now lost forever. Adam shook his head in despair. Monte turned away never to look again.

Out of the air, the Lord's Angel army ushered in hordes of demons in chains to fill in the rest of the valley floor in front of the White Throne. These demons were grotesque beyond words, surpassing even the most vivid monster imagination. Each was distorted, malformed, ugly, deformed, disfigured; all with jagged wings, wart-covered bodies and gaping wounds oozing green or red puss.

The Saints shuddered and moaned. Many began to shake.

The demons struggled and fought against the chains that held them, snarling and spitting venom at the angels who kept them in check. Loud curses issued from their mouths, accusations against the Saints were hurled in every direction. They screamed filth, lies and berated God's Word, insulted the Bride of Christ, the church and yelled putrid profanities at God's chosen people.

To the Saints' surprise, Christ did not silence this demonic rabble but let them go on. He wanted every living being to see the true nature of Satan's host. Not deceptive angels of light, but this. Not familiar spirits they sought advice from, but this. Not spirit guides they channeled and let direct their thoughts and actions, but this. Deep, dismal groans rose from the ranks of the lost. Christ needed no words of explanation. All saw for themselves.

Jesus raised His Hand. The valley became deathly still. No one moved. "Bring him," Christ ordered.

Angels opened a pathway from the very end of the masses of the lost all the way through the rebel millennials and the hordes of demons to the White Throne. A disturbed silence began at the far north and progressed slowly down the path. Saints strained to see what was happening.

The amazing part of what was taking place did not generate sounds or movement, but garnered a stone-cold, icy stillness. Even as the procession along the path moved forward, there were no reactions, only gasps. There were millions of millennial rebels and demons between the open pathway and the Saints. They could not see exactly who was on the opened path until the angels reached the White Throne and stepped aside. A collective response burst from the Saints!

Standing before the Judge was the scrawny, pathetic, twisted remains of a once beautiful, powerful angel. Now his wings were boney and bent. Deep wrinkles enveloped his skin. His body was thin with long skinny arms and legs. His hands had claws not fingers. He did have horns and a broken tail; however, his color was tawny, not red as imagined for centuries. He snarled and hissed at Christ, not daring to look at Him.

"Satan," the Lord addressed the devil. "You are exposed before all the angels in heaven and every human who was ever conceived and lived. Once you were greatly favored and bestowed with magnificent beauty and strong powers. You hovered over God's Throne and led in worship of the Most High. But you allowed pride to control you, and you sought worship for yourself. One day, you declared you would rise up and become as the Most High, a god, which you can never be. You are a created being."

"No!" Satan argued. "I would be a god."

Jesus held up his hand and Satan was silenced.

"And all you angels who followed and fell with him to become demons. Look at your leader. Look long and hard. Now see yourselves, and what your rebellion has gotten you? Look!" Jesus roared.

The demons shrieked and screamed profanities and accusations at the one they once followed. Satan railed on them bitterly and tried to use his powers, but had none.

Now, Jesus directed Satan's attention to the Martyred Saints he faced.

"These are all those who refused the unholy mark of the man you possessed and attempted to make into me. You incited their murder and their blood cries out from the ground. They stand as witnesses of your condemnation. Each will live forever in the Presence of the Almighty. Now turn around and face all assembled here."

Satan shook clinched claws at Jesus, but turned to stand before the vast millions.

"Behind your demons is your millennial army and all those you deceived with your tricks and lies. Here before you Millennials is the one you gave you devotion to." Jesus' words blazed into each of their minds and souls. The stark realization that they were forever doomed ate into them like a fast-spreading cancer.

"Millennial Rebels, there is no provision for any trial for you. You lived in a perfect world and I was King. You are without excuse. Over and over I tried to reach you with love, and you rejected Me. Now, I reject you.

"And demons, you were created by God and thrived in His Presence. Heaven was your home. My death on the cross was not for you and could not remake heaven your home. You are without excuse.

"Those of the Second Resurrection. This is who lead you on the broad path to destruction. Look long upon him for you will remember him and what he did to you for countless eons of endless time.

"Resurrected Saints, my beloved. Behold, the one written in my Word, which says: *'they will shake their heads in amazement. So this is the one who tore up nations and brought such destruction and chaos upon the earth.'* Now you see him who battled the saints, the church, and believers through the ages, who thought he could rule the world. Here you see his true nature."

Jesus stood up. "Face me," He ordered.

Satan spun around, defiance in his twisted face.

"Who am I?" Jesus asked.

"Teacher," Satan snarled.

"Who?" Jesus demanded.

"Rabbi," Satan yelled.

"You know who I am, and you will bend your knee and confess it before every living soul both in the Heavens and on the earth."

"Never," Satan began cursing profane blasphemy.

Blinding light filled the valley. There was a clap like thunder but no clouds.

"You will bend your knee. Your reign and kingdom are finished. Who am I?" A power of undeniable strength sprang from the Lord. This was power against power as Satan fought and resisted.

He struggled against his chains. His body jerked in wild convulsions. He screamed, strained, fought, until his body wreathed in such contortions as to go out of joint, throwing the demon down on one knee. He thought to jump up, but could not. All his strength left.

"Who am I?" Jesus again asked.

Satan's face contorted into the most evil, hateful expression and his mouth was yanked to one side as if some force would pull it from his face. He struggled to get the words out.

"Jesus, you are Lord," Satan confessed for all to hear.

A cheer rose up from the Saints and Angels, which resounded through the Universe.

CHAPTER 91

JUDGMENT BEGINS

The final judgment of Satan, his fallen demons, and his millennial following would be swift and decisive. The end had arrived for the beautiful cherub who covered the Throne of God, and the inevitable finish of fallen demon angels he had deceived into wicked rebellion against Almighty God. They were all blessed with heaven as home, but were cast forth in shame to the earth. Each now without excuse would make their abode in darkness and torment.

The millennials were tested under the personal reign of Jesus Christ as King. The whole earth existed in a perfect state and all had access to the Son of God. Yet many turned their hearts, eager to listen to Satan's voice of deception. Like the demons, they, too, rose up in rebellion in one last angry effort to de-throne their King and thwart the very purpose of God. Others simply ignored or put off any decision for Christ and thereby neglected so great a salvation. They also stood before the judgment throne without excuse.

As it is in a court of law, when a guilty verdict is rendered and sentence passed, there are different reactions. With some there is no indication of remorse, repentance, only angry defiance. That was so with Satan and his demon army. They only continued to fight and spew filth. Was evil and blackness of spirit so imbedded into their beings; no sign of sorrow, repentance, or even the slightest hint of departure from hatred detected?

However with others, when sentence is rendered, horror fills their faces as they realize they have no hope. Regret floods their thoughts as they see the high price of their folly. When the gavel bangs, there is no chance for mercy; there will be no more second chances, no appeals to change the verdict. Emotions of fear, horror and remorse swept through the condemned millennials. The verdict of guilty had already been rendered and now the sentence of eternal punishment was given. A sentence, they realized, that would have no end. A million years and it hadn't yet begun. Empty silence filled the Valley of Destruction.

In the Bible, there are more references to Hell than to Heaven. Jesus knew the unspeakable punishment that awaited all who went there. He wanted His word to contain ample warning. Now, Jesus points to the far distant smoke bellowing upwards from earth The abyss it is called, inferno, Hades, bottomless pit, place of torment, place of the wicked dead, purgatory, this feared and dreaded place that has been referred to as Hell. Yet, there remains a stronger word of definition: one of mortal terror. Christ uses it now in passing judgment on Satan, the demons and the unbelieving millennials.

"Cast them in the Lake of Fire," He commands.

Millions of angels descend on those that have been sentenced. Two archangels grab up Satan to cast him into the deepest, darkest part of the Lake.

Next, each angel takes hold of one demon to carry them off. These demons attempt to resist, but have no power. The command demon angels, principalities, powers, and rulers of darkness were in chains. They hurled insults, threats, and curses and struggled against their bonds and captors, but they, too, were carried off to be cast into the Fire.

The looks of terror and screams of the millennials were witnessed and heard by the rest of the assembled lost. They all cried aloud and trembled in sheer fright.

The scene was truly difficult for the Saints to view. Among the condemned millennials were many family members and friends. The huge Trevor family descendants were not left untouched by such deep, painful feelings of sorrow and loss. A massive unsettling rippled throughout the Valley of Destruction among the lost and saved alike. This grew until Christ spoke again.

"Throughout human history, man's tendency to sin has been recorded over and over. I will reveal that your sin is absolutely without excuse," Jesus began. "Tested in the Garden of Eden, man broke my one and only prohibition. The only 'thou shalt not' amidst all the 'thou haves.'

"Tested under the conscience of man, corruption and violence filled the earth until I destroyed it with a great flood.

"As mankind repopulated, man was tested under my appointed, restraining influence of governments. What did you do? You went into idolatry and turned your back on Me. You gave yourselves to false gods.

"So, I tested man under the law, but any and all restraint was thrown away, and man crucified Me on a cross.

"On the cross I paid the penalty of sin, but now the test was under grace. All I asked was for all to repent, believe in Me, and accept that I took your sin upon Myself. But under that test, man showed himself utterly unable to embrace such mercy and again chose to reject Me.

"On this mountain, I gave my law to Moses. Hear Me now. I came to fulfill that law and gave Myself an atonement for sin; so, by your rejection of Me as your Savior, you will be judged by My law. My Word declares that if you are guilty of any part of the law, you are guilty of all.

"Now, let me be perfectly clear what a guilty verdict will mean. Your sentence will be an eternal banishment from My presence. That includes a place of darkness. There is no light, except from the flames that would consume you, but can only inflict terrible pain. In your darkness is no fellowship with family or friends. You are left to your own memories, thoughts and remembrances that you will rethink and regret a million times over. You will cry out in loneliness that never goes away, and scream in terror, but no one cares or hears. Love is gone, hate has no place, only torment. And torment is heightened because your resurrected body is most sensitive as worms eat from the inside and crawl over your body. They never die nor are they satisfied. And the flame burns your flesh but is never able to consume you. Eternity has no end. Your punishment will never diminish or end. You will curse a million times the day you were born and wish you never existed. All faith, hope, and love will completely depart when you are cast into the Lake of Fire.

"Bring the lost of the ages to Me that their judgment might begin."

CHAPTER 92

THE GREAT WHITE THRONE JUDGMENT

In the entire Universe, the saddest day in all of history was when Jesus Christ hung between heaven, earth and hell. But when He gave up His life a willing sacrifice for all mankind, a sense of loss pervaded among men and angels. Yet hope was not lost because they believed Sunday would come.

This day, the day of the White Throne Judgment, will be known as the second saddest day in the Universe. No shouts of victory will be raised. There will be no angel choruses, no peal of trumpets. Yes, a deep grief of loss will be felt. Panic and horror will possess the condemned. The worst part for all: when love is gone, nothing is left. The separation to follow will be forever. How does one live with that? The Saints or the lost?

As the lost were brought near to Christ, they attempted to shrink back before their Judge. Who could know the exact thoughts and feelings of the condemned, as they fully realize they will face the Son of the Living God alone? One-by-one? There would be no mass sentencing like the Millennial rebels before. To know with certainty they would be cast into the pit of flames and torment, no hope to come out—who would know but to read it in their faces?

"Bring the books," Jesus ordered.

Angels brought forth two large stands and set each one on either side of the Throne. Next, the books were carried in and placed upon the stands. Both were very large and heavy; one trimmed in silver; the other overlaid in beautiful gold.

"Open them," Jesus pointed. Angels pulled the covers back and stood by.

"All will be judged by my law and the deeds written in that book." Jesus pointed to the silver-trimmed book on His left. "The final verdict is determined by the Book of Life on My right. A search will be conducted for each name. Let me explain how listings are placed in the Book of Life for all to hear and understand. Every human who was ever conceived is written in this book. Their name remains for as long as they live. Upon their death, if they trusted in Me and what I did for them on the cross, by their faith, their name is still recorded in this book. If my sacrifice was neglected, ignored or rejected, their name is blotted out."

There was a stirring among the lost as they examined their own lives. 'Did I do that?' Many began to justify and rationalize their innocence. 'Maybe I'll get off,' some convinced themselves or those around them. 'We'll state our case and Jesus will go easy on us. We weren't evil like lots of these,' they said to each other.

"Case one," a magnificent angel read from a scroll.

"Adam, Eve and Abel come forth."

A shocked gasp rose among the Saints. Surely these three were not on trial.

Abel panicked. "Oh, no!" he cried aloud. He started to make his way out onto the valley floor.

"Not you," Adam grabbed his son. "They want your namesake."

Two angels wrestled a wild man out to the foot of the Throne. "The accused, Cain," they spoke loudly.

Cain stood up to face Jesus. He shook his fist at the Judge and shouted, "You promised to protect me."

"From those who would do to you as you did to your brother Abel, not from your punishment. Abel's life was stricken from him by your hands. Read from the Book of Deeds," Jesus instructed.

"Ruled by pride and envy. Was enraged that God rejected his offering while accepting Abel's. He murdered his brother. Caused great distress to his mother and father."

"Adam my son, Eve my daughter, come closer. Abel, come. Cain, look long and well at your parents, who bore and raised you. The image you see now will be infused into your mind forever. As you are racked with pain and torment, you will see them and remember they are with me in Paradise. Look now at your brother Abel, whom you murdered. His blood cried out to me from the ground where it was spilt."

Cain attempted to charge Abel and strike him, but angels blocked him. "You always loved him more than me." Cain's accusations were razor-sharp. "You chose him!" he growled. "Now I must pay all over again."

"No, no," Adam and Eve tried to reach out to their condemned boy. Grief flooded their souls and shook them to the very core of their beings.

"I never wanted to hurt you," Abel pleaded. "I loved you and looked up to you."

"Enough," Jesus ordered. "Is Cain recorded in the Book of Life?"

After a thorough search, the angel addressed Jesus. "Cain's name is not found."

"You stand guilty of murder. Cast him in fire that will burn him forever." The Judge pronounced Cain's sentence.

The look on Cain's face as angels came for him was beyond any description. Adam, Eve and Abel all screamed at a level of pain and grief they had never known. They reached out to Cain, but he was gone—never to be seen or heard from again. Adam fell to his knees and Eve collapsed. Abel stood, head hung low. Ministering angels helped strengthen the broken family and led them back into the ranks of the saved.

Moans of fear and stress swept the vast mass of the lost. Sorrow unspoken passed through the saved.

Thus began the long process of justice. One-by-one the lost were brought before the Judge, Jesus Christ. They were forced to face witnesses. The Books were opened to expose the life lived, and to pass sentence. Screams of terror, horror, sheer fright and panic filled the Valley of Destruction hour-by-hour. People of all ranks and stations of life would stand before the Throne and face the Judge. None were exempt.

King Saul in chains was made to look in the face of David, whom he hunted like a dog to kill because of jealousy. Samuel stood as witness to Saul's headstrong disobedience. The deeds recorded were clear: pride, fear of rejection, manipulation, selfishness and consulting a medium. He was drug to the pit as his name was not in the Book of Life.

"Appears ta me they be workin' through Old Testament people," Farmer commented to Emile.

"Oh Farmer, I'm frightened. Do you think we will have to go to the Throne?" Emile asked.

"Reckon we will fer somebody, but not ta be afraid, Emile. We must remember how Jesus came ta us in Paradise. Seeing how He loved us in the Jerusalem Temple. He never changes. Not fer us ta ferget. He be Judge now, but not of us. Think of thet as we go down there."

"What a movie this would have made," Janee muttered.

"Wonder how long we have been at this?" Caleb mentioned. "Continual day, no time, no calendar. What year is it? A century could pass by and we'd never know."

"We must be on an eternal time schedule," Sarah deduced. "We don't need to eat or sleep, and don't tire of standing. The trial is so intense; we can't say we are bored. It seems each condemned, the witnesses, the deeds, all become personal to me."

"Yes!" Emile agreed. "I cry and ache for them."

There came a slight pause when judgment of the Old Testament accused was complete. Now the trial of New Testament, Church Age lost would commence.

King Herod, plus all who carried out his vicious orders must stand before Judge Jesus Christ. Herod's thirst for power and grasping attempt to hold his position caused him to send troops to Bethlehem to kill all male babies under the age of two. The Book of Deeds read.

Several dozen of those babies, now as the Resurrected men they were meant to be, faced Herod in stark testimony to his murderous act.

Herod's kingship stripped away, he now confessed that Jesus Christ was the true, Supreme King. His eternal damnation was sealed when the Book of Life revealed the absence of his name.

Judas lay prostrate on the ground, unable to look up at John and the other disciples who confirmed the deeds' record of betrayal.

"My Word says of you, Judas, *'that it would have been better had you never been born.'* For time eternal, you will wish that very thing." Jesus pronounced sentence when Judas Iscariot's name was not found. "Cast him away into Hell Fire."

Caesar, Emperor of Rome, Nero was hauled before the judgment Throne. When he saw Paul and countless others waiting to witness about his wicked rule, the dictator raved like a lunatic. He demanded Paul come bow before him.

"And who am I?" Jesus interrupted. "Tell me! The devil who possessed you has already confessed it. Who am I? You, who I gave office and authority, are the one to bow to Me."

Nero shrieked in defiance but dropped to his knees. "You are Jesus Christ the Lord, the one Paul, the Jew told me about."

Jesus nodded to the angel at the Book of Life, who searched the pages. "Not here," the angel answered.

"Great is your punishment, Nero. Throw him into the hottest depths of the flames near the Beast Antichrist and his False Prophet," Jesus passed sentence.

Time progressed as one-by-one unbelievers over two thousand years of the Church Age, small and great alike, each faced the Mighty Judge. Scenes of this nature were never before observed in all the annals of the Universe. Well it was spoken of the Judge that He was just, but so terrible and horrible that the lost begged for the mountains to fall on them and cover up their very existence. Truly they wanted to flee if possible from this court.

The sorrow, regret and loss to the Saints was immeasurable. None of the Resurrected would be unaffected. As witnesses were called forth, those leaving the ranks of the saved kept creeping closer to Farmer and Emile. He could see that Emile was nervous as the obvious judgment moved ever closer. The Trevor family would be included with those who were already experiencing such painful loss. It would traverse from just observance to actually facing family or people they knew. For some it would at least be justice meted out. Others, it would be unspeakable grief over those who should not be banished forever, but were supposed to be next to them forever in heaven.

As for the day, hour, month, year, century, no one had any inkling of how long this trial had lasted, but the time came to engage the Trevors.

Franklin, Allison, Farmer, Emile, Jacob, Dorothy, William and Phyllis were to come forth. They all made their way to the Judgment Throne. Farmer was thrilled to see family again, but painfully aware this was no time for a reunion. They had all foreseen and dreaded this moment for a long time.

"Bring Stella," Jesus ordered.

Swiftly an angel brought Farmer's sister into their midst. The instant Stella saw them, she whimpered, shook her head no, holding out her hands in a pitiful tear-filled plea for help. The family moved to console, and surround their loved one, but were prevented by the angel.

"Read her record," Jesus asked for evidence.

"Attended church faithfully during youth. Rebelled against her parents and ran away at fifteen. Heavily involved in drinking, smoking and sex. She became unclean in body, mind and spirit. All family members and others tried to reach out to her, but she was unresponsive. Her brother and sister-in-law went to visit her. She chided them for coming to preach about her sins."

"Oh, God, no!" Stella moaned.

"She wished to celebrate her drunkenness. She judged Farmer and Emile as pious. She called her mother 'spineless,' her Pa 'a cruel tyrant' and wished him to burn in Hell. She mocked her brother and said she would have a reunion in Hell and a party."

The family wept openly and cried out. Stella hung her head in shame. Farmer and Emile felt a spiritual ripping of their insides. They all stood helpless.

"Is she recorded in the Book of Life?" Jesus asked.

"No," the angel answered after searching.

"It has to be!" Stella screamed. "I went to church, every service."

"True. However, you only listened to sermons and sang hymns faithfully, never giving your heart to Me."

"No. No. I loved you. I prayed, please, I really did. I read my Bible. I loved you, please, I swear. Please . . . check again," she begged.

Jesus nodded and the angel went over columns of names with the same verdict.

"Take her to the pit." Jesus pointed to the far distant smoke.

The family wailed. Franklin and Allison fell to the ground. Stella hopelessly reached out to them as she was whisked away. Farmer felt he and Emile could take no more of this.

Still, Farmer, Emile and Betty Jean were called as witnesses a short time later.

A shock bolted across Farmer's mind as he heard his best friend, Benjamin Harrison, called before the great Judge. Farmer hardly recognized his friend, his appearance disheveled in clothes so unlike Benjamin, who was very conscientious about his appearance. Tears streamed down their faces. They made eye contact when he passed Farmer. Betty Jean cried out in distress of soul and heavy grief when the love of her life stopped near her.

While Benjamin's deeds were read, Farmer bravely attempted to review pleasant and happy scenes of their youth. It was vivid now, but would it be a million years from now? He would choose to remember these times, excited over maps on the table planning their Oregon trip; his friend laughing, full of love of life, good times, but not today.

He was jerked to reality at the mention of his letter.

"Farmer wrote he was 'yernin' ta see his friend Benjamin know Jesus Christ, and then told him how to receive Christ," the angel disclosed. "Benjamin brushed the request off in his reply letter. 'What's God done for me? Church's not my interest, maybe when I'm old and grey. I want to make money.' Parties, drink and greed became his god. He shunned the woman who loved him and befriended sinister people who turned on him and contracted his murder."

"I was a fool," Benjamin sobbed. "Please have mercy and forgive. I can do better if you will only give me a chance."

Jesus answered sternly, "The time of mercy is over. Your only course of forgiveness was through Me. Surely, you have heard enough cases to understand second changes ended upon your death. You are guilty under the law. Look at Me, Benjamin."

The condemned man tried to hide his face.

"Look. At. Me." Jesus ordered.

Benjamin yelped in destress.

"Farmer and Emile were witness of Me to you. Now they are witnesses of your guilt. By your union, Betty Jean was your wife and loved you faithfully. She found Me and has been with Me while you abode in the place of torment. You joked about a party in Hell. I assure you, there are no parties. Now look at your witnesses. The plight and hurt you see in their faces are stamped into your mind to fill you with the deepest sorrow and regret forever."

"Don't bother to look for my name," Benjamin spoke from a broken spirit. "It's not there."

Jesus nodded for the search. No sentence pronounced. Benjamin admitted his own condemnation. In a few seconds, he was taken from them to the fire, never to be seen or heard from again.

Janee was called to be witness several times, but two were most noteworthy. The first was with Seth. Aaron Mocknour was called to the Judgment Throne. Janee had no interest to even seeing this man. Many years ago she forgave him and found peace with the past.

Mocknour would not look at Janee and ignored the young man beside her. Aaron's suit was worn and tattered, but still he maintained that familiar air of brash confidence and arrogance.

"I can pay you," he shouted out. "I have tons of money."

"You do?" Jesus questioned. "Are you bribing me?"

"Of course not. Just a friendly gift."

"What price would you put on your freedom?"

"Name your price."

"The giving of a life, the shedding of blood."

"Not acceptable. Come on now, come on, Judge, name a price. Let's deal."

Jesus sighed. "Truly I say to you, Aaron Mocknour. You have no money for your life is bankrupt. In fact, you are a prisoner. The price of redemption cannot be measured in dollars, but in blood. I shed my blood for you and you would have no part of my gift."

"I, I didn't know," Aaron stammered.

Jesus glanced to the angel at the Book of Deeds.

"After Janee was born again, she arranged a meeting with Mocknour on his phone. She told of her salvation through Jesus Christ. How she accepted Him as her Savior and her whole life was changed."

Mocknour beat his face as he remembered.

"Janee told him she forgave him. Aaron berated her with accusations and belittled her. He also mocked her salvation experience as a crutch. Aaron threw her out of his life and said, 'Hollywood will be a better place when you are dead and gone.' So Mocknour is without excuse. He is rejected."

"You knew and you rejected me as you did others," Jesus confronted Aaron with the truth. "Turn and look at Janee. Face her."

Mocknour slowly, reluctantly faced Janee. He was unsettled and puzzled.

"This woman loved you and gave you her love. She only expected love in return. Yet you abused her. Lust for her body blackened your heart. You pushed her away with loathing after you got the sex you wanted. You hurt and confused her. She found me and accepted me. You rejected me as you did her and your son."

"What?" Mocknour gasped.

"Your son, Seth, whom you stripped away before he could have a chance to live. Observe how fine a man he became, in Paradise."

Seth wanted to come to Mocknour, but the angel restrained him. "I've wanted to know you," Seth cried out. "Why didn't you want me?"

Mocknour was speechless and dropped his head for the first time.

"I can answer that," Jesus continued. "He counted his reputation of more value than his child."

Jesus motioned for others to come and face Mocknour. Six young people came to stand with Seth; three with their mothers.

"You stand accused of seven murders: three sons and four daughters. You could have enjoyed a full, rich life with any of them, but you decided it more convenient to rid yourself of your 'little problems.' Behold, your children, Mocknour."

"Their mothers could have refused. They are as much to blame as me."

"A mean, powerful man like yourself? Full of threats? You bullied them into submission."

The list of deeds for Director Aaron Mocknour was long. He left a trail of devastated lives along the path he walked. Even his movies revealed little substance to change lives in a positive way. Jesus called for a verdict from the Book of Life. Aaron Mocknour was taken in terrified screams and cast into the Lake of Fire.

Janee was one of many witnesses brought out on this individual. Her part would be brief. She was totally taken when Talk Show Host Theon Dice was pulled by an angel to the foot of the White Throne. Stubborn to the core, he maintained his innocence. Theon insisted he lived a clean life, gave donations to the needy. "I kept your law to the tee," he declared loudly. "Agents voted me and gave me an AOK, so you have nothing on me. No record, no infractions. You got nothing on me."

"We shall see," Christ spoke calmly. "Read his deeds."

"His recorded life did reveal an honest, generous, kind man. He treated his staff fairly and above all, he was a faithful friend. Never married, no sexual relations, attended church on a regular basis. But his downfall was not in these acts, but would be exposed in another area."

Theon eyed the Judge and thought a minute. The Lord waited. "Wow!" Theon spoke loudly. "What a Show we coulda' had with You as guest. Never thought to have my people give You an invite."

"I was on your Show, Theon," the Lord answered.

"What? When?"

"I came with Janee Stemper Swift. Janee, come, child. Do you recognize Janee and remember that night, Theon?"

"Yes," Theon hesitated. "But I didn't see you?"

"By My Spirit, I dwell in my children. What you spoke to her you said to Me."

Theon gulped.

"You delighted to pin her down. You were smug and aloof. You loved exposing raw portions of her private life. When she talked about me, Jesus Christ, and how I gave her life and freedom, what did you do?"

"Don't recall," Theon mumbled.

"You lie. Of truth, you remember. Speak it."

"I took a commercial break."

"And?

"I asked her not to talk about religion and threatened to embarrass her with personal questions if she defied me. I declared war."

"You painted an ugly picture of a fractured woman. Blind, you were. Trouble figuring out what she stood for? Blind guide, she was standing for Me."

"She wanted to ruin my show. Make me a network running joke. She would destroy my career."

"If you were so worried, why did you rub your hands together in glee backstage over the high ratings you were pulling in?"

Theon couldn't answer.

"Look at Janee, Theon. She faced you on your Show and testified of my death on the cross. How I washed away guilt and shame. Something you never had, Theon. No, you made ratings and your image the god in your life."

"I'm sorry," Theon muttered low.

"Did Janee not invite you to pray to receive Me as your own Savior? She encouraged you to do it then, on camera. You balked, she begged you."

Theon shook his head. "I couldn't. Not a good time or place."

"And so you never did, Theon." Jesus was somber. "Let me speak clearly. If you would have taken courage, heeded Janee's pleas to pray with her and opened your heart to receive so great a salvation on camera, millions would have followed your example. You would be rejoicing with Janee. Great would be your reward; instead I must send you to eternal damnation."

"Oh, God, No! I accept you, I believe in you," Theon's expression turned to one of sheer terror.

Janee broke into tears as Theon Dice was carried away to his eternal abode in the pit of flames.

Trials moved forward at a steady pace. Each was horrible, emotionally wrenching in different and unique ways. The numbers of the lost kept dwindling as they inched closer to the Great White Throne.

Next called to witness were Caleb and Sarah. 'Who could this be?' Sarah wondered. 'No doubt an enemy.' They could never have guessed Destini Polovi, the physic. Her verdict would no doubt be decisive and quick.

Destini fought, clawed and kicked at the angel, who administered physical force to bring her before the Judge. "Read her deeds," He commanded.

"Throughout her lifetime she deceived many souls with her witchcraft. She led others to channel their spirit guides who controlled all they did. Hundreds, she turned away from Jesus Christ to familiar spirits. The Lord directed Caleb Hillag by one of His angels to warn the people not to go to the resort but to go up the mountain to Saint Marcos Church. His son disagreed out of ignorance, but she was controlled by demons and urged the people to the resort. She called God's missionary a fraud."

"What about his stupid son? He should be punished like me," Destini hissed.

"Come, Mark Hillag. Come, Chris Fowler. Both were there that night. They are witness to your evil advice.

Physic Polovi was shocked at Mark's radiant beauty.

"Mark Hillag accepted Me and I saved him. You hated Me, my sacrifice on the cross and you rejected My salvation." Jesus addressed the once-powerful physic.

"Her name is not found in the Book of Life," the angel reported.

"Where are all your possessing demons and spirit guides to help you?" Jesus inquired.

"In the pit of Hell, and I shall find them," she growled and spit.

"As you say. Take her from my presence and throw her down into the lower part," Jesus gave Destini's sentence.

The Lord dismissed Chris to return to the Saints. He instructed Caleb, Sarah and Mark to remain, while He called Sarah's mother Hannah, Sarah's sister Penny and Mark's wife Nikki forward as witnesses. A vast number of witnesses against this next accused filled in behind Caleb and his group.

Jesus motioned with His Hand to bring the defendant. "Stoner Howser," his name was announced. A collective response of shock and fear came out of the witnesses.

Stoner was escorted by two strong angels. The once-powerful Enlightened One in heavy chains hobbled slowly. His resurrected body was gross. It bore little resemblance to the muscular handsome man he once was. He walked in deformed fashion, and appeared almost bloated. His clothes were full of holes, his exposed skin dotted with burn marks. When he glowered at the witnesses as he passed through, it was with blood-red eyes. Caleb's family whispered in shock. Stoner stopped to stare.

"What?" he snapped. "What were you expecting? Me to act and talk like Destini Polovi? She was play-acting you. When all the demons were captured and dumped in the pit, she lost her voice and all her power, same as me. Drama and a fancy show was all she ever did. I was the real deal."

The angels urged Stoner on to the Throne.

Mark held his head. It was almost like he could hear those whirling sounds and feel those awful warping waves trying to invade his mind. He shook it off.

Stoner drug his chains and stood alone before the Judge. He looked intently into the eyes of Christ, then dropped down on both knees. "Jesus is Lord," he muttered, before standing up. "Wanted to get that out of the way."

Stoner pulled his chains closer. He addressed the Lord.

"In human court the condemned was always given his final word. Some time to speak to his accusers. So let's cut to the chase here. I have no doubt your deeds book will list more than enough to render a guilty verdict. Let me talk and your angel can keep track, if I covered all the points." Stoner looked up at the Judge.

"Why should I grant this to you?"

"Because this will be the last time I see these people. I want to set some things straight and maybe answer some questions, theirs or mine. I can't appeal to your mercy, just asking this favor."

Jesus studied Stoner a few seconds before making His decision. "You may speak but the witnesses may not."

Stoner turned to face the vast throng of his accusers. He began his address to them.

"I shall begin with my biggest sin, which affected many. When I was young I dabbled in witchcraft. Even then, I felt its intoxicating invasion into my mind and soul. I gained power like physic Polovi had, but I wanted more. I offered many sacrifices and begged demons to possess me. I wanted them not only in my head, but also in my heart. I progressed from animal sacrifices to human, yes, even infants. I was elevated ever higher in position, wealth and power. I no longer heard from demons, but Satan himself. I became one of his elite, an Enlightened One. I took whatever I wanted: property, money, positions of leadership, women and even lives. I became obsessive and ruthless, leaving a stream of devastated lives along the way.

"The first was my family. I began using my powers on them. My dad wrote me off as crazy, but I faced my first resistance with my stepmother and sisters Penny and Sarah. When I came against Sarah's boyfriend Caleb, I hit a wall I could not

395

penetrate. I removed myself from them but would return secretly to torment or harass.

"Later, I returned to declare war on them. I especially wanted Caleb dead and his son Mark to offer in a sacrifice. Satan offered me greater power and a place next to him. I smelled victory at the Concert Crusade. I had four hundred satanic priests with me and would have taken Caleb out were it not for the interference of a mystery man. But I was certain I had Mark on my side. I could sense his yearning for the power I had to offer.

"Then millions disappeared. A new leader emerged and I declared war on those who refused him to follow Christ. My dad, Gary, who is out there among the lost, was easy prey. He fell victim as soon as he saw and felt my power. He sold his soul for that, and money.

"I wanted Mark, but it seemed that he and his friends were always an elusive bunch. However, a few at a time, I took their lives. I thought I had Mark and his friend Nikki trapped in Colorado, but they disappeared. Word came to me they were spotted in Oregon. That's when the hunter was hunted and killed. I've wondered for a thousand years who got me. I think I deserve to know."

Shag was called to face Stoner.

"I gotcha," Shag bellowed.

Stoner eyed him a long time. "The old Vet. But how?"

"Ye were so intent on your wicked plans for Mark and Nikki you left yer back door unlocked." Shag smiled with satisfaction.

"There is someone else you must face, Stoner," Jesus said. "Someone you hunted with murderous hate."

Timon walked from the witnesses to face Stoner.

"Ah, a worthy opponent, the Jewish Witness. I tracked you down and beheaded you."

"Without God my Father allowing it, you could have done neither," Timon answered.

"Perhaps." Stoner looked away. "I fear I indeed won that battle, and lost the war."

"Are you finished, Stoner?" Jesus asked.

"I have one last thing," Stoner continued. "All of you may be wondering if I could do my life over, would it be different? I am not sure. I received a grand rush from the power. I got super-charged to have men and women fall at my feet. With my wealth I could go anywhere in the world and do whatever I desired. I remember how all that felt and even now it pulls me.

"However, a change did happen to me. With all the demons snatched away and their hounding voices silenced in my mind, I became a kid again. I was aghast at how I had shattered or destroyed your lives. Especially those I loved the most. Looking at you is the image I must carry in my mind. I can't ask you to tell me of your forgiveness, but if you can, if you will, I know it will show in your faces. If I can leave you with some sense of vindication, and I have even the slightest degree of forgiveness given, let us part with those memories."

Stoner turned to face his Judge, who nodded to the angel at the Book of Life.

"Stoner Howser is not written."

Without word, the once-feared and powerful Stoner was carried away to suffer in agony for his crimes. Alone, in flames, never to be seen or heard from again.

All the witnesses returned to their places among the Saints. Caleb and his group did not quite know what to think or how they felt about the turn in Stoner. They had mixed emotions. Some were glad and thankful he was gone. Others grappled with loss and wished they could have known him all their lives as he was at the end.

Meanwhile, the trials at the Great White Throne Judgment continued on into the Tribulation years. Many of Mark and Nikki's Global Missions friends were called on to witness against Combats; those who took Christo's mark or took part in their capture or murder.

Mark and Nikki were witness to the traitor Baylor Kane's demise. Later they faced the Combat Mark shot and killed.

One-by-one at a steady pace, the lost came before the Judge until there was only a single case left. The vast Valley of Destruction was emptied out. When this final accused was sentenced and thrown in the Lake of Fire, it was as though the whole curse of sin and its darkness and wickedness was emptied into the burning flames as well.

The Judgment of the Great White Throne was concluded.

EPILOGUE

The Saints were all called to Old Jerusalem to await the arrival of the New. It was an exciting time of great Joy.

The City was full to overflowing and Jesus was in their midst. Time was non-existent; day was constant. Tech gadgets were of no use, because a whole new lifestyle was about to begin.

The anticipation of a New Heaven and Earth filled the Saints with wonder and stirred lively, reflective conversations. Imaginative thoughts and ideas of how the new world and the City would appear were tossed around.

Families were gathered, and Farmer and Emile's could easily make a small city. The couple sat on a high porch looking out over all their kin below. At this moment their emotions were high.

"Do you believe we will remember all that has happened? The victories, excitement, joy, happiness, the pain, struggles, hurts and sorrow?" Emile's eyes teared up. "Will we even remember we were a husband and wife?"

Farmer pondered her question a long time as he watched their family. A thousand memories flooded his thoughts. Many were great, others no so.

"Reckon some events be best forgotten," Farmer answered slowly. "So maybe as we step inta our ferever, the Lord jus' might filter out all the bad stuff. But I pray, Emile, we never ferget the good. Ta take away remembrance of those we love and have gone through so much together, ta me, would erase who we are—as a couple—as a family."

"But we still cry," Emile brushed tears away.

"Well now, in thinken' on it, the Good Lord tol' o' some things thet would cease. Those be no more tears an' no more

399

sorrow, no separation ever again. How can there be separation ifen we don't remember who we be? So, sad thoughts an' memories may go away, but the happy ones be fixed in our minds."

"I know. Just look at our family."

"Makes me pleased an' proud," Farmer murmured. "I reckon God done gave us a legacy. All thet has happened ta us is part of our legacy. Our history. But more then thet, legacy is people. Precious ones we hev met along our journey, an' especially our own, which has growed. Thet be our legacy, Emile, an' the one thing thet will keep going on forever.

"You and I grabbed hold o' a dream an' started our fantastic journey in 1925. Today, this journey be complete, but us an' our legacy will go on."

THE END

Printed in the USA
CPSIA information can be obtained
at www.ICGtesting.com
LVHW041251151023
761121LV00001BB/63